A ruthless fire vampire. An unsuspecting human. A bargain that will cost them everything.

Blood Mosaic

Tatyana Vorona has no idea that she just made a deal with a vampire. When the naïve human bookkeeper offers to help locate embezzled funds for a wealthy CEO, she doesn't realize she's being set up as bait.

Oleg Sokolov is a fire vampire as ancient as he is vicious. It's bad enough that his daughter stole money from him, but now she's sought refuge with one of his bitter rivals. He wants her back under his control, and he doesn't mind using Tatyana to draw her out.

But as Oleg spends more time with Tatyana, he begins to want her for more than just revenge. When Tatyana is attacked, Oleg is forced to reveal his true nature to save her. Can he convince her to stay in his bloody world when he's the reason she's in danger?

Dark and compelling, BLOOD MOSAIC is the first in a new series from USA Today Bestselling Author Elizabeth Hunter, set in her popular Elemental universe.

Never bargain with Fire.

Praise for Blood Mosaic

I give five, flame-snapping stars to this absolutely riveting first installment in The Firebird and the Wolf series. I'm aching for book two already!

— Lisa Conant, Goodreads Reviewer

There are not enough stars! What an epic start to the series. Blood, gore, conflict, romance, it has it all.

— Tanja, Goodreads Reviewer

The bond between the two main characters was SWOON worthy and I love how deep it goes because of their supernatural existence.

— OM, Goodreads Reviewer

BLOOD MOSAIC

BY

ELIZABETH HUNTER

Blood Mosaic

The Firebird and the Wolf
Book 1

Elizabeth Hunter

Recurve Press, LLC

I've lived to bury my own desires,
      And see my dreams corrode with rust;
      Now all that's left are fruitless fires
      That burn my empty heart to dust.

— Alexander Pushkin

Author's Note

When I began to establish the canon of the Elemental Universe in 2012 (Oleg's first appearance in A Fall of Water) I did not anticipate the war in Ukraine or the Russian invasion. To place this book in context, please understand that the events depicted in Blood Mosaic take place around 2016, after the Russian incursion into Crimea (where Sevastopol is located) but before the full-scale war that started in 2022. My heart is with the Ukrainian people and every innocent person affected by the tragedy of this war.

Chapter One

The vampire traced a finger over blood-red tesserae set into the intricately composed mosaic that lined the walls of his day chamber.

Sire.

Lover.

Mate.

Brother.

Friend.

Each one singular. Each unique.

Each one dead by his hand.

One after another after another, each tessera flashed in the light of his fire before dissolving into the shattered pattern that made up his endless night.

He spread a thin layer of cement next to the newest section of the mosaic—a jagged landscape filled with deep blues and greens—and placed a large glass tile onto the wall, red glass snipped and melted into the shape of a half-moon.

The new tile positioned, he quickly placed smaller tesserae around it, counting each like the victims of the vampire he'd helped to kill. He turned the solitary moon tile into a burst of scarlet bleeding into the blues and greens.

After the tesserae were placed, he stepped back and looked at the rhythm and balance of his work. The pattern was even and blended well with the larger motif.

He would wait until the cement cured before he set the grout that would fix the glass tiles into place among the ceramic and stone tesserae he'd used over the centuries.

The cold stone walls of his castle in the Eastern Carpathian Mountains had been gradually decorated over centuries by his own hand. The fortress rose from a river valley and spread into the surrounding mountains, a grey stone citadel teeming with vampires and the humans who served him, all of them surrounded by the intricate art that covered the corridors and ceremonial rooms. Even his armory was decorated with mosaics.

But this particular chamber was his alone, and few had trespassed in nine hundred years. This chamber was locked against the sun, barricaded against those who might harm him, guarded by loyal humans during the day and his own fierce reputation during the night.

Oleg Sokolov, the fire vampire lord of Kievan Rus, heir of Truvor the Red, and anonymous head of numerous multinational corporations, stood shirtless in his day chamber, playing with a lick of fire that danced in his hand and contemplating how he would finish the border of the pattern that had occupied his mind for over a week.

The mosaic in his day chamber was a record of his life, the only one he hadn't destroyed, and it covered two-thirds of the stone walls with scenes of blood, conquest, and victory over his enemies.

The chamber was as much studio as bedroom, the wall behind him lined with strictly organized shelves containing glass in all colors, ceramic tiles, and carefully cut stone. The tools of his art were a mix of ancient and modern, but most had been custom made for him and had lasted for centuries.

He heard a firm knock on his door. Only one of two people would disturb him in his private rooms. Walking toward the heavy oak door, he tossed the dancing flame in his hand toward the fireplace in the corner, then flipped open the wooden cover over the small window cut into the door.

The grim face of his current chief financial officer stared back. "I need to talk to you."

He'd told Elene he wanted the week to himself, and she wouldn't have disturbed him if it wasn't important.

He let out a short grunt and snapped the window closed, then walked back to his workbench and pumped water into a basin to wash his hands before running a damp rag over his bare shoulders to remove any dust. Finally he forced a comb through his wavy russet hair.

Glancing in a small oval mirror tacked to the wall above the basin, he made sure his beard hadn't grown wild in the heat and humidity of his chamber, then threw on a shirt hanging from a peg and buttoned it halfway up his chest.

Oleg kept no modern technology in his day chamber—the magic of the current world had its uses, but not where he rested during the day. This stone room was illuminated by multiple braziers he lit himself. He had no need for electric lights that would buzz and irritate him like summer insects.

Neither did he have need for hot water to bathe when he preferred the cold mountain stream water that soothed the elemental fire running under his skin. A simple pump carried the water to his chambers for washing and to keep his rooms damp enough to control his element.

Warm air was circulated by vents designed by a wind vampire four centuries before, and plumbing consisted of concealed drains along one wall.

"Oleg!" Elene shouted through the door. "I don't have all night."

"I'm coming." He had no need for modern communication devices when he hired humans to keep in touch with the modern world so they could report to him.

The most important human was the woman on the other side of the door.

Oleg grabbed a bottle of blood-wine from a sturdy cedar cabinet before he walked to the door. He hadn't fed in a week, and it wouldn't do to let his fangs down around Elene. She'd only be irritable.

He fed on the blood of the people who served in the castle and filled his belly with game from the forest around him. Elene was a trusted adviser and partner, not a blood donor.

His life had changed little over the centuries, the biggest shock wave being the death of his mate a decade before, but he and Luana had been estranged and she'd never spent much time at his citadel in the mountains, preferring to be near her own element and live by the sea.

Oleg opened the door and stepped into the antechamber where Elene waited.

The competent human usually had a briefcase with her and a portfolio of papers for him to read and sign. There were contracts and tax forms and any number of legal documents involved in being a legitimate businessman in the twenty-first century, and he had to sign all of them with one alias or another. It was Elene's job to keep all that straight.

That night there were no papers spread on the carved oak desk. No briefcase. No terse recitation of tasks he needed to accomplish to keep the human money and vampire gold flowing.

Elene sat on a velvet settee with her hands folded on her lap. "You need to come to Odesa with me."

"Why?"

"To meet an accountant."

His irritation was immediately pricked. Sitting across from Elene, he leaned back and stretched his arms across the back of the sofa as a servant brought in a tea service.

Oleg handed the servant the bottle of blood-wine, and the woman silently walked to the sideboard, opened it, and handed him a full goblet before she continued serving Elene tea.

"I'm sorry," Oleg said. "Say that again because I think you're mistaking me for someone who deals with minor financial issues."

"Which is me?" Elene raised an arched black eyebrow at him.

"Which is your assistant's assistant, Elene. Or do you need to hire more people?"

She sighed and took the tea the maid held out. "Thank you, Serena. You may go."

The maid silently left the room, and Elene waited a few minutes as her steps retreated down the hall.

Oleg heard when the double doors to his wing of the citadel closed. "We're alone."

"You need to meet this accountant." Elene sipped her tea.

"Why?"

"Because she might know something about your daughter."

THE BENEFIT OF OLEG'S CITADEL WAS ITS REMOTE LOCATION, which was also its liability when it came to business matters. Luckily, Elene had come by the same car that took her back to the private airstrip where a plane waited for her and Oleg.

As they were flying to Odesa, Elene handed him a file. "Tatyana Otsana Vorona."

Oleg flipped the file open, and the image of the woman in the photograph arrested his gaze. She was blond and blue-eyed, a pale beauty with delicate features and a wide mouth set in a firm line. Faint lines surrounded her eyes, more from stress than age because the woman looked to be in her late twenties at the most.

"Miss Vorona attended the national university in Kyiv and graduated with honors with a double major in accounting and mathematics. She also studied computer science during an internship, and Mika's sources say she was casually involved in the Kyiv hacker community when she was in school. She's currently unemployed."

The resemblance to Oleg's late mate was unmistakable, and Elene had to have seen it, but she didn't say a word.

"Where is she from?" He couldn't take his eyes off the photograph. The twist in his cold heart was unwelcome, and he felt his fangs aching in his jaw.

"We're not sure. Her mother is from the Crimea, but the parents are divorced and her father wasn't involved in her life past putting his name on her birth certificate."

Crimea, where Luana had died but not where she was born in her human life. Maybe it was all a coincidence. Maybe he was seeing ghosts where none existed.

"You said she knew about Zara?" Oleg had numerous vampire children, but none as maddening or problematic as Zara.

"Don't rush the story," Elene muttered.

Oleg snapped the file closed. "Then get to the point."

"She worked as an entry-level accountant for a financial firm in Kyiv for a time—very typical job—then it appears that her mother started having health problems after her grandparents passed away. She moved back home, and there is no record of work for about a year. Then..."

Oleg crossed his arms over his chest as the plane bumped over some turbulence in the mountains. He could feel his skin heating as he waited. "The point?"

"She started working for an import-and-export company in Sevastopol a few years ago. She was a bookkeeper."

"The firm?"

"A small company called ZOL Enterprises."

"Fuck." ZOL was the subsidiary he had set up for Zara to run after Luana's death. It was supposed to be something to keep her busy but had turned into a front for any number of schemes his daughter had used to undermine him.

"Yes, and even better, the official records we have for ZOL don't have Miss Vorona anywhere on them."

Oleg frowned. "What does that mean?"

Zara had disappeared two years before, leaving Oleg with a financial and political mess in a region that was quickly becoming even more unstable because of human politics. He and Mika had been trying ever since to sort out all those she had offended and the human and vampire victims she'd left in her wake.

Technically Zara hadn't disappeared. She'd fled to the protection of a powerful vampire lover in Istanbul, taking millions of dollars of Oleg's money with her.

Elene continued, "She wasn't on ZOL's books because she was keeping Zara's *real* books, not the official ones with the reports she was sending to us."

"So Zara *was* skimming money."

"We already suspected she was, but this confirms it."

Oleg picked up Tatyana's file again, paging through the school records, tax receipts, and credit reports, all very typical documents for a law-abiding woman who looked like she was very accustomed to following the rules.

How had this rule-follower become involved with his criminal daughter?

"Well..." Oleg pursed his lips. "As Zara's sire, I would be disappointed if she *wasn't* skimming money."

"You were always too lenient with her."

"Luana loved her." It was all he had to say to make Elene stop her chiding.

"Still." Elene looked out the dark window. "She left a lot of chaos, Oleg."

"I know that." And he would clean it up. Eventually.

The vampire world didn't have governments like the human world. What it had was a complicated network of secret fiefdoms and territories run by powerful vampires and those who served them. Trusted people were often placed in human governments to protect secrets the immortal world wanted to remain hidden.

Zara had used Oleg's connections to fool and humiliate powerful vampires. She'd used his connections to cheat him and others, only to run away to a new protector.

Oleg was powerful, but he wasn't the only dangerous vampire in the world. Zara had seduced Laskaris, a water vampire who ruled a territory that stretched from Athens to Istanbul and controlled the Bosporus, which was Oleg's only access from the Black Sea to the larger world.

"You know Zara is probably cheating the Greek now that she can't cheat me." The idea gave him perverse pleasure.

"I imagine you're correct," Elene said. "No matter how much your daughter had, she always wanted more."

Oleg had been diverting some operations to his export subsidiary in Saint Petersburg, but the human government in Moscow was a constant headache with delusions of empire that regularly got in the way of his business dealings.

The Black Sea ports were more central and far more lucrative. So for Elene to grow his legitimate operations, Oleg was forced to pay millions to Zara's lover Laskaris to obtain access to the Mediterranean Sea.

If he failed to pay the bribe, the ancient Greek immortal would sic human authorities on his largest shipping company, SMO International, forcing Oleg into the light or out of business.

He hadn't worked for centuries building careful alliances and eliminating rivals to have all of it taken away by one errant and vengeful child.

Oleg would find Zara and he'd find the money she'd stolen. And once he found her, he would teach her a lesson that all his children and the entire vampire world would witness.

He flipped to the front of Tatyana Vorona's file again. "If this woman worked for Zara, why is she coming to us?"

"Zara didn't pay her," Elene said.

Oleg looked up from the file. "You are joking."

Rule number one of a criminal enterprise was to pay your accountant on time.

"I am not joking. Tatyana Vorona worked remotely for three years, sent all her work to Zara directly, and then Zara didn't pay her for six months. She claimed that there was something holding up her accounts in Sevastopol—"

"*I* was holding up her accounts," Oleg muttered as he looked back at the human's file. "But Zara always had money."

There were school pictures in the file along with copies of awards Tatyana Vorona had won. A promising dance practice had been abandoned when the mother couldn't pay for classes. Anna Asanov was a government clerk who had grown up in the country, graduated from local schools, and hadn't attained entry to a university. She had a government pension and no particular skills of note.

Tatyana Vorona didn't come from a family with money or power. A human who didn't come from wealth was not going to abandon six months of wages without trying to recover it.

His daughter had made a dangerous mistake.

"Zara thought she could cheat the human out of her wages." The corner of Elene's mouth turned up. "Luckily for us, Tatyana doesn't seem to be an ordinary human."

Oleg narrowed his eyes. "She knows about our kind?"

"About vampires?" Elene shook her head. "Not that I can tell."

Elene had been raised by humans already involved in the vampire world. She'd known about and worked for immortals her entire career, and Oleg had stolen her from a rival decades ago. After a short romantic relationship, they'd decided they were much better suited to be friends and business partners instead of lovers.

"She doesn't know about the immortal world," Elene said. "But she did manage to connect ZOL to SMO when she realized Zara had cheated her."

"You said that would be difficult to do."

"It *was* difficult to do."

"So she's intelligent." Oleg shrugged. "She can't find Zara, or she wouldn't have come looking for me. So why is it so important that I meet her?"

"Because according to the accountant that met with her, Tatyana Vorona claims to have her own copies of all of Zara's books."

"The real books?" Oleg asked. "Not the doctored reports she sent to us?"

"Exactly."

So the human woman was suspicious. Oleg approved.

"If we play this right," Elene continued, "Tatyana Vorona might give Zara's bookkeeping records to us in exchange for six months of wages."

"I'd get my money back," he muttered.

"And if there's something in the books that proves Zara is cheating Laskaris, we might even get the Greek to abandon her too."

For the first time that night, Oleg smiled.

Chapter Two

Tatyana Vorona sat in the waiting room of yet another corporate office in downtown Odesa. The chairs were immaculate and far nicer than any office she'd worked at. There was little attempt at looking new or modern. SMO was clearly a firm backed by old money, with rich wooden doors, warm gold lamps, and hardly a fluorescent lamp in sight.

She tugged on her black pencil skirt, trying not to be intimidated and knowing she looked like a poor country mouse in this luxurious office. The woman delivering coffee around the office was better dressed than Tatyana was.

Then again, she wasn't accustomed to paying close attention to her wardrobe. At her first job, she'd worn smart wool slacks, white shirts, and a few different sweaters to work. It was a medium-size firm in Kyiv that employed mostly young people, many of whom wore sneakers to work instead of heels.

After she'd had to move back to Sevastopol, Tatyana had worked from home and gradually given away or sold most of her professional wardrobe save for this ill-fitting pencil-skirt-and-sweater combination.

It shouldn't matter how she was dressed. Her hair was neatly coiled into a bun at the back of her head. She'd put on a little bit of makeup, and most importantly, she had paperwork, digital and paper files, and a printed record of her work history along with her former employer's ties to this firm.

And the laptop.

Zara had been adamant that the laptop Tatyana used for her bookkeeping not be tied to the internet in any way. She'd only gotten the job after she could prove to Zara that no one would be able to hack her computer and that all the information she needed could be stored in paper files.

The woman was paranoid, but she was paranoid with good reason because Tatyana had made numerous backups for her work. She hadn't told Zara of course, but Tatyana knew that paper could be lost and digital backups lasted forever.

Working for the paranoid woman was the only job that Tatyana had been able to find in her childhood home, and after her grandparents had passed, she and her mother desperately needed money if they wanted to keep their home.

Zara was eccentric, but she'd paid well.

Until she didn't.

Tatyana took a deep breath and tried not to tap her foot with impatience.

The secretary glanced up and offered a kind smile. "Ms. Beridze is on her way into the office. She was traveling last night and sends her apologies for being late."

"It's fine." Tatyana gave her a tight smile. "I appreciate her time."

"Of course."

Beridze was a Georgian name. Since she'd walked into SMO International, she'd met Ukrainians and Russians, of course, but she'd also heard accents from Armenia, Romania, and other Black Sea countries. Muted phone conversations around her were conducted in English, Russian, Chinese, and other languages she didn't recognize, but all that made sense for an international shipping conglomerate like SMO.

Elene Beridze was the chief financial officer for the labyrinthine corporation that Zara's company had operated under, which Tatyana had found out once she'd picked through layers and layers of paperwork.

It had taken months to find the connection between SMO International and Zara, even after calling in favors from old friends. SMO seemed to be as archaic in some of their practices as Zara had been, and hardly anything was online. No website. No email addresses listed.

Nothing.

Tatyana cleared her throat. "If there's someone else I could meet about compensation so I don't have to take Ms. Beridze's time—"

"No, no." The secretary was quick to jump in. "It's no trouble. She wanted to meet you personally."

So you don't report us to regulators.

It was the unspoken subtext to all her conversations thus far. First she had to convince the receptionist in the front office that someone in Accounting really *did* want to talk to her. It was only when someone in a suit walked by and overheard Zara's name that she'd gotten attention.

Then she had to convince the person in Accounting that she wasn't speaking fiction.

Five people later, she'd ended up on the fourth floor of a luxurious office situated in an old mansion located in the north end of the Prymorskyi District. She could smell the ocean outside, and a deep breath of Black Sea air shored up her confidence.

She had worked for six months without pay.

She deserved her money. Her family needed it.

And judging from the crystal water goblets by the decanter on the sideboard, this company had more than enough funds to pay her.

Muted footsteps sounded in the hallway as Tatyana looked away from the cut-crystal decanter and back toward the door.

An attractive woman with a chic grey bob and a burgundy suit walked over the threshold, accompanied by a tall, dark-haired man carrying a briefcase. She appeared to be in her mid-fifties, and her appearance shouted money in the most low-key way.

In Sevastopol, Tatyana was accustomed to women with money displaying that wealth with designer handbags and jewelry that could blind you. This woman was the opposite of that.

"Miss Vorona?" She smiled graciously. "I'm Elene Beridze, and I apologize for keeping you waiting." The woman spoke in English with a demure British accent and reached out, offering Tatyana a handshake.

Tatyana took her hand, responding in English. "It's no problem. I only hope we can settle this. I know it's a very awkward situation."

"Thank you for your patience while we sorted things out." She reached back for the briefcase her companion was carrying. "Why don't we speak in my conference room?"

"Of course." Tatyana glanced out the window as she followed the executive down a wood-paneled hallway. She'd been waiting so long the sun was already setting. "What time do you think—"

"This shouldn't take much longer, but to go over all the paperwork to settle your back pay, you might need to come back tomorrow morning. Again, I am so sorry for the wait. I had to travel unexpectedly last night. You're staying in town, yes?"

Tatyana nodded. "At a hotel." A run-down tourist trap, but it was cheap and clean.

"I hope you realize we will be compensating you for all your travel expenses as well."

Elene Beridze ushered her into a conference room dominated by a wooden table carved with a rose detail. There was a crystal chandelier overhead, and a gilt-framed mirror dominated the longest wall.

Tatyana tried not to stare. A gold flower from the edge of that mirror could probably pay her mother's expenses for a month.

"You never should have had to track us down as you did," Elene continued, "so the expenses related to that will be reimbursed. We have a standing agreement at the Admiral Hotel for employees who need to work in town. Can we put you in a room there on our account?"

Tatyana blinked. "That's all right. I only want to settle this as quickly as possible so I can return to my mother."

"Of course." Elene motioned for her assistant to pull out a chair for Tatyana before she dismissed the man. "Please join me. I've seen the copies of the paperwork you've already submitted, but I have a few questions."

"Of course." Tatyana took a deep breath. "Are those questions related to all the money Zara stole from you?"

Elene froze, and her only movement for a few moments was a long blink. "You're direct, Miss Vorona. I appreciate that."

Tatyana looked around the office and decided that she currently had nothing to lose. "I'm not interested in dishonesty, Miss Beridze. I approached SMO because I need to be paid but also because I knew that Zara was probably running two sets of books." She placed her hand on her messenger bag. "I have the real accounts. I would like to be paid the salary that I am owed, but I want to make things right. If you would like, I can make myself available to help you find the money that Zara stole."

There was a flicker of amusement in Elene's eyes. "As I said before, I appreciate directness."

"Then you should also appreciate that whatever money I recover for you, I would expect a percentage of it." It was a huge gamble, but day after day in SMO's offices made Tatyana bold. "A finder's fee."

And desperate.

Elene smiled a little bit. "You want a finder's fee for telling us you helped Zara embezzle money from our corporation?"

"I'm only a bookkeeper, Ms. Beridze. I embezzled nothing. In fact, I worked for six months without pay."

Elene lifted her chin. "This is true."

Tatyana kept her hand on her messenger bag. "I compiled accounts and organized money, which I believe I can help you recover. It is not illegal to receive a consulting fee in this situation, but it *is* illegal to file false tax reports as Zara must have done under your corporate aegis."

Elene cocked her head. "An interesting choice of words," she murmured. "So you are saying that if we cannot come to an agreement, you will be reporting SMO to regulators in Sevastopol?"

"As an employee who could also be held responsible for any trespass of the law, I would feel a responsibility to come forward if I knew illegality had been committed by my employer."

"Are you attempting to blackmail us?"

Tatyana didn't flinch. "Not at all. I am very sure that all of Zara's actions were taken without your consent, and" —she chose her words carefully— "I *trust* that a firm with the reputation that SMO International carries would correct all those reports once the theft has been reported and the money is recovered."

Fat chance that they would, but that wasn't Tatyana's responsibility.

"Of course," Elene said. "If a violation was proven to us, we would report it to the proper authorities."

"But to prove SMO is not involved, the company would have to recover the money first."

Elene leaned forward. "And you can do that for us?"

Tatyana fixed a confident and cool expression on her face. "I can."

The corner of Elene's mouth flicked up. "I hope you don't mind late nights, Miss Vorona." She glanced at the darkening sky out the window. "Because if you want more than your back pay, there's one more person you will need to meet."

TATYANA HADN'T SMOKED SINCE SHE GRADUATED FROM secondary school, but she wished she had a cigarette as she paced in the cobblestone courtyard of SMO's offices while they waited for Elene's boss to arrive. Apparently the man was traveling from the north and kept odd hours because of jet lag.

Tatyana wasn't going to question it when she felt inches away from success.

Offering to find the money for a finder's fee was a gamble, and she wasn't nearly as confident as she'd presented to Elene, but it was the only play she had.

Yes, she wanted to get paid, but she also needed a job, and those were few and far between in Sevastopol, which was where she needed to be. Her neighbor could only look in on her mother for a few more days before Tatyana would need to return because the woman could not take care of herself.

She felt her phone buzzing in her pocket and reached for it, knowing without looking who it was going to be. "Hallo."

"Tatyana, are you flying home now?"

She squeezed her eyes shut. "No, because you wouldn't be able to call me if I was flying, Mama."

"I know that. Are you still in Kyiv?"

"Odesa, Mama."

"Odesa." Anna Asanov whispered the word like a curse. "And are they going to pay you?"

"Yes, it's a good company. It's a real company, Mama, don't worry."

Her mother had always been suspicious of Tatyana working from home. She worried that the job wasn't legal. That Tatyana was doing something illegal by not going into an office even after Tatyana explained that much of her work back in Kyiv was also online and could be done from anywhere.

Sadly, with things the way they were, no firm in Kyiv was going to keep paying someone who had to live in Sevastopol even if they wanted to.

"The electricity bill is due, Tanya."

Fuck. Where was she going to get the money for it? How fast could SMO reimburse her for travel expenses? Maybe she should have taken Elene up on the offer to stay at the company's preferred hotel and send the rest of her travel money back to her mother.

No, no, no. That gave SMO too much power over the situation. Better to be independent until some kind of contract was signed.

"Can you borrow a little bit from Karol?" Their neighbor knew the situation—a little of it anyway—and the old man held Tatyana in great affection because of her grandparents.

"I mean, I can try. He's going to want something from me if I borrow money though."

Tatyana tried not to roll her eyes, but then she gave in to the impulse because what the hell? Her mother couldn't see her. "Mama, Karol doesn't want to have sex with you."

"Why not? I'm still a beautiful woman, Tanya."

"And he's a sweet old man who was friends with your father. He doesn't see you that way."

Her mother muttered something about old men still having balls even if they were saggy, and Tatyana let out a slow, even breath and tried not to listen because the last thing she wanted to think about was her neighbor's balls. "Mama, just borrow the money from Karol and tell him I'll pay him back as soon as I get home."

Because maybe money would magically materialize in her pocket as she went through security.

You'll figure it out, Tatyana. You always figure it out.

She told herself the same thing every time she woke up in the middle of the night, wondering how she and her mother were going to make it through the winter without Tatyana having a job.

She sucked in a hard breath and let the sea air fill her lungs. It was Friday night, and beyond the stone and wrought iron wall of SMO's headquarters, she could hear young people heading into the night with friends. She heard faint music in the distance from a club and the pulse and retreat of pop music pumping from passing cars.

You used to have that life.

Well, not exactly that life. But she'd had friends in Kyiv. She'd had a job and a little extra money for fun on the weekends. She'd had friends she could call and boys she dated when she wanted to feel sexy and seen.

Tatyana was twenty-seven, but she felt like she was a decade older. Maybe more. She had no one but her mother now. She didn't even have a job.

"Miss Vorona?" a voice called from the front of the office. "They're ready for you."

She took another deep, bracing breath of sea air and said, "I have to go, Mama. Borrow the money from Karol and I'll pay him back soon."

"Okay but—"

"Mama, I have to go."

"Fine, fine." Anna muttered something under her breath and hung up the phone.

"Good night to you too." Tatyana put her phone in her pocket and walked into the building and through polished wooden doors that could pay her mother's electric bill for a year.

Maybe a decade.

Tatyana was back in Elene Beridze's conference room, her hand resting on the messenger bag in the seat next to her, when two people walked in.

One was Elene, and the other was a man.

No, more than a man. A *presence.*

Tatyana wasn't impressed by men. Growing up without a father made her keenly aware that men held too much power over most women's lives. Her mother pined for a man who'd never loved her. Her grandfather had been the rare, stable exception in her life, but she'd never become attached to a boyfriend or a lover because, in her experience, men were not dependable.

But the man who took the seat next to Elene was magnetic.

He was dressed in a dark grey suit the color of charcoal and wore a wine-red shirt under his jacket that was open at the collar. No tie.

Dark, reddish-brown hair was swept back from his face, and a trim beard covered his jaw.

He sat across from her, staring at Tatyana with keen grey eyes the color of storm clouds. He was tall, even while sitting, and she knew he'd tower over her if he stood. He was also handsome, but it was the least impressive thing about him.

Whatever cologne he was wearing smelled like cedar and sweet smoke, and she was tempted to lean toward him. She resisted. Power radiated from him, and in her gut, Tatyana knew he was dangerous.

Her research had told her that SMO International was a legitimate multinational company not connected to organized crime, so why did this man have the bearing of a gangster?

Elene said, "Miss Vorona, this is my employer, Mr. Sokolov, the CEO of SMO International."

His voice was low and curt. "She knows who I am." He spoke in Russian, not English.

"I don't know who you are," Tatyana responded in Russian too, "but you look like the boss."

The corner of his mouth curled up. "Then you know who I am."

Sokolov. He *looked* like a bird of prey, ready to snatch up the pale little girl sitting in front of him. He appeared to be in his late thirties or early forties, but something about him told Tatyana he was older than he looked.

His gaze on her didn't waver; Tatyana felt like she was under a microscope.

"Elene thinks you can find the money Zara stole. Is she right?"

Tatyana glanced at Elene. "I think Ms. Beridze is rarely wrong."

"That's not an answer."

"I think it is."

He didn't look away, and his constant attention felt like a burn on her skin. "I don't like it when people lie to me."

Tatyana narrowed her eyes. "You think I'm lying?"

"I think Zara is very smart and very conniving."

"Agreed." Tatyana leaned forward. "But I'm smarter than she is.

And I found the connection between ZOL Enterprises and SMO International, so I'm smarter than whoever tried to hide her company, don't you think?"

"I'm the one who tried to hide her company." His mouth twitched again at the corner, almost as if he wanted to smile. "So you think you're smarter than me?"

Well, shit. "Maybe I'm just better at sorting through paperwork."

"Don't back away now, volchitsa. I like your teeth."

What was happening? Was this absolutely terrifying man... *flirting* with her?

No, no, no, no, no.

That was not going to happen.

Tatyana met his terrifying grey eyes rimmed with lashes black as ink, and she kept her gaze fixed, trying to project stone-cold confidence. "I can find the money Zara hid. I'm the one who did the transfers, and I know how to find my way through paperwork mazes. If you try to use a blunt instrument, you will get nowhere. You need a key, and I'm it."

Sokolov finally broke their locked gaze and glanced down to the chair at Tatyana's right side. "What's to stop me from taking that bag with all your documents and your computer and getting rid of you tonight?"

"Oleg." Elene's voice was a sharp rebuke.

He looked at his financial officer and shrugged. "Maybe I don't want to give her a percentage of thirty million dollars she didn't earn."

Tatyana nearly choked, but she tried not to lose her cool expression.

Thirty million? Dollars? US dollars?

Dear God, what had she gotten herself into?

This was a mistake. This was a horrible, horrible mistake. There was no way she could find thirty million dollars anywhere. There was no way she would be able to—

"Five percent," Sokolov said.

"Fifteen," she blurted.

No! What was she doing? She was negotiating for something she couldn't do! It was decided. She was going to die. She was absolutely writing a check that she had no way of cashing.

"Seven percent, and you'll work from Elene's office so she can supervise you. Don't fool yourself that you can find thirty million without some help."

"Thirteen percent. I can find my own help, and I'm not working from here. I have family obligations in Sevastopol."

"Sevastopol is Zara's old neighborhood, and she probably still has people there watching you. Don't underestimate how dangerous she can be. You're safer here." He leaned forward and held out a hand. "You can have ten percent, volchitsa, but I'll be keeping my eye on you."

Ten percent of thirty million dollars was three million dollars.

Three. Million. Dollars. US dollars.

It was enough for the rest of her life. Enough to keep her mother out of poverty. Enough to pay back every loan she'd ever taken and enough to say fuck you to her father forever.

Tatyana reached out her hand to the most dangerous man she'd ever met. "Ten percent *and* my pay for the last six months of work for Zara. My mother needs it and it's what I am owed."

"Done." His hand closed over hers, and Tatyana felt a wave of something... wrong. Foreign, wrong, inhuman.

She looked into Sokolov's eyes, and there was a dark, swirling energy coming off him that caught her breath. "What are you?"

He frowned, narrowed his eyes, and then everything went black.

Chapter Three

"**D**id you have to completely knock her out with your amnis?" Mika Arakis, Oleg's head of security, liaison to the Sokolov crime family, and chief boyar of Oleg's druzhina was bitching about carrying a woman who probably weighed less than an average steamer trunk.

"Relax, Mika." Oleg held the heavy wooden door as Mika walked the small human woman out to the waiting car in the courtyard. "I tried to use a nudge, but she resisted my influence."

The elemental energy that fed his fire and had kept him alive for eleven centuries was commonly called amnis. It ran like an electric current under the skin and was the reason Oleg could manipulate fire, thrive on blood, and influence the cerebral cortex of ordinary humans.

Of course, different humans had different natural shields.

"She resisted your amnis, so you used a hammer instead?" Mika grunted as he put the woman in the back of the car. "Bodies aren't heavy—they're just awkward to carry."

"You've gotten soft," Oleg muttered. "Too many minions jumping to do your bidding. I'm going to tell Ludmila to stop coddling you."

Mika snorted.

The Estonian water vampire was more than an employee to Oleg. He was the spear tip of Oleg's druzhina, the collection of his oldest friends and most trusted warriors, vampires who had been with him for centuries. They were comrades-in-arms—brothers and sisters by oath—and Oleg trusted them more than his own blood.

And Ludmila—one of the oldest members and Mika's most trusted sniper—was about as nurturing as a wolverine.

"Fuck off." Mika straightened and looked at Oleg. "Why did you use your influence at all? I was watching, and she agreed to your terms."

Unfortunately, amnis didn't work on other vampires, which was why Mika was such a pain in his ass.

"She could tell something was different about me."

Mika lowered his voice and stepped close. "Tatyana Vorona suspected... that you are a moody bitch who needs to get laid?"

Oleg smirked and patted Mika's cheek. "It's good that you amuse me." He walked to the other side of the antique Mercedes where one of Mika's men was holding the door. "The Admiral Hotel."

"Right away, Mr. Sokolov."

The man closed the door after Oleg slipped inside, glancing at the unconscious human before Mika joined them in the front passenger seat.

"She's going to be a problem," Mika said.

"She's going to be a solution." Oleg examined Tatyana Vorona's sleeping face. "She's going to find thirty million dollars for me."

"Thirty million," Mika muttered. "You spent that last year on good caviar."

"The money isn't the point, and I don't think that's correct. *You* like caviar, not me."

"Like I said," Mika repeated, "you spent thirty million on good caviar last year."

"I'll probably kill you." Oleg stretched out his legs, grateful that he had a fleet of antique vehicles to enjoy rather than the cramped, modern cars that humans used. "One of these nights I'll probably decide to kill you."

Vampire amnis acted like an electrical current to modern technology. That meant nothing digital and no computers. There were companies who had adapted modern technology for immortal hands, but Oleg didn't use it. He hired humans to use technology for him, humans like Tatyana Vorona.

"Even if she can find the money, she's going to be a problem," Mika said. "She's seen your face."

"And?" He waved a hand over Tatyana's pretty blond head. "I can make her forget me."

"But will you?" Mika turned around and switched from Russian—which their driver spoke—to his own native Estonian. "Don't think I missed the resemblance. She could be Luana's sister."

Oleg glanced at the woman. "The resemblance is only passing when she's awake. Plus this woman was born twenty-seven years ago in a government hospital in Kerch, not to a wealthy merchant in Vienna."

"Details."

"Details matter."

"Don't pretend you didn't notice."

Oleg glanced at the limp woman beside him. In repose, she looked younger and the lines around her eyes had relaxed. Her hair had come loose from the neat bun at the base of her neck, and the vivid blue eyes that had captured him during their meeting were closed; light brown lashes rested against her cheeks.

"I noticed." He looked away. Resemblance to his dead mate or not, he would use Tatyana Vorona to claw back what Zara had stolen from him, and then he would wipe her memory and let her resume her simple human life, richer by several million dollars. "Make sure she gets the money Zara owed her."

"I'm sure Elene will take care of it."

"See to it personally," he snapped. "Elene has enough to do."

"And I don't?" Mika's eyes were stormy. "You think it's easy dealing with all the shit your daughter left in her wake? I'm still sorting out allies in the east whom Zara fucked over when she left Sevastopol for Laskaris's mansion in Istanbul."

"How much last week?"

"She increased the tariffs again." He snapped his fingers. "No, sorry. *Laskaris* increased the tariffs through the Bosporus. It's definitely not your daughter."

As irritated as Oleg was about the extra money Zara was leaching from his businesses, he had to admire her cunning. He'd left his own sire once, and it had been just as brutal to create his own reputation in the vampire world.

If she weren't a sociopath, he'd be proud of her.

"I have an idea," Mika said.

They were pulling up to the luxury hotel where Oleg kept a dedicated suite of rooms for humans who worked for him.

"Later. Let's get this one situated." He snapped his fingers and touched a spark to Tatyana's cheek. "Miss Vorona."

At his touch, the woman's eyes flickered open, but they were confused. "Where—"

"We're at the hotel, Miss Vorona. You passed out in the conference room, and we're making sure you're delivered safely to a hotel."

"No I want..." She sounded exhausted. "My bag." Her voice grew in strength. "My bag is—"

"Right next to you." He patted the shabby messenger bag. "We have a deal now, Miss Vorona. We're partners, and I don't steal from my business partners."

Her fingers closed around the handle of the bag, and he saw her trying to sit up.

"Relax." He touched her hand, and the natural shields that had been so strong before were weak and soft against his touch. He saw her hand relax and ignored the quick burst of pleasure it gave him to see her surrender. "Relax, Tatyana."

Her blue eyes flickered open and found his own. "Who are you?"

"Oleg." He used the Russian pronunciation, so it sounded more like Alec.

Mika opened the passenger door and held Tatyana's back so she didn't fall out. "The concierge is bringing a chair over."

"Excellent." He kept his eyes on Tatyana's. "My assistant has called for the concierge. She's a lovely woman named Marina, and she'll see you to your room and make sure you have everything you need."

"I don't know…" She closed her eyes. "I'm tired. Why am I so tired?"

"It's late and you had a stressful day." He touched her hand again. "Sleep, volchitsa. I'm sure your fangs will be back when I see you tomorrow night."

He smiled and allowed a hint of his own fangs to peek out, but Tatyana's eyes were already closed.

"I STILL HAVE MY DOUBTS WHETHER THIS WOMAN CAN FIND THE money Zara stole," Mika said, taking Tatyana's seat in the back of the Mercedes as they headed toward Oleg's private penthouse near the city center.

Oleg had a large compound in Odesa, but he kept a secure apartment near SMO's offices for the times Elene needed him to work. Mika had a room in the same complex, as did Elene for the times she didn't want to make the commute from her house outside the city.

There was no sea view as there was at his larger compound, but Oleg wasn't a water vampire who needed to see the ocean every five minutes or he would expire.

"You have doubts," Oleg said. "I have doubts. Elene has *fewer* doubts, and she's the only who's been trying to figure out how Zara did it, so why don't we trust the smartest woman we know, huh?"

"Not as smart as Tatyana, according to your little wolf."

Oleg chuckled. "You caught that."

"I like a woman with ego, but this feels more like bravado." Mika shrugged. "Still, I have an idea."

"Which is?" Oleg made a habit of hiring smart people and then listening to them. It had helped him build an empire, and it was the only way he kept it.

"The human finds the money or she doesn't find the money. Either way, we can use her to draw Zara out."

"Use her as bait?" Oleg was intrigued.

Zara taking up with Laskaris meant his own child was out of his aegis because the old Greek was wealthy, influential, and powerful with the old guard in Athens and Rome. And since vampires were slow to come into the modern world, the Athenian immortal court still held an enormous amount of sway among vampires.

"As long as she stays in Istanbul, we can't touch her, but the moment she steps back into your territory..." Mika shrugged. "Laskaris might complain, but there would be nothing he could do."

"Zara's left the woman alone this long. Why do you think she'd bother to come after her now?"

"Before now, Tatyana Vorona wasn't revealing all her secrets to you."

"I like your thinking." Oleg nodded. "Instead of keeping Tatyana's identity a secret, we make it known that she's working with us. That Zara's secret bookkeeper came to us and is helping us track her money."

"She has her financial settlement from you, but she knows she can't touch it."

Oleg smiled. It was one of his finer ideas. No sire in the immortal world would send their progeny off without some kind of financial settlement, usually something around five percent of their wealth, which in Oleg's case was a treasure gathered over a millennium of conquest along the richest river cities in Europe.

And five percent of that immense wealth was sitting in several nondescript trunks in his mansion in Saint Petersburg, the heart of Oleg's business empire.

All Zara had to do to claim her inheritance was return to Oleg's territory.

Mika continued, "With your permission, Oksana and I will put the word out among the immortal gossips of the world that Tatyana is our new favorite human and she has all the information we need. Whether it's true or not, it will draw Zara out."

"It could put the human at risk."

Mika frowned. "Do you care?"

"An excellent question."

Oleg kept strict standards on who could be subjected to harm in his world. Mundane humans simply living their lives were a resource. They created the economies that fed his wealth and produced the blood he needed to live. To harm them was as foolish as salting his own fields.

Humans who willingly entered into the vampire world were another matter, which made Tatyana a bit of a conundrum. She had been working with vampires, but he was fairly sure she had no idea what Zara was, which should have made her immune to immortal violence by his own rules.

But...

"Put her name out," Oleg said. "We'll keep an eye on Miss Vorona, but getting Zara away from Laskaris is more important. Once she's not whispering in his ear, we'll be able to negotiate more reasonable tariffs for our shipping partners."

"And Zara will finally be under your control."

"Exactly." He glanced at Mika again. "Hang Tatyana Vorona out the window and let's see who comes after her."

"Done." Mika smiled. "I'll start making calls tonight."

He called Elene on the video chat system built into his office at the penthouse. She must have already arrived at her residence, because he could see her husband in the background mixing a drink and she was dressed in a blue housecoat.

A maid was hanging his coat and then gathered the papers Mika had handed her, stacking them silently on the console table.

"Thank you for calling Marina and filling her in," Oleg said. "I told her to put the woman in the employee's suite."

"I've already sent a note over so she won't be confused when she wakes up."

"She'll be confused, but I don't think she'll run." Oleg remembered the firm handshake the woman had offered before she was triggered by his use of amnis.

Elene said, "I have a good feeling about Miss Vorona."

"You think she can find the accounts?"

Mika lifted a hand to wave goodbye before he departed the room.

Oleg nodded at him, then returned to Elene.

Elene continued. "I think she's a meticulous record keeper—from what I could see of her paperwork—and with the reports she has and the reports Zara submitted from ZOL, we should be able to figure out not only how much money was actually taken but how Zara was doing it."

"I know that's been bothering you." He snapped at the maid who was just about to leave the room and motioned her over. "I haven't fed," he said to Elene. "Do you mind?"

"As long as you don't." She reached for the glass of red wine her husband handed to her.

The maid began to unbutton her collar, but Oleg shook his head and pointed to her wrist.

"I had a conversation with Mika on the way home," Oleg said.

The woman pushed up the sleeve that covered her left wrist and wound a kitchen towel around her arm. Then she held it out to Oleg, who grasped it in his left hand.

Elene sipped her wine. "What did Mika think of Tatyana Vorona?"

"He thinks we should put her name out." Oleg licked along the maid's wrist, squeezing the flesh and plumping the blue vein visible under her pale skin.

"Do you think that's wise? This early, I mean. We don't have all her records yet."

"It will take time for word to spread." Oleg brushed his lips along the maid's arm and felt her body relax as his amnis took hold. His fangs grew long in his mouth, and his breath heated the woman's skin. "How much are we losing every month in bribes to Laskaris?"

Putting his lips to the woman's wrist, he bit down and felt her flesh give way. Her iron-rich blood poured into his mouth and sang for his senses, flooding his body with pleasure as he tried to concentrate on Elene's side of the conversation.

Elene sighed. "The taxes are the same, but the bribes are double what we used to pay before Zara moved in. I spoke with Radu the other day, and he claims she's taking three times as much as Laskaris did."

Oleg took four strong pulls on the woman's wrist before he stroked her arm in appreciation and pierced his tongue to heal the small wounds he'd made in her flesh.

"Now, Radu loves to exaggerate," Elene continued, "but it's not out of the question that she could be bumping the price for our allies even more than she's gouging us."

Oleg glanced up to see the woman's mouth flushed and parted. Her eyes were fixed on his fangs, but he placed a light kiss on her wrist before he used the towel to wipe his lips and then wrap her arm.

"Find Mika if you like," he murmured. "I'm finished."

Sexual arousal was a common response to feeding, and if he weren't on a call with Elene, he might have offered the young woman some release, but his mind was occupied with other matters.

"Radu exaggerates, but he's not the only one complaining." Oleg felt the living blood flood his system. He was alert. Primed for action he couldn't take.

At least not at that moment.

"We put Tatyana Vorona's name out," he said. "We use her as bait to draw Zara out, and then we take control of the situation. Laskaris is an ancient, but he's not a god."

"You don't want to go to war with Athens," Elene said. "That won't end well for anyone."

"We shall see," he said. "It wouldn't be the first time I've fought an ancient. Water vampires have their vulnerabilities."

"As do you."

"Nonsense." He smiled a little bit. "Don't you remember, Elene? I'm the monster in the night."

"You're going to be a monster to Tatyana if she gets hurt."

"If she had come to you asking for her pay and nothing else, I wouldn't have even noticed her. She's hunting now, and she knows there are other predators in the forest."

"You know she has no idea what she's getting into."

"She struck a bargain, Elene." His mind flashed to the clear blue eyes and the direct challenge on the young woman's face.

Bold. Tatyana was bold, and he admired those who took chances. "If this all works out the way I want it to, Zara will be neutralized, you and the bookkeeper will recover my money, and Laskaris will be forced to back down."

"And Tatyana?"

Oleg shrugged. "She'll walk away with what I promised her. Ten percent of anything she can recover. I told her earlier tonight: I don't steal from my business partners."

"She's human."

"So are you." Oleg brought his hands together, steepling his fingers and resting them against his chin. "I've learned more than a little over a thousand years, Elene. Never underestimate a human."

Chapter Four

Sevastopol
Three years before

Was karaoke ever a good idea?

Tatyana sat at the back of a lively club near Ushakov Square. It wasn't smoky. The drinks were good, and the groups on stage were like any karaoke club, a mix of amazing and terrible.

"Another drink?" A friendly server walked over. She was wearing a black apron and her hair was tied back in a neat twist.

Tatyana stared at her. "Do you like working here?"

The woman shrugged. "It's okay. Are you looking for a job? The waiting list for this place is pretty long."

"Right."

That was the answer everywhere. She'd had to leave her job and move back to her mother's city when her grandparents had passed. Her mother couldn't be alone, and now Tatyana couldn't find work.

Just go apply at the city somewhere, Tanya.

That was her mother's attitude. Find a nice government job somewhere that paid pennies but offered the security of never being fired.

The problem was, if they were going to pay the bills, she needed the kind of money she had been making in Kyiv. The kind of money that no one in Sevastopol was going to pay her these days.

But she couldn't live in Kyiv because her mother couldn't be alone.

Life was... impossible.

"Did you want another drink?"

"Sorry." Tatyana quickly finished her vodka tonic and nodded. "Yes. Sure." At least the drinks weren't terribly expensive here. She hadn't planned on ordering a second, but she felt guilty about staring into space in front of the server. "It's mostly tourists here, right?"

The woman smiled ruefully. "Mostly, yes. In this part of town, it's pretty much all tourists."

Perfect.

She'd gone out after another passive-aggressive exchange with her mother in the hope that going to a karaoke bar would point her in the direction of some people her own age who might be friendly.

She was twenty-four, not eighty. She hadn't had a huge group of friends in Kyiv, but she'd met other people at the university and stayed in touch. She'd been rooming with a nice girl from the north. She went out on the weekends. Her friends from work invited her to bars and concerts.

Then life and politics became horrible and everything went to shit. Instead of working at a nice accounting firm in a city she loved, Tatyana was living with her mother, everything in the world was upside down, and she couldn't find a job. Her mother's pension barely stretched through half the month.

She muttered under her breath, "People had to pay their rent when the Roman Empire was falling too."

A sharp laugh came from the table next to her, and a woman with long, dark hair glanced over. "You're right."

Tatyana shrugged.

The woman was with a half a dozen people, most of whom seemed to be watching and cheering the woman singing on the stage. Tatyana saw her look away, then look back at Tatyana. Her eyes locked on her face.

Did Tatyana know her? Had they met? She had the strange feeling the woman knew her, and she wondered what kind of awkward conversation was coming. It was inevitable that she would run into people she knew when she was younger, but it rarely went well because her memories of school were terrible.

Tatyana tried to ignore the dark-haired woman's stare. She glanced at the singer on the stage. "Is she your friend? She's good."

They were probably tourists, but that was no excuse to be rude.

"We're friendly." The woman looked at the empty chairs at her table. "Can I join you?"

Oh no. This *was* going to get awkward.

Then again, the woman seemed friendly enough, and she was around Tatyana's age. This could be a new friend. Wasn't that why she got dressed up and went out in the first place? She wanted to meet people.

"Um, sure." Tatyana moved her purse to the chair on the other side. "Why not?"

"I'll buy the next round." The woman rose and walked over. She wasn't tall, but she was stunning with legs that almost looked too long for her body, further elongated by four-inch heels.

The woman was glamorous. She looked rich, and she clearly spent far more time and money on her appearance than Tatyana did.

Tatyana was racking her brain, trying to figure out where she might know her from as she sat in the chair to Tatyana's left.

She put her own purse in the remaining chair and leaned an elbow on the table. "It was getting loud over there."

"If your friends don't cheer you on when you're attempting 'The Greatest Love of All,' are they really your friends?"

The woman held out her hand. "I'm Zara."

"Tatyana." She shook the woman's hand and felt a strange wash of giddiness rise up.

Well, the vodka was finally kicking in.

"Are you visiting the city?" Zara asked.

"No, I just moved back. Right before all the..." She waved a hand. "You know."

"Ah." Zara nodded. "We live in interesting times."

"Isn't that a way of cursing someone?" Tatyana asked. "To wish that they live in interesting times?"

"It's better than being bored." Zara had beautiful dark eyes that glinted in the lights of the club. "Don't you think?"

"No, I like boring." Not boring exactly. "I mean, I like knowing what to expect. Then again, I'm not working, so maybe that's why."

"Really?" Zara raised a manicured hand and waved for a server. "What do you do?"

"I'm a bookkeeper." She clarified. "My degree is in accounting and mathematics, but I was working as a bookkeeper before I had to move back."

"Why did you move?"

"Family reasons." She didn't want to elaborate. "Do you live here?"

Zara smiled. "For the moment. My family is rich. Very rich."

"That must be nice."

"It is." Her smile was coquettish. "But I wanted to see if I could make my own money, so my father set up an import-and-export business for me to run here in Sevastopol."

"Wow." Tatyana couldn't conceive of having so much money you'd set up a company for your daughter like playing at a tea party. "How is it going?"

Her family must be in organized crime. Maybe they were connected to the government. She had better watch what she said. Tatyana suddenly wished she'd never offered a seat to Zara.

Then again, was it better to ignore a rich man's daughter or make nice? She had no idea what was the best idea, so she quickly downed the drink the server set in front of her.

"Are you looking for a job?" Zara asked. "To pay the rent while the empire falls?"

Tatyana snorted. "Something like that."

Zara narrowed her eyes. "Are you good at being a bookkeeper?"

"I'm very fucking good at it." Maybe it was the vodka talking, but Tatyana wasn't lying. She was very good at her job. She was actually underutilized at her last position.

"I like that." Zara's full red lips curled into a smile. "I like confidence."

"My former boss said my ego was too big."

"That sounds like a man." Zara leaned forward. "Women need to be confident, don't they? If we don't believe in ourselves, who else will?"

No one. No one believed in her. Not anymore. "My grandmother used to say the same thing." The sadness hit her like a sudden wave. "I'm sorry." She reached for her purse. "I'm in a strange mood tonight, and I shouldn't burden you with that when you're out with your friends. I should go."

Zara reached out and put a hand on her arm. "Don't."

"Okay." Tatyana sat down and relaxed back into her chair. What a ridiculous idea. She should stay with Zara. Zara hadn't made her sad; it was just her memories.

"You're sad." Zara kept a kind hand on her arm. "Did I say something?"

The story poured out before she could even think about the words escaping her mouth. "My grandparents passed away about six months ago. My grandmother had a heart attack, and then my grandfather died four days after her funeral. He just went to sleep and didn't wake up the next morning."

Zara's hand was soft and soothing on her arm. "I'm so sorry."

"I can't believe I told you that." Tatyana blinked back tears. "I don't... I usually don't talk about them."

"They were important to you." Zara cocked her head and moved her thumb back and forth over Tatyana's wrist. "I'm jealous. My family isn't very close."

"That can be a blessing sometimes." Tatyana wanted to pull her arm away, but she didn't. It was as if she heard a voice in her mind, telling her that Zara was someone she could trust.

"I suppose you're right."

Tatyana laughed ruefully. "At least your father set up a business for you. You must be a little bit close."

"Yes, he did." Zara's eyes sparkled. They were so beautiful. She was beautiful. Tatyana was so lucky that Zara even noticed her.

"You're so kind." Tatyana was starting to slur her words. "I shouldn't have another drink. I'm feeling it."

"Don't be silly. I am enjoying our chat."

Tatyana didn't know why this stunning, glamorous woman was paying attention to her when there were far more interesting people at the club.

"Speaking of my father's business though, I have an idea." Zara leaned closer. "If you're really fucking good at being a bookkeeper, I mean."

"Yeah." Tatyana nodded through the haze. "I am."

Chapter Five

Tatyana woke up swathed in luxurious cotton sheets, her shoes missing and her wrinkled skirt stiff around her body. She sat up slowly, trying to piece together what had happened.

She didn't have a headache. She didn't feel any aches at all save for the uncomfortable sensation that occurs when you sleep in dress clothes.

"What the hell happened last night?" She remembered her meeting with the terrifying CEO of SMO International, the cool professionalism of Elene Beridze, and shaking hands...

Shaking hands on thirty million dollars.

"Oh fuck!" She swung her legs out of the bed and set her feet on the floor, looking for her shoes.

She didn't know where she was, but she had to get out of there. Forget her back pay. She'd been insane to go after it. She had to get home. She had to get back to her mother. Being a waitress was an option. Working in a soul-sucking job at the utilities authority was an excellent option.

Tatyana just had to get away from that handshake.

She raced around the hotel room only to come up short when she saw her battered suitcase sitting in the closet next to her shoes, her trainers, and the slippers she'd stuffed in her carry-on.

"What is happening right now?"

She walked over to the bathroom, and all her toiletries were laid out on the counter, supplemented by high-end hotel items. A robe was neatly folded on a cushioned bench.

Tatyana stepped back and looked—really looked—around the hotel room where she'd been sleeping.

Gold and marble and gilt mirrors.

A giant king bed, a generous sitting area near draped windows with a view of the city. What looked like French doors leading out to a wrought iron balcony that curved around the room. Persian rugs over dark, polished wood floors.

There was an espresso maker in the small kitchenette with a stack of shiny aluminum coffee pods and a giant bowl of fruit next to a tray of fresh pastries.

On the table near the kitchenette, her messenger bag was sitting next to something that looked like a letter. Tatyana walked over and rifled through her bag to check that everything was still in place before she picked up the letter.

Dear Miss Vorona,

I hope you're feeling better this morning. My greatest apologies for the stressful day you experienced yesterday. According to my secretary, you failed to take a lunch or dinner break while you were waiting for me, and that might have contributed to your illness. I sincerely apologize for my late arrival, and I hope you're feeling rested today.

I took the liberty of booking a room for you at the Admiral and having your bags moved over from your previous accommodation to make sure you are comfortable in Odesa since you'll be staying for an extended time. Please speak to the concierge, Marina, should you need anything.

Ring the front desk when you are ready for breakfast and it will be delivered.

Your accommodations and all travel expenses while you are in Odesa will be covered completely by SMO International, of course, as all of us are eager to work with our new consultant on her upcoming project.

I have included my personal number at the bottom of this letter when you feel ready to come back to the office. Please use it when you're rested and ready to proceed.

Sincerely,

Elene Beridze

P.S. The entirely of your wages for your last six months working for ZOL have been transferred to your personal accounts in Sevastopol on Mr. Sokolov's direct orders, but I would appreciate if you could fill out the employment paperwork I have sent to your email address as soon as possible. I'm sure you can appreciate that my own bookkeeper would prefer that the necessary paperwork for your official intake is filled out promptly.

Mr. Sokolov has also instructed me to issue you a small retainer for your upcoming work to cover your expenses while you are consulting with us. We can discuss details when you come into the office later.

TATYANA DROPPED THE LETTER ON THE TABLE AND IMMEDIATELY looked for her phone, which she found plugged into the wall with a charging cord she didn't recognize.

"Oh God, oh God." She tapped furiously to open her banking app, only to see all the money she was owed was already in her account. Along with an additional seven hundred thousand rubles.

And a separate transfer of eight million rubles.

Tatyana dropped her phone, and it rattled when it hit the marble counter.

Sokolov had deposited roughly one hundred thousand US dollars in her bank account overnight. She had no idea how or why the man had done it, but—

Of course you know how.

Of course you know why.

Sokolov was as corrupt as Zara had been. Probably more.

Tatyana picked up her phone and sat down on the sofa overlooking the harbor as morning light poured through the gauzy drapes and her toes rested in the plush carpet of the luxury hotel suite.

She stared at the number again.

It was much harder to back out of a deal when doing so meant returning money. And, of course, it was a large reminder that one hundred thousand was only a fraction of the money Tatyana could make should she find the money Zara stole.

"Checkmate, Mr. Sokolov." She felt a band tightening around her chest.

Tatyana, what have you done?

Someone knocked on the door, and she blinked back the tears that were threatening her eyes. She smoothed her hair back, shook out her wrinkled skirt, and tried to straighten her sweater before she opened the door.

A young woman in an elegant navy-blue suit was standing in the doorway next to a rolling rack filled with clothes in black garment bags. A pile of shoeboxes was lined up under the hanging rack.

"Good morning, Miss Vorona. My name is Lorala, and I'm the hotel stylist. Marina asked me to bring these clothes up for you to try on. She had to guess your size, but she's usually very accurate. I brought a range of items from the boutique downstairs for you to try on."

Tatyana stared at the rack of black garment bags, then glanced down at her wrinkled shirt. "Ms. Beridze ordered clothes for me?"

She couldn't decide if she was relieved or embarrassed. Probably both.

"Oh no, Miss Vorona. Mr. Sokolov asked Marina to help you dress." Lorala glanced at the polyester skirt Tatyana had bought years ago and her creased sweater. "He mentioned that you would be working at SMO and told her a more appropriate professional wardrobe was necessary. All of this is compliments of the hotel."

"Mr. Sokolov ordered the clothes." Tatyana's cheeks were burning. "How... thoughtful."

Lorala's chin tilted up. "But if you'd be more comfortable in your own clothes, I would be happy to have yours dry-cleaned. We have a one-hour cleaner nearby, and I will take them myself."

Tatyana felt her embarrassment wane in the face of the woman's generosity. She had a spare shirt and a pair of summer trousers in her bag, but she knew they were shabby compared to the wardrobe of everyone in the SMO corporate offices.

"That won't be necessary." She opened the door for Lorala to come into the room. "I will be in Odesa longer than originally planned. This is very convenient and will save time. Thank you."

Tatyana would be shooting herself in the foot if she passed up the opportunity for some better clothes. She needed to be taken seriously, and clothes were part of that. She couldn't let her pride get in the way of professionalism.

The woman was clearly in her element. "I'll order breakfast for you, and then I can lay out some outfits while you get cleaned up. We're going to make you look amazing."

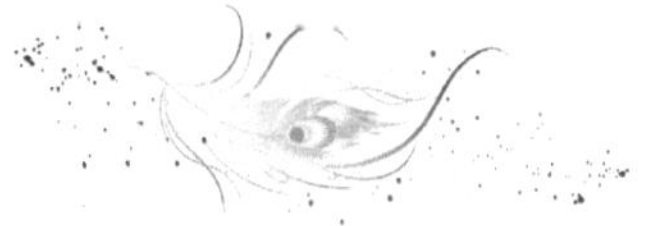

TTATYANA WAS DRESSED IN A MUTED GREY-BLUE SUIT THAT complemented her eyes when she slipped into the car that would take her back to SMO International. Her battered messenger bag was unchanged, but her hair was carefully twisted into a neat chignon, her feet were cushioned in a pair of stylish low-stacked heels, and her makeup was understated and elegant.

By the time Lorala was finished, Tatyana hardly recognized herself, but the stylist was clearly satisfied and promised to bring even more clothes the next day.

"They brought clothes to your hotel room?" Her mother was almost shouting into the phone.

Tatyana held the phone away from her ear and hoped the driver couldn't hear her mother's voice. "I'm going to be staying in Odesa longer than I thought. I'm sure this just saves time. That's why I'm calling."

"How long will you be gone?" The nerves were evident in Anna's voice. "I thought you could be a bookkeeper from home? Do you need a new computer? Is your old one not good enough?"

"It's not about my computer." Her hand rested on the laptop as if it was a talisman that could protect her. "I'll know more after I meet with Ms. Beridze this afternoon, but the good news is they've already paid all my back wages."

"Of course they did. Didn't I tell you they would? There are laws about this, Tanya. They cannot refuse to pay people. That's not *legal*."

"You did tell me." Tatyana sometimes envied her mother's simple views in life. Anna knew that corruption existed, but it was something that happened to big people with big money, not ordinary people who worked as bookkeepers. "And you were right, Mama. So I already transferred money to your account, okay? You can pay back Karol and the bill at the grocery. There's also enough in there for next month's electricity too, and if you want to go to the movies or something with Gabi, you have some money for that too."

"Gabi was gossiping about me."

"I don't know about that." This was typical of her mother. She was highly paranoid.

"No, she was. I can tell. She was talking on her phone, and when I walked into the restaurant, she got off her phone and was quiet, so obviously she was talking about me."

She had no idea what was going on with her mother, but Anna had been like this as long as Tatyana could remember. "We'll talk about it when I get home. If you want to go to a movie, you could go on your own."

"What fun is that?" Anna huffed out a breath. "There's nothing good at the cinema anyway. All the movies are too loud."

"Okay." She closed her eyes and rubbed a circle on her temple. "I'm just telling you there's a little extra money if you want to do something fun, okay? Take the car to the farm for a visit if you want." They'd spent all their savings paying the taxes on the place. Anna should enjoy her childhood home. Sometimes it was the only place that made her happy.

Tatyana continued. "In fact, you could take Pushkin and go up to the farm for a week or so. The weather will be better than the city."

"You think I want to listen to that cat howling for three hours?"

Tatyana pressed her eyes closed. Her mother had been given a grey Siberian kitten when Tatyana was twenty and away at school. Even though she hadn't known the cat from birth, Pushkin immediately took to Tatyana when she came home for holidays, and Anna had never truly forgiven the animal for preferring Tatyana when Anna was the one who fed and brushed him.

"I know Pushkin doesn't like his carrier, but he loves being at the farm. Three hours isn't that much if you're staying for the week. It's just an idea." She noticed the driver turning onto the tree-lined street where SMO was located. "I need to go to work."

"Don't cause trouble."

"I won't, Mama." She ended the call and noticed the driver watching her in the rearview mirror. "Parents."

"I have two of them." He shrugged. "I know."

She muttered, "I only have the one, but most days she feels like three."

The driver chuckled. "What would we do without them though?"

It was a horrible thought, so Tatyana didn't even entertain it. "Do you only work for SMO? Is this a company car? I didn't even ask if I should pay you."

"No, no." He waved a hand. "I'm always on call. A lot of the upper-level executives don't drive. At least this car has power steering."

Tatyana blinked. "Some of them don't?"

"Mr. Sokolov and Mr. Arakis prefer antique vehicles."
A flash of something in her memory.

"Relax, Tatyana."
    "Who are you?"
    "Oleg."

Another voice from outside the luxurious old car.

"The concierge is bringing a chair over."

She'd been in an antique car with Mr. Sokolov the night before.
"Oleg Sokolov?"
The driver nodded. "Yes, Mr. Sokolov."
But that was... impossible. The Oleg Sokolov she'd met couldn't have been over fifty. If he was over forty, she would be shocked.

"What's to stop me from taking that bag with all your documents and your computer and getting rid of you tonight?"
    "Oleg."
    "Maybe I don't want to give her a percentage of thirty million dollars she didn't earn."

Caught in the shock of thirty million dollars and the stressful negotiations with Sokolov the night before, the man's first name had hardly registered.

It was a coincidence. It had to be a coincidence. Oleg wasn't a common name. It wasn't uncommon either.

Because there was no way that the Oleg Sokolov—the beautiful and terrifying man who ran SMO International—was Zara's own father.

Chapter Six

Oleg watched through the two-way glass of the mirror in Elene's conference room as papers were spread out over the table and Elene's secretary—Maria? Margret? He couldn't remember—talked the little wolf through the intake paperwork that would make her officially Oleg's property.

Not property exactly, but once she'd signed those papers, she was well and truly part of his world, which made her fair game for all sorts of interesting possibilities.

His fingers itched as the fire under his skin begged to come out, just to play a little bit, but he pushed back his instincts. Light like that might betray his presence.

Someone cracked open the door. Oleg glanced over his shoulder and saw Mika with his second-in-command, another water vampire named Oksana.

Oleg snapped his fingers and motioned them in. "Get inside and close the door."

Mika walked to Oleg and Oksana shut the door behind them.

"What's happening?" Mika asked.

"She's signing her intake paperwork for Elene."

Mika glanced at the mirror, then at Oleg. "And you're watching this why?"

Oleg cocked his head. "She's interesting."

Oksana peered through the glass, seeing Tatyana for the first time. "She looks like Luana, doesn't she?"

Mika made a rumbling sound in the back of his throat. "She's not Luana."

"Obviously not," Oksana said. "But she does look a little bit—"

"It's not the resemblance that makes her interesting." Oleg wished both of them would keep quiet. "The more I look at her, the more I see the difference. The coloring is the same." He shrugged. "A bit around the eyes. But her mouth, her personality—completely different."

Mika nodded slowly. "Yes, she seems rational and not insane."

Oleg's lip curled. "Did you have something to tell me?"

Mika reached his hand out and Oksana handed him a file. "We found more on her father after you and I spoke last night. He's Czech— no known relation to Luana's people—and was in Sevastopol on holiday when he met her mother. Basic sad tale for the woman. He has his fun and takes off home. She's left with a baby and no father. End of story."

The end of the story on paper, but Oleg had a feeling it was more complicated for the human in the ice-blue suit.

Tatyana examined everything. She noticed everything. She'd glanced at the two-way mirror more than once, and he suspected she knew she was being watched.

She asked question after question, but there was nothing to detect. There was no secret agenda—at least not on paper.

Tatyana Vorona was agreeing to a contract to be a paid consultant for SMO International, a forensic-accounting consultant to be specific. She would receive a base pay, lodging, and a meal stipend while she was in Odesa along with a percentage of monies recovered during her employment.

She would pay taxes on it. She'd have part of it deducted for SMO's mandatory investment program and would be covered under the company's standard employment benefits and obligations umbrella while she was a contractor.

His little wolf could pick apart every contract he handed to her, and she would find nothing that went against the law.

"She likes rules." Oleg fixed his eyes on her as she read through the last bit of her contract. "She likes order and predictability. She's ambitious but a little bit afraid of it. She wasn't raised to think much of herself, but she does and she's not sure how she feels about that."

Mika leaned against the wall and looked at Tatyana. Then at Oleg. "How much time have you spent watching this woman?"

He caught Oksana's smile, even though she tried to cover it, but the vampire said nothing.

"Enough to read her." Oleg was fascinated by Tatyana's mouth. It was wide and expressive. She didn't conceal much even though she probably thought she did. Her mouth told every story. Annoyance with the rote corporatespeak that Elene's secretary was spewing. Awareness of the bag that carried her computer and papers. She kept glancing at it with a small frown. Not unhappy, just serious.

"She doesn't know how to find that money," Mika said.

"How do you know?" Oleg kept his eyes on Tatyana but raised an eyebrow. "She knows more about computers than either of us. She might find it."

"It doesn't matter if she does. As of tonight, she is bait for Zara."

Oleg grunted as he glanced at Mika. His second-in-command was cold-blooded, and that's why Oleg trusted him. Mika Arakis was loyal to Oleg, to the druzhina, and to his own interests. That was all, and that was everything Oleg needed from the vampire.

He looked back at the woman. "Miss Vorona might not be as clumsy as you think."

"It would be better she tripped *some* of Zara's traps," Oksana said quietly. "We need to get your daughter out of Istanbul."

"And if she doesn't?" The corner of Oleg's mouth ticked up. "Whatever will you two do if the woman manages to steal back my money without tipping Zara off?"

Oksana curled her lip. "That would be inconvenient."

"It won't matter," Mika said. "I've already leaked her name to some of your brothers in Moscow."

Oleg felt a twitch under his right eye. "Why?"

"Because your criminal relations gossip more than old soldiers." Mika straightened. "I know Zara keeps in touch with the Albanians too. Word will get around, and we'll be ready."

Oleg didn't know why there was a sour taste in the back of his throat. That was exactly what Mika was supposed to do.

"Don't worry." Mika smiled a little bit. "I have people watching her. Day and night. Zara and her minions won't be able to get to her without us knowing."

"I don't want her hurt." Oleg turned back to the window to see Tatyana signing the last paper.

She smiled a polite, professional smile at Maria. Miriam? Whatever the secretary's name was. Then she glanced at the mirror again.

Her eyes narrowed, and Oleg had the oddest feeling that the woman could see right through the glass. He met her intense blue gaze and felt as if she were looking right through the wall.

Elene walked into the room, and Tatyana looked away.

Oleg turned the volume up on the speaker feed from the conference room.

"...get you situated in a proper office."

"I don't mind this room as long as it's private." Tatyana looked at the mirror. "I do need privacy."

So she knew someone was there. Maybe not Oleg, but someone.

"Of course," Elene said smoothly. "Which is why I'd prefer you to work in one of the offices that adjoins mine. This conference room can have people coming and going. You need someplace where you'll have privacy and can leave your computer if you need to go out for a break."

"My computer stays with me." She touched the strap of the messenger bag. "I don't leave it."

"Ever?"

"Never." She rested her hand on the worn leather. "I have backup equipment in other locations. Encrypted drives with people I trust, but my primary computer I keep myself."

What a suspicious little thing she was. Oleg approved.

"She doesn't trust any of us," Mika said. "She might survive this after all."

"Yes." Oksana's nose was nearly on the glass. "She seems smart for a human."

Elene continued in the conference room. "That's very security conscious." She nodded. "I approve. Marta says you've completed all the paperwork we need."

Marta. The secretary's name was Marta.

He'd forget it by the next night. There were too many women with M-names in the office at the moment.

Elene continued. "I'm assuming you've checked that your back pay was transferred into your account. If it's not, we can wait before we proceed. Sometimes bank transfers can take a few days."

"The money is already there, but I think there was some mistake. The amount I received was far more than what I was owed." Tatyana lifted her chin. "I was not asking for an advance."

"The advance is standard with contracts of this kind," Elene said. "As you will not be paid the full commission until your contract is complete, you'll need money to live on, and that's what the advance is for."

"But the money Zara owed me—"

"Was also correct," Elene said. "You were paid for your six months of wages. We calculated your per-day rate based on that amount and paid you for the six months of workdays—roughly one hundred and twenty days minus bank and government holidays—for that period and added that amount to your payment. It's standard back pay. Mr. Sokolov insisted. He wants no problems with the Ukrainian or Russian labor authorities, and he trusts that SMO has remedied the situation to your satisfaction."

She blinked. The icy little wolf blinked, and Oleg smiled.

He'd surprised her. Good.

"Of course. You are correct." Tatyana nodded. "I appreciate how quickly you resolved this, Ms. Beridze."

"She didn't say thank you." Mika glanced over his shoulder. "Ungrateful human."

"No thanks are needed when a debt is settled," Oleg said. "I paid her what Zara owed."

Elene was just as brusque. "Excellent." She handed Tatyana one last form. "If you could sign this, we will make a copy for both SMO and your own files so that we have a record you have received your back pay from ZOL and that any outstanding wages have been settled before the start of your current contract."

"Of course." The little human signed on the line, and Elene snatched up the paper and handed it to the secretary.

Your foot is well and truly in my trap now, volchitsa.

"She's mine now," Oleg said.

Mika raised an eyebrow. "What does that mean?"

Oleg shrugged. "Exactly what I said. She's mine."

Oleg was walking toward the conference room when he nearly ran into Elene's secretary. He looked down at the dark-haired woman who only came up to his chest.

"Marta."

The young woman blushed. "Mr. Sokolov."

"Thank you for staying late tonight."

The secretary stammered. "It's always a pleasure... I mean, it's no problem, Mr. Sokolov."

He'd fed from her once. Enjoyed her innocent attempts at seduction before he wiped her memory. She would have been embarrassed to look at him otherwise.

He lifted his chin and looked down at the woman. "Is Elene finished in the conference room?"

She glanced over her shoulder. "I believe Ms. Beridze is showing Tatyana to the office she wants her to use."

"Thank you."

"It's the one right behind my desk." Marta blushed a little. "If you want me to show you—"

"No need. I remember where your desk is."

Marta smiled. "Of course." She blushed harder, and Oleg took a deep inhale of the light, floral scent of the human's blood.

Was she a vegetarian? Possibly.

He moved past the blushing human and walked down the hall, turning quickly into another office where he spotted Elene and Tatyana behind a half-open door.

"...not sure what you mean, Miss Vorona." Elene's voice was low and cautious.

Oleg paused at the door, scanning the room for other ears. It was late and there was no one else around since Marta had left.

"Zara said her father had set up the company for her," Tatyana said. "And I thought it was... I mean, there's no way that Mr. Sokolov...?"

"What exactly are you asking?"

Yes, what are you asking, little human? Oleg paused in the doorway and leaned against the wall, waiting to hear how his newest employee would explain her prying. This was interesting. He hadn't considered what Zara might have told her bookkeeper. The woman might know more about the vampire world than she realized.

"I'm not being intrusive." Tatyana's voice was defensive. "If I am to understand the financial structure of ZOL and start searching for the money Mr. Sokolov is owed, I need to know where the initial funding came from and if there is another person who might have been working with her. If someone else had access to those funds—"

"I will have to speak to Mr. Sokolov about this," Elene said. "There are some matters that are—"

"Personal," he said in a raised voice.

Tatyana and Elene both swung their heads toward him. Tatyana's mouth gaped in surprise. Elene's expression was blank. She had probably known he was there the entire time. For a human, she had incredible instincts.

Oleg stepped into Elene's waiting room. "I believe you were asking personal questions about my relationship with Zara, Miss Vorona."

Elene opened the office door wider and looked at Oleg with a lifted brow. "Oleg."

"Zara said her father's name was Oleg." Tatyana's arms were crossed over her chest. "That her father set up the company for her. I am not trying to invade your privacy, but I had to ask because I need to know—"

"It's a perfectly understandable question," Oleg said. "Have you eaten tonight, Miss Vorona?"

The little wolf blinked again. "I have not."

"Neither have I." He'd fed the night before and he was old. Very old. He only needed to feed on human blood every week or so.

But Oleg had other appetites.

"I'll take you to dinner. After we've eaten, you may ask your questions."

Elene's voice was sharp. "That's not necessary."

Oleg kept his eyes on Tatyana. "Consider it your welcome dinner to SMO. If you're curious about me, you can ask whatever you like. Directly."

Tatyana glanced at Elene, then back at Oleg. "I would be happy to join you and Ms. Beridze for dinner."

"Elene has a family." The corner of his mouth inched up, and he had the urge to bare his fangs. "And she's already stayed long past office hours. I don't want to keep her." He held out his arm and hitched his fingers at Tatyana. "Come. My car will take us to a restaurant I know near your hotel. How does that sound?"

She didn't want to agree; Oleg could see it in her eyes. She wanted to get away. She wanted someone else to answer the questions she had about him. But then again...

Tatyana Vorona was a curious little thing.

"Thank you, Mr. Sokolov." She forced a smile. "Give me one moment to get my papers together and I'll join you out front."

"I'll wait." He glanced at Elene. "I can be patient when I need to be."

Elene's expression was asking what her mouth refused to say. *What are you doing, Oleg?*

He shrugged. He would do as he wanted, and that night he wanted to dine with Tatyana Vorona.

Tatyana rushed to put the stack of contracts in her worn satchel along with her precious computer.

As curious as he was about what she kept on her cherished machine, Oleg would have to remember to keep his distance. Valuable information was locked in that electronic device, and his elemental energy would fry it.

The bookkeeper finished and closed the clasp on her bag. "Thank you for explaining everything so clearly, Ms. Beridze. Will I see you tomorrow?"

"Of course. Now that you've signed a nondisclosure agreement, our first order of business will be to get you copies of all the accounts Zara forwarded to us from ZOL so you can compare them against your books."

Back on surer footing, Tatyana relaxed. "Of course. As long as she was using the same software, I can compare them very quickly."

"Dinner," Oleg barked.

Elene lifted her chin and looked at Oleg, her eyes shouting at him. Then she turned back to Tatyana and smiled. "I'll be in the office at nine."

"I'll see you then."

Oleg held out his hand, snapping his fingers at Tatyana, who nearly jumped at the sound.

Elene barked at him in her native Georgian. "Don't be a barbarian."

He responded in the same language. "I am a barbarian, remember?" He turned to Tatyana. "It's late and you haven't eaten. You're pale."

"I'm always pale."

She wasn't afraid of him now that she had her computer under her arm and business with Elene to discuss. Good. He didn't like people who were afraid of him. They were useful but boring.

Oleg hated to be bored.

Chapter Seven

"Do you generally order your employees' food for them?"

Oleg sipped the glass of red wine the sommelier had just poured for them. "I know what's good at this restaurant. You don't."

"That didn't answer my question." She was sitting across from him, her hair a little bit loose around her face, in the steakhouse around the corner from her hotel.

The host had seated them in a velvet booth in a corner of the restaurant after he recognized Oleg, assuring him that they would have the most private corner of the restaurant.

Tatyana looked at the full tables on the far side of the room. "Are the tables near ours off-limits?"

"I prefer privacy when I'm eating." He'd ordered both of them steaks and told the waiter to bring a variety of side dishes for the table.

"Do you always order for your employees?" She wasn't giving up.

"I don't. I do order for women though."

She leaned back and lifted her chin. "I am not your woman."

He felt that annoying twitch under his eye again. "It's a courtesy. As I said, I know this restaurant; you do not."

"What if I'm a vegetarian?"

Your blood doesn't smell like a vegetarian, but you are iron deficient.

Probably best not to answer her that way. "You don't eat meat? Is that why you're so pale? You ordered a full breakfast at the hotel this morning."

Her eyes went wide. "They told you what I ordered?"

Oleg picked up his wine again. "I didn't ask. It was a guess, but I was right, wasn't I?"

That brought some color to her cheeks. "I would prefer to pay for my own lodging and meals while I'm here."

He swirled the bright red wine in his glass. "It's part of your employment since you're required to be in Odesa while you work. The advance is for..." He waved a hand. What did humans have to pay for? Rent. Car things. She wasn't spending her money on red meat, that was for sure. "...your personal expenses. No need to lose your residence in Sevastopol because you're working here."

"That clause wasn't specifically in my contract, and I checked," she said. "Staying in Odesa the entire contract time isn't going to be possible. I *will* have to go back."

He took a gulp of wine and poured more into his own glass and then into hers even though she'd barely touched it. "Why?"

"Because I have family obligations."

"Your mother is an adult, and you don't have children."

She sat back again. More color on her cheeks. "You don't know everything about me."

"You've searched *my* name, haven't you?" He nodded at her computer bag. "On your computer."

She narrowed her eyes. "Yes. I had to search for you when I was trying to get paid."

"And yet you still have questions about me." Oleg relaxed into the lush velvet of the booth. "So ask them."

"Are you Zara's father?"

He raised an eyebrow. "Did she call me her father?"

"Occasionally. More often, she called you 'fucking Oleg' or 'that criminal bastard.'" Tatyana sipped her wine. "*If* you are the Oleg she was referring to."

He felt a laugh rumbling up from his chest and was surprised when it escaped.

Tatyana blinked, and her cheeks flushed again.

Oleg asked, "Did you think I was incapable of laughing when I hear something funny?"

"I don't think I've even seen you smile."

If I smile, you'll likely see my fangs. He bared his teeth, fangs firmly retracted. "I can smile when I want to."

"No." She frowned at him. "No, it doesn't suit you. Scowl again please."

The playful part of his little wolf was coming out, and he had to fight the urge to smile again. "When you say things like that, I cannot help my laughter." He swirled his wine, enjoying the deep purple-red color in the candlelight. "I am not Zara's biological father."

She exhaled. "I didn't think you were, because you can't be more than..."

"Continue." He was curious. "How old do you think I am?"

"I am very bad at guessing ages." She shook her head. "But not old enough to be her father."

"No? I'm eleven hundred and thirty-seven. I think that's old enough."

It was her turn to smile, and the expression softened the curve of her stern mouth. "So you're thirty-seven. And Zara was my age. So unless you were a very, very precocious ten-year-old, you're not her father." She narrowed her eyes. "But she did call you that."

"Hmm." How to answer the woman? She'd brushed off the reveal of his true age as if it were a joke. Which was what most humans would assume.

He was surprised he'd told her the truth. Not even Mika knew how old he really was.

"You could call me her guardian. Of a sort. I am older than you think, but as I said, I am not her biological father. I was close with him though." *I killed him.* "And after he died, I committed to helping raise Zara. I helped her establish herself. That's why she calls me her father. I am intrigued by the 'criminal bastard' label though." He paused to sip his wine. "I've done some criminal things in the past, but my parents were married."

Tatyana's mouth was gaping. "You're a criminal?"

"Not in the way you might think." The corner of his mouth ticked up. "And definitely not in this country."

She looked around the restaurant. "I... This was a mistake. I should have gone to the authorities when I realized—"

"Which authorities?" Oleg kept his voice low and leaned across the table. "The... Russian ones? Ukrainian? Things are complicated now, and they would be far more likely to arrest you than Zara. After all, you compiled a fraudulent set of corporate accounts."

She sucked in a sharp breath. "Zara told me *I* was keeping the correct accounts. That you were the one telling the others at the company to manipulate the real numbers to avoid taxes, and she could only confirm her suspicions if she had an accurate set of books to take to the authorities when she reported you."

So that was how Zara had lured the little rule-follower into her employ. Clever girl. Then again, Oleg had never thought his youngest child was anything but brilliant.

"Relax, volchitsa." The woman looked like she was about to bolt from the room. Oleg reached over and poured more wine. "You don't need to bare your teeth at me. I'm here to help you." *And myself.* "If we follow Elene's lead, there is no reason that you should face any legal consequences. This will all be sorted. Nothing you're doing is illegal."

She seemed to relax a little bit, but the color that his teasing words had brought to her cheeks had fled again.

Oleg used his most soothing voice. "You're doing the right thing, Tatyana. The good thing."

She nodded, but he could see that her previous playfulness had vanished, and he wanted it back. Her hands were twisted in her lap, and she was looking at the other diners on the other side of the restaurant again. Glancing at the door. Then at the floor.

Oleg said, "So the next time we go to dinner, what restaurant do you want to try?"

The corner of her mouth twitched up. "I'm not going to dinner with you again. It's not appropriate."

"Neither is a twenty-seven-year-old pursuing an eleven-hundred-and thirty-seven-year-old, but you don't see me running from the room. I can't help it. You're an intriguing woman."

She shook her head, and her lips curved into a full smile. "Sorry, Mr. Sokolov. I need a job more than I need a man."

I'm not a man.

"Call me Oleg. Mr. Sokolov is very impersonal. And what you need is food." He could smell the perfectly grilled steaks in the kitchen. "Which they will be serving shortly."

"I don't eat red meat much, but thank you."

He lifted his glass. "Welcome to the company."

"WHAT DO YOU DO FOR FUN IN SEVASTOPOL?" HE WAS KEEPING his distance, but after a hearty Western-style steak with roasted potatoes, braised carrots, and other side dishes that had Tatyana's eyes going wide, he told her he'd walk her back to the hotel.

Tatyana kept glancing over her shoulder as his driver followed them at a distance. "This is ridiculous. You don't have to walk me back to the hotel. We're in a safe part of the city, aren't we?"

"Yes, but I enjoy a good walk when the air is fresh." The night air was cool, and he could smell the sea. "What do you do for fun?"

"I..." She seemed to be at a loss. "I work."

"That is not an answer. You can't work all the time."

"I take care of my mother. She has a cat. And she keeps pigeons on the roof. It annoys our neighbors, but I think they remind her of the country."

"She grew up in the country?"

"Yes. She moved to the city to work. Like me. I grew up in Sevastopol."

"But you went to university in Kyiv."

A smile touched her lips. "I liked Kyiv."

"Then why move back?"

"My mother can't be alone for long." Her eyes took on a distant, internal look. "I don't really do much for fun. I'm quite boring."

"I doubt that." He remembered that she had been a dancer when she was a child. "There are clubs in Sevastopol. Dance clubs. Discos?"

She smiled and crossed her arms over her chest. "Uh, yes. Discos." She smirked. "Yes, there are clubs, but mostly they're for tourists. I met Zara in a club."

"Was she dancing?" He hadn't known his daughter enjoyed dancing unless it was over the graves of her enemies.

"No, it was a karaoke club."

He stopped in his tracks. "No."

Tatyana laughed. "Yes. A karaoke club. She was there with a number of employees from ZOL, but I didn't know it at the time. She was just friendly, and I was alone."

"Why were you alone?"

"I don't..." She narrowed her eyes and cocked her head when she looked at him. "Do you ask all your employees such personal questions?"

"You asked me personal questions."

She sighed. "Most of my friends were from university. I don't know many people in Sevastopol anymore. My old school friends mostly moved away."

"The current political situation?"

"And work." She shrugged. "It's beautiful, but it's not my favorite place."

"What is your favorite place?" He didn't know why he wanted to know, but he did.

"No, it's my turn. What do you do for fun?"

Oleg blinked. "I don't think anyone has asked me that in a decade."

"Seriously?"

"I work."

She smiled and shook her finger at him. "No, no. You didn't let me answer with that. There has to be more."

"I work on my art." Why had he told her that? It wasn't a secret, but he didn't share his mosaics with everyone.

Her eyes lit up. "You're an artist?"

"Eh..." Yes. Why was it so hard to say it? "I'm not a painter or anything like that. It's something I learned to do a long time ago, and—"

"What is it?"

"Mosaics." He forced the words out. "I create mosaics."

Her mouth dropped open. "Really? That's amazing. I've never met a mosaic artist before."

"That impresses you?" His eyebrows went up as he pulled his billfold from his coat pocket. "Not the planes or the yachts or the multinational corporations but the mosaic art?"

"How many people can do that?" She stepped closer as she saw his billfold. "Do you have pictures?"

"Yes, I'll show you." He was already pulling out a picture of the armory at the citadel. "This is from my castle in the north."

"Of course you own a castle," she muttered as she leaned closer. "This is so strange."

"My mosaics?" He pulled the picture away.

"No, looking at a picture that's not on a phone." She smiled and put her hand on his arm, tugging him toward the streetlamp. "Move into the light. I can't see it."

Oleg grunted and walked with her. "I don't have a phone."

"How do you not have a phone?"

He nodded at the driver. "I have people who have phones. I don't need to carry one."

"That is definitely the richest thing you have ever said to me." She lifted the picture from his hand. "That and the castle thing." She gasped. "Oh my God. You made *this*?"

"Yes."

"By yourself?"

"It took some time."

It had taken roughly forty years. The mosaic decorating the main wall of his armory was an expansive forest scene with riders chasing a white stag as a firebird perched in the trees overhead.

"This is stunning." Her eyes were glued to the photograph. "It looks *hundreds* of years old."

It was.

"I enjoy using historical elements and techniques in certain pieces."

"This must have taken so long."

He tried to take the photograph back, feeling oddly exposed with her keen blue eyes on his work.

She looked up, the gold light of the streetlamp casting a warm glow on her skin. She was verdantly alive, and her heart was beating quickly as her eyes met his.

"It's incredible," she whispered. "Thank you for showing me."

He frowned. "Please don't mention it to others. It's not something I share outside of—"

"Of course not. I'm honored that you showed me. Thank you." She put her hand on his as he took the photograph back, her skin warm and violently alive against his cold hands.

Tatyana stared at his hand, then up into his eyes, and Oleg could see when the inhuman energy hit her.

Her eyes went wide and her pupils dilated. "What are you?"

Oleg sent a wave of amnis straight to her cerebral cortex, catching her as her knees went out and lifting her into his arms.

"Infuriating human," he muttered. "Why does this keep happening?"

Chapter Eight

Tatyana blinked her eyes open to rays of warm morning sun touching her face. She sat up in a panic, realizing as soon as she did that once again, she was waking up in her clothes from the day before, shoes removed, in a bed at the Admiral Hotel.

"What the hell is going on?"

Why was this happening? She had a vague memory of Oleg walking her into the lobby last night and Lorala and Marina helping her to her room and getting her into bed, but why was her memory so cloudy?

She'd had *one* glass of wine. Why wasn't she able to remember anything after the restaurant? Was it stress? Was she sick?

It had to be the stress.

She took a deep breath and swung her legs over the side of the bed, glancing at the clock and noting she had an hour and a half before she needed to be at the office. It was more than enough time to get ready.

At least she didn't have a headache. And the bed in the hotel was so comfortable even sleeping in her suit didn't seem to have bothered her.

Maybe once her mind adjusted to not having to count every penny and watch every word with her mother, Tatyana would sleep better. She hadn't been sleeping well for months. Maybe her body had finally given up.

She rubbed a hand over her eyes and stood.

How embarrassing! What must Oleg Sokolov think of her when she'd passed out twice in front of him? Was that why he'd forced her into a steak dinner? The man probably thought she was malnourished.

She'd never eaten at a Western-style steak house before, and she had to admit, so far it was the most enjoyable aspect of the extravagantly wealthy world she'd stumbled into. The food had been delicious, the wine was better than any she'd had in college, and Oleg's company had been surprisingly pleasant. She couldn't remember much of their conversation, but she had a warm, positive feeling about it.

Her phone buzzed on the counter. As soon as she saw the screen, panic leaped into her throat.

Five missed calls from her mother and one from Karol.

"Oh God." She unlocked her phone and hurriedly tapped on the button to return Anna's call, ignoring the voicemail alerts. The phone rang twice before her mother picked up. "Mama?"

"Tanya." Her mother sounded surprised. "Aren't you supposed to be at work?"

"Mama, there were five missed calls."

"From who?"

"From you!" Tatyana let out a breath and leaned against the counter. "What is going on?"

"Mrs. Lipovsky was yelling at me last night, and I couldn't sleep. Why does she complain about my angels?" Anna started whining about her birds. "They're on the roof. She's on the first floor. She doesn't even hear them. I promise you that."

"Mama—"

"And Popov, that old bastard, he's going to raise the rent again. I know it."

Tatyana closed her eyes. "Mama, we own our apartment, remember? It's paid for. He can't raise our rent. He's not our landlord anymore."

"But he'll charge us more somehow. The second toilet is broken. I know it is and—"

"Mama!" She barked at her mother, then winced.

That won't help. That will only make it worse.

She took a deep breath. "Mama, I'll be home soon. I'm going to come home today."

She should have been back yesterday. She'd been gone for a week, jumping through hoops at SMO like a trained dog, and now she was wearing designer suits and eating extravagant meals while her mother fought her demons alone.

"I'll be home tonight."

"Are you sure?"

"As sure as I can be."

Somehow she'd find a flight. She had money, and if there was anything she'd learned from growing up poor, money could make things happen.

She'd call the office and tell Elene that she needed to go back to Sevastopol and work from there. All the files she was supposed to check were electronic anyway. There was no reason she needed to work in Odesa save for Oleg Sokolov's suspicious and controlling nature.

"Mama, take a breath."

Anna gasped and let out a slow breath over the phone.

"Okay good. Are you feeling calmer?"

"Yes. As soon as you said that you were coming home, I felt like my heart just went very easy, Tanya. And my blood pressure. I think my blood pressure was bad like Papa's this morning."

"No, we checked it right before I left, remember?" She walked to the closet and opened the door to see four more garment bags lined up with notes from Lorala pinned to each and a neat line of office-appropriate shoes underneath them. "Mama, I need to go into the office and work for a little bit, and then I'll be able to come home."

"Are you sure?"

"Yes." She grabbed the nearest garment back and unzipped it to reveal a pale yellow sheath dress with a jacket. "My new boss will be in at nine o'clock and I need to get some files, and then I can work from home again. Won't that be nice?"

"So nice." Her mother's voice instantly transformed. "Okay, okay. I'll go to the store and buy some pork cutlets and make that for dinner like Baboolya made, right? Does that sound good?"

Tatyana pressed her eyes closed, fighting the tears at the memory of her grandmother. "Yes, that sounds perfect."

"I'll see you tonight." Her mother hung up the phone, and Tatyana's arm dropped to her side.

Love shouldn't feel like a trap. Her grandmother's words battered her memory like a bird caught behind a window.

She'd been fifteen and convinced that her first boyfriend was her true love. That she had to bend to his ridiculous demands because she "loved" him. As if a sixteen-year-old boy's whims should dictate her life.

Her grandmother had wisely taken her arm, hugged her, and told her that loving her grandfather made her feel free. "Love shouldn't feel like a trap, Tanya. That kind of love will have you carving off parts of yourself until there is nothing left."

Love shouldn't feel like a trap, but Anna wasn't a sixteen-year-old boy. Anna was her mother. The only parent she had. Anna was the last of her family.

She tossed the dress on the bed before she went to the bathroom to get ready.

This was going to be a long day.

"For how long?" Elene Beridze was clearly not happy with Tatyana's request.

"I'm not sure, but when I left, she was expecting me back in a week maximum, and it's been eight days."

Elene frowned. "Is your mother in poor health? Is she disabled in some way? Does she have a nurse?"

"No." Tatyana let out a breathy laugh. "Even if she was, we couldn't afford... No, it's not that. My grandparents died a few years ago, and that was very hard on her. She depends on me, but I will be able to get her settled if I go back today."

"Hmm."

Tatyana was twisting her hands, knowing how unprofessional it looked to show up on your first day at a new job and immediately tell your supervisor that you had to leave.

"As I said, I was only supposed to be gone for one week. We hadn't prepared for an extended absence, and then this new contract happened so quickly that I wasn't able to—"

"Oleg won't be pleased," Elene muttered. "But I can't argue with your logic. Being away from home for a week and being gone for months are very different things."

A tiny spring of hope. "Thank you for understanding."

"Go." Elene waved a hand. "The files are on your desk and we've emailed them to you as well. But this is a break to get your mother situated, not a permanent situation. You do need to work from this office."

"I understand." She didn't know how she was going to make it work, but she'd have to think of something.

She would have to.

"You have your advance," Elene continued. "So if coming back to Odesa means hiring someone to look after your mother or be her companion, take care of it. You're not doing yourself any favors coddling her like a child, and it's going to hold you back professionally." Elene's frown was severe. "I understand family, but who pays the water bill if you don't work, hmm?"

"I agree, and I will make my mother understand." How, she wasn't sure, but the idea of hiring someone to take some of the load off her own shoulders sounded like heaven. "I'll work just as hard there as I would here. I promise."

"I'm not worried about that," Elene said. "Just go and do what you need to do, then come back and we can focus on following Zara's breadcrumbs."

"Yes. Thank you." Tatyana nodded and grabbed her phone. "Flying is complicated now. Hopefully I can find something this afternoon. I'll probably have to go all the way to Krasnodar, but—"

"Don't be silly," Elene said. "You can take the company plane. Oleg's flights always receive special permissions, so you should be able to fly directly. That will be much faster."

Tatyana froze. "No, I couldn't possibly—"

"Of course you can. It's not efficient for you to spend all that time jumping through governmental nonsense when you could take advantage of SMO's connections. Besides, the plane is sitting at the airport right now and we're paying the pilots whether they fly or not." Elene put her reading glasses on and turned to her computer monitor. "I'll call them and have them ready for you at three o'clock."

"Are you sure? Is that... legal?"

"It will be legal when I call them and tell them that Oleg's plane is coming." Elene scribbled a number on a note and handed it to Tatyana. "Call this number an hour before you're ready to go and the steward will give you directions."

"Are you sure?"

"Tatyana, please don't waste my time." Elene was looking back at her monitor, already tapping on her keyboard. "It's a small jet, so don't set your expectations on the moon. We're a shipping company, not rock stars. They will be waiting for you this afternoon. Now please work until noon so I can answer any questions you might have before you leave."

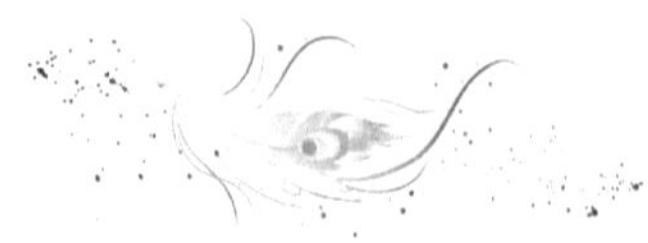

Sevastopol
Nearly three years before

"It doesn't add up for me." Tatyana felt a headache starting in her temple. "And I can't tell you why. But there is a discrepancy in the numbers and it's driving me crazy."

She and Zara were back at the karaoke club. This time they were talking in a corner booth at the back of the club while the regular employees from ZOL took turns on the stage.

"What are you saying?" Zara's eyes were wide and shocked. "Are you saying" —she glanced at the data management supervisor on the stage— "you think someone is embezzling?"

"I don't know." She couldn't think of any other reason though. "I don't want to point fingers, but at most companies, there are separate accounts for fees, taxes, customs, all the payments that have to be made to the government, and I'm not seeing any of that in what you've given me so far. Maybe if I could get a look at last year's books—"

"They're a mess," Zara said. "That's why I hired you. I wanted an independent audit because I suspected..." She sighed. "Tatyana, you're the only one I can trust."

"Why?" She didn't know any of the in-office employees other than to wave at them, but they seemed fairly nice.

"Everyone else at the company was either hired by my father or his right hand, this frigid old woman who's obsessed with him." Zara waved a hand. "Boring family drama."

"So I'm the only one you've hired?"

"Of the main team?" Zara nodded. "Yes."

Tatyana had asked Zara multiple times if she could work from the office, but her new boss told her she wanted Tatyana to be independent of the rest of the group. She was the bookkeeper, so being in the office wasn't essential.

Of course, Tatyana knew she wasn't the *only* bookkeeper, but according to Zara, the bookkeepers at ZOL worked more for her father's company than for hers.

"I'm a little bit worried that…" Zara sighed. "It's my father. I haven't told you much about Oleg, but he's always been very secretive about where he made his money."

"He didn't inherit it?"

The kind of wealth that Zara exhibited, Tatyana just assumed that her family had always been wealthy. Even during the Soviet era, Tatyana knew that some in Sevastopol lived much better than others, especially if they had military or international connections.

"My father didn't grow up wealthy, but somewhere along the way…" Zara let the idea trail off. "You have to know what I suspect, right? I mean, who makes that kind of money honestly?"

"Do you think you should" —Tatyana dropped her voice to a whisper— "report him? I know he's your father, but if you're worried he's breaking the law—"

"What would I report?" Zara snorted. "I'm not saying it's not the right thing or even that I'm afraid of him. Oleg would never hurt me." The corner of her mouth curled up. "Never."

"So?"

Zara shrugged. "Right now all I have are feelings and suspicions." She slid her hand across the table and put it over Tatyana's. "That's why what you're doing is so important, Tanya. I trust you. I'm *depending* on you."

Tatyana felt a surge of purpose in her chest. If Zara could be brave enough to investigate her own father, Tatyana could help. "If you can get me the receivables and the deposit account information, I think I can figure out what's going on."

"Thank you." Zara's eyes were sparkling. "Thank you so much. I know you could find another job so easily, so thank you for sticking with me. I know this is… far from normal."

She felt her cheeks flush. "You're welcome. I'm just happy I could help."

Tatyana's eyes opened when the plane bumped as it touched down. As soon as the bumping stopped, the automatic shutters that had slid down the moment they took to the sky opened, flooding the small jet with late-afternoon sunshine.

She looked out the window and realized they were on some kind of military base, but no one seemed alarmed to see the SMO plane.

An elderly steward who had introduced himself as Roman walked over with a warm towel on a tray. "I trust you were able to rest, Ms. Vorona."

"Just for a little bit, but it was nice to close my eyes."

The flight had been just over two hours, longer than it would have taken a few years ago because they had to fly what Roman had called "a creative route" to avoid trouble. Nevertheless, it was far easier than the complicated series of flights Tatyana had been forced to take to get to Odesa in the first place.

She looked out the window. "How do I get to my house?"

"We have people on the ground waiting for you," Roman said. "It's all been arranged."

Tatyana pressed the warm towel to her face, refreshing her cheeks and neck. "Thank you."

Professional clothes brought to her door. Bags packed for her by hotel staff along with an entirely new suitcase with all the clothes Lorala had picked out for her. Cars from hotel to airport. An entire cabin to herself.

It was hard not to feel like a princess in a fairy tale.

"It's been a pleasure to serve you." The old steward nodded kindly. "Miss Beridze said we will see you again to take you back to Odesa when everything has been arranged here, and we look forward to that."

It would be easy—so, so easy—to accept all this without question, but Tatyana had questions. So many. "How long have you worked for Mr. Sokolov?"

"I've worked for SMO for nearly forty years." His blue eyes crinkled at the corners. "As you can imagine, I have seen many changes during that time."

"Forty years?"

"Mm-hmm." Roman picked up the damp towel with a pair of gold tongs and stood. "They will roll the stairs to the door soon," he said. "You will be with a driver named Kiril. Please follow all his directions. He already has your address and he will get you home."

Tatyana stood and registered faint shouting from outside the plane, but it didn't sound dangerous. She suspected it was just loud outside.

Roman began to retrieve all her luggage and place it by the door. "Kiril will transport your bags, but I understand you will hold on to your computer bag yourself. Is that correct?"

"Yes, thank you."

Roman smiled and waited with her as the door opened and the roar of military jets filled the air. "I will see you next time, Miss Vorona."

"Please call me Tatyana."

She couldn't hear how he responded as she was swept off the plane and into the long shadows of the afternoon sun, hustled toward a black car, and quickly shuffled inside.

Moments later the doors shut and everything went quiet again.

She couldn't see her driver through the black divider in the front of the car, but she recognized the streets they were driving a few minutes later, even through the near-black windows of the luxury sedan.

Eventually they turned onto the rutted street north of downtown where Tatyana and her mother lived in a three-story house that had been divided into three flats with generous balconies that looked over the ocean when the sky was clear.

She tapped on the divider and it rolled down. "This is fine. You can drop me off here."

"I've been instructed to take you to your front door and help you with your luggage, Ms. Vorona."

"Oh my God," she muttered before she sighed. "Fine, but my mother is going to interrogate you. Don't say I didn't warn you."

As soon as they pulled onto the street, Tatyana saw curious eyes peering out.

It was a perfectly nice, perfectly safe neighborhood of middle-class retirees and civil servants like her mother. Nothing was too run-down. Nothing was too fancy. Walled compounds were common, but there were still a few brightly painted summerhouses with metal roofs and large gardens with fruit trees in the yards.

Kiril opened her door before he went to the back of the car and retrieved her two suitcases.

"We're on the third floor." She pointed to the tall building painted an optimistic yellow. "Stairs are on the left, so you can—"

"Tatyana Vorona." The grating sound of Mrs. Lipovsky's voice stopped Tatyana in her tracks. "Your birds are shitting in my fruit trees again."

She sighed and turned to the middle-aged woman who lived on the ground floor. "I'm really not sure how you know that it is our birds who are shitting, Mrs. Lipovsky. Unlike the government, we don't control the airspace."

Kiril snorted and started up the stairs as Mrs. Lipovsky looked her up and down.

"Did you get a new boyfriend?" Her smile was twisted. "He looks rich."

"I have a new job." Tatyana turned to go. "Have a good afternoon."

The woman grumbled something about Tatyana's mother before she turned to go inside. Kiril was already at the top of the stairs and waited for her.

Tatyana opened the door and immediately called out, "Mama?"

The house was so neat you could eat dinner on the floor, but her mother was nowhere to be found. Still, the old car was sitting in their spot and the house smelled of pork cutlet and her grandmother's gravy. Anna was definitely at home.

She turned to Kiril as he set down her suitcase. "Thank you. I don't know if I'm supposed to tip you."

"You're not." He gave her a hint of a smile. "Mr. Sokolov pays me enough. I'll see you next time." He tipped his head, then backed out of the doorway and closed the door behind her.

With a purr, Pushkin the cat walked down the hall and wound his grey tail around her legs.

And Tatyana was home.

She gave Pushkin a quick pat, then quickly moved her suitcases into her room—better that her mother not see the new one—before she walked to the back balcony where the stairs to the roof were located. She walked out the back door, sliding it closed quickly to keep Pushkin from escaping up to the pigeon loft.

She could hear the soft cooing of the birds as soon as she stepped outside.

As she climbed the stairs, a few of them flapped out to greet her, and she called them by their names, old Hollywood royalty from the classic American movies her mother loved.

"Hello, Audrey." She recognized the bright purple feathers of a favorite. "Cary Grant, you handsome devil. It's good to see you."

Cary Grant landed on the edge of the wall that encircled the roof and started strutting, his bright purple head flashing in the setting sun.

Anna glanced over her shoulder as she cleaned out the aviary. "You're back. The food is ready when you're hungry."

"I'm fine for now. Just wanted to watch the sunset."

Her mother wasn't an expressive woman—she reserved most of her affection for her feathered pets—but the neat house and the food told Tatyana that Anna was happy and relieved that she was home. "How is Rex Harrison?"

She nodded toward the coop. "Healing. I let him out last night, and he flew around the neighborhood a bit before he came back." She touched the head of a shining white male pigeon who had injured a wing a few weeks before.

"Did he shit on Mrs. Lipovsky's apples before he came back?"

"I certainly hope so," Anna said.

"Me too." She watched the sun slip past the horizon, and the sea settled into a deep blue green that pricked at something in her memory.

"You did this?"

"Yes."

"By yourself?"

"It took some time."

It was a faint memory that drifted away before it clarified. Was it a movie? A conversation she'd overheard? Something about the garbled memory gave her a warm, contented feeling.

It's not something I share...

Her mother turned and brushed off her hands, taking off her work gloves before she walked toward Tatyana. "Why don't we go inside and eat? I'm done up here. The boys will put all the girls to roost. Tell me about the new job."

"I will." Tatyana stood and followed her mother down the steps. "But let me unpack a few things from my bag and plug my computer in before I set the table."

"You and the computer." Anna muttered something under her breath. "Don't be long."

She followed her mother inside the house and went to the back bedroom that she'd claimed for her office with Pushkin tagging at her heels. Her suitcases would be fine as they were, but there was one thing she needed to check before she did anything else.

Tatyana took her computer from the messenger bag and set it on the desk that looked over the back garden of the house. Then she plugged it in, grabbed the small screwdriver from her desk drawer, and crawled under the desk to take off the register cover over the heating vent in the floor.

She carefully set the small screws to the side and shined her phone's flashlight into the cavity she'd cleared the year before.

Her heart stopped.

No.

She shined the light into the corners even though she knew there was no way her backup laptop should be anywhere but exactly where she left it before she flew to Odesa.

Oh God.

Oh no.

No one knew about this hiding place, and nothing in the rest of her office was out of place, but her backup computer, an external hard drive, and all her micro USB drives were gone.

Chapter Nine

Oleg's larger compound in Odesa was an expanse of modern construction northeast of the historic center, stretched over a coastal property that was walled off from the city and the tourists who flooded to the Black Sea for holidays.

He'd built it for two reasons: his younger brother who oversaw Odesa in his absence was mated to a water vampire who wanted to be near her element, and Oleg usually didn't spend much time there.

He'd built four houses on the property, one for himself, another for his brother Klaus, one for Mika and any of the druzhina who happened to be in the area, and the last for his human staff who ran the compound. There was a private dock and a high wall around the entire compound; golf carts for the security staff; cameras, surveillance equipment, and many, many weapons.

Klaus's house was gaudy and modern in the way that many vampires enjoyed with large windows that could be blocked off with metal shades during the day, large stretches of marble, and lavish modern luxuries.

Oleg's was nearly empty. There were too many windows, too much concrete for his liking, and too many bare walls.

He was trying to remedy the last problem by working on a mosaic in his living room that overlooked the water. There was a modern fireplace that ran on natural gas and a massive balcony that wrapped around the seaside portion of the house. He'd decided to cover the fireplace wall with a mosaic that brought the marine sunset into the house.

Oleg was using a combination of angular and round tesserae on the project in oceanic colors like blue and green but adding in accents the color of his element. Blood-red, vibrant orange, and rich golden yellows all in transparent glass tiles.

When it was finished, it would flicker and come alive in the light of his fire. It was a moody project, one that he'd been working on for roughly five years.

That night Oleg stood shirtless in the living room, enjoying the cooling marine layer that washed in on the evening wind and working on an icy blue curl of waves hitting a grouping of rocks he'd created from stones his servants had gathered from the beach.

He was also trying not to think about how much the light blue glass he was using reminded him of Tatyana Vorona's eyes.

Why did the damn woman have to be so perceptive?

He spread a thin layer of concrete on the wall and placed the pale blue tiles around the circular center of the wave. He picked up his tile nippers and adjusted the angle on one tile, then set the pieces to dry, heating his fingers to speed up the process.

He pulled his hand away and frowned at the wall. No, that wouldn't do. Using fire to speed up drying always resulted in a weaker set.

Patience. The old human who had taught him how to create this art had admonished him for decades. *Patience.* Waiting had value. Suffering had value. The hawk that waited would end the night with a full belly.

Oleg pulled his warm hand away from the glass tiles and reached for the next grouping on his worktable.

The old human's wisdom had served him well for centuries. Oleg had waited for the right time to surpass his sire. He had waited for the right moment to strike out at his enemies and take their territories. He had waited until others saw him as a banked fire before he chose to ignite. Now his immortal territory stretched from Saint Petersburg to Sochi and all the way across to North America.

Oleg believed in patience because patience had served him well. So what did patience teach him about the little wolf nipping at his mind?

Tatyana Vorona had folded in seconds when he flooded her mind with amnis. She would wake up for the second time in two days to hazy memories and confusion. If he wanted to keep her innocent about the vampire world, he needed to keep his distance.

Most humans interacted with immortals without suspecting a thing. Zara was far more inhuman than Oleg, and Tatyana had worked with Zara for two years.

Then again, perhaps Zara had wiped the woman's mind as well. There could be a reason that she perceived something different about Oleg.

Tatyana's mind could be fighting back against too much intrusion. Amnis could work to wipe human memory, but the mind was sharp and adaptable. Given too much vampire influence, it would learn to work around their usual tricks.

Which was probably what had happened with Tatyana and Zara.

Once again proving that the ways that his daughter could fuck him over were nearly endless.

She will have to die.

The sinister little voice whispered in the back of his mind, but he tried to ignore it.

She will have to die, and you will have to do it.

"No," he whispered to himself. "Not another. Not again."

"Are you still working on this thing?"

Oleg glanced over his shoulder when he heard Mika's voice. "Of course I am. It's not finished. What are you doing here? Does Klaus need something?"

"Not that I know of." Mika approached but kept his distance. "I'm here trying to figure out why you sent your new bookkeeper to

Sevastopol in the jet when I just put the word out what she's in Odesa." Mika sounded annoyed. "Oksana and Ludmila were already tracking a group of Albanians in the city. Is there something I need to know?"

Oleg spun, feeling the fire burst to life on his shoulders as he rounded on Mika. "She went where?"

"Back to Zara's old territory," Mika said. "And she took the plane, which means that either you, I, or Elene sent her. I'm guessing from your expression and all the smoke that it must have been Elene."

Oleg's fangs dropped, and he snarled at Mika. "Get my driver. We're going into the office."

"I cannot keep the girl captive, Oleg." Elene looked over her reading glasses, just as annoyed as Oleg was. "She had a perfectly reasonable request to go home and sort out her family and living situation before she returned to work. I thought it would be more efficient to use the plane. She'll be back next week." She returned to her computer and started typing again. "She's working while she's there. I gave her copies of ZOL's records for the past three years and she's—"

"I don't give a damn about the work," Oleg barked. "She's part of a..." He glanced at Mika, who walked over and poked his head out of the office to ask Marta to get him a coffee from a café down the street.

Once the office was clear, Oleg sat in the chair across from Elene. "She's part of a larger plan. Mika already put the word out that the woman was here."

"There are Albanians," Mika said. "They look promising."

"If Zara has already sent people after the girl, they're not going to pack up and return to Durrës because she went home for the weekend. And they don't have the connections you do, so they're not likely to jump over to Sevastopol, are they?"

"They could." Mika leaned against a wall and kept an eye on the outer office. "They're primarily water vampires. Albanian vampires travel fast when they want to."

"And Zara could still have people in the city."

"So do we," Elene said. "I told Kiril to keep an eye on her."

Oleg only relaxed a little bit. Kiril was a competent human, but he would be no match for Zara. He looked at Oleg. "Our people in Istanbul, have they reported any movement from her?"

Mika shook his head. "Nothing. She's sitting in Laskaris's house and ruling it like a queen. If anything, she's probably busier than you are juggling the shipping traffic."

"She'll have people watching all her old haunts though."

Elene said, "I doubt she thinks Tatyana is a threat. Do you think she would have neglected to pay her if she thought the bookkeeper was a threat?"

"God only knows," Oleg said. "It's Zara. Sometimes she schemes for a decade, and sometimes she tosses mud at the devil just to see how he'll react."

Elene raised her eyebrows and Mika shrugged.

"You're not wrong," Elene said. "But it was the right thing to do. Tatyana has some issue with her mother, and she wouldn't have been able to concentrate until she had her settled. I don't want to deal with a distracted accountant when I'm trying to find thirty million dollars."

"The money is hardly worth noting," Oleg said. "It would be nice to recover, but—"

"Do you know how much we're paying in bribes now?" Elene raised her voice. "We're dealing with three different hostile human governments on any given day and also paying Athens. Thirty million isn't something to be ignored."

Oleg saw Elene's phone light up. "Someone is calling you."

Elene picked up her phone and shot a look at Oleg and Mika. "It's the bookkeeper."

Oleg sat back and crossed his arms over his chest. "Answer it." He'd had to put on a suit to come into the office, and the collar of the shirt raked against his skin.

Elene rolled her eyes, but she tapped a lit-up button on the phone console. "Hello, Miss Vorona. I trust the flight was—"

"There is a problem."

Oleg sat up and leaned forward. He'd heard Tatyana's voice clearly, but he snapped his fingers and pointed at Elene's phone. She tapped something on the screen so Tatyana's voice was louder for Oleg and Mika.

"What problem?" Elene said. "I trust Kiril delivered you home safely."

"Yes, but when I arrived, I went to my office to check on my backups."

"Your backups?"

"I had a backup computer. An external hard drive. Some USB drives with scans of files that Zara had given to me. They were all gone."

Mika gripped his hand and shook his head, baring his fangs at Elene, who shook her head and put a finger over her lips. The message was clear.

Quiet.

"Your backups were stolen from your office?" Elene asked. "Is there anything you don't already have?"

"No. And I do have other backups, but these were stolen from the office in my home. In my *mother's* home. It's very possible that Zara knows I'm working on finding the money."

Mika scribbled something on a piece of paper and handed it to Elene.

"Did your mother realize someone had broken in?" Elene read the note Mika handed her. "Have there been any workmen in the house? Anyone who might have been posing as someone they were not?"

"I don't know. I'll have to ask her. Do you think Zara is watching me?" A tremor of fear in Tatyana's voice. "What if she—"

"Volchitsa, I'm flying to you." Oleg spoke before he realized what he was doing.

Mika's eyes went wide, and Elene's eyebrows went up.

"Mr. Sokolov?"

A low rumbling in his chest, and his fangs grew long. "You called me Oleg last night."

"I didn't know you were on the call." Tatyana's voice had turned from frightened to suspicious. "How long have you been listening?"

"We were talking about a billing issue when you called," Elene said. "I understand you're frightened, but I can send Kiril back to the house if that would make you feel more secure." Elene was staring at Oleg, silently shaking her head.

She mouthed, *Do not go to Sevastopol.*

He narrowed his eyes. "Mika and I can both go."

Mika's head swung around. "What?"

"We'll make some inquiries and see if any of ZOL's employees might still be in contact with Zara. If anyone is, they might offer some insight into the embezzlement. And to her location."

Elene was silently cursing him, and Mika was furious.

"We'll be there before dawn," Oleg continued, ignoring his two closest associates.

Tatyana tried to protest. "That's really not necess—"

"I'll see you tomorrow night." He snapped his fingers at Elene. "Hang up. This is not a discussion."

Elene tapped the phone and disconnected the call, then sat back and stared at Oleg. "What the hell are you doing?"

"Exactly what I want." He stood and walked out the door. "Mika, tell Grigor to pack some clothes for me. We'll leave as soon as my plane is ready."

It always amused Oleg when Mika was annoyed. The man was normally as even-tempered as you could desire in a second-in-command, but when his temper was riled, he could be as pissy as a wet cat.

"—didn't even consider that I might have commitments I didn't want to cancel," he was muttering.

Oleg paged through a fashion magazine Roman handed him and noticed that a model he'd had a brief affair with was doing a campaign for a new perfume. "Good for you, Sofia." He showed Mika the ad. "Look at that. She looks beautiful. I should send her some flowers. She liked tulips."

"Are you really bragging about one of your women right now?"

Oleg muttered, "I wouldn't call it bragging."

A cutting rain was pounding against the side of the plane as Mika cut his eyes across the cabin. "This plane may be fireproof, but there's more than enough rain to bring it down."

His empty threat made Oleg truly laugh for the first time in days. "You wouldn't do that to Roman."

Mika snarled. "Why are you in such a good mood?"

"Because you're in a bad one. It's about balance." He glanced at Mika, then back to the magazine. "What was more important than making me happy by accompanying me to Sevastopol?"

"A screen call with Ivan and Alexey."

Oleg grunted. "The two most criminal of my brothers. What do they want?"

"They want to buy out our interests in Serbia."

"I'm assuming not the legitimate ones."

"Of course not."

Oleg had a smuggling hub outside Belgrade that had served him well for two centuries, but it was in need of massive investment to keep it updated, and he wasn't sure he wanted to spend his money on smuggled cigarettes, liquor, and electronics when he had legitimate opportunities with his freight companies that required less graft.

"How much are my brothers offering?"

"For the hub?"

"And the networks."

Mika's eyebrow went up. "They were just offering for the hub, and it was ten million US."

"See what they'll offer for the network. Dollars, not local currency." Oleg flipped through the magazine and saw another former lover. "Oh look, Ingrid is in here too."

Oleg enjoyed the occasional human lover. Human women were amusing and easy to please. He had a feeling that Tatyana Vorona would have sharper teeth.

Oleg snapped the magazine closed and tossed it on the seat next to him.

"You want to sell the liquor network?" Mika asked. "Really?"

He waved a hand. "It all goes together. If they make a decent offer, give them a timeline. We'll have people working there who won't want to work with Ivan, so we'll need to put them in other positions."

"Fine." Mika was still pissy. "Maybe you should have asked me what I had planned for tonight before you committed me to flying off to rescue your new girlfriend."

"My girlfriend?" Amusing. "Your bait, you mean? I would think you'd want to keep her safe."

"She's still my bait even if she gets a bit damaged," Mika said. "You're obsessed with the woman because she looks like Luana."

"I honestly don't see the resemblance." He was slightly preoccupied with the woman, but it wasn't about her looks. He was far more curious why she continued to see him as anything more than a man. "Am I becoming less human?"

"Peko's balls." Mika rubbed a hand over his face. "Is this because you're going to therapy now?"

"Fuck off." He spoke to a friend who was a therapist. That didn't mean he was in therapy. "She's not my therapist. I've been trying to seduce her."

"You've been trying to seduce her once a month for the past five years," Mika said. "Her ass can't be that alluring."

The corner of his mouth curled up. "You've been trying to seduce Elene for twenty years."

If looks could kill a vampire, Mika's glare would have decapitated Oleg.

"I'm just saying." Oleg shrugged. "We all have our distractions."

"You called this bookkeeper *yours*."

"Because she is." He felt the plane start to descend. "Just like *you're* mine. And Elene. And Grigor and Roman and Marta at the office." He spread his arms. "My people, Mika. *Mine*."

And those that were his were not to be harmed save by his own hand.

Especially Tatyana Vorona.

Chapter Ten

Tatyana was in her office, tapping away in a private chat room with one of the few friends she'd kept in touch with from her university days while Pushkin slept on the futon behind her, purring furiously.

The friend was a young man who went by 6R1M4C3 or Grimace online, and he called her P1dg3n or Pidge, which was a name no one in her real life had ever heard or ever would.

—*still have all the drives you sent me,* Grimace typed. —*they're safe.*

—*thank you.*

—*want me to send them somewhere?*

—*not now. not yet. not sure where this is going.*

—*you know how to get in touch.*

Tatyana was fairly sure Grimace had intended his name to sound dangerous and menacing when he chose it, but all Tatyana could think of was the giant purple monster who stole the hamburgers of her youth.

She threw out an idea. —*if you wanted to hide thirty million dollars, how would you hide it?*

—*not in russia.*

—*no kidding.*

She was pretty sure Grimace was still in Kyiv, but she had no idea if that would last. His post office box was in Kyiv, but there were forwarding services and he was paranoid.

—*real estate and gold,* he finally typed back. —*definitely gold. real estate if I have lawyers in other countries.*

Tatyana took a deep breath. Zara had lawyers, she was sure of it. Zara probably had lots of lawyers at her beck and call. After all, she had thirty million dollars of Oleg's money.

—*remember the job I was doing last year?* she typed.

—*the whistleblower thing?*

—*I think I might have been the bad guy.*

—*pidge!*

—*I know.*

—*I taught you to use your powers for good. you said you and Z were taking down a billionaire.*

—*I thought I was, but I think I was really helping Z embezzle money.*

—*fuck.*

—*I know.*

—*are you in trouble?*

—*not if I help the billionaire.*

—*FUCK.*

—*I know.*

—*what are you going to do?*

The man was probably already in Sevastopol, lurking and waiting to find her. She'd been sitting in her house all day, stressing out and trying to figure out who had broken in. She'd touched base with everyone who had backups like Grimace and another online friend in the UK. She'd gone out and immediately bought another laptop and cloned her working computer to that, hiding it in a brand-new location.

And all day she'd felt like someone was watching her.

Maybe it was Oleg's people, maybe it was Zara's, but Tatyana felt like she had a target on her back, and she was more and more certain that tracking down Zara's father had been a stupid idea.

You could run.

One hundred thousand dollars might not be millions, but it would be enough to get her and her mother away from Sevastopol. The question was, where would they go?

No, the real question was: How would she ever convince her mother to *keep* running? Anna might run for a short time, but eventually she would start whining to go back to her house and her birds.

Tatyana felt as trapped as poor Rex Harrison with his broken wing.

—what are you going to do?

Grimace's question lingered on the screen.

—I'm going to help the billionaire find the money. Then I'm going to try to forget all this ever happened and hope he and Z both forget I exist.

—don't be too good at your job.

—I learned your lesson.

According to Grimace, he'd hacked into a military database only to be recruited to some shadowy arm of the government when they caught him. They didn't want to put him in jail. They just made him work for them.

—did Z have lawyers?

—she paid enough money to offices with three last names, so I think yes.

—any of them international?

Tatyana frowned and flipped open her laptop, scanning the expenses for the first year she'd been doing Zara's books.

—three different firms, she typed to Grimace. *—one in Russia, one in the UK, and one in the US.*

—real estate. Easiest way to hide money overseas. She could have claimed them as offices or put them into an entirely different name. Invest in the right real estate and your dirty money starts getting cleaner.

Tatyana double-checked the ledgers that Elene had given her, the ones Zara had submitted to SMO, and noticed that only two firms had been paid in that ledger, the one in New York and the other in Saint Petersburg.

—the UK firm isn't on both sets of books.

—*Londongrad, babee.*

—*you might be right.*

—*you know I'm right. I'm always right.*

Tatyana rolled her eyes. She had a sneaking suspicion that Grimace was barely in his twenties. When she'd first met him online, he struck her as a teenage boy and kept wanting pictures of her even though he offered nothing of himself.

Tatyana refused. Obviously.

But maybe Grimace could help her with something else.

—*any idea how to get access to accounts that I set up for Z? I'm sure she changed the passwords.*

—*my paws are itching.* Grimace sent a gif of a cat furiously typing on a laptop. —*give it to me.*

Tatyana couldn't stop her smile. She glanced over her shoulder at Pushkin but couldn't imagine an animal less interested in typing. It felt good to smile, but she was reluctant to drag Grimace into anything involving Oleg or Zara.

—*I don't want to get you involved. These people...*

A memory flickered in Tatyana's mind.

Cool skin and callused fingers.

Memories of trees and a shining bird on a jewel-green background.

Eyes the color of woodsmoke, rimmed by thick black lashes.

What are you?

She shook her head and kept typing. —*these people are really dangerous.*

—*I don't like this. Someone broke into your house. They know where you live for real.*

—*my boss flew into town last night. I don't think Z is going to cross him.*

—*you trusted Z.*

—*I won't make that mistake again.*

—*be careful, pidge.*

Sevastopol
Two years before

ZARA LEANED OVER HER, KEEPING ONE HAND ON TATYANA'S shoulder while she worked. "Tell me what you're doing."

"Okay, so I've identified all the income streams that ZOL should be paying taxes on but they aren't."

"Okay." Zara could be surprisingly affectionate with Tatyana. She did it with everyone in the office, but Tatyana knew her family was Albanian originally. It must be a cultural thing.

"And I've written a program that will skim a small percentage from each of those transactions once they're entered into accounts receivable."

"And you can do that on this computer program?"

Not with the factory settings. She didn't tell Zara that part. It was a slight tweak in the code that Tatyana had created, and she would only ever use it with Zara's permission.

It was Zara's company. She wasn't doing anything illegal. She was helping her boss prove to authorities that her father was corrupt and that she'd been trying to do the right thing.

Zara brushed a hand over the back of Tatyana's neck. "You're too stressed."

Tatyana let out a nervous laugh and felt an immediate wave of relaxation. "I feel like I'm breaking the law."

"You're not. I promise." Zara laughed too. "This probably isn't even enough to cover what all the fines and everything will be when I turn him in, but at least we'll be able to show the police that we were trying to withhold something."

She took a deep breath and nodded as she uploaded the program into the accounting software at ZOL.

"This will funnel a percentage of each transaction into an outside account." She sat back and stared at the screen as lines of code started to fill the monitor.

"How much?" Zara said.

"Just under one percent. I've programmed it to choose randomly between point seven and point nine percent so nothing will seem too regular. And unless someone at your father's company is checking every line in the receivables, it's not going to be enough to notice."

Zara squeezed the back of her neck and straightened up. "You're brilliant."

"I'm really not." She watched the code running and let out a deep breath. "I'm just a bookkeeper."

"You're a whistleblower," Zara said. "When we go to the authorities—"

"Are you going to have to tell them it was me?" Tatyana spun in her chair. "I don't want... I don't think I want the police knowing it was me unless they really have to."

"I'm not sure." Zara sat on the small futon on the other side of Tatyana's home office, and her eyes were wide. "I've never done anything like this before either. I don't even know how much evidence they're going to need."

"What if you go to them now?" Tatyana asked. "Maybe there's a way that you could meet with them and they could tell you what kind of paperwork or documents they might need to—"

"And chance Oleg finding out?" Zara shook her head. "He has people everywhere. Like I told you, all the people originally hired at ZOL were hired by his staff." She huffed out a breath. "I don't even know why he gave all this to me. I'm starting to think he's trying to set me up to get arrested or something."

"Why?" Tatyana's eyes went wide. "Your think your own father would try to set you up?"

"He can be very... practical." Zara's mouth twisted into a grimace. "And cruel. He hasn't been the same since Luana died."

"Is that your mother?"

Zara cut her eyes to Tatyana. "Luana was *not* my mother." Her gaze turned to the dark window where the yellow glow from the street-lamp illuminated the cobbled street. "Luana was his wife though. We were close. She loved me." Zara's eyes turned a little bit pink. "I think she loved me more than she loved Oleg, and he's never forgiven me for that."

"I'm sorry." Tatyana swallowed the lump in her throat. "My father... My mother thinks he disappeared, but he didn't. He found me when I was at university, and he started emailing me. He tries to pretend he's interested in my life, that he wants to have a relationship, but I think he just wants money. He emailed me right after my grandparents died and was asking all these questions about their property."

"That's your mother's country house, right?"

Tatyana nodded. "It's just a farm. There's actually quite a lot of property, and it's very near to the sea. So there are developers who have wanted to buy it over the years." Tatyana shook her head. "My mother would never sell. She's really only happy when she's there."

There was a clatter of pots and pans in the kitchen down the hallway, and Zara turned her head. "Why is she in the city then? She's retired, isn't she?"

Her lip was curled in disdain, and Tatyana had that random thought burst into her mind again. *You're a bad person.*

She blinked and turned back to the computer. "She knows I need to work. I already moved back so she wouldn't be alone, but there's nothing in the country. The house doesn't even have a phone line. Definitely no internet. I wouldn't be able to work anywhere but as a server at a tourist hotel."

"Hmm."

Tatyana glanced over her shoulder. Zara was staring out the window again, looking bored. The woman was strange, but Tatyana tried not to judge her too harshly. Everything Zara was trying to do was honorable, so why did she make Tatyana's hair stand on end?

At first she'd been dazzled by Zara's laughter and quick wit. Her passion for discovering what he father was up to. Tatyana had been swept up with the idea of being a secret superhero, fighting crime with her computer and accounting skills. It was so much more exciting than keeping books for a shipping company.

But the more time she spent with Zara, the more she realized that—while their project was noble—Zara was just not a very good person.

She was spoiled and selfish. She wasn't kind to people and she was rabidly judgmental, writing off anyone who offended her with embarrassing swiftness.

People don't have to be good to do good things.

"You look stressed again." Zara jumped to her feet and came over to rub Tatyana's neck. "Relax. We're doing the right thing. You're not going to get into trouble. I promise."

ANNA WAS STARING OUT THE WINDOW AT THE BLACK CAR THAT had just pulled up next to the house. "Are you in trouble?"

Tatyana glanced out the window and saw Oleg Sokolov looking up. He was wearing a black overcoat, and his piercing grey eyes found Tatyana's before she could hide from his view.

I am in so much trouble.

"It's my boss." Tatyana spun around. "Why is he coming here *now*? I was waiting all day." Her eyes raced around the small living area. Had the sofa always been so threadbare? There were scratches on the coffee table, and the stack of books under the lamp was crooked.

She walked over and straightened them.

Pushkin sensed Tatyana's tension and ran down the hall, probably to hide under a bed.

"What are you doing?" Anna asked. "This house is clean. We have nothing to be embarrassed about." Her mother lifted her chin. "We may not be rich foreigners, but we are honest people."

"I know." Her heart was racing. Why was he here?

A sharp rap cracked against the door, and Tatyana's pulse jumped.

"Tanya, are you in trouble?" Anna walked over to her, her eyes narrowing as she looked at Tatyana. "Should I call the police?"

"No!" Tatyana hissed. "Besides, he probably owns the police. His plane? We landed at the military base when I came back."

"You landed in a military plane?" Anna's eyes went wide. "What are you telling me? Who are these people? I thought this was an honest—"

"Mama, shhh!" She had to calm down. Oleg was standing outside her door, and the longer she waited to answer it, the more awkward it would be. "I'm answering the door."

"Good." Anna crossed her arms over her chest. "I'm not afraid of them." Her sad, irritable mother suddenly had an antagonist and turned into a mother bear.

It had always been this way. When things were smooth in Tatyana's life, Anna always looked for something to go wrong. But when things actually did go wrong? Her mother came to life. She was in her element during an emergency.

Tatyana walked to the door and pulled it open. "Mr. Soko— Oh."

It wasn't Oleg; it was the other man, the one who was always following a few steps behind Oleg. The man who seemed to blend into the background and raised the hair on Tatyana's arms.

"You."

"Mika Arakis." The man walked past her and swept his eyes around the room. "And you are Tatyana Vorona. You had an intruder?" He stopped in front of Anna and looked her up and down. "You're the mother."

Anna's chin went up. "And you're not the boss. I can tell."

Mika cocked his head. "I approve."

"I don't care. Why are you here?"

"Because someone broke into your house." A deep voice came from the doorway.

Tatyana turned toward Oleg's voice, surprised by the warmth that surged through her when she met his gaze.

He nodded deeply. "Tatyana."

"Mr. Sokolov."

There was a twitch under his eye. He kept his hands in his pockets as he entered the room until Kiril the driver stepped behind him. Then he held out his arms and Kiril took off his overcoat, draping it over his arm and leaving Oleg in an immaculate charcoal sweater and a pair of black trousers that highlighted his trim hips and powerful thighs.

Oh dammit, why was she looking at her boss's thighs? That was not okay. Tatyana immediately looked anywhere but at him.

While Mika wandered around the living room, inspecting the windows and lamps, Oleg approached Tatyana's mother.

"Ms. Vorona, you must excuse our sudden arrival. I am of the old tradition, and I tend to visit without announcing it with phone calls or texts or any of that nonsense." He reached back and snapped his fingers.

Kiril stepped forward and handed Oleg a pink pastry box marked with the logo of a luxury hotel in the city center.

"Chocolate smetannik." Oleg held the box out with a charming smile. "I hope you'll accept it as my apology."

Tatyana's eyes went wide. Her mother loved the rich sour cream cake and often made it for holidays. Oleg was being... charming?

This was so dangerous. Her mother automatically distrusted charming men. If Oleg wanted to impress her mother—which was unlikely—he'd go much further being his usual domineering self.

"Hmm." Anna took the box reluctantly. "It will taste better tomorrow."

"Mama," Tatyana said, jumping in. "Why don't we make some tea?"

"No, she's correct, of course." Oleg's eyes were warm and his voice wrapped around Tatyana like a cashmere scarf. "Your mother must be a baker. Smetannik is always better if it is chilled overnight. In fact" — Oleg straightened and shifted his shoulders back until his tall frame seemed to fill the room— "I have some business to discuss with Tatyana while Mika takes a look around the house to improve the security for you and your daughter, Ms. Vorona."

Anna sniffed and held on to the box. "She says someone broke in, but I don't see anything missing."

"That's Mr. Arakis's specialty. He's a security expert." Oleg finally looked at Tatyana. "I wonder if it would be better to leave Mika to his work while we speak about the accounts. I haven't eaten this evening, have you?"

Tatyana wasn't able to answer before her mother jumped in.

"Are you here as her boss or something else?" Anna asked. "Is that appropriate? Asking her out on a date and pretending it's for work? She's not stupid. You think she can refuse you? What kind of company do you run?"

"It's fine." Tatyana stepped toward her mother. "Mr. Sokolov traveled all the way from Odesa. If he wants to eat while we talk about the accounts, I'm happy to join him." She glanced at Oleg. "I know it's a *working* dinner, not a..." She could barely say the word because the thought was terrifying. "Not a date. Obviously not a date."

"I wouldn't presume that a lovely young woman like your daughter would be interested in an old man like me, Ms. Vorona."

Old man? Was he joking?

"I'll get my coat," Tatyana said. "Just give me a moment. I'll get my coat and my briefcase."

"Briefcase?" Oleg narrowed his eyes. "Ah yes." He reached back and snapped his fingers again.

Kiril handed Oleg a large bag with ribbons for handles.

Oh no. No no no.

"I saw that your computer bag was shabby, so I took the opportunity to get you a new one," Oleg said. "For work."

A bag with ribbons like that meant money. So. Much. Money.

And there was no way she could reject the gift graciously while Oleg Sokolov was standing in her mother's living room, wearing a cashmere sweater and a wolflike smile.

"Thank you." Tatyana reached out and took the bag, which had cream-colored tissue paper sticking out from the top. Whatever it was, it probably cost more than her car.

Anna humphed. "Not a date. Of course not a date. How could I possibly think it's a date?" She muttered something under her breath and walked to the kitchen. "Security man, if you're going to poke around my house, I'm going to make tea."

Chapter Eleven

"You know I'm returning this bag." Tatyana was sitting back in her chair, her eyes fixed on Oleg as he watched the sommelier pour two glasses of red wine.

"You're keeping the bag." He glanced at the soft V of flesh visible at her neckline. She was wearing a blue-green wrap dress that was both professional and sexy as hell. He really needed to buy Lorala some flowers. "Lorala picked it out to go with your new wardrobe."

"I'm not going to pretend that I do not like these clothes, but I need to pay for them." She leaned forward as the sommelier left the table. "People at SMO are going to think I'm your mistress if you keep paying for things. I'm working for you now and—"

"You're working for Elene. If I tried to fire you, she wouldn't let me." Oleg waved a hand. "You're going to keep the clothes and the handbag and you'll continue staying at the hotel. Shopping for a wardrobe or looking for an apartment would distract you from your main objective, which is finding the money Zara stole from me."

She narrowed her eyes. "I won't have my fellow employees thinking that you're favoring me because—"

"Don't be ridiculous, Tatyana."

"You think they won't notice? Do you buy every new hire fancy clothes and handbags? Do you fly to their houses because they had a break-in?"

"Of course I don't. And I'm obviously favoring you. There's no point in hiding it." Oleg tilted his head to the side. "I hired you as an independent contractor, and you're working on commission."

Tatyana shook her head. "And?"

He leaned forward, matching her posture. "None of my employees are independent. None of them bargain with me for their position or their pay. Most of the employees at SMO don't even know who I am."

Tatyana blinked. "You're the CEO."

"I'm the CEO of several companies, and those companies are run by very competent executives. The only reason you know me at all is because you worked for Zara. So no, this is not a typical employee-and-employer relationship, and there is no reason to pretend it is."

Oleg sat back and picked up his wine, sipping the Spanish red, rolling the rich liquid around his mouth and imagining what her blood tasted like. Her scent was an intriguing blend of salt and something green. It would be sharp and biting on his tongue.

His mouth watered at the thought, and his fangs ached in his jaw.

There was nothing floral or sweet about Tatyana Vorona. Despite her looks, her body chemistry was elemental. Earthy. Her limbs were slim, her shoulders square, her neck long. Oleg suspected she was stronger than she looked and most people would underestimate her.

He did not.

For a human, she was smart and perceptive. She was headstrong but logical. She reminded him of a predator, pursuing her goal with focus but not forgetting that there were dangers lurking in the forest.

The corner of his mouth inched up. "I would enjoy seducing you."

Tatyana covered her mouth as she nearly spat out her wine. She immediately put her white napkin to her mouth to dab her lips. "That is... That will not be happening."

Now that the words had escaped him, Oleg was determined. This was an excellent idea. He hadn't had a proper paramour in years. "Why not?"

Her eyes went wide. "You are my employer."

What a ridiculous argument. "You're an independent contractor, and Elene is in charge of you. Do you like music?"

"Yes." She blinked. "Not that it matters. Why would you tell me something like that?"

"About music?"

"About..." She sputtered. "Not the music thing."

"So you mean" —he leaned forward— "*seduction?*"

Her lips were flushed. From anger or desire?

"Yes," she hissed. "That."

"Because I thought it. I prefer being direct in these matters."

"And I prefer to keep a professional relationship with my boss."

Oleg smiled. "You've never had a boss like me."

She rolled her eyes. "I've known plenty of men like you."

He could only smile. "No, you haven't." His fangs were lengthening, but she didn't notice.

Tatyana sipped her wine and met his eyes with unflinching candor. "It will not be happening."

"I agree. Not unless both of us want it."

She opened her mouth, but whatever she was going to say was choked by something that was trying to be indignation and failing miserably.

She wanted him too.

Oleg kept his eyes on her, enjoying the rapid parade of expressions on her face.

Shock.

Interest.

Embarrassment.

Curiosity.

Denial.

One expression was noticeable in its absence.

He said, "I like that you're not intimidated by me."

She took a long drink of wine and set her glass down with a decided thunk. "If you do anything to annoy me, I will tell Elene and I have a feeling she would take care of it."

"You're not wrong." Elene wouldn't approve of any of his words or his actions. Tatyana had judged that relationship one hundred percent correctly.

"You do that."

"I do what?" Oleg let his eyes travel over her shoulders, wondering how she would look in candlelight. Electric light was too harsh for her skin. She deserved fire.

"You tell people they're not wrong. But you don't tell them they're right or correct."

"A habit of speech." He shrugged. "Russian isn't my first language. Shall I tell you what I noticed about you?"

She pursed her lips. "Why start being polite now?"

The corner of his mouth tilted up. "I noticed that you didn't say you wouldn't *also* enjoy a seduction, just that you think it isn't going to happen."

"Because it won't." Two spots of red at her cheeks and the hint of a smile.

Now they were playing.

Excellent.

He set down his wineglass and rubbed his thumb across his lower lip, letting the corner of his tongue peek out to taste a lingering drop of red wine. "I didn't say I was *going* to seduce you. I said that I would enjoy doing so."

Her mouth twisted. She was fighting a smile. "And I'm sure many women would be flattered by that."

"Not you?"

She rolled her eyes. "Do you think I'm an innocent country girl?"

Of course she was an innocent. At least she was in his world.

"You don't want to be flattered, but you are." Oleg could feel her heart racing, but her direct gaze told him it wasn't from fear. "You suspect—correctly, I will confirm—that I am particular in my pursuits. Don't pretend you aren't attracted to me."

The little wolf snapped her teeth. "Who I am attracted to is none of your business."

"It is if we're considering a seduction." His fingers slipped up and down the stem of his wineglass, and he saw her eyes move to them. "I am a very skilled lover. We would both enjoy it."

"You're shameless." Her lips were pouted and swollen; a red flush touched the V of skin at her neck. She crossed her arms over her chest, but that only pushed her breasts forward.

Delicious.

Tatyana asked, "Does this actually work on women?"

"The direct approach? Yes." *It's working on you.* Oleg leaned forward, rested his forearms on the table, and tilted his head to the side as he took a deep breath of her scent.

Delicious.

"What was that?" Her eyes went wide. "Did you just... *smell* me?"

"You're wearing some fragrance. I like it."

"I didn't put on perfume before dinner."

"This morning then? Maybe your shampoo." He shrugged. "Whatever it is, it's lovely."

She looked around the restaurant. "Is the food coming? Soon?"

Oleg snapped his fingers and a few moments later, a waiter brought out the first course. "Now that we've had a chance to enjoy the wine, we can eat."

Tatyana stared at his hand. "The snapping thing is going to annoy me."

"I'm not going to snap at *you*." He used a thin fork to pick up an oily black olive from his plate. "You'll find I have much better things I can do with my fingers."

Oleg reached out and caught the olive that went flying from Tatyana's plate, placing it on the edge the table without a word.

Her entire face was the color of a ripe red pepper.

"No." Tatyana was trying not to laugh and only halfway succeeding. "You think you've charmed her, but I promise you have not."

Oleg was feeling surprisingly relaxed. He and Tatyana had enjoyed a delectable meal of Spanish food, which she had never had before, and he'd guided the conversation back toward less... stimulating topics.

He'd suggested walking off some of the rich food with a leisurely stroll along the waterfront. It was before midnight and humans were walking in couples and groups, perusing the white-fronted restaurants popular with tourists.

The scents of humanity surrounded him, and Oleg realized it had been years since he'd spent time among this many humans who didn't know who and what he was.

It was not unpleasant.

Now that Oleg had determined to seduce Tatyana, he'd also decided he could be patient. She was young and he had eternity. If she wanted to finish her current job for him before they took their relationship to the obvious next level, that was fine.

But he'd try to convince her not to be so hesitant.

"I may not have charmed your mother completely," he said, "but she liked the smetannik."

"You did help yourself with the smetannik," Tatyana admitted. "But don't try to charm her. That won't work at all. She'll be very suspicious."

"No? What about with you?"

Tatyana laughed, and it was the first time he'd heard her laugh with her whole chest.

It was a riveting sound. The light in her eyes and the red flush on her cheeks. Tatyana Vorona laughed with her whole body.

Enticing. Delicious.

Oleg could grow addicted to the sound. There was no madness in it, no mania or dark edge. Just the full-throated laughter of a woman who'd drunk a little too much wine and heard something that amused her.

"Is that what this is?" She lifted her chin to meet his eyes. "This is you being charming? You have the charm of a bulldozer, Oleg Sokolov." She blinked, and her eyes cleared when their gazes met. "Why don't I remember what happened after we went to dinner in Odesa?"

Damn it. Her mind was fighting his amnis. "I don't know. You didn't drink that much. Stress maybe?" He'd avoided touching her skin, wondering if direct contact was the catalyst for her preternatural perception.

She smiled again. "So you admit that you're stressful?"

"Not at all. I am trying to reduce your stress." He touched the handle of her handbag. "See? I even replaced your briefcase for you."

"This?" She held out the smooth Italian leather satchel. "This isn't because you're trying to reduce my stress. This is you showing off."

"Is it working?"

Her laugh turned rueful. "I can't tell you that—it will only encourage you."

"By all means." He reached out to steady her as she walked up a step, putting them eye to eye when he tugged her around to face him. "Encourage me."

Her mouth was slightly open, and the scent of wine was on her breath. He leaned in, considering what it would taste like to kiss her.

He wasn't sure he wanted to kiss this woman anyplace that was public.

"You don't need" —her voice was a little breathless— "any encouragement."

"You could always opt for showing me your teeth," he murmured. "I like those too."

"What are you doing to me?"

Oleg wanted to touch her so badly he felt the ache in his fingers. "I'm seducing you."

"Without a single touch?"

"We'll get there." He leaned forward, her lips inches from his own, and he felt his skin heat.

"What is that cologne?" She breathed in.

"Did you just smell me?" The corner of his mouth turned up.

"Stop." She smiled again, and it nearly snapped his control. "It smells like smoke and cedar trees."

"Ah." He breathed out. "I did put fragrance on before I came to your house. I'm surprised you didn't smell it before. Do you like it?"

She blinked and pulled back. "It's... good."

"Good?" A burst of laughter from a group farther down the waterfront broke the spell she'd cast over him. "Good is boring."

"Maybe I'll buy you a cologne then."

Oleg stepped up next to her, forcing Tatyana's eyes up to his. "You're going to buy a fragrance for me?"

"As a thank-you." Her cheeks were red again. "For my boss."

"Yes, that's a very professional gift," he said, nudging her arm with his own to urge her into walking again. "I approve. Nothing with roses, please. I'm allergic."

"Fine." The color on her cheeks died down when they passed a clutch of soldiers standing in front of a tourist restaurant that had been built to look like an old wooden ship. They were holding military rifles, passing around cigarettes, and taking pictures with their phones.

Tatyana stared at them. "My grandfather loved that restaurant. Their fried fish is good."

Despite their uniforms and weapons, the soldiers reminded Oleg of boys on a school trip. They were watching the pretty girls strolling along the waterfront and joking among themselves.

"It's different." Oleg touched Tatyana's back to urge her away from the soldiers. "It's different than the last time I visited here."

"Yes." Her expression fell a little bit as they walked away from the waterfront and down an alley that would lead them back to the restaurant where his car was parked. "It's different."

They walked in silence for some time, turning away from the brightly lit waterfront and into the shadows where Oleg could relax.

He wasn't a creature of the light, though he might wish to see the sun in Tatyana's hair. Her smile had fallen away, and he knew her mind was fixed on the boys playing soldier by the harbor.

He stopped and watched her walk up another couple of steps before she noticed he wasn't beside her.

"What?" Tatyana turned. "What is it?"

He walked toward her. "The world will always change. Change is the only constant."

She offered him a slight smile. "For the worse?"

"No." He shook his head. "I'm older than you. It gets worse. It gets better. The worse may seem more obvious, but the better is surprisingly more enduring."

Tatyana's eyebrows went up. "Are you an optimist, Oleg Sokolov?"

"I have to be." Shadows flickered in his memory. Red-tinged shadows that would claw in and take over his mind if he allowed it. "I have to be, or I would go quite mad."

Oleg walked forward and stepped into the gold cast of a streetlight bouncing off a storefront window.

Tatyana blinked, and the look she gave him was missing the edge of suspicion she usually carried. "Did you show me a picture of something beautiful once?"

Oleg's attention was fixed on her. That was his only excuse for overlooking the threat that emerged from around the corner and quickly surrounded them.

It was a gang of young men, nine of them and three already had blades out.

"That's a beautiful purse, pretty girl." The leader of the small gang lifted a gleaming blade. "Why don't you give it to me?"

Oleg put his arm around Tatyana and scanned the circle of young men. "This is a mistake," he told them calmly. "You do not want to bother me and my friend."

Tatyana wouldn't hand over her bag. Her computer was in that bag, and she'd sooner hand over her right arm.

She was clutching it to her chest, and her heart was racing in fear. The stench of adrenaline spoiled the air, coming from both the woman at his side and the group of boys around him.

Oleg regretted what was going to happen because these men were drunk and eager for a fight. A few of them were unsure and wary, looking at their leader for cues, but none of them stood up to the twitching man holding out the knife.

That one had the taste of violence on his tongue, and he wouldn't be satisfied until he'd fed.

Knowing what was about to happen, Oleg felt the world slow to a crawl, his preternaturally alert senses absorbing everything at once.

The cobblestones were wet from evening fog that had rolled in over the city at nightfall. He could hear the footsteps of the men shuffling behind him.

A car raced by on the street where they'd been headed, the rise and fall of music telling him they were utterly alone.

There was a siren in the distance, an ambulance speeding in the opposite direction.

There were no other humans nearby. This small gang of violent men had happened on Oleg and Tatyana and seen them as an opportunity.

They would die because of their foolishness.

"This is a mistake," he said again slowly, moving his arm from around Tatyana. He removed his coat and let it fall to the ground. "You should leave now or I will kill you."

Tatyana's breath caught.

A few of the boys laughed nervously, but the leader's eyes glittered on Oleg. "I'll take that coat. And your money. I think I will take your woman too. Maybe you can pay to get her back."

"Oleg, no." Tatyana was panicking. "Please, you can have the bag but I need my computer and—"

"You will give them nothing." Oleg stared at the leader, whose eyes were shining with intoxication. Something more than vodka was at work in his mind, and he was not going to leave them alone without blood. "Close your eyes, volchitsa."

She sucked in a breath, and Oleg had no idea if she closed her eyes or not. He was keeping his gaze on the ringleader.

There was a dripping sound as a drop of water fell from a nearby roof and landed on the street. A slap of footsteps on cobblestones and someone coughed.

Oleg snapped his fingers, twisted his hand to gather his element, and threw a flaming ball of fire in the face of the bloodthirsty human.

The leader screamed and fell back, but not before he threw his knife at Tatyana.

Oleg's hand shot out, stopping the blade before it could reach her, and then he stepped away from her and let his element burst to life around him, enveloping his sweater in flames and transforming it to singed rags that floated to the ground around him like burned paper.

Tatyana screamed and ducked her head down, hiding her face from the fire.

Their attackers shouted and turned to flee, but Oleg flung the knife that had been meant for Tatyana into the back of one man as he ran, then pulled another man into his arms, embracing him and grabbing the man's blade as the human's clothes burst into flame and he fell screaming and writhing to the ground.

Tatyana crouched down as Oleg moved calmly around the alley at vampire speed, disarming each man, twisting their necks, and letting them fall to the ground in smoking heaps as he destroyed each and every human who had threatened them.

His fangs were down, and at one point he sank his teeth into the neck of one man, ripping out his artery with a fast jerk of his teeth as blood sprayed in the face of the man next to him.

By the time that human could suck in a blood-misted breath, his neck was cut, blood was pouring down his front, and he collapsed at Oleg's feet.

Within moments, the nine humans who had tried to attack them were dead, and Tatyana was running out of the alley, her bag clutched to her chest, not even sparing a glance as Oleg picked up a body, tore off the human's shirt, and wiped his face and chest to clean off the blood.

She left him alone in the alley, his wool pants singed and hanging loose on his hips, his shirt and sweater utterly destroyed. The evening fog rolled in, soothing the biting pain of his heated skin as his fire died back, kissing the edge of his jaw before she melted away. He smelled the acrid hint of burned hair and knew he'd lost a little bit of his beard.

Pity.

Oleg listened to Tatyana's footsteps racing around the corner and down the street. He heard her panting breaths and panicked hiccups as she ran toward the brightly lit intersection where the ambulance had passed a few minutes before. There were cars waiting at the light.

"Taxi!" She screamed it from a block away and he heard that too. He closed his eyes and waited for the door to slam and the car to speed away.

Oleg let her run.

She'd seen the monster now. He would find her soon enough.

Chapter Twelve

This cannot be real. That was a fever dream. A nightmare.

Her wrist was bruised from the pinch of her own fingers.

This is a nightmare and I'm going to wake up.

"Lady, you need help?"

She stared straight ahead, afraid to look out the windows in case Oleg was chasing her.

"Can you take me home, please?" Her voice sounded like she was speaking into a hollow tube.

"Give me the address and I'll take you anywhere." The man turned around, examining her, even as the cars started to honk behind him. "You need a hospital? The police?"

"Just go," she whispered. If she closed her eyes, would she wake up? "Please go very fast."

"Is someone chasing you?"

"Please just go!" She recited her address by rote, and the drive didn't even balk at how far away from the city center he was going to have to drive.

"Okay, okay—relax." He started moving. "See? The traffic is going now."

Tatyana's heart would not slow down.

Oleg knew where she lived, but she had to go home. Her mother was at home. She needed to get her mother and run.

But how was she going to run... from *that?*

Oleg didn't have a phone. Mika probably did. Maybe she could get to her mother before Oleg could call Mika.

"Close your eyes, volchitsa."

"Oh God." Tatyana bent over, resisting the gagging urge to vomit when images flashed in her mind.

Dead eyes. Showers of blood. There had been an arm—a torn-off arm—on the cobblestones and rivulets of blood running down the seams of the street like rain.

Tatyana hadn't known blood was dark like that. It hadn't looked red, it had looked black, and when she dared to steal a glance at Oleg, all she could see was the black stain down the front of his bare chest as fire danced in his arms and his lips curled back, revealing a set of long, thick fangs.

Fangs.

"Please pull over," she whispered.

"What?"

"Pull over!"

The moment the car reached the side of the road, she pushed the door open and—gripping her bag to her chest—vomited her fancy dinner all over the sidewalk.

The cab driver ran around and put a hand on her shoulder. He was a round man who reminded her of her grandfather except he was wearing a Yankees baseball cap.

"Girl, you need to go to the police. Or the hospital. Whatever happened, it wasn't your fault and you need to report—"

"I can't." She shook her head, and her heart rate spiked again. "It's not safe." She wiped her mouth with the sleeve of her jacket. "Please, I just need to go home before he can find her."

The driver's eyes were wide and sad. "Whatever this is, I am so sorry it has happened."

Tatyana felt tears threatening, but she couldn't break down. "I'm sorry we had to stop; I didn't want to puke in your cab."

"Don't even think about it." He helped her to her feet and back to the car. "You're more considerate than the average drunk asshole." Once she was back in the car, he carefully closed the door, then rushed around and got driving again. "I'll get you home fast. I know a shortcut or two."

Even with shortcuts, it was fifteen long minutes before they reached her neighborhood.

The driver nodded to the left when they came to a stop. "Is that it?"

"Yes."

Tatyana had told him to drive up the street behind her house. She didn't want anyone watching the house to see her return. She was just praying her mother was safe.

"You don't want me to get you closer?"

"I can go through the neighbors' fence. I know where the gate is."

"There's a car in front of your house." He turned to look at her. "They'll see you leave."

"We don't park our car at the house. It's at a small garage nearby," she said. "I need to get my mother and we can sneak out the back. They won't know we're gone."

He kept his eyes on her. "Do you want me to wait here?"

Tatyana racked her brain. The man had been more than helpful, and she didn't want to involve him any more than he was.

Then again, she didn't have many allies right now.

"If you want to help, can you go and sit at the end of the street?" she asked. "You don't have to talk to anyone or even get out of the car. Just act like you're waiting for a fare maybe?"

"I can do that." He nodded. "I'll park in the middle of the road. They won't be able to drive out of there with me parked like that."

"Are you sure?" She had no idea if Oleg's drivers carried guns. Then again, when your boss had fangs and could control fire, probably guns were not all that necessary.

"It's not a big deal. Are these guys mafia or something? Is that what it is?"

"I don't know, but they're dangerous." She opened the car door and ducked out quickly as the overhead light came on, shoving far too much cash in his hand. "Please be careful. And if they come near you, just drive away. Quickly."

He reached out and grabbed her hand, dropping the cash to the floor of his cab. "I still think you should go to the police."

"He knows them." It was the easiest thing to say; the easiest explanation that she knew he'd believe. "But I have a place to hide. I promise, I just need to get my mom."

"You're a good daughter."

That was debatable, but she didn't have time to argue. "Thank you."

"Be careful. I'm going to drive away so they don't look at me too long. I'll just circle around and wait at the front of the road."

"Thank you."

She had pulled her sweater out of her bag and used it to cover her hair, which was far more visible than she'd like in the moonlight.

Tatyana hurried over the rough ground on the side of the neighbor's house and ducked under their clothesline until she made it to the back stairs of the old three-story house.

Climbing up, she tried to be as silent as possible to avoid waking the neighbors, and eventually she made it to their back balcony and the kitchen door where she saw her mother snoozing under a lamp with her glasses falling down her nose.

Tatyana eased the door open, noticing the shadow at the front door of the house.

She tiptoed over to her mother and bent down, touching her knee and putting a finger to her lips when Anna's eyes flew open.

"Mama," she whispered, "I can't tell you what's happening right now, but you have to trust me. Grab a few things, all the cash you have, and we need to go out the back door. Now."

Anna's eyes went to the silhouette of the man standing outside the front door, and then she looked back at Tatyana, nodded, and silently stood.

THEY DROVE OUT OF THE CITY ON BACK ROADS, AVOIDING THE motorways until they were well away from Sevastopol and heading northeast.

When they were past Simferopol, Anna finally spoke. "It's another two hours to the farm. Are you going to tell me what's going on?"

"My new boss is not who I thought he was." Hopefully that would be enough.

Of course it wasn't.

"What a surprise. The wealthy, handsome man who buys you designer coats and Italian leather bags isn't a typical businessman. I am so shocked."

"Mama, can you not?"

"I don't know what you expected. First you take this very strange job working for that crazy girl who didn't even let you go into the office, and then when she stops paying you, you find the one who helped her start her company and expect him to be an honest person."

"Yes." Tatyana sighed. "This is obviously all my fault."

"If you had applied for a job at the city office, none of this would have happened."

"If I'd applied for a job at the city office," Tatyana snapped, "the farm we're driving to right now would belong to a developer."

That shut her mother up.

So far the escape had been seamless, which made Tatyana somehow even more nervous. Her mother had cooperated. So far.

Anna was suspicious by nature, so disaster never really took her by surprise. She'd grabbed Pushkin and put him in his carrier, taken the backpack she kept in the pantry for emergencies, and retrieved all her cash from the garish pink shoebox she'd hidden in her closet.

Tatyana had grabbed her backups, a change of clothes, some extra underwear, and nothing else. She dumped the fancy leather bag that Oleg had given to her, suspecting that it could have a tracker, along with all the clothes she'd brought from Odesa.

She pulled on a black hoodie to cover her hair, a ratty old barn coat, and her baggiest jeans. By the time she and her mother were sneaking out the back, she felt like even if Oleg stepped right in front of her, he wouldn't recognize her.

Then again, maybe he could track her by smell.

"Did you just... smell me?"

"You're wearing some fragrance. I like it."

"I didn't put on perfume before dinner."

"This morning then? Maybe your shampoo. Whatever it is, it's lovely."

She'd been *flirting* with the man.

The monster.

She'd even entertained the ridiculous idea of taking him up on his offer to date. Not while she was working for him, of course, but she'd allowed herself to wonder if something might be possible when the job was done.

He was charming.

Intriguing.

Tempting.

And yes, wealthy and competent and successful. Oleg took charge of their every interaction, and for someone who'd had to be the care-taker for too many years, it felt amazing to have someone else steering the ship.

Tatyana had allowed herself to daydream about being with a man like Oleg.

When she'd thought he was a man.

Anna sat up straight and looked out the window. "Why are you going this way?"

Tatyana had passed the old turnoff for the local road. "I'm taking the highway, Mama."

"Hmm." Anna set her lips in a grim line. "If the police are looking for us—"

"I don't think he's going to go to the police."

"All those gangsters have police in their pocket."

"Maybe." Tatyana didn't think Oleg could be classified as a gangster. He was something... much worse. "Mama, have you ever seen something... like something out of a story?"

Anna frowned. "What kind of story?"

"Like a folktale. Or a... a myth. Something unnatural."

"I see a million things that seem unnatural just by turning on the television these days." She looked at Tatyana from the corner of her eye. "What are you talking about?"

"Nothing."

"If it was nothing, you wouldn't have asked."

"Fine. I saw... saw something impossible."

"If you saw it, it's not impossible."

"It was... something unnatural."

"Criminals aren't unnatural," Anna said. "They're evil, but they're not unnatural."

What Tatyana had seen went far past the criminal. "Do you believe in monsters?"

"I believe in human monsters; my grandparents survived Stalin." Anna glanced at Tatyana. "Take the next exit and get off the highway."

She sighed. "Mama—"

"Do it. It'll take longer, but if anyone is following us, there are places we can hide on the local roads. There is nothing on the highway."

She had a point. Tatyana exited the expressway and turned back toward the small town they'd passed. The local road that would take them toward the area around Feodosia, which Anna called home.

Her mother had been born on that farm, and while most of the land was rented out to a local farmer who cultivated almond trees and lavender, the house, the old barn, and the garden was theirs alone.

It was isolated, and as far as she knew, it was still in her grandfather's name. Maybe it would be enough to keep Oleg's people from finding it immediately.

"So you saw something criminal," Anna said. "Did you even think of going to the police?"

"What I saw went far past criminal."

"Don't be ridiculous. He's a man, like all men. Maybe he's an evil one behind that charming smile, but he's just a man."

No, Mama, he is not.

Tatyana swallowed the lump in her throat. "I just need to get away and think for a little bit, okay? Those people were in front of our house."

"And whose fault is that?" Anna snapped. "You brought them to our home."

The cat decided that was the perfect time to start howling. Pushkin had been surprisingly amenable to this entire adventure when they were escaping the city, but one and a half hours in his carrier was quite enough.

"Yes!" Tatyana shouted over the yowling animal. "I'm sure this is entirely my fault."

"You never should have taken a job with that crazy woman."

"Of course not! In fact, I never should have moved away from Kyiv," Tatyana snapped. "I had a good job there. I would have had a promotion in six months if I hadn't left."

Anna clamped her lips together and said nothing.

But Tatyana was on a roll. "Then again, why would I want to stay in Kyiv with my friends and my good job that paid half your bills when I could move back to the place I was desperate to get away from?" Her voice rose to shout over Pushkin's.

Anna spoke with a clenched jaw. "You have family responsibilities here."

The cat was howling directly in Tatyana's ear, the country road rocked and rolled their little compact car, jolting her jaw so hard that she bit her cheek.

Tatyana snapped. "What I have is a paranoid mother who has no friends, no job, and is completely incapable of living on her own like an actual adult. A mother who is determined to keep a farm we can't afford to pay taxes on because it's the only happiness she ever had. But you won't move back, so we have to pay for an apartment in Sevastopol too. But yes, Mama." She turned and shouted at her mother. "It's completely my fault that I ended up working for a vampire!"

THEY PULLED INTO THE FARM AT THREE IN THE MORNING AFTER taking the old twisting roads through the hills and valleys of the Crimean peninsula, dodging skunks that crossed the road and a few drunks in tiny towns that had once been throughways and were now backwaters because of the highway.

They skirted the scattered lights of Feodosia and headed into the hills. The farm where Anna had grown up was only ten miles from the historic town and seven kilometers from the sea.

Tatyana turned off the paved road and came to a stop near an old metal gate. Anna jumped out of the car and went to open the gate while Pushkin finally settled down.

Her mother hadn't said a single word about Tatyana's blurted confession. She either thought her daughter was losing her mind, or she was too furious to speak.

Very possibly both.

Tatyana pulled the car forward as Pushkin's yowls turned to happy meows.

"Oh, you know where we are now, do you?" She glanced over her shoulder. "She'll let you outside now that you can't attack her birds."

Pushkin chirped.

"Oh no, that was entirely your own fault. Rex Harrison was your friend and you maimed him."

She couldn't blame the cat; he was an animal. It was in his nature to attack birds, even birds his mistress loved.

What was Oleg's nature? Was he compelled to attack humans? To feed from them? He hadn't attacked Tatyana. In fact, the more she thought about the strange night she'd experienced, the less it made sense.

Anna closed the gate and walked back to the house.

Out in the country and miles away from the bloody alley in Sevastopol, Tatyana finally took a breath.

"I'm sorry for what I said," she told her mother. "I don't want you to be alone."

"Humph." Anna crossed her arms. "Tell me about the vampire."

"I'm probably going crazy."

Anna shrugged. "All myths come from somewhere, Tanya."

"You don't think I'm delusional?"

"You?" Anna snorted. "You didn't even like to read the stories about the wizard boy when you were young because you thought they were silly. You read Crime and Punishment when you were thirteen. You have no natural imagination, so you wouldn't make something like that up."

She didn't know whether to be insulted or relieved. "I am so boring."

"Not boring. Practical." Anna nodded. "So you saw a vurdulac?"

Oleg was so far from tales of hairy wolf-men who drank human blood she nearly laughed. "I don't think he's anything we know about."

"So what did you see?" She raised a hand. "You know what? Don't tell me; no good for both of us to have nightmares."

"In an odd way, he was protecting me."

"What do you mean?"

"We were walking along the waterfront after dinner—"

"So he eats food?"

Tatyana had to think about it. Yes, Oleg had definitely eaten food. He'd also drunk wine.

At least she thought it was wine.

Of course it was wine—her glass had been poured from the same bottle.

"He eats food, and he drinks wine."

"Vampires don't eat food," Anna said.

"Maybe this one does. Maybe he's not a vampire."

"How was he protecting you?"

Tatyana steered the car through a narrow alley of ash trees and up the hill to the old house that was nestled in the rolling orchards and lavender fields that surrounded it.

"We were walking back, and I wasn't paying attention. We turned in to an alley and there was no one around. Then these men—there were eight or nine of them, I think—they just walked into the alley and they were drunk. I'm sure they were drunk and maybe high too. Some of them had knives."

"Oh Tanya." Anna reached across and put her hand on Tatyana's arm. "They could have done anything."

"Oleg told them to leave us alone."

"This is a mistake. You do not want to bother me and my friend."

"This is a mistake. You should leave now or I will kill you."

"He told them twice, Mama." She turned past the last ash tree and into the farmyard where a low stone wall surrounded a beautiful cottage. A barn was built across from it, and a rusted tractor was silhouetted by the full moon.

She parked the car between the house and the barn, finally able to think clearly. "He told them twice to leave us alone. But they ignored him, and he killed them all. He was so fast." She shuddered. "It all happened in moments. Just... minutes. Maybe less."

"Then he came after you?" Anna was reaching for Pushkin. "How did you escape?"

"He didn't come after me." Tatyana blinked. "I ran away. He was on fire and I ran."

"Fire?" Anna's eyes went wide. "I thought fire would kill vampires."

"I don't know, but he was…" She spread her arms out. "Throwing it. He shot fireballs, like a dragon."

"But he had fangs, yes?"

She nodded. The fangs were burned into her memory. "Yes. He definitely had fangs, and he definitely ripped a few necks open when he—"

"Ah, da da da da." Anna held up one hand and took Pushkin with the other. "I don't need to know."

Tatyana unclasped her seat belt and got out of the car. "I'm not going to be able to sleep until the sun comes up. Do you think we should hide the car?"

"Who says this vampire dragon man is even going to come after you?" Anna seemed oddly unconcerned. "If he wanted to kill you, he would have done it right then." She walked toward the front door of the cottage. "I'll get Papa's shotgun from the barn, and then we'll take turns watching out for this monster until daylight."

Tatyana grabbed her bag and slung it over her shoulder, oddly reassured that her mother seemed to be taking all this in stride.

Then again, Anna was always happier at the farm. Tatyana paused by the car, looking at the battered old compact with the rack on the roof. The dirt was crusted on it from rain on the road, and there was a crack in the windshield.

The house behind her was snug and cozy, but the furniture was the same as it had been for the past thirty years. And all the tools in the barn were left over from when her grandfather had farmed twenty years ago.

With the faint smell of cow manure in the air, gourmet dinners, private jets, and luxury suits seemed about as fanciful as vampires.

"Come on, get inside," Anna called. "We'll prepare things better tomorrow, but right now you're ready to jump out of your skin and there's not a soul around."

Tatyana wandered into the farmhouse, grateful that at least something seemed familiar when everything in her world seemed upside down.

Chapter Thirteen

Oleg waited in the car as his driver Seban called for a cleanup crew in the alley and took care of paying off the human authorities that needed to be bribed. A light rain was falling over the city, and he thought about Tatyana running through the rain. She'd been wearing a dressy coat, but it didn't look warm, and he made a mental note to tell Lorala to buy another, heavier, garment for her.

Had she lived in another century, he would have enjoyed hunting foxes or trapping ermine so a furrier could make her a coat from animals he'd provided, but she was a modern woman and women in the twenty-first century did not appreciate furs as older centuries did.

Oleg hadn't worn fur since he was human. He found it too warm for his element.

"Finished, boss."

"Good."

The driver's door clicked shut, and Seban turned to look at him. "I called Mika when I was finished with the police. He said they're gone."

"Both of them?"

"Yes."

"Good." He would have been surprised if Tatyana had left her mother when she ran.

"Mika wanted to know if he should follow them, but if they've had a head start—"

"It's fine." He plucked at the freshly pressed pants Seban had procured for him. A crisp cotton shirt had taken the place of his cashmere sweater. He'd have to order a new one since he'd liked the texture of the one that burned. "Take me to the house."

"Are you sure?"

Oleg glanced at Seban, then flicked his fingers, pinching back the burst of flame that wanted to escape. "Just go."

The human turned around and put the car into gear.

Oleg supposed it was natural for the man to be skeptical. Seban had been Oleg's personal driver for three decades, and he remembered when his boss had spent more time in Sevastopol. Even after he and Luana had grown distant, they were not truly estranged.

Vampire unions could take many shapes, and while his and Luana's mating had once been highly passionate, Oleg had been supportive of her desire to have some distance after several hundred years. They remained close, but their sexual relationship ended so their blood bond could wane.

Seban drove through the city as it grew quiet and cold. The tourists had returned to their hotels. All but the hardiest clubs were shutting down. It was three in the morning, and Oleg spotted a blue moon hanging low in the sky as his car turned on familiar streets toward the oceanfront villa Luana had loved.

She was a water vampire and had always reveled in her element. She wanted waterfalls flowing through the house and massive fountains in the garden. Oleg had spared no expense creating the perfect getaway for his mate and delighted when she was pleased.

He'd created a mosaic fountain in the entryway that was one of his finest works, but he hadn't crossed the threshold of Luana's house in over a decade.

When Zara had secured Luana's affections, Oleg had been relieved.

His mate was happy. In time, their blood bond would recede and Oleg would finally be free of the woman who had been his dream, his nightmare, and his obsession for centuries.

Fate, of course, had other plans.

They pulled up to a white mansion with classical Greek columns and arches that surrounded the three-story building. The whitewashed walls glowed in the moonlight, and the scent of the Black Sea surround him.

Seban opened the door, and Oleg stepped onto land he'd bid farewell to centuries before.

Mika was standing in the doorway of the house, his arms crossed over his chest. "This night didn't go the way I expected."

Oleg patted him on the shoulder as he walked inside. "Wouldn't it be worse to be bored?"

"Seban told me to let her and the mother go." Mika was sitting on an immaculately kept lounge chair on a veranda that over-looked waves crashing over rocks. "Why?"

Just because the house had been empty for a year didn't mean it wasn't well-kept. Perhaps someday he might want to visit this place again. It was isolated enough for his liking, and the upper stories were completely light safe. There were extensive rooms built into the bedrock as well as passages leading back to sea caverns where Luana and Zara had enjoyed their private swims.

He also suspected they'd lured humans there at times, but that was none of his business as long as they cleaned up after themselves.

"She saw me kill the humans."

"Yes, I sensed a bit of pent-up tension at work there from the pictures Seban sent." Mika leaned forward and rested his elbows on his knees. "Feeling better?"

Slightly.

He had been tense, but it had nothing to do with Zara this time. It was the tidy little human with her facts, her figures, and her stubborn determination to lodge herself in his mind that was throwing Oleg off.

"I'm fine." He'd prefer to be fucking the woman and sinking his teeth into her neck, but that could come later when she wasn't afraid of him. "Do you have concerns, Mika?"

"I have concerns that you let her run off like a scared rabbit. Why on earth didn't you wipe her memory?"

It wouldn't have worked.

He didn't tell Mika that. "I've decided that I want to take her as a mistress, so I'd prefer she know my true nature."

It wasn't *un*true. But Oleg also didn't want any other vampires to know that Tatyana's mind was becoming resistant to vampire manipulation. If immortals thought she couldn't be fooled, she would become a danger to them.

"You want her as a *mistress?*" Mika gaped. "We're using her as bait."

"We can continue using her as bait. I'll just depend on you to protect her so she's not damaged."

Mika shook his head. "We're talking about Zara. I can't guarantee anything."

"I think you can if you want to keep me happy." Oleg leaned forward and took the glass of wine that a silent servant set down. "She's going to be working intimately with us. I decided it was more convenient for her to know my true nature."

"That was definitely one way to show her," Mika said. "You ripped off several limbs in front of the woman and killed nine men."

"Who were trying to rob us," Oleg said. "And they were not interested in just her purse."

Now Mika looked amused. "She still might see that as an overreaction, but maybe I'm misreading her. No doubt young accountants are accustomed to violent and deadly retribution for common street crimes."

"The human world would be far safer if thieves had to fear death if they assaulted a woman." Oleg shrugged. "Their deaths will not sit on my conscience, semu."

The old nickname seemed to cut the tension between them. Mika sighed and sat back in the lounge chair. "This is a great house."

"It really is." Oleg looked around. "And without Zara here, it's quite peaceful."

"I'm hearing whispers from Istanbul."

"What kind of whispers?"

"Zara hasn't been seen in two nights."

Oleg's eyebrow went up. "That coincides with your putting the word out that Tatyana was working with us, correct?"

"Correct. Are you sure we shouldn't be chasing the woman right now?"

"Relax." Oleg snapped his fingers, and the servant appeared at his side. "They took their car, correct?"

"Yes, and headed northeast toward Simferopol."

"Then they're going to her grandparents' old farm, I imagine." He kicked his feet up on the edge of the stone table as his wineglass was refilled. "It's in the Feodosia region, correct?"

"Yes. We already have people in the area. I'll call them and tell them to keep an eye on the place until we get there."

"Good. Let my little wolf catch her breath and try to convince herself she didn't see what she saw tonight." Oleg looked out toward the low-slung moon on the edge of the horizon. "I'll find her soon enough."

Two nights later, Oleg sat in the back of an old Land Cruiser as Seban drove it up a narrow dirt track that wound between bare almond groves and trimmed lavender fields. The land was cool and quiet, but the rolling fields that rose up from the Black Sea coast were green even as winter approached.

"It's no wonder that they went into debt to pay the taxes on this place," Oleg said.

"It's beautiful country."

"Human inheritance laws are cruel." He didn't know the details, but it irritated him that Tatyana had been forced to use her money to pay the taxes on land that her grandparents had farmed for decades.

"Human governments are corrupt," Seban said. "That's why I prefer working for vampires."

"Even when I create messy situations for you?" The corner of his mouth turned up.

"But I never have to worry that you'll fire me." Seban glanced in the rearview mirror. "If you're not happy with me, you'll just kill me. All my worries will be over."

"And your grandchildren would receive excellent educations." Oleg nodded. "Remind me to update the employee benefit handbook when we get back to the citadel."

Seban chuckled. "I have a feeling that kind of benefit isn't going to appeal to a woman like her."

"It might. She's a practical one." He saw a yellow light at the top of the barn as they crested a hill. "No mirrors hanging from the trees?"

"No, but all the lights are on in the house."

"And thorns in the windows, no doubt," Oleg murmured. *Come now, volchitsa, do you think you can rid yourself of me so easily?*

Seban pulled into the yard between the house and the barn and brought the car to a stop. "Cross on the door."

"Maybe they're just religious."

Seban chuckled. "Do you want me to come with you?"

"No. Stay in the car, but you don't have to keep it running. Call Mika. Tell him I'm here."

Oleg had dressed himself in a sweater the color of birchwood and a pair of brown wool pants. Lighter colors made him appear more human, and he needed to set Tatyana at ease.

He walked calmly to a wooden gate set into a stacked stone wall, noting the bowls of water set on either side.

Consecrated water did nothing to Oleg. In fact, he used it to cool his fire when he worked on mosaic pieces in churches.

He cleared his throat and made sure to step loudly when he opened the gate. He could smell the faint scent of gunpowder nearby and suspected that an old farm like this would have at least a shotgun or a rifle on hand.

A gun wouldn't kill him unless it managed to precisely sever his spinal cord at the neck, effectively decapitating him, but gunshot wounds were painful and took elemental energy to heal. He'd just burned up one favorite sweater and didn't want to wreck this one as well.

"Tatyana Vorona."

The faint sound of a shotgun racking.

Oleg smiled and raised both hands. "You can't kill me with a shotgun, and I'm not here to harm you."

"Why are you here?" she yelled through the closed door.

"I can hear you very well," Oleg said. "You don't have to yell. My hearing is excellent."

The door to the old farmhouse swung open slowly, and Tatyana appeared in the doorway.

"Why are you here?"

Oleg was momentarily speechless. Gone was her professional armor of poorly fitting business clothes and fashionable new suits. She was dressed in a plain white T-shirt, a black hoodie, and a pair of worn jeans. Her golden hair glowed in the yellow electric lights, and her blue eyes were fixed on him.

She looked younger. And she looked fierce.

Oh, I will have you, my little wolf. You will most definitely be mine.

"Are you here to kill me?" Her voice was flat and emotionless.

"Why would I kill you? You work for me. Have you betrayed me?"

"No."

"Good. So whatever you think you saw—"

"I saw you bare your fangs, rip out the throats of nine men, and set them on fire with flames you pulled from nowhere," Tatyana said. "Tell me I was imagining it."

She might smell afraid, but she wasn't showing it. He liked her bravado, and it was a little bit disturbing how attractive she was carrying a weapon. He glanced at her feet to see a pile of freshly hewn wooden stakes piled near the door.

They couldn't kill him, but he was impressed by her effort.

"You weren't imagining anything." Oleg opened his jaw, rubbing his beard as he let his fangs grow long. He tilted his head back so she couldn't miss his extended canines in the darkness. "Your mind wasn't tricking you, Tatyana Vorona. But you knew that already."

She gulped, but her gaze never wavered. "I want out."

"Out of what?"

"Out of our contract. Out of SMO. I don't care about the money; I'll return it. I want nothing to do with you."

"It's a little bit late for that," Oleg said. "Zara already knows you're working with me."

Her face grew pale. "How? Was she watching my house? Did she steal my backup computer?"

It would have been easy for Oleg to let her believe that. He could be the protector then. He could trick her into thinking that all this was for her own good and that despite his monstrous nature, she could trust him.

"No." Oleg decided that she'd be more persuaded by the truth. "Mika put the word out days ago that you were working with us to find the money Zara stole. I'm sure that's why someone broke into your house."

The barrel of the shotgun rose, and Tatyana's face grew red. "You were going to use me as bait."

"Yes." He took a step closer. "I'm still going to use you as bait, but you won't be unprotected. Neither will your mother. We were watching this house before you even arrived."

"Why?"

"I protect my assets. And you are one of my assets now." Oleg lifted his chin. "And, of course, bait is useless if a trap isn't well-set."

A voice called from inside the house. "That I will believe."

"Mama," Tatyana barked, "be quiet."

Oleg smiled. "You're right. She doesn't trust charming men. And I don't think you do either."

The barrel of the shotgun dipped a little bit. "Are all those men dead?"

"Yes."

"And you don't feel bad about that, do you?"

He took another step forward. "Not even a little bit. I warned them. Twice."

She nodded a little bit. "And you're a... what? What are you?"

He took another careful step. "I am Oleg Sokolov, immortal lord of Kievan Rus, sired of earth and born to fire, vampire heir of Truvor the Red... and your boss."

Tatyana's face leached of the bright color her temper had provoked. "Zara *is* your child, isn't she? And she's a vampire too."

"Unfortunately yes."

"And she stole money from you. Thirty million dollars."

Oleg nodded. "It's probably closer to fifty million, but it's not the amount that's the issue. It's the fact that she stole, and she cannot be allowed to get away with that. Not in my world."

Tatyana nodded for a long time, staring at him without saying anything; Oleg could see a thousand questions racing through her mind.

"Invite me in." He walked up the steps to the old wooden porch. He could smell her now. Smell her mother. Smell the memories in the house and the sour scent of fear in the air. "I'm not going to hurt you. I'm going to protect you. I can tell you have questions, and I'm willing to answer them. But you have to invite me in."

Her eyes lit up. "You can't come in, can you? You can't enter my house without an invitation, so if I—"

Oleg stepped his foot over the threshold, and Tatyana gasped. "I can come in."

She cursed under her breath.

"But I won't without your permission," he continued, "because I prefer it."

"Invite him in," Anna called from inside the house. "You're letting the cold in, Tanya. Just invite the vampire in."

Tatyana lowered the shotgun and set it by the door, then stepped to the side and said nothing, her jaw clenched in anger.

"Come in, Mr. Sokolov," Anna said. "I'll make some tea."

As Oleg walked past Tatyana, he leaned down and whispered in her ear. "You know, I don't mind the garlic but it's not my favorite perfume."

"Fuck you," Tatyana whispered.

"Oh, volchitsa." Oleg smiled. "I do look forward to your teeth."

Chapter Fourteen

Tatyana spent the night listening to Oleg reassure her mother that Tatyana would be safe with vampires. All his arguments were rational, and her mother had seemed reassured, and Tatyana felt like she was in the middle of someone else's life.

When he was finished telling her mother how things would be, Oleg walked down the porch steps and looked over his shoulder. "I will see you in Sevastopol tomorrow night, Miss Vorona. Please be ready to travel." Then he turned to Anna, who was peering over Tatyana's shoulder. "Miss Asanov, your new assistant will meet you in Sevastopol on your return." He glanced at Tatyana. "She's a professional and will be able to assist you with anything you need while I am borrowing your daughter."

Bookkeeper acquired. Mother assuaged.

He was efficient, Tatyana had to give him that.

After Oleg left the farm, efficient professionals appeared as if by magic, setting up a communications center near the barn, sending out dark-clad individuals to patrol the orchards, and bringing in a black Land Cruiser to drive Anna and Tatyana back to Sevastopol the next morning.

Anna stared at the midnight bustle on the quiet farm. "I hope they don't disturb the neighbors."

Tatyana stared at her mother. "Are you actually okay with this?"

Her mother spared her a glance before she returned to surveying Oleg's people. "You made an agreement with a vampire. He's not asking for your blood or your firstborn child, is he?"

"No."

She shrugged. "You were a bookkeeper for a packaging manufacturer, you can be a bookkeeper for a vampire. You needed a job, didn't you?"

Part of Tatyana couldn't believe her mother was being so casual about this, but the other part of her realized that Anna Asanov had seen more change in her life than Tatyana could imagine. A new dictator rolling in to run her life probably felt more normal than not.

"That assistant is probably a bodyguard," Tatyana said. "She'll be watching your every move. You know that, right?"

Anna looked at her. "And? I'm still going to make her clean. Your boss said she was going to work for me. So she can watch me while she cleans pigeon shit."

The allure of a private jet was significantly less impressive on Tatyana's return to Odesa.

The plane was just as luxurious, but instead of going home, Tatyana was returning to Odesa for an unknown period of time to work with a creature she didn't fully understand, trying to accomplish a job she wasn't sure she could actually do.

The plane was dimly lit and occupied by four other passengers: Oleg's driver Seban and three other people she didn't recognize. No one was speaking to the others; all of them appeared to start working the minute they sat down.

Tatyana sat on her own in a seat that faced backward, staring at a soft taupe curtain. Her messenger bag was next to her, but she didn't open it.

She had things to do. She had a book her mother gave her and the files Elene had sent with her to Sevastopol, but she found herself staring at the curtain, determined to *not* work as long as possible.

"Miss Vorona." Roman, the lovely steward, bent down and spoke softly. "Would you like a drink while the pilots prepare the plane?"

"Yes," she said softly. "Just water, please."

Nothing in Tatyana's life seemed real, but as her mother had pointed out the night before, there were countless times when Oleg could have killed both of them and didn't.

She'd become a target, and Oleg was probably the only one who could protect her.

Even though he'd been the one to make her a target in the first place.

"You were going to use me as bait."

"I'm still going to use you as bait."

Her mother, ever the pragmatic, reminded Tatyana that she had signed up to work for Oleg and she had to finish the job. As much as Tatyana had wanted to argue, she couldn't.

Besides, if a monster was chasing her, she needed a monster to protect her.

"He's coming." A woman's voice cut through Tatyana's exhausted daze.

A female steward walked to the back and drew a curtain aside, revealing a strange contraption built into the back of the passenger compartment.

What the hell?

It looked like a very fancy silver... cage. The cage extended around four seats at the back of the passenger compartment, wrapping around everything—the floor, the windows, everything. There were large openings between the metal strips and a large door.

Just as Roman brought her a bottle of spring water and a cut-crystal glass, she heard footsteps on the stairs leading to the plane. Glancing over her shoulder, she saw Oleg enter, followed a few moments later by Mika.

"Mr. Sokolov, welcome." Roman gave him a deep nod. "Good to see you, Mr. Arakis."

Pleasantries were exchanged, but Oleg's eyes scanned the plane with clear intent, settling on Tatyana immediately. He gave her a curt nod, then greeted the other passengers like a courteous boss and ignored Tatyana.

He walked down the aisle, opened the cage, and sat in a seat, picking up a newspaper and opening it. Mika followed a few minutes later, chatting with no one but Oleg's driver before he also entered the cage and closed the door behind them.

The moment the compartment closed, it was as if a switch flipped.

Dim lighting brightened, and the hum of electrical appliances and instruments started.

Roman and the second steward started moving around the compartment, handing out drinks and securing the compartment for flight.

Oleg called from the back compartment. "Blood-wine, Roman. Two glasses and a bottle."

"Right away, Mr. Sokolov."

Tatyana looked up and realized that Oleg's seat was opposite hers, separated by four rows, but she was directly in his line of sight. Was it intentional?

"I protect my assets. And you are one of my assets now."

She didn't feel like an asset. She felt trapped.

Tatyana looked away from the strange man who now dictated her life and back at the book in her lap. It was a bestseller that her mother had picked up and shoved at Tatyana as she walked out the door.

Roman walked down the aisle with an open bottle of wine and two wineglasses, passing them through the slats of the metal cage without opening it.

"Thank you, Roman."

"Of course, Mr. Sokolov."

Oleg caught her curious stare. "It's a Faraday cage. The only way I can fly."

Tatyana said, "I thought vampires could fly."

There was a low sound of laughter around the plane, and she felt her cheeks heat.

Oleg looked at her, the hint of a smile touching his lips. "Come." He flicked two fingers at her in a come-hither gesture. "Take one of the back seats and talk with me. I cannot open the cage while the electronics are active, so you'll be very safe."

More quiet laughter.

Tatyana was tempted to ignore Oleg, but she had questions and she didn't want people laughing at her. She grabbed her old messenger bag and her glass of water, moving to the farthest seat in the back that butted up to the cage where Oleg and Mika were sitting.

As soon as she sat, he held his hand out.

Tatyana stared at the hand. Mika was studiously ignoring both of them, sitting across the aisle in a chair that faced to the back and reading a book.

"Come on." A snap of Oleg's fingers and he held out his open palm. "You can reach in; I cannot reach out."

"I told you the snapping was going to annoy me," she muttered.

The corner of his mouth turned up, and Tatyana tentatively put her hand into the cage. She looked Oleg in the eye. "Why do you need a Faraday cage on an airplane?"

"It's a special modification so I can fly." His fingers wrapped around her hand. "Do you feel it?"

Tatyana frowned. The moment Oleg's hand touched hers, there was a slight buzz, as if she were touching a covered wire. Gradually she felt the buzz move up her hand and her arm. At the same time she felt her heart start to race, and the hairs on her arm stood up. Her skin was impossibly sensitive when he rubbed his thumb over her knuckles. Her lips tingled.

Tatyana pulled her hand away, shocked by the sudden arousal Oleg had provoked with a single touch. "What is that?"

"Amnis. Human stories call it glamour. Magic. Enchantment. It's the current that connects us to our elemental power."

"Your fire."

"Not all of us are flammable," Mika muttered.

Oleg smiled. "Mika draws strength from water. My sire drew it from earth. Every vampire in the world gains their power from an element."

I am Oleg Sokolov, immortal lord of Kievan Rus, sired of earth and born to fire.

Tatyana said, "You were born to fire."

"A genetic quirk if you can believe it. Vampires also have their... recessive genes."

"I thought vampires gained power from blood."

"Blood is the embodiment of all the elements." Oleg leaned back and lifted the wine bottle that Roman had brought, tipping it. "Iron, water, oxygen." Brilliant red wine poured into his glass, but it was a little darker, a little blacker than most wine she'd seen. "And of course the heat of living fire."

He handed the wine to Mika and reached for another glass.

"Blood-wine is exactly what you think it is," Oleg continued. "Human blood preserved in fortified wine."

Tatyana watched the glass. "So you drink that instead of fresh blood?"

Mika chuckled a little as he sipped his wine. "Like a weight lifter surviving on Caesar salad."

"That's not a bad comparison," Oleg continued. "Blood-wine is convenient, and it will sate your hunger for a time." He put the bottle in a bucket on the side table. "But it's not a true meal."

Tatyana watched him take a long drink, then lick a drop of blood from his lower lip before he spoke again.

"We still need to feed from humans," he said. "Depending on our age, we don't have to drink very often. Maybe once a week or so."

She opened her mouth and closed it again.

Oleg had already guessed her question. "I don't drain a human unless I want to. I don't have to kill to survive."

She kept her voice soft. "But you do kill."

"When the situation warrants?" He lifted his chin. "You should be glad I killed the other night."

Tatyana didn't know how to feel about that night. She glanced at Oleg's wineglass and remembered the black blood dripping down his chest and the scent of iron in the air.

She looked away. "I saw you eat food too."

"We have stomachs, don't we? If your stomach is empty, it groans. Besides that, our tastes are heightened. Our senses are better than yours. Good food is highly enjoyable."

Tatyana glanced at him again and saw his eyes settle on her face.

He said, "Anything that appeals to the senses is more pleasurable for vampires."

She didn't like the way her cheeks flushed. She sat back and crossed her arms over her chest. "Clearly the stories are not correct if you can't fly."

Oleg smiled. "Disappointed?"

"Some of us can." Mika glanced over his shoulder. "Wind vampires, remember?"

"And you're a fire vampire." Tatyana looked around the plane. "You have electrical currents under your skin. If you weren't in that cage, you'd short-circuit all the electronics on this plane, wouldn't you?"

"You're very bright."

"That's why you hired me."

"No," Mika said. "He hired you because Zara will want to kill you when she hears that you're working for us." He glanced at Tatyana. "Don't worry. I won't let you die. He'll be annoyed if I do."

Oleg barked something at Mika in a language Tatyana didn't understand, and the other vampire muttered something, set his book down, and closed his eyes.

"Forgive Mika," Oleg said. "He has no manners. He will protect you though. All of my people will protect you."

"Why?"

"As I told you last night, you're an asset to me. And you are very bright. I fully expect you to find my money."

Tatyana swallowed. "If I can't?"

"Given enough time and resources, I have every confidence in you." He lifted his glass. "I will give you everything you need."

"But until then I'm a captive?"

Oleg took a long drink of wine, and Tatyana saw the corner of his fangs peek out from behind his lips. "I suppose that depends on how you define captive."

OLEG'S DRIVER DROPPED HER OFF AT THE ADMIRAL HOTEL, AND Tatyana collapsed in a room that felt at least a little bit familiar even if it didn't feel safe. She dragged pillows and blankets over to the window and fell asleep with a guard outside her door.

When she woke, she felt the warmth of the late-morning sun bathing her skin.

She rolled over and closed her eyes, reveling in the security of the light.

She hadn't asked anyone directly, but judging by the fact that she'd only seen Oleg and Zara at night, she suspected the stories about sunlight burning vampires was based on fact. In the sunlight, she was safe. During the day, she didn't have to worry about monsters lurking.

A tap at her door. "Miss Vorona?"

The voice was familiar, and when Tatyana went to open the door, she was pleased to see Lorala's bright smile.

The woman was also holding another rack of garment bags. "Coats," she said. "Mr. Sokolov said you needed a coat."

Tatyana looked down at her sweatpants and her favorite black hoodie. The coat she'd been wearing that fateful night in Sevastopol had stayed in her bedroom, stained by mud and vomit from her traumatic night.

"Come on in." She opened the door. "It's been a rough few days."

"It's nice to see you again." The woman bustled into the room and immediately went to the kitchenette to turn on the coffee maker. "Marina tells me that you are aware of Mr. Sokolov's nature. How are you feeling?"

Tatyana gaped. "You mean... You know Mr. Sokolov is..."

"Vampire." Lorala smiled politely. "Of course. This hotel is actually a converted mansion that once belonged to a vampire. It's owned by the Wallace Conglomerate and caters to all guests but specifically those in the immortal world—vampires and their day people."

"Oh my God." She sat on the edge of the bed. "They're everywhere, aren't they?"

"Take a moment and breathe." Lorala brought her over a cup of strong black coffee. "I can see that you're still processing all this. I put two sugars in your coffee. If you'd prefer something with milk or tea—"

"No, this is good." Tatyana sipped the coffee and immediately felt better. "This is great." She looked at Lorala with new eyes. "Are you a vampire?" Tatyana shook her head. "No, of course not. It's daylight, so unless I'm wrong about—"

"No, you are correct." The woman nodded. "Vampires cannot be in sunlight without damage, and most of them sleep very deeply during the day. Almost as if they're dead."

She took another long drink of coffee. "But there are a lot of them, aren't there?"

Lorala walked to the table and angled a chair toward Tatyana. "Not as many as you probably think but more than you knew before. If you have questions, I'm happy to answer them."

Tatyana blinked. "Uh... how do you know about all this?"

"My father worked for an immortal. I've known since I was quite young. There is a whole community of day people in most large cities."

"How many vampires are out there?" Had she been passing them in the streets her whole life and not knowing?

"I have no idea. I doubt anyone does." She smiled. "I'm sure it's very overwhelming. And you might be scared, but there is no reason to be. Mr. Sokolov is a very powerful man. Taken under his protection, you're probably one of the safest women in the world right now."

Safe from others maybe, but what about from him?

Tatyana finished her coffee and set it to the side. "He's *very* rich, isn't he?"

Lorala said, "I would assume so. He's the vampire lord in this area."

"This area?"

"Vampire territories rarely follow human borders. Mr. Sokolov has been the immortal ruler of Odesa, Kyiv, and much of the northern Black Sea region for far longer than it has been part of any modern state."

"How old is he?" Tatyana asked.

Lorala shook her head. "I have no idea. Most vampires hide their age because it's an indication of power, but I know he's quite old."

Hundreds of years? Maybe longer?

How old do you think I am?

I am very bad with guessing ages.

I'm eleven hundred and thirty-seven.

Tatyana had thought he was joking, but she had a suspicion that she knew exactly how old Oleg was.

Why had he told her?

And how did anyone wrap their mind around being that old? "Is he Russian?"

Lorala cocked her head, considering the question. "He would probably be considered Russian now. I believe his corporate headquarters are in Saint Petersburg. But remember modern borders—even modern languages—are new for many immortals."

I'm a captive?

I suppose that depends on how you define captive.

Who was Tatyana in comparison to someone who was more powerful than human governments? She was a state-educated accountant.

"My life is over," she whispered.

"I *promise* you, it is not." Lorala's face was sympathetic when she rose. "Ms. Beridze left a message that you'd be going into the SMO corporate offices today but she didn't expect you until later. Would you like me to have one of your suits pressed while you get ready and eat breakfast?"

She looked up at Lorala, suddenly suspicious. "Are you here to make sure I follow directions?"

Lorala smiled and her eyes were soft. "I understand your suspicions, but I'm here to help. I hope you can trust me even though I know that everything must feel very strange right now. I promise though, you're quite safe at the Admiral. This is neutral ground. All humans and vampires are safe in this hotel, and no violence is allowed on the grounds, not even between rival vampires."

"Neutral ground?"

Lorala nodded. "I don't work for Mr. Sokolov. I work for Marina, and Marina works for Wallace Hotels. And Wallace Hotels are neutral territory. You can trust us."

Tatyana had no way of knowing if Lorala was lying or not, but she wanted to trust her. She had no idea if she was being a naive fool, but the woman seemed honest.

"And who is paying the bill for my room?" Tatyana asked.

"SMO International has an account at the Admiral."

"Right."

And SMO International was Oleg.

Tatyana was going to find out how much her room cost—or maybe how much a smaller room was. As long as Oleg controlled her money, he controlled her.

"Still, I think it's quite telling that Mr. Sokolov brought you here." Lorala walked back to the kitchenette. "He has multiple properties in Odesa, but instead of taking you to his people, he brought you to the Admiral."

"Why?"

"I have no idea." Lorala started the coffee maker again. "But if he wanted to control your every move, he wouldn't have brought you here."

Chapter Fifteen

She looked sick. When Seban had dropped the woman off at the Admiral, she had looked sick to her stomach. Was Oleg repulsive to her now?

He should probably give her a few nights to recover before he resumed his pursuit, but a voice inside Oleg told him that would be a mistake.

He stared at the round blue tesserae he'd set into the mosaic at his house. The color of the tile mirrored the ocean in sunlight, a sight he only ever saw in paintings or on screens now.

What color would Tatyana Vorona's hair be in the sunlight?

He pressed his fingers against the cool concrete wall and heated it very slowly with his amnis. He was out of patience with this project and with the entire situation. Tatyana Vorona should be grateful. He was going to make her a lot of money.

The water in the sea air slowed the rate that the concrete set and clung to his skin. "Seban?"

His driver spoke from his chair by the door. "Yes, boss?"

"Where is Mika?"

"Probably at his place. He said he and Oksana had a bunch of calls to return at nightfall."

Mika's calls could wait. "Fetch him for me."

"Yes, boss."

Seban walked away, and Oleg continued slowly curing the cement he'd used to affix the new pieces of the mural. After those pieces were secure, he picked up a handful of pebble-like glass pieces in a greenish hue and began to imagine how he would place them in the emerging seascape.

"Seawater at dusk," he murmured to himself. He closed his eyes and tried to picture the exact hue, but his imagination flew toward the woman again.

Interesting.

Oleg was over a thousand years old; he didn't question why his mind became preoccupied with certain people or subjects. Perhaps it was indulgent, but he'd lived long enough at the mercy of others' whims.

If he wanted to fixate on a mural, he would. If he wanted to seduce a human, he would seduce her. If he wanted to shower her with gifts, he had more money than he knew what to do with.

"Is there a problem?"

Oleg didn't turn around when Mika walked into the room. "You and Oksana have the Vorona woman under surveillance, correct?"

"Twenty-four hours."

"Good." He spread a thin skin of cement over the wall. "Find a picture of her in the sunlight. I need to see the color of her hair."

Mika walked closer. "You interrupted an important call with Radu because you want to see a woman's hair in the sun?"

"It won't be exact, but it's the best I can do," Oleg muttered. "Video would be better."

"You're obsessed."

"I'm interested." He glanced over his shoulder. "There's a difference."

"You're intent on making her your new mistress?"

He shrugged. "Why not?"

"Because I thought we had agreed that she is my bait to catch Zara."

He delicately placed the smooth glass pieces in a starburst pattern. "She can be both."

"And if it comes down to it, will you choose to neutralize your daughter or protect the woman?"

Oleg paused and turned slowly to face his second-in-command. "Are you saying you're incapable of protecting the woman?"

Mika pursed his lips. "I'm not saying that."

Oleg felt his neck heat. "Then are you incapable of neutralizing Zara?"

"You told me that I'm not allowed to kill her. That she belongs to you."

"You know what I mean." His eyes bored into Mika. "Well?"

The water vampire lifted his chin. "I will not fail you, Knyaz."

"Good." Oleg turned back to the mural. "If you're doing your job, I won't have to make any choices like that."

"There has been a development."

Oleg let him stew in the silence for a good ten minutes as finished placing the green tiles into a star, then oriented seed pearls into the space between. "What is the development?"

"Zara has left Istanbul. It has been confirmed."

Oleg blinked, set his tray of tesserae down on his worktable, and slowly turned, crossing his arms over his chest. "Are you sure?"

"Radu said his informants in the palace confirm she has left. He doesn't know if Laskaris threw her out or if Zara left on her own."

"But the timing coincides with your Albanian rumors." Then he remembered who Mika had been talking to. "Radu *gave* you this information?"

"He offered it in exchange for discounted passage for the camvasa when they travel through our territory."

Oleg smirked. "That's what I thought."

The Romanian vampire was one of three leaders of the Poshani, an itinerant clan of humans and vampires who roamed across Eastern Europe and Southern Russia.

Though they had various lucrative businesses in Romania, Bulgaria, Ukraine, and Belarus, the Poshani clan's main source of income was a moving safe house they ran for immortals called the Dawn Caravan. They guarded vampires by day and by night. They were smart, brutal, and most of all, secretive. If a vampire wanted to thoroughly disappear, the Dawn Caravan was where they would go.

And if Zara had been allowed in, Oleg was going to murder someone.

Possibly Radu.

Oleg gritted his teeth and felt his fangs aching in his jaw. "Is she in the caravan?"

Mika shook his head. "According to Radu, she isn't."

"But if she was, he wouldn't tell us."

Secrecy was the key to the Poshani.

The Poshani took hospitality to a supernatural level, telling no one who was traveling under their protection, not on threat of death and not for a bribe.

Vampires had tried to manipulate the minds of human Poshani to get information and were found with their heads taken off for daring to violate their honor. Few ever attempted to cross them, knowing that someday they might need that safety themselves.

"They wouldn't allow Zara in the caravan," Mika said. "She's cost them too much money since she moved to Istanbul. They have to let you in, and I guarantee Radu hates Zara far too much to allow it."

"So she's missing." Oleg's mind started to whirl. He turned and picked up his tesserae palette again, stepping back to look at the pattern as a whole. "You'll increase the guards around Tatyana and her mother of course."

"Obviously," Mika said. "She's our bait."

This was an opportunity. His daughter had soiled his name in the vampire world, and Oleg had taken a hit to his reputation because of it.

Immortal progeny usually attained a level of independence from their sire at some point, but a bond remained, usually an affectionate one. Stronger than that of biological children, it was a relationship of shared blood and elemental power.

Zara had been Luana's lover, but Sokolov blood ran through her veins.

There was one brutal lie he could tell that would shore up his reputation and isolate his daughter at the same time.

"Tell Radu that I've killed her." He started placing a new row of square blue tiles.

Mika blinked. "Who?"

"Zara. I want you and Oksana to tell everyone you know, everyone you've met, everyone you can think of, that I have killed my child."

Mika took a step closer. "That *you* killed her? Personally?"

"With my bare hands." His extended clan would be horrified.

The Sokolov clan that their sire had left behind was bonded—despite all their internal rivalries—by the trauma of surviving Truvor. Killing those outside the clan? Expected. Completely reasonable in fact. Killing anyone directly related by blood?

Heinous.

It was something not even his own sire would have done, as brutal as Truvor had been. He would capture his sons, keep them captive, set his children against each other, make them battle and brawl—even provoke them to walk into the sun to end their own life, which many of them did.

But not even Truvor had killed his own blood.

Vampire children killing their sires on the other hand?

Technically it was forbidden—as taboo as killing a child of your blood—but there were ways around it. Oleg had personal experience with that.

Mika asked, "Are you sure you want to do that? It will make allies question their trust in us."

Oleg's organization didn't have a *kind* reputation, but they were considered trustworthy. A wolf would always eat their kill first—that was the nature of things—but they left plenty on the bones for the ravens who came after.

Killing his own child might call his character into question, but it would make Zara desperate.

"It will isolate her. Even if she shows her face, people will question her. It will sow confusion, and many of her former allies will cut her loose."

"And Laskaris?"

"He either threw her out or she left him." Oleg smiled. "He won't take her back."

"They'll call you a monster," Mika said. "Beyond the Sokolovs, we might lose some goodwill in our legitimate channels. Your brothers will cut you off."

"Cut off by a gang of thugs with concrete for brains in Moscow?" Oleg drawled. "How terrible."

Mika persisted. "Let me do it. I'll say that I fought her and—"

"No." Oleg picked up a blood-red tile and placed it on the wall. "Dead by my hand, Mika."

His second was quiet for a long time. "You're sure?"

"Yes." Oleg stepped back and stared at the lone scarlet tile in the middle of a sea of blue and green. "She's dead to the immortal world anyway," he said. "Because once I find her, she'll never see the sky again."

OLEG WENT INTO THE OFFICE AGAINST MIKA'S ADVICE. He wanted to see Tatyana, and he knew she was working with Elene that evening.

While Elene didn't exactly keep vampire hours, she usually worked in the evening and went home at midnight, leaving her time to supervise both the human and the vampire employees of SMO.

When Oleg walked into her office that night, he saw the door to Tatyana's office closed, but Elene's was open.

He strode past a fluttering Marta and tapped on Elene's door.

She kept her eyes on the file she was reading but waved him in. "I didn't think you were coming in."

He closed the door and took a seat in the chair across from hers. "Zara is in the wind."

Elene looked up. "When?"

"Two nights ago. She's left Laskaris."

"Does Mika know why?"

"Maybe because we are looking for the money. Maybe she was stealing from him too. It's Zara, so it could be anything."

Elene's expression was grim. "Do you have any idea where she is?"

"If I knew that, I wouldn't have increased all your security." He crossed his arms over his chest. "You and Dmytro should move into the compound here in town."

"You know he won't agree to that."

"Does your husband know how much Zara hates you?"

She shrugged. "My children are grown. I'm not that concerned about my life." She glanced to the right. "What about Tatyana?"

"How successful do you really think she'll be?"

"Well..." Elene flipped over the file to show him. "She's already discovered how Zara was skimming the money."

"How?"

"She programmed an automation to skim random percentages off incoming receivables. Always under one percent. Nothing regular, so it was very easy to miss. And in addition to that, there were other minor scrapes. Ninety-nine cents skimmed here. Overcharges for travel. Nothing big enough to raise flags."

"Smart."

"And because ZOL and SMO's software was linked, she didn't just skim from ZOL but from SMO too. Thousands of microtransactions every day added to accounts with high interest rates that banks offered based on their relationships with you. At the end of the day the total amount was probably closer to fifty million than thirty."

"So she stole from her own business and from mine?" Oleg scanned the documents but knew he'd have an easier time reading Ancient Greek. "I don't understand any of this."

Elene rolled her eyes. "You would be sitting in your castle, stacking gold coins like a dragon if you didn't have me."

"You're correct." He handed the file back to Elene.

"Zara was greedy." She set the folder to the side and leaned back in her chair. "It's hard to hide that much money. Tatyana is smart, and she has relationships with specialists who can find hidden things online. We'll find the money."

"A fox is most dangerous when she's cornered." Oleg stared at his old friend. "Stay at the house."

"Focus on Tatyana." Elene jerked her head to the side. "I've had three people from rival organizations ask me if we really have Zara's bookkeeper. Apparently Zara bragged about the bookkeeper's skills even though your daughter had no idea what Tatyana was doing."

"She managed to help Zara skim money for three years without your discovering it."

Elene scowled. "Sometimes I hate that I'm..."

"Human? We could have fixed that years ago." Oleg smirked. "But you wanted to have babies."

"I wanted Dmytro," Elene said. "And I like my children well enough. As their godfather, I would hope you like them too."

Oleg smiled, and eventually Elene smiled back.

"My friend," he said softly. "I would feel much better if you stayed at my house. Just until I have taken care of this problem. Think of your family."

"I have work and you have people," Elene said. "Mika's guards are ruthless and very discreet. Worry about the new girl. She's..." Elene shook her head.

"Still panicking?"

"You turned her head and then turned her world upside down," Elene said. "What did you expect?"

"I expected to seduce her *before* I told her about my fangs." He lowered his voice. "There was some unfortunate violence after our last dinner."

"Ah yes, your *business* dinner. Mika told me about that."

"There was an interruption. I will still seduce her."

"She reminds me of myself when I was younger, so you might have a chance, but she's even more cynical than I was."

"A delicious challenge then."

"Are you going to tell her Zara is missing?"

"Yes. There is no point in lying to her now. She realized Zara is a vampire as soon as she realized what I was. And she knows we're using her as bait."

Elene's eyes flew open. "You told her?"

"I have no interest in lying to my future lover. It would insult us both."

"You've never lacked confidence, but this is extreme. Even for you. Why her?"

"She's beautiful."

"Ordinary beauty bores you."

That was true. His most interesting lovers had rarely been conventionally beautiful, and while Tatyana was very beautiful by human standards, it wasn't her looks that he found intriguing.

"I appreciate her loyalty to her family," he said. "She's clever and bold even when she lacks confidence."

Elene leaned back and crossed her arms over her chest. "You like bold."

"I do." Oleg glanced toward her office wall. "If she was listening in, I wouldn't be surprised or offended."

"She might be too smart for you."

"Immortal minds process faster than human minds. It is highly unlikely that she is smarter than me."

"I didn't say smarter than you, I said too smart for you. As in she will be too smart to get involved with an old man like you."

Oleg leaned forward and leaned his elbows on Elene's desk. "If I recall correctly, I had enough youthful vigor to keep you satisfied when you were younger than her, kitten."

"Stop." Elene shook her head. "Digging up ancient history to prove a point." She waved him away. "Go and seduce the girl, Oleg. Just remember that you have to keep her alive until she finds all this money."

Oleg rose. "It's fifty million. It won't break us."

"Spoken like someone who is not the chief financial officer of your company. Go."

He tapped on Tatyana's door and waited to hear her footsteps on the other side.

She opened it and looked up. "You."

"May I come in?"

"What a nice captor." She opened the door wider. "Of course. How polite of you to ask."

"I'm not your captor." He sat in the chair in front of her desk and stretched his legs out, crossing them at the ankles. "But if that's a fantasy of yours—"

"Absolutely not." She waved a hand in his general direction. "You may have flirted with me before all this happened, and I might have even entertained it then, but now?" She shook her head.

"You need a job more than you need a man?"

"Yes." She narrowed her eyes. "I need to find all this money, return it to you, and try to forget all this ever happened."

"I also like most of those goals, but I do want to point out that I am not a man." Oleg spread his arms. "So your reasoning doesn't hold up."

"You are a man in every way that counts."

Oleg lowered his voice. "Very glad you've noticed."

Tatyana's cheeks burned. "Of course you think a vampire would be less trouble than a man."

She had looked sick when he'd dropped her at the hotel the night before. Now she was spitting fire and he loved it.

"I told you I like your teeth. Do you really think you can find my money?"

"No." Her eyes went wide and innocent. "You should probably just let me go back to Sevastopol and forget all this ever happened. Would you like to wipe my memory? Please. According to Elene, you've done it before."

Damn that woman for telling his secrets. He reached back and pushed the door closed, giving them even more privacy.

Tatyana's eyes went to the closed door, and her shoulders grew stiff.

"I'm not going to hurt you," he said. "Remember?"

"I know enough now—"

"Really? After two whole nights you know enough?"

She pressed her lips together.

"Here is what *I* know after barely a week of knowing you exist, Tatyana Vorona." Oleg dropped his voice to barely over a whisper. "I know that Zara manipulated your mind. Far more than you realize, I think. I know that your brain is quite clever and it was fighting against my amnis—"

"The glamour?"

"Call it whatever you want, but amnis is more accurate."

"That's a Latin word. Latin was the imperial language of the Byzantine Empire."

Oleg smiled. "Are you trying to discover my age now? I already told you."

She sat back and wiped the inquisitive expression from her face, putting another stiff mask in its place.

He *had* told her, and it surprised him a little bit. He usually didn't do that, but she was quick and he'd let it slip.

"Your mind is strong," Oleg continued. "It was fighting against my influence. That's why you passed out twice when we were together."

She frowned. "That's why that happened? I don't remember—"

"Of course you don't."

"So you manipulated my memories already. So why am I...?" She clamped her lips shut, and her cheeks grew red.

"Still attracted to me? Still *tempted*? Still having warm feelings for the monster who has captured you?" Oleg lifted his chin. "I can manipulate memories, not feelings. I can make you tell the truth, but I cannot make you attracted to me. I cannot force you to care for me. That's not what amnis does."

"I don't believe you."

He narrowed his eyes. "Tell me, how did you feel about Zara?"

She opened her mouth, then pressed her lips together.

Oleg uncrossed his legs and leaned forward across Tatyana's desk. "How did you feel about her?"

"I didn't like her." Tatyana's voice was soft. "She could be... enthralling. It was impossible to ignore her when she walked into a room. When she was talking to you, paying attention to you, it was as if you were the most fascinating person in the world."

"But how did you *feel* about her?"

Tatyana swallowed hard. "I disliked her. I didn't trust her. I got a sour taste at the back of my throat every time she came to my house, and I could never understand why."

"Because she manipulated your memories, but she couldn't change your heart or your intuition. Your mind is strong, Tatyana. It's one of the things I find so attractive."

Her cheeks burned with red, but she leaned forward on her desk, boldly entering his space. "I still don't need a man."

"And as I pointed out before, I am not a man." His eyes dropped to the perfect curve of her upper lip. "If I kissed you—"

"I'd bite your lip so hard you'd bleed."

Oleg was instantly aroused. His cock grew heavy at the thought. "Good. Let me know where I can bite *you*. It's only fair."

She sucked in a breath and leaned back. "Stop."

"There's a particular spot on the inside of a woman's thigh where the taste of her blood and the taste of her—"

"Stop." She put her hand over his mouth.

Oleg parted his lips and gently took her finger between his teeth, teasing the inside of her knuckles with the tip of his tongue while his elongated fangs dug into the soft flesh.

Her heart was racing, and the scent of her arousal bloomed around her. Sweet blood. Sweeter honey between her thighs.

I will take you on the desk, fuck you with my fingers, and drink your blood when you're coming over my hand.

He had to be careful with human women. The first time they had sex, Oleg probably wouldn't be able to fuck her properly, but he could sate his hunger a bit and bring her all the pleasure she wanted.

Sexual novelty did not breed self-control, and he was a fire vampire.

Oleg held his hand up and snapped, bringing the warm glow of fire to his fingertips. He kept the flames light, tickling along his fingertips as he ran them over her wrist. She wouldn't feel the burn, but she'd feel the sensation of his element.

The hairs on her forearms stood up, burning away at the touch of his fire.

He pressed his lips to her fingers in a lingering kiss before he pulled away. "I look forward to your bite, little wolf."

"You're manipulating me now." Her heart was pounding. "This is your amnis. This is—"

"It is not." Oleg smiled a little bit. "And you know it."

She opened her mouth as if to protest again, but he cut her off before she could speak.

"Zara is missing."

It was as if a frosty wind blew through the room. Tatyana's face drained of color. Her hand dropped to the desk.

Her eyes went wide. "My mother—"

"I have already contacted her bodyguard, and Mika called in reinforcements in Sevastopol. It's a precaution. Zara still has allies in the region, but your mother should not be a target. Her people already have the computer" —he waved a hand— "things that you stored there."

"Files. A backup hard drive. A laptop and USB—"

"Yes, all those things. Your mother knows nothing, and Mika has already spread the word that *you* are here. So your mother will be safe."

"But not me." Her smile was bitter. "Because I'm the bait, right?"

"The bait that is under my protection," Oleg said. "I have no plans to let Zara get her hands on you, Miss Vorona. You belong to me now, and I'm a very possessive vampire."

Chapter Sixteen

Hours later, Tatyana made it back to the hotel and stumbled into her room. She was exhausted and keyed up with numbers and spreadsheets dancing in her mind, but she dragged her pillows and blankets to the bay windows and curled in front of them, eager for sunlight even though the morning light would make it harder to sleep.

She dreamed about Oleg, and in her dream, fire danced over his naked flesh. He held her against a wall, licking down her body as her back arched in pleasure.

He was whispering things in a language she didn't understand, and when he knelt in front of her and looked up, blood was dripping from his lips. Instead of making her afraid, it only aroused her more.

When Tatyana woke, she was sweaty and her hair was tangled.

What was happening to her?

"Vampire glamour," she muttered.

Not for a second did she believe that Oleg wasn't using his influence over her mind to seduce her.

She grabbed her phone from the charger and quickly navigated to the internet.

She searched "vampire glamour" and got various links to websites for popular shows, book series, and online games. She even got an ad for something called a "vampire glamour facial" and really didn't want to know what that was.

Tatyana sighed. The problem with finding information about vampires was that they were fiction.

Except that they weren't.

What was the other word Oleg had used?

Amnis.

She searched for "vampire amnis" and got absolutely nothing but random fan art, pop-culture wikis, and a few miscellaneous blog posts.

Whoever was doing online scrubbing for the vampire world, they were earning their money. There was very little information about any of it online, not even on conspiracy sites.

She searched "Wallace Conglomerate" and only got listings for a few Scottish tourism companies and one events company in New York. SMO's listings she was intimately aware of because she'd searched it out when she was trying to get paid and there was nothing suspicious about it.

Fascinating.

So vampires like Oleg couldn't use technology because they would short it out, but they clearly had people who knew how technology worked.

Yes, Tanya, like you.

What was she except an extension of Oleg now? She was finding his money for him and dangling herself as bait for him to catch his vampire daughter.

"What is my life now?" Tatyana stared out the window at the deep blue waters of the Black Sea.

The sea had always brought her comfort.

When she was a child, it was the place where she was happiest. She would run down the hill to the seaside every morning at her grand-parents' farm, spend all day with the kids from town, and hike back home when the sun went down, exhausted and grubby from a full day of sunshine and salty water.

In Sevastopol, her only comfort in leaving her old life was being back near the water after the urban sprawl of Kyiv. She loved the ocean and was always happier when it was in her sight.

But now when she looked at the depths spreading out before her, she wondered what was below the surface. The glistening waves danced in the sunlight, but beneath that light were vast depths she had never seen.

Water vampires.

Wind vampires.

Earth vampires.

And of course fire.

She thought she'd known about the world around her just like she'd known about the sea. But what she had known was only a thin skin along the surface of a depth so vast and dark she was beginning to think there was no way not to drown.

I have no plans to let Zara get her hands on you, Miss Vorona. You belong to me now, and I'm a very possessive vampire.

She was losing it, because a week ago, those words would have set off every alarm in her mind. Now? They seemed reassuring.

There was a friendly knock at her door, and she threw on a robe before she went to answer it, unsurprised to see a uniformed waiter rolling a breakfast cart into the room.

"Good morning, Miss Vorona," the waiter said in English. "I've brought your usual breakfast, but is there anything else you'd like this morning?"

He set out trays of steaming eggs and sausages, a basket of French-style pastries, and a bowl of fruit.

She looked at the small mountain of food on the table, all of it for one person. "Does everyone eat in their room here?"

"Not at all, miss." He glanced up. "There are two eating establishments at the Admiral—a restaurant on the mezzanine and a steak house on the fourteenth floor. And there is an excellent and exclusive nightclub on the roof. As a guest at the Admiral, your name will be on the list every night you stay here."

"Huh." She watched him clear the table and organize everything on the rolling cart. "And everyone here knows about vampires, right?"

The server blinked. "I... Well, it's not something we speak about openly. We're welcoming to all guests, Miss Vorona."

"Right." That was a yes, but keep your mouth shut, thank you. "I think I'll take my meals at the restaurant starting tomorrow. Can you let Marina know?"

"Of course, Miss Vorona." He looked slightly uncomfortable. "I will pass that along."

"Thank you." With that small step into independence—such as it was—Tatyana felt good enough to get up and face the day.

ELENE WAS STANDING OVER HER SHOULDER, LOOKING AT THE computer screen where Tatyana and Grimace were typing. "And you trust this person named after a blue cartoon character?"

Tatyana pressed her lips together. "He's actually named after a purple hamburger mascot, but yes."

"Why is your online name Pigeon?"

"Because no one would guess it." She really hated that Elene was standing over her, but she understood that she was going outside the secure and background-checked employee pool at SMO and Elene had reservations. "I promise he doesn't know where I'm working or who I'm working with, but he's the best at getting into secure servers, and that's what we need to do. We need to access the account information and reset the access codes and passwords so we can—"

"None of that will make any sense to me." Elene cut her off. "I simply need to know that this purple person is not going to be able to get into our servers while he's working on this project."

"He won't." Tatyana couldn't say he wouldn't be able to. Grimace could get nearly anywhere, but she trusted that if she threw enough red meat at the boy, he wouldn't be interested in a boring shipping conglomerate like SMO. "I'm giving him something far more fun with this project."

She tapped out a message in the online shorthand that she suspected was completely foreign to Elene. "I've got the account numbers for three different banks where Zara moved money, back-tracked from the mortgage payments for the London and New York properties. Now all Grimace has to do is hack in and reset those pass-words and we'll have access."

"Good." Elene patted the top of Tatyana's chair. "But don't think I didn't notice that you didn't answer the question."

She looked up, her eyes wide and innocent. "What question?"

"Can this man get into our servers?"

Tatyana opened her mouth and hummed a little bit. "He can. I can't think of a server he wouldn't be able to access with enough time and attention. If he wanted to, but he won't. It's not enough of a chal-lenge for him."

"We have excellent firewalls." Elene crossed her arms. "Are you saying—"

"Every server has vulnerabilities," Tatyana said. "Even the Pentagon has been compromised. What you don't have is a sexy image, right?"

Elene narrowed her eyes. "What do you mean?"

"Unless a hacker became obsessed with logistics in the Black Sea, SMO is not going to be a target. Maybe for finances, but that would be taking on the bank servers, and we don't have access to them. The infor-mation that you deal in is simply" —she shrugged— "not very sexy for a hacker. Who cares about a Ukrainian shipping company?"

Elene smiled. "Excellent. We are safe by being boring. Don't tell Oleg and Mika, but that's perfect."

"Okay, great." She pinched her lips. "I won't mention it to your boss."

"He wouldn't understand half of what you told me anyway. He's a dinosaur when it comes to technology."

"Aren't all vampires?" She was typing with Grimace again, and he sent her a cat gif that made her smile. "They can't even touch a phone."

"There are devices now that they can use. They're clumsy and slow, but they are available."

"Why doesn't Oleg have one?"

"He's not interested." Elene sat down in Tatyana's other chair and stretched her arms over her head. "The last thing he wants is to be more available. Years ago he'd take me away to the citadel and we wouldn't see a screen or hear a radio for a month. Sometimes more."

Tatyana looked up. "What's the citadel?"

"His castle. I thought he'd mentioned it. It's his main residence for most of the year."

"And you and he would go for work? What if you needed to call the office or...?" Tatyana looked up and saw Elene's amused expression. "Or... not for work."

Elene raised an eyebrow. "What do you think?"

Tatyana's cheeks felt hot. "So work relationships are not foreign to him, I see."

"They're not particularly common either. When we were together, I was working for a rival organization." Elene smiled. "You might say he seduced me away for his own purposes."

"I see."

Elene smiled. "He's an excellent lover and an even better former lover. We're good friends now. Oleg doesn't have serious relationships with humans."

Tatyana dropped her voice. "Can I ask a question?"

"You can ask." Elene sat up straight. "I'll decide if I want to answer after I hear it."

"Oleg's attitude toward Zara... Were they ever involved? Is that why she hates him so much?"

"Oh God no." Elene wiped a hand over her face. "This is important to know, so it's good you asked. Vampire sires and their blood children are *never* romantically involved. It's as taboo as it is in human society. A relationship like that would be considered monstrously perverse."

"I didn't know," Tatyana said. "I didn't want to imply—"

"If Oleg had ever turned me, his feelings would have immediately gone paternal. It's a complicated bond, just like with mates, but it is intensely paternal."

"Mates?" Tatyana frowned. "What are...? Someone mentioned a mate, but is that like a marriage? Kind of?"

"Sometimes yes. Sometimes no. Mate relationships are different for everyone. Oleg's was..." She fell silent. "It's not my place to say."

Wait, Oleg had a mate? Did that mean that her sexy and terrifying boss was the vampire equivalent of a widower?

Elena continued, "Vampire matings—hypothetically—can be formed for as many reasons as human marriages. And some are very much like a human marriage. Oksana and her mate Ludmila, for instance."

"Oksana?" Tatyana thought the name sounded familiar, but Oleg wasn't exactly introducing her to his friends and family.

"Oksana and Ludmila both work with Mika. If you see two very tall women who look like soldiers hanging around Mika, that's probably them."

"Okay." Tatyana avoided Mika. She couldn't put her finger on it, but the man felt dangerous.

"Some mates are affectionate and highly possessive. Many are political or business based. Some are friendly. Others are antagonistic even though the blood bond is there."

Tatyana's mind was whirling. "I guess relationships get complicated when people live for hundreds of years."

Elene rolled her eyes. "Can you imagine? I adore my husband, but we've been together for over thirty years. I couldn't put up with *anyone* for two hundred."

A door slammed somewhere in the office, and someone shouted, "Elene!"

Stalking footsteps and Marta's squeaked directions had Tatyana's door flying open and Oleg storming in. He glanced at her, looked her up and down in a cold, raking stare, then turned to Elene.

"I need to take care of some business in Saint Petersburg," he said, "and then I'll be going to the citadel."

"Understood." She nodded. "Anything I need to know about?"

He glanced at Tatyana, then back at Elene. "I'll call you with details when I know more."

"Okay." Elene shrugged. "Is Mika going with you?"

"Of course." Oleg turned to Tatyana. "I will be calling you too."

"Why?" She looked at Elene. "You don't need to."

"I will if I want to." Oleg scowled. "If you don't want to talk to me, don't answer your phone."

"Okay." Tatyana didn't know how to respond to that, and by the time she wrapped her brain around what Oleg was saying, he was gone, leaving the faint scent of smoky cedar in his wake.

"He seems fond of you." Elene had that amused expression again. "This might be interesting."

Chapter Seventeen

One month later

Tatyana sat at the bar on top of the Admiral on a Friday night, sipping a glass of red wine and looking at the pictures her mother had sent her of Rex Harrison and her newest bird, a clever female Anna had named Brigitte Bardot.

She's beautiful.

And so smart. I've already taken her to the park north of the city, and she found her way back to the home roost. After only two weeks of settling.

She smiled at her mother's obvious excitement. She'd been worried that Anna would start texting her obsessively after a week, but her assistant must have been providing enough distraction, because her mother was happy and focused on her birds again.

You went to the farm last weekend?

Just for the weekend, but now that I'm
training Brigitte, I'll be home for a while.

That's great. You're going to breed her
and Rex?

I hope so. He lost Ava last year, and he's
been lonely. He needs a new lady and seems
interested in Brigitte.

Then I hope Cupid takes aim. Rex is a
sweetheart.

I miss you, Tanya. When will you finish?

Soon I think.

Tatyana set down her phone and closed her eyes when she took a sip of the rich red wine the bartender at the club had recommended.

The music stayed at an easy level because vampire hearing was so sensitive, and the lights were kept low. The club wasn't too crowded, but it was only nine o'clock. The real action would start around midnight when immortal business was done for the week and the vampires showed up.

Over the past month, Tatyana had slowly learned to recognize the creatures of the night that moved in her orbit. Most of them had far less presence than Oleg, but there was a way they walked and moved that was different from humans. They moved deliberately. They were watchful, and their senses were keen.

If there was any animal that vampires reminded her of, it was a lion. A lazy predator by all accounts, with little movement until it was ready to burst into speed. Most vampires held that quality in her eyes. They were watchful and waiting, ready to break their human shells as soon as it became necessary.

Not that it was ever necessary at the Admiral. Even when things got tense at a table, violence never broke out.

Tatyana had quit early that Friday and was trying to get her mind off work when her mother texted. She'd located the third of five accounts she and Elene had identified from Zara's files that afternoon. With Grimace's help, Tatyana had been able to access two of them in the past month, and Elene had emptied around ten million from Zara's coffers.

She picked up her phone and texted her mother again.

I'm making good progress.

And you're safe?

So safe that life is very boring right now.

"Who are you texting?"

Tatyana spun around and blinked when she saw who had spoken. Her boss was back in Odesa and wearing a scowl.

"Oleg." Tatyana tried to keep her face blank, but her heart leaped and her body immediately reacted to his presence.

And Oleg knew it. His scowl died away, and the corner of his mouth turned up. "Tanya."

He was wearing a moss-green sweater that gave his grey eyes a hint of green. His hands hung loosely in the pockets of a pair of grey trousers, and as soon as she turned toward him, she caught the smoky cedar scent that had haunted her dreams for weeks.

"Only my mother calls me Tanya." She didn't like Oleg doing it. "Find another nickname."

He held out a hand. "Join me at my table. They're setting it right now."

She glanced at the bartender. "I'm just going to finish my drink and—"

"I don't sit at the bar." He snapped his fingers. "Come."

Since Oleg was the one paying for her wine, her room and board, and the millions of dollars that she was going to earn by finding Zara's accounts, sitting with him for a drink wasn't too big an ask.

She quickly typed.

Mom, my boss is back. I will text later.

Be careful.

Tatyana slid off the barstool and grabbed her wine. Oleg snapped his fingers at a server and one hurried over to take Tatyana's wine from her hand to carry it to the table.

Tatyana sighed. "I can carry my own wine."

"Not when you're with me."

"I see that you're just as demanding as you were a month ago."

"Why would I change?"

He put his fingers at the small of her back, guiding her through the crowded tables in the club, and it was all Tatyana could do not to shiver at his touch. The hair on her arms and neck was already standing up.

Her dreams of him had been relentless over the past four weeks, and he'd called her three times. Two of those times, she'd picked up the phone.

"You didn't answer my call last week." He leaned down and whispered in her ear. "Where were you?"

"Sleeping. In my bed. You called at three in the morning."

"I was in Ireland."

"And I was here.

"Hmm." He put his hand on her elbow and slid his fingers along the crease where her arm bent. "You smell of saffron and amber. A little bit of black pepper."

She barely managed not to shiver. "I got the perfume you sent, and I like it. Thank you."

"Good." He slid into the booth beside her. "I have a friend in Greece who makes it."

"Vampire friend?"

"Yes, her nose is exquisite. We may form a business venture together if she wants to expand. Which she should because she's very talented."

Tatyana sat back and looked at him.

The server set down her wine, and Oleg ordered a bottle of what she was drinking for the table.

"What is it?" He lifted his chin and narrowed his eyes. "I enjoy it when you look at me, but I can tell your mind is spinning."

"You like women."

His eyebrow went up. "I do. I'm glad you have noticed."

"Not just sexually."

He smiled a little bit. "I like them sexually. And obviously in other ways too."

"No, not obviously." She picked up her wine. "Many men do *not* like women. Trust me, they will pretend to be your friend, but they don't want to be your friend, they just want to have sex with you."

"I plan on having sex with you, so I can't blame them."

She ignored his boldness and pressed on. "Yes, but you're open about that. You've never pretended not to want to sleep with me."

"We won't be sleeping."

She closed her eyes. "You know what I mean. But you like women. You and Elene are close friends. You have multiple female executives at SMO in positions of authority. You have a friend who makes perfume that you might invest in."

"I have also had sex with two of the women you have mentioned, but you are correct. I enjoy women in many ways, not only sexually."

The waiter came back and poured Oleg a glass of wine. He lifted it and held it out to Tatyana. "To women. Who are fascinating and beautiful and maddening at the same time."

"I take it you still haven't found... her." Tatyana glanced at the crowd in the club and lowered her voice. "Elene told me to keep my mouth shut."

As far as anyone outside Oleg's inner circle knew, Zara was dead and Oleg had killed her. Tatyana was still wrapping her mind around being in Oleg's inner circle in any way, but she understood how to be quiet.

She didn't know why Oleg had been traipsing around Europe for a month, but Elene said that was normal. He had many businesses and interests in other places and had multiple disputes to either settle or negotiate as a vampire lord.

"No, I haven't found our mutual friend." He slid closer to her and bent down to her ear. "But I did come to a realization, which is why I returned before all my business was concluded. Do you want to know what it is?"

Tatyana couldn't stop her shiver. "Do I really have a choice?"

"You always have a choice with me." His breath was cool on her heated neck. "When it comes to *this*, you always have a choice."

Her heart was pounding in her chest when she whispered, "What was your realization?"

"I left without claiming you, little wolf." His lips hovered over her neck. "That means all these vampires might think you're fair game."

Chapter Eighteen

Oleg drew in Tatyana's scent, alternately pleased and annoyed by it. She'd been an irritant in the back of his mind for over a month as he traveled around the world, forming agreements and soothing allies who'd heard he'd killed his child.

Reactions had been mixed.

While everyone agreed that Zara's loss was nothing to be mourned, more than one vampire expressed concern about his actions setting a precedent in a precariously balanced world of predators. Even more were worried that Laskaris would find some way to avenge his lover, plunging the Black Sea region and its abundant resources into vampire war.

In the end, immortal politics usually came down to money.

Oleg's brothers in Moscow were no longer speaking to him, but that was more a relief than a problem.

But through all the political wrangling, this human woman had lingered in Oleg's thoughts, rubbing at his memories like a burr. And like a burr, the more she lingered, the further in she'd dug until he found himself rejecting his usual blood donors because their scents were... wrong. He'd taken nothing but blood-wine since she hadn't answered his call the week before.

An unacceptable situation.

"Claiming me?" she finally whispered. "What does that mean?"

As Oleg breathed in the scent of her blood, Tatyana's heart raced like cornered prey, provoking his instinct to hunt.

"What does it mean to claim you?" He roused his amnis and warmed his body, making his breath warm against her skin. "To drink from you, of course."

Her body went immediately stiff. "No."

Oleg had known it wouldn't be an immediate yes. He was prepared for that. She was new to his world and didn't know how the hierarchy worked. "You will think about it. The vampires in this city know you are my employee, so they will respect that, but personally you belong to no one."

"And I'm fine with that." Her voice was cutting. "I belong to myself."

"That's not how it works, little wolf. You're a human in the vampire world. If you don't belong to me, that means you're fair game for their pursuits." He pulled away, tipping her chin up until she met his eyes. "And some of them might be quite persuasive."

Her eyes were haughty. "If I work for you, they wouldn't dare. Aren't you their lord?"

The corner of his mouth turned up. "I am. But in this place, I'm simply a humble immortal like everyone else."

"I don't believe you."

"I don't lie to you. You may not want to believe me, but I do not lie." He took the opportunity of touching her chin to rub his thumb over her jaw.

Delectably soft skin.

"I don't believe you're humble," Tatyana said. "Ever."

His mouth curved into a full smile, and he felt the cold night air touch his fangs. "I do enjoy your teeth."

"Oleg."

"Yes, volchitsa?"

She whispered, "You're still holding my chin."

"And you're not pulling away." He moved a little closer. "Maybe you *do* want me to claim you."

Her lips were flush with blood as her heart rate picked up. "You'd feed from me in the middle of the restaurant?"

"Oh no. When I take blood from your pretty neck, I don't want to share the experience." He moved a little closer. "But I will put my mark on you, Tatyana Vorona. If you want it."

He felt her hesitation in the set of her jaw.

"I don't want anyone else—"

"That's excellent news."

"—to bother me," she continued, "while I'm just trying to have a drink."

"Hmm." He nodded. "So you're saying that if I kissed you right now, it would be... convenient?"

"It would be for show. To keep others away. Would that be enough?"

"For me? Of course not." He glanced to the side. "For them? Yes."

She was already his. Not a single vampire in that club would touch her; everyone knew that Zara's bookkeeper belonged to Oleg Sokolov now. No one would attempt to bother her, and only a fool would try to get near her while Oleg's scent was even a hint on her skin.

But she didn't need to know that.

He could smell her arousal and her resistance. The combination was heady. His cock was hard and wanting, but he ignored it for now, focusing on the delicate flesh at her neck where he could see her pulse fluttering.

"A single kiss..." He bent down and brushed his lips against her pulse, his amnis touching her skin and spreading near-burning heat. "... would be enough."

Not too much. Just enough to excite her senses. Her hand lifted to his shoulder and her fingers dug in, drawing him closer even as the rest of her body was frozen with indecision.

"Do you like that, Tatyana?" He could feel her soften, could sense her surrender as her body grew wet and heated for him.

So tempting. He could have her alone in seconds.

"Shall I give you more?" he murmured against her neck.

Oleg lifted his head, meeting Tatyana's hooded eyes in the dim light of the corner booth. A single candle flickered on the table. One hand gripped his shoulder, and the other dug into the smooth velvet of her seat.

"Do you think" —she swallowed hard— "a kiss like that will be enough?"

She wanted more.

Oleg lowered his head, sliding his hand to the small of her back, letting a single finger trail lower to the curve of her ass. Her breasts arched up and touched his chest as her lungs pumped air into her heated body.

She was on fire. Bending to her neck, he trailed the tip of his tongue along her collarbone, letting his fangs scrape along her skin without breaking the surface.

If he tasted her blood, he'd try to take her in the club. And in the state she was in, Tatyana might let him.

Oleg didn't like to share.

He lapped up her neck, and the hand that was at his shoulder moved to his nape, stroking the hair that fell over his collar and pressing into his skin.

In a single movement, he circled her wrist in his fingers and brought her hand to his chest. It wouldn't do to let others in the club see her hand at his neck.

Other than fire, the only way a vampire could be killed was to take their head off. That made the neck a singularly vulnerable position, and no vampire was going to see Oleg with Tatyana's hand on his neck.

She didn't seem to notice the gesture, because her fingers gripped the front of his sweater and her head fell back.

He felt the flame under his skin, his element aching to release.

Enough.

Enough.

Oleg pulled back from teasing her neck with his tongue and fangs. He put both his hands on her cheeks, framing her face before he angled her head to the side and bent down, placing a firm, closed-mouth kiss on Tatyana's lips for a few long seconds.

Then he pulled away and glanced around the rooftop club.

Every immortal eye was on them along with those of quite a few humans.

Tatyana didn't seem to notice, but her eyes weren't as sharp as his. She probably couldn't see.

"There." He stroked her cheek. "No one will bother you now."

"Good." She sat up straight and angled her body away from his, picking up her wineglass with trembling fingers. "I like to come up here to read at night. I don't want anyone talking to me."

What a good actress you are, little wolf.

"They won't." He picked up his glass of blood-wine and adjusted the hard cock in his pants. "I'll finish this glass of wine, and then I have another meeting tonight."

"About... her?"

"Don't worry." He touched her chin again. "I'm very good at cleaning up messes."

A HAUGHTY GREEK WATER VAMPIRE NAMED KASTOR SAT ACROSS from Oleg in the luxury of Oleg's suite at the Admiral, his legs spread wide and his arms stretched across the back of the velvet sofa, taking up as much space as possible.

How utterly common.

Oleg glanced at Mika and Ludmila in the corner and saw his two boyars heroically suppressing their smiles.

If Kastor had lifted his leg and pissed on the coffee table, his need to assert dominance might have been more subtle.

"Tea?" The hotel server held out a delicate cup she'd prepared from the brightly painted samovar on the side table. They were enjoying a full tea with all the accompanying sweets prepared by the excellent bakery at the Admiral.

Kastor was unimpressed, but he took the tea and sipped it before he set it down on the table between them. "Just because Zara is gone doesn't mean anything will change. Your tariffs to Alitea remain unchanged."

Alitea was the hidden island fortress in the middle of the Aegean Sea where Laskaris and a council of ancient vampires ruled. They had dominated shipping traffic in the Mediterranean for centuries, growing lazy and greedy under Laskaris's leadership.

"Is this because I killed his newest plaything?" Oleg sipped his tea, eyeing Kastor's abandoned cup on the table. To not partake in this hospitality told Oleg all he needed to know about the grating immortal. "It was a family matter. Nothing personal."

Kastor shrugged. "Laskaris enjoyed your daughter's company, but this has nothing to do with Zara or your" —he curled his lip— "barbaric discipline."

He glanced at Mika, who raised a single eyebrow and shrugged as if to say, *I told you so.*

Oleg smiled at Kastor. "Consider it a favor to all our kind. She was probably stealing from your boss just as she stole from me."

The slight twitch in Kastor's expression told Oleg that Zara had definitely been stealing from Laskaris, and they'd probably only found out when she fled.

"If she was stealing from us, even more reason to keep your tariffs as they are." The vampire leaned forward. "Or perhaps we will raise them to compensate for the loss."

"Tell Laskaris to keep pushing and see what happens. A hungry wolf is stronger than a well-fed dog."

"Are you calling yourself a dog?"

"I'm calling myself a businessman who has ports in three oceans while Laskaris rules one." Oleg smiled a little bit. "Tell him to think twice about what will happen if I divert my business. I have my own resources, and I don't need to ruminate for a decade with an ancient council to make decisions."

Kastor's fangs dropped in his mouth. "Are you threatening Alitea?"

"I am simply reminding you that once, my sire ruled the rivers of this continent, and while I choose to conduct my business with more" —Oleg sipped his tea— "modern practices, I am not without the people and the resources necessary to control and exploit my territory." He finished his tea and set down his cup before he looked the Greek emissary dead in the eye. "The Bosporus is one strait. Istanbul is one city. A far eastern outpost for your master, is it not?"

Kastor's eyes narrowed. "You *are* threatening us."

"I am suggesting that you return to Alitea with a proposal to ease the tariffs through the Turkish Straits for all the immortal organizations who must use them as a shipping channel. Not only me. Everyone. Consider it a gesture of goodwill. After all, it's only with cooperation and *peace* that all of us can prosper."

"Barbarian." Kastor curled his lip and stood up. "I see that you're as unreasonable as the Poshani bastard and the Georgian bitch."

"Please keep complimenting my allies, Kastor. I'll be sure to pass your praises to all the vampires of the Pontos Axeinos. Let Laskaris continue insulting our people and he will discover just how inhospitable we can be."

Kastor turned his nose up and stormed out of the hotel suite, no doubt retreating to his own accommodations at the hotel before he returned to Athens the following night. Or maybe he would go jump in the ocean.

Oleg didn't care either way.

Mika strolled over and sat in Kastor's seat. "That went so well. Ever the diplomat, my lord."

Ludmila snorted from her perch near the door.

"The man is a peon." Oleg held his teacup out, and the server began to mix him another glass of tea. "He has no power."

"But Laskaris does. Do you really want to start a fight with Alitea? Their allies are formidable."

Oleg looked at Ludmila. She was one of his oldest boyars, and while the sniper enjoyed her silence, when she spoke, it was always perceptive. "What do you think?"

Ludmila looked at Mika, then back at Oleg. "Alitea is weak. And they are ripe for takeover. The council are slow to make decisions, and they rest in victories that are centuries old."

Oleg turned his eyes back to Mika. "I agree with her."

"You're going to do what you want, no matter what I say." Mika picked up Kastor's teacup. "He didn't even finish his tea."

"Terrible manners." Oleg snapped his fingers at the server, and the young woman came over. "Thank you, my dear." He held her hand and flooded her mind with amnis. "What a boring meeting that was. Nothing at all was said, and he spoke about olive oil shipments the entire time."

The young woman's eyes swam as she smiled. "Such an odd man."

"Very odd." Oleg squeezed her hand and smiled as he released her. "You may go. Please tell Marina we won't need anything else tonight."

"Of course, Mr. Sokolov."

Ludmila opened the door, and the young woman wheeled the samovar and the cart out of the hotel suite, leaving Mika, Ludmila, and Oleg alone.

"Laskaris will keep pressing," Mika said. "Even with Zara out of the picture, he has no motivation to negotiate when he's had control for so long."

Ludmila moved from her sniper's perch in the corner to sit on the arm of one sofa. "Laskaris isn't the only power in Alitea."

"But he is the dominant," Oleg said.

There were five immortal powers in the Black Sea region. The Poshani exercised a surprising amount of control for an itinerant clan, but that was mostly in coordination with Oleg and Petre, the vampire lord in Bucharest. That left Alina in the East, and the Greeks controlling the southern coast and the straits.

Oleg, Petre, and Alina were all fed up with Laskaris.

"An alliance would not be out of the question." Mika leaned forward and rested his elbows on his knees. "But in the end, it would still come down to one power controlling the straits."

The chokepoint of their access to the wider world was the Turkish Straits, two narrow ocean channels that bordered the Sea of Marmara. Whoever controlled those straits controlled the Black Sea.

And for thousands of years, that control had rested in Alitea.

"Tell me..." Mika and Ludmila exchanged a look before Mika turned back to Oleg. "Are you willing to meet with someone much older and more powerful than you are?"

"If you're talking about Arosh, I want nothing to do with the Fire King."

Arosh was the oldest fire vampire known to the immortal world, and he was situated far too close to Oleg's territory for his liking. The ancient fire vampire's favorite castle was in the Caucasus Mountains, less than five hundred kilometers from Oleg's eastern compound in Sochi.

Luckily, for the past millennium the Fire King had been content to rule his small territory and collect beautiful human women for his harem. He had little use for any interaction with the outside world.

Which was good for everyone because if Oleg faced Arosh—even for a parlay—the chances that one of them would try to kill the other were high.

"Not Arosh," Mika said. "But someone who knows him. Someone I think might be able to help."

THE FOLLOWING NIGHT, OLEG WAS STANDING IN FRONT OF THE sea again, listening to the waves crash on shore as he danced with the fire that burned in a hearth overlooking the ocean.

A tall glass enclosure protected the decorative fireplace from the ocean breeze, but when Oleg was around, the fire had more than enough energy to combat the wind.

His shirt was removed and he wore loose canvas pants that hung low on his waist. The air was crisp with an icy edge, but the fire warmed him and the ocean air soothed the prickling sensation that lived under his skin.

The flames danced as Oleg listened to the memory of an orchestra in his mind. He could see her, dancing in an eerie white gown across a stage in Vienna, playing the part of Giselle as the dancer she had once been.

With the image of Luana's arms outstretched, Oleg spread his own to catch her in a flaming pas de deux, his fire courting the memories of his dead mate.

On nights where the moon was full, he felt the emptiness in his blood where Luana had lived, her passion, her talent, and her madness inextricably linked.

She had been everything to him.

Everything.

At one point in time, Oleg would have died for her. He had killed for her many times. He would have crawled through mud and scraped his hands to the bone to make her smile.

And Zara carried the last of Luana's amnis in her rotten, conniving veins.

"You told me that I'm not allowed to kill her. That she belongs to you."

Oleg coaxed the flames higher, building them and making them dance as Luana had danced, circling above him as his fire leaped across the celestial stage.

He closed his eyes and saw his mate rise up from the grave, ghostly smoke around her, her arms crossed over her chest and her golden-blond hair glittering in reflected candlelight.

She came to his memory like a *vila*, her ghost intent on revenge. She rose and danced in mad whorls, laughing with the agony and betrayal of love.

His mate was a beautiful monster with a shattered mind, one that Oleg couldn't forget even though she had been dead for years.

"Luana never should have stopped dancing."

Oleg turned and saw Mika standing at a distance, watching his element pirouette above the shore, a swirling company of red-gold flames.

"All the performances were at night," Mika continued, watching Oleg's fire dance and whirl in the darkness. "She could have kept dancing."

"She would have killed the entire company. Sucked the blood from the tiniest ballerina." Oleg whispered to his element, and it calmed from its mad performance, settling back into the hearth where it flickered and snapped at the wood. "She would have sucked the marrow from their bones."

Mika leaned against a stone wall. "I see that you're feeling sentimental tonight."

Oleg cut his eyes at the impertinent man. "She was too beautiful after she changed. No one would have believed she wasn't a witch."

Nothing about Luana's features had changed when she turned into a vampire. Even her eyes, which often changed color with immortality, had stayed the same sky blue. But her body had changed, as had her abilities.

Vampires did not tire or faint from exertion. They had no need to catch their breath because oxygen was only necessary to speak.

"True." Mika sat on a bench a small distance away. "Saba has asked to see you."

Oleg turned to look at Mika. "Saba? Saba is the ancient you were speaking about?"

"The Alitea problem may not be a problem for long." The corner of

Mika's mouth ticked up. "Laskaris seems to have pissed off the wrong vampires."

Saba of the Simien Mountains was the oldest immortal known to their kind. According to legend, she was an earth vampire of unspeakable power and one of the creators of the only poison that could destroy them. A poison that his mate had once encouraged him to reproduce.

If Laskaris had angered Saba, that could be very good for Oleg.

"What does she want with me?"

"A favor." Mika shifted on the stone bench. "There were whispers and then a message from her people."

"Am I going to Ethiopia?"

It wouldn't be a convenient trip, but if the mother of all immortals asked to meet, no vampire would refuse unless they wanted to die.

"No." Mika grimaced. "She's coming to see you. She'll be in Sevastopol next week."

That was either a good sign or a very, very bad one.

Oleg stared at the sky swirling with gold and ice-white stars. "I see fate is coming for me."

"Do you think she wants you to atone for your sins?"

"I don't know, but I'm sure she will tell me." He crossed his arms over his bare chest. "I'll take the woman."

Mika sighed. "I really wish you wouldn't."

"She can visit her mother. It will be good for her."

"That's not why you're taking her."

Oleg smiled a little bit. "Oh? Then why am I taking her?"

"Just fuck her and get it over with. The fascination will die, and she won't be a distraction anymore. It's been far too long since you've had a proper lover. Just get the woman out of your system."

Oleg had a sneaking suspicion she might be even more distracting after he'd fucked her. "And then you won't have to worry about dangling my little human farther out on a tree branch?" He stretched out his arm and flicked his fingers in a coaxing gesture. "Here, kitty, kitty. Come get your bookkeeper, Zara."

"You want me to protect the human and catch your daughter

without killing her." Mika narrowed his eyes. "These are not complementary goals."

Oleg leaned against a rock wall that faced the sea. "I'm sure you'll figure it out. When was the last sighting?"

"There was a rumor that she showed her face in Plovdiv a few nights ago. Someone reported it to Radu as if he'd seen a ghost."

"Do you think Radu knows she's alive?"

"Knows? No. Suspects? Probably. He won't say anything."

Oleg nodded. "I'll take the woman to Sevastopol. She can meet Saba. After she meets a vampire like that, nothing in our world will scare her."

"And she might just run into your arms for protection?"

"She might." His mouth watered at the memory of her scent, and his fangs ached in his jaw. "And once she comes to me, I will do as I wish."

Chapter Nineteen

"Who are these people?" Her mother was staring out the window at the car waiting in the lane. "You can't stay in your own home? Even with all these guards? Mrs. Lipovsky was asking about them the other day, you know. She thinks you're working for the mafia now."

"Oh my God." Tatyana was exhausted by her mother. She loved her, but she was exhausted. "I'm staying at Oleg's house because I'm working and all the other people in the accounting department are staying there too."

Which made it sound like there was a gaggle of people in Sevastopol when really it was only Tatyana and Elene.

Still, when her mother was like this, Tatyana couldn't regret having an excuse to have some space.

"Tell me about the birds." Tatyana glanced at the clock. She had ten more minutes before she would need to go, and she didn't want to spend it listening to her mother complain. "How is Rex Harrison?"

"A champion, of course. I took him to the farm and he was back before I arrived." Anna looked out the window again, her arms crossed over her chest. "These vurdulac—"

"Vampires." These were not the monstrous creatures from folk-tales. "Vampires, Mama."

"Same thing." Anna walked over and picked up the cat from the back of the sofa, putting Pushkin in her lap as she sat across from Tatyana. "Can they hear us?"

"Maybe." There was at least one vampire guard out on the landing in back. "Probably."

"So they're monsters, but they're" —she twisted her mouth— "*civilized* monsters?"

"They're people," Tatyana said. "At least as far as I can tell." She'd spent over a month observing the various types of immortals she'd run into at the Admiral. It was an interesting study.

"What do you mean they're people? Of course they used to be people, but—"

"I don't know that becoming a vampire changes your character all that much." Tatyana shrugged. "Except for the blood thing."

The moment she said blood, she felt Oleg's hot breath on her neck. His firm lips on her mouth.

Anna looked down at Pushkin, stroking his back as he purred. "You should go to church."

"You don't go to church."

"No? I don't work for vampires either."

Tatyana couldn't stop her smile. "I've watched them. They are mostly like normal people. There are bosses and employees. There are quiet, introverted vampires who keep to themselves. There are outlandish and generous ones who prefer human company more than that of other vampires. Water vampires are sneaky and always seem to be plotting silently. Earth vampires are loyal and friendly. Wind vampires are hard to judge. Of all of them, they seem the most strange to me."

"And your boss?" Anna's hand paused on the cat's tail. "I see the way he looks at you."

Tatyana felt her cheeks burn. She'd tried her best to forget the experience of Oleg "claiming" her in front of a hundred staring eyes, but she couldn't forget it, and the thread of pleasure that shot through her blood whenever she remembered his lips filled her with shame.

He was a monster. He was her boss. No matter what he said or how determined he was, any kind of relationship with him would be a disaster.

"Fire vampires are something else," Tatyana said. "They don't fit into neat categories."

"Fire vampires," Anna muttered. "Working for a fire vampire sounds like a fast way to die." For a moment Anna's hand clutched the back of Pushkin's neck and trembled. "Do you want to die, Tanya? Is that what this is about? Do you hate me so much?"

"It's not about you." That was enough; Tatyana stood. She couldn't take any more of her mother's selfishness. "I need to go."

"You just got here."

Pushkin gave a loud chirrup and leaped off Anna's lap.

"I have to go." She walked over and bent down, placing a kiss on Anna's cheek. "I'll call you if I have time before I go back to Odesa."

"It must be nice," Anna said, "to travel like that." Her mother's eyes lifted to the ceiling. "Like the birds. They can fly anywhere. They don't know borders, do they?"

Tatyana's anger cooled, and she saw her mother for the worried, trapped woman she was, bound by her own anxiety, unable to leave a home that brought her little pleasure because to give it up meant losing her daughter.

Anna was right. Her pampered birds had far more freedom than she did.

"I'll try to come back," Tatyana said, "before I leave the city."

"Promise?"

"Promise."

"You didn't stay with your mother long." Oleg was paging through a magazine about race cars. "You had more time."

"My mother is complicated." Tatyana looked out the window as they sped out of the city and toward the outskirts of town, taking the road along the shoreline where vast estates were reserved for the rich and powerful. "You have a house here?"

He didn't look up. "Yes."

"Do you enjoy spending time in Sevastopol? It's beautiful in the summer."

"I can't really sunbathe." Oleg glanced at her. "Which steals some of the charm of the seaside."

"I suppose you're right." Tatyana smiled a little bit. "So is it an instant 'burst into flames' kind of thing, because I've seen you on fire and you seem to handle it well."

Oleg chuckled, and the sound warmed her belly.

"But that is *my* fire," he said. "She belongs to me. The sun is the mother of humanity and has no love for those who feed on them."

She glanced out the window at the rising moon. "So is the moon the mother of vampires?"

"No, but you're going to meet the mother of vampires tomorrow night."

Tatyana blinked. "What?"

"You're going to meet the immortal Eve." Oleg glanced at her. "Don't worry. You won't be alone."

If Tatyana's brain had been a computer, there would have been a spinning disk in her eyes. "Who is vampire Eve? What if I don't want to meet her?"

In fact, Tatyana was fairly sure she did *not* want to meet vampire Eve. She had a vision of a naked woman wearing fig leaves and baring bloody fangs, even though she was certain she was wrong.

"Saba is the oldest known vampire on earth. She is tens of thousands of years old, and she comes from the Rift Valley in Ethiopia." Oleg closed his magazine. "If Saba asks to meet with you, you meet with her."

"Tens of thousands of years old?" Tatyana couldn't imagine it.

"Probably. No one really knows."

"Why would she want to meet me?"

"She doesn't want to meet you." Oleg set his magazine to the side, leaned his head back against the seat of the car, and closed his eyes. "She wants to meet me."

"So why do I have to meet her?"

"Because you're coming with me. Don't worry; you won't have to talk. In fact, I forbid it."

"You *forbid* it?" What century did he come from?

The ninth century, Tanya, you know this already.

Tatyana tried to change the subject. "So the house we're going to—"

"I built it for my mate," Oleg said. "Who is dead."

Oleg's driver glanced in the rearview mirror and quickly looked away.

"I'm sorry." Tatyana scooted toward the window. "So a mate is like a husband or wife, right?"

"In human terms, yes." Oleg kept his eyes closed. "But as I said, mine is dead. And she wouldn't care if I had sex with you if she were alive."

Well, that was a raft of information in three small sentences.

She'd known that he'd had a mate, but what did losing one do to a vampire? Did they mate for life? That was a cruel fate for an immortal.

But he also said his mate wouldn't have cared if Oleg cheated on her.

That surprised Tatyana. Vampires seemed like the possessive sort. Then again, maybe male vampires were expected to keep mistresses like powerful human men. They had to drink from humans, didn't they?

Tatyana already knew from the brief physical contact she and Oleg shared that he could make drinking from her neck intensely pleasurable.

"So you cheated on your wife," Tatyana said, "and she didn't care?"

He opened one eye, looked at Tatyana, then closed it again. "It's not cheating if it's not a secret."

"Would you have cared if she had sex with someone else?"

"If you're wondering whether I make a habit of sharing the women I have sex with, I do not. When you and I are lovers, you will not have relationships with any other men."

"Hypocrite."

"Hardly."

The car turned right and paused at a set of wrought iron gates with a guardhouse next to it. Two men stepped from the shadows and started to pull open the door.

"Even mates can grow apart." Oleg kept his head back, his eyes closed and his hands folded loosely on his lap, as if he were discussing the latest business trends in Japan and not immortal infidelity. "Luana thrived on novelty, so I indulged her."

Tatyana tried not to think about it.

She didn't follow gossip columns. She didn't read internet news about actors or athletes. She was intensely uninterested in other people's love lives because she had none of her own. It would be miserable to dwell on what she couldn't have.

"As for you, once we are lovers, I would prefer you avoid any contact with other men, but I know that's not practical. Family is acceptable. Business associates will be tolerated. Random friendships with human or vampire men will not be."

"You arrogant—"

"We're here." His eyes flew open as if he were one of her mother's homing pigeons who had found his way home. "The human quarters are on the first floor. Pick whichever one you prefer. The others can wait until after you've chosen yours."

"I *don't* want preferential treatment." There were at least half a dozen other mortal staff traveling with them. "I'm the most junior employee; I can go last."

They were driving through an alley of arching palm trees, and the moon was at its apex, shining over the water with an eerie blue glow.

Tatyana stared out of the window at the hidden luxury she never could have imagined was only a few short miles from where she'd grown up.

"If you don't pick a room for yourself, volchitsa, I'll put you in the locked closet attached to my day chamber." Oleg smiled. "Don't worry, it's very spacious and has a washroom and a bath."

Absolutely not.

The car came to a stop in front of a massive whitewashed mansion, and Tatyana pushed her door open before Seban or Oleg could open it for her. "I'll pick something right now."

THEY WERE SITTING IN A TAVERN ON THE OUTSKIRTS OF THE CITY, a place where fishermen mingled with luxury-yacht owners and most people kept to themselves.

Tatyana was sitting at a table with Mika while the tall vampire named Oksana stood near the door, watching the tavern with sharp green eyes.

Oleg waited in a booth by himself, sipping a cup of tea and ignoring the pretty server who was trying to catch his attention.

The young woman was dressed in a low-cut V-neck top, and her breasts were nearly falling out of it. Her jeans were skintight, and Tatyana had the distinct urge to yank her hair and drag her out into the drizzly night.

"You're possessive."

She turned when she heard Mika speak. "What?"

The vampire was smiling a little bit. "You're glaring at that server like she kicked your cat."

Tatyana looked away and stared at the door. "When is this person coming?"

"Whenever she wants to," Mika said. "She doesn't answer to anyone."

Tatyana glanced at the vampire, then looked away. She didn't want him to think she was studying him even though she was. Mika Arakis was an utterly average-looking man. He was just handsome enough to wear a suit without looking awkward. Yet if she had put him in a fisherman's sweater and work pants, he wouldn't look out of place either.

He was tall but not taller than Oleg. His accent was vaguely Baltic but not strong. He had brown hair and blue eyes. His features were even and somewhat forgettable.

But those keen blue eyes saw everything in the tavern, and he communicated seamlessly with the humans and vampires who had come with them and filtered through the pub.

The fact that Oleg had asked Mika to sit with her probably grated on the man, but she was also grateful. It was hard to be a woman alone in a place like this.

Tatyana didn't have a phone or a book with her, so she tried to make conversation. "How long have you worked for Oleg?"

"I don't work for him." Mika looked amused. "I am his boyar."

"I don't know what that means to vampires."

Mika narrowed his eyes as if trying to decide if she was worthy of the information. "You don't know much about history, do you?"

"I was a mathematics person."

"A boyar was... is a title. The English would probably call it a duke or something like that. But we are the leaders of Oleg's druzhina."

She opened her mouth, but Mika kept speaking.

"And the druzhina is something like Oleg's immortal army. Some carry blood relation to him. Brothers. Children. But most are simply very old, very loyal vampires who would follow Oleg into battle should he need us to do so."

"Aren't modern vampire battles fought through business?"

The corner of his mouth turned up. "Not always. And Oleg controls a great amount of territory. He keeps it together through his boyars."

"Like you?"

"I am personally attached to him, but my own territory is nearer to Tartu in Estonia. Others oversee it in my absence."

Tatyana was getting a better picture of this complicated world. "Is this vampire really the oldest vampire in the world?"

Mika was looking over her shoulder when he answered. "Maybe."

"And does she have territories?" Tatyana glanced at Oksana by the door. "Does she have boyars of her own?"

He smiled. "I suppose she does. At one point this vampire and three others ruled most of Europe, Central Asia, and Africa. It was the age of vampire emperors, before humans became more advanced."

"What happened? Why aren't they still the emperors?"

Mika shrugged. "Maybe they became bored."

"Bored?" Tatyana almost laughed. "Of being emperors?"

"Being a leader is a lot of work." Mika glanced at Oleg, who was still sipping his tea and trying to look inconspicuous. "Particularly when you're trying to rule vampires, who all think they're minor gods."

"Actually, you're right. That sounds horrible."

Mika smiled a little bit. "I think I don't hate you."

Tatyana picked up her tea, which had gone cold. "What a glowing compliment."

"You're welcome."

Tatyana looked over at Oleg, who was still alone. "I would assume there are no vampire history books with her face in them." Tatyana glanced at the bar, noticed the waitress sashaying away from Oleg's table, then turned back to the door. "How will you know it's her?"

"From what I have heard, there will be no question." Mika glanced at her, then back over her shoulder at Oksana. "She is rumored to be very... other."

"You blend in with humans well," she said. "If I didn't know about vampires, I'd never guess you were anything but a banker or something."

He cracked a hint of a smile. "See? You can give glowing compliments too."

"Isn't blending in the goal?"

Mika stared at her. "You're quite clever, aren't you?"

"That's why Zara hired me."

"That's why Oleg hired you too."

"Let's hope Oleg is smarter than Zara."

Mika shrugged. "He is. Zara is reactionary. Oleg plans."

"And he has me for bait."

"You came to him."

To get paid! She didn't say it. Getting into an argument with Oleg's boyar was as pointless as being annoyed at the server who was literally dangling her breasts in Oleg's face as she placed a bottle of vodka on the table.

She turned her flushed cheeks away from his table. "You didn't answer my question before: how long have you been Oleg's boyar?"

"Long enough to know when he's distracted."

She looked at Mika. "Distracted?"

"Yes. You distract him. You should make your intentions more clear. If you're interested in being his mistress, he will be very good to you. But if that is the case, I should kill Zara before she can kill you."

"Wait, he's really going to kill her?" Tatyana blinked. "You don't kill someone for stealing."

Mika looked amused. "What do you think she would do to someone who stole from her?"

Kill them. Knowing how unpredictable Zara could be, imagining her murdering someone for stealing anything was not a stretch.

"There are neutral spaces for vampires, aren't there? Places like the Admiral?"

Mika cocked his head. "What are you getting at?"

"Aren't there..." She tried to think of a better word but couldn't. "Aren't there vampire prisons? Of some kind? I mean, Oleg has basically trapped me. Couldn't he do the same thing to Zara?"

"Oleg has allowed you a surprising amount of access and freedom. Too much freedom if you ask me, which he rarely does when it comes to women." Mika lowered his voice. "And no. There are no vampire prisons."

"So you're just going to kill her?"

He was looking over her shoulder again. "She's near."

Tatyana's heart leaped to her throat. "Zara?"

"Saba." Mika narrowed his eyes. "Don't say her name in front of her. Maybe don't even think it."

Tatyana whispered, "She can't read my mind, can she?"

"I don't know what this vampire can do." He glanced at the door, then looked away and sucked in a breath. "Tatyana, don't look."

"Why?" She felt a tug of energy like a hand in her chest, wrapping around her lungs and drawing her attention to the woman in a black overcoat who was walking through the door. "Oh..." Her lungs heaved, and she closed her eyes. "Who is that?"

Whoever she was, she wasn't human.

"It's *her*," Mika whispered. "Don't look."

Tatyana didn't look at Saba, but she did look at Oksana, who was frozen with her eyes locked on the woman walking toward Oleg.

Even the humans around the bar had fallen silent to observe the woman with a giant at her side.

She was small, shorter than Tatyana even, but her presence was massive.

Her skin was the color of ebony wood, and her large eyes took in everything around her as she scanned the tavern. Her lips were full and wide, her cheekbones set at a sharp angle drawn up from a pointed chin.

The man at her side—an immortal if Tatyana had ever seen one— looked like a statue of Poseidon, russet hair falling over his shoulders, and a heavy beard. He walked in long strides, but there was something soft about his energy that the woman didn't have.

Saba's energy was rumbling and precarious. Tatyana had the sensation of the earth moving beneath them as the woman walked across the room and sat across from Oleg with the giant at her side.

Mika said. "I don't know the man with her."

"That isn't a man."

"You're not wrong." Mika kept his eyes on the table. "I don't want to look at her, but I can't look away." He swallowed hard, and his eyes took on a glassy sheen. He whispered something under his breath in a language Tatyana didn't recognize.

"Mika."

The vampire couldn't look away from his boss. Saba had some kind of hold on every immortal in the room.

But while the vampires were enthralled by her power, the humans around them were vaguely intrigued but soon returned to their previous conversations.

"What is going on?" Tatyana lifted her foot under the table and slammed it down on Mika's. "Stop it."

The vampire curled his lip, baring his fangs at Tatyana before he blinked and seemed to wake up. "What kind of power does this vampire have?" he whispered. "I've never felt anything like her."

"If she's really..." Tatyana dropped her voice to a whisper, glancing over at Oleg and the two ancient vampires who were deep in conversation. "If she's really vampire Eve, she's like a mother to all of you. You're all kind of... descended from her, right?"

Mika nodded slightly. "Yes."

The vampire slowly began to look more like himself even though he continued to glance at the corner booth toward Saba and Oleg.

Tatyana tried to distract him. "How does that work anyway? Oleg said she's an earth vampire. You're a water vampire. He's fire. How does an element choose a vampire?"

"We don't choose." Mika continued to stare at Saba as he spoke in hushed tones. "Amnis is inherited in the blood. Water vampire to water vampire. Earth to earth."

"Fire to fire?" Tatyana could understand that. "So is Zara a fire vampire?"

"No. Fire vampires are..." He glanced at Tatyana, then looked over her shoulder again, clearly trying to avoid Saba's magnetic energy. "I suppose it's not a secret. Think of it as a recessive trait. Fire vampires can be born from any element, and they're not very common."

She frowned. "So if Oleg had a child—"

"Vampires cannot father children," Mika said. "Eliminate that thought immediately. You will never have children with him, Tatyana Vorona."

She sat back, and her face was burning. "I wasn't talking about *babies*. The last thing I want is to have Oleg's—"

"Oleg's immortal children are earth vampires because his sire was an earth vampire."

She frowned. "Zara's not an earth vampire, is she?" The earth vampires she'd run into at the club had been the most human of all the immortals. They were friendly and seemed to like humans, far from Zara's predatory attitude toward nearly everyone she crossed.

"No." Mika was staring at the booth again. "Zara is a water vampire like me."

"Then how—"

"It's complicated. Ask Oleg." He dropped his voice to a whisper. "They're finished."

Tatyana glanced over her shoulder and saw Saba holding Oleg's hand.

The vampire had a familiar expression on her face. It was the face of a mother chiding her child.

And Oleg's face was even paler than usual.

Moments later, her boss was striding toward the door, and Mika, Tatyana, and all the vampires in Oleg's retinue were running to catch up.

Chapter Twenty

"*You're speaking of Zara? She was nothing to me.*"

"*She was your blood.*"

"*She was nothing.*"

Oleg walked to the car, catching Seban's eye as he approached. "Back to the house." He glanced over his shoulder and saw Mika, Tatyana, Oksana, and his people following. "The woman with me. The rest of you in the other car."

Tatyana froze, and Mika nearly ran into her. "What?"

Oleg held out his hand, snapped his fingers, and pointed at the car. "You? In. Mika—"

"Leaving." His enforcer walked back to the other car with the rest of his men.

Tatyana carefully approached the black sedan, and Oleg opened the car door for her.

"Did something happen?" she whispered.

Less than I expected and more than I wanted. "Old business."

She got in the car, and Oleg walked around to the other side. Seban held the door for him and he slid into the back seat.

The old vampire really hadn't asked for much. In a way, it was business that had already been concluded, or would be when Zara was dead.

The only problem was now that he'd told a bold-faced lie to the oldest vampire in the world, Oleg felt compelled to actually kill his child.

The thought put a sick feeling in the pit of his stomach.

His fangs ached in his mouth, and the fire that usually warmed him felt like it was biting the inside of his skin.

Your blood comes from the earth. From one of my line. So, Oleg Sokolov, you are mine whether you want to be or not.

His sire was dead. He owed loyalty to no one but himself and the allies he chose. But now the mother of their race thought Oleg had killed his own child, and she approved because Zara had been conspiring with Laskaris, whom Saba hated.

Which meant that Zara had to die. When he finally found her, she would have to die, and the last of Luana's blood would be gone from the earth.

"Oleg?"

Warm fingers touched the back of his hand, and the biting sensation under his skin eased away.

Tatyana kept her voice low. "What did she say to you?"

She patted my head, called me a good boy, and made me afraid.

"Seban," he snapped.

"Yes, boss?"

"Call Mika and tell him to fly with the others back to Odesa. Immediately. Tatyana and I will stay at the house tonight and fly back tomorrow."

"Yes, boss."

"And raise the screen," he muttered. "I want to think."

Tatyana was watching him carefully. "Let me sit in front with Seban. That way you can—"

"No, you will stay with me."

Oleg didn't know why he wanted her except that arguing with the woman made him feel like less of a monster. Which made no sense because he was using her as bait and holding her captive to lure his daughter out of hiding.

She knew nothing about him. Nothing. But he'd made her trust him enough that her heart wasn't racing in fear as she sat beside him, and Oleg was more than on edge. He felt vulnerable for the first time in a very long time, and feeling vulnerable made him feral.

But as Seban raised the black privacy screen, she reached across the car and took Oleg's hand in her own.

He looked at her hand holding his. "Why?"

"You seem upset."

He wanted to strip her naked, fuck her, and sate his hunger with her blood.

And she was being kind.

Oleg looked at her face, her velvet skin and blue eyes gentle with human emotion.

He imagined her throat red with blood, only instead of Oleg's fangs in her neck, it was Zara's blade at her throat.

He murmured, "She will never touch you."

Tatyana's eyes went wide. "What?"

"Zara should die, little wolf."

"I don't want her dead though. She stole *money*," Tatyana said. "You have so much money. You don't need to do this."

Didn't he? He'd spread the rumor that Zara was dead to isolate her, but now he was backed into a corner. His options became more limited after lying to an ancient. "I no longer have a choice."

"I'll find your money. I promise I will find your money."

Why was she so insistent? Why was she protecting Zara of all people? Zara wouldn't hesitate to cut Tatyana's throat to keep her quiet.

"This is not something we will debate," he said. "She stole from me, she's as insane as my dead mate, and she's a threat to me." *And to you.* He squeezed her hand and released it. "This is not your decision."

"You could keep Zara locked up. You have a castle, don't you? Castles have dungeons. You don't have to kill her."

Oleg cocked his head, watching the strange human beside him.

"You think locking Zara up would be more merciful than killing her?" Perhaps his little wolf was more vicious than he'd thought. "That would be even crueler than death for an immortal."

Her cheeks flushed a little bit. "Wouldn't that be a better punishment then?"

He grunted. She wasn't wrong.

"If Zara *has* to die, make Mika do it."

Oleg narrowed his eyes. "Why does it matter?"

Tatyana opened her mouth, then closed it.

"Tell me what you're thinking." He took her hand and gripped it. "Or I will make you."

"It will hurt you," she snapped and pulled her hand away. "She's your child. You might hate her, but Mika told me how it works. She's literally your own blood. What would it do to you to kill your own blood?"

This strange, strange woman.

"You're *worried* about me?" In the space of a heartbeat, Oleg unlatched her safety belt and yanked her across the bench seat. "You're worried about *me?*"

Tatyana fell into his lap. She gasped and braced her arms on Oleg's chest. Then she looked up at him, and his eyes locked with hers.

"You don't worry about me," he murmured. "You don't take care of me. That's not how my world works. I take care of you. I take care of all my people."

And she was his. For now. Maybe forever.

Oleg was going to keep her.

She was staring at his mouth and her heart was racing, but there was no smell of fear or adrenaline. Her body was reacting to his with desire. Her scent bloomed around him, filling the car with her perfume.

Oleg's body was hard, and he shifted her so she was sitting on his lap, his cock pressed up against her thigh. Her lips parted, and her cheeks flushed with blood.

With her sitting on his lap, her lips were aligned with his, and he moved closer, letting his fangs fall as he delicately bit the edge of her lower lip, bruising the skin without breaking it.

She squirmed in his lap, her body hungry for his. Her thigh brushed against his cock again, and a small, needy sound came from her throat.

"Do you want that, Tatyana?" He pulled her closer. "Very soon you'll have my cock in your mouth. You'll be able to taste me with your pretty little tongue. Kiss me with your lips." He reached up, nudging her mouth open with his thumb. "Until then, taste this."

She reacted with such beautiful submission he nearly tore off her clothes in the back of his car and gave her everything she wanted.

Instead, he reveled in the feeling of her tongue stroking his thumb, her little teeth hard on his knuckle as he angled her head to the side and licked up her neck, slowly running his fangs over the muscle there.

His right hand moved to her rounded ass, cupping the swell in his palm as he pulled her harder into his groin and rubbed her body against his.

She was wearing a neat little suit, a silk-and-wool blend he had picked from a selection the stylist sent to him. Luckily, that suit had a skirt instead of trousers.

Oleg pulled his thumb from Tatyana's mouth, and she sucked hard against the loss, her mouth begging to be filled.

She gave a small cry when he took his hand away, so he turned her face and took her mouth in a predatory kiss, stealing her breath and swallowing the moan of pleasure as the hand that had been in her mouth moved to the gentle rise of her pert breast.

It was small and deliciously round. It reminded Oleg of a ripe peach, and he wanted to sink his teeth into it.

Soon.

He wouldn't feed from her in the back of a car even though they had come to a stop. They were at the house, and he heard Seban quickly exit the vehicle, leaving Oleg and Tatyana alone.

He reached his amnis out but felt no one around, no human and definitely no vampire.

Just Oleg and his little bookkeeper, her proper suit on the verge of falling apart under his greedy hands.

Her kiss was hot and drugging, and Oleg felt his senses swim. Did she have amnis of her own? Impossible.

He was conscious of the fire under his skin, eager to burst out as his senses rose and his elemental power built from the electricity between them. He clamped down on his control, surprised by the surge of chaotic emotions.

He wanted to fuck her. He wanted to feed from her. He also felt intensely possessive in a way that sent up a dozen red flags in his mind.

Sex with Tatyana was going to be a challenge.

Her hand came to the back of his neck, but he didn't move it. She stroked the curls where they fell over his collar and pulled him even closer as his tongue invaded her mouth.

She was riding the line of his cock, her body surging against his as she tried to reach for release. With her mouth firmly on his and one of his hands gripping the outside of her thigh, he took his left hand where it caressed her breast and reached down, shoving her knees apart as she gasped and arched toward him.

"Do you like that, volchitsa?" he murmured against her lips.

All she could do was nod. Her breath was coming in hard pants. "Please. Please."

"Do you want my bite?"

Her blue eyes went wide as his hand slid between her thighs. "There?"

"Not tonight." He teased the soft fabric covering her pussy, then pinched the inside of her thigh, smelling a hint of blood as a bruise rose on her delicate skin. "Soon I'll bite you there. Drink from you and eat your pussy with your blood in my mouth. Would you like that?"

Ever the honest human, she blinked and said, "I don't know."

Oleg's lips curved into a smile as his fingers moved back to her sex. "You will like it very much."

He took her mouth again, sucking on her full lower lip as his fingers moved her panties from the hot, wet flesh at the juncture of her thighs.

Oleg's mouth watered, but this was not the place to feed from her. Her body was inches away from climax, primed by his kisses and the low vibration of energy he sent over her skin. Not to influence her mind but to heighten her arousal.

As he slid two fingers inside her, he realized he wasn't ready to make her come yet. She was deliciously open to him even though her body was fully clothed. He wanted to tease her a little bit.

He broke off their kiss. "Do you like a lover to lick your breasts, little wolf? Shall I use my tongue next time?"

Her hand reached out, searching for something to grab, but there was nothing.

"Touch yourself," he told her. "Touch your breast the way you want me to touch it next time."

"Oleg—"

"Do it." He watched her grab the pert little breast and squeeze hard, desperate for release. "Mmm. You don't need soft touches, do you?"

Good. Oleg could be gentle if he needed to be, but he preferred a shout over a whisper.

Her pussy was swollen and weeping around his fingers. He removed his hand, and she bit her lip in frustration.

"Bastard," she panted.

Oleg smiled and followed her eyes as they watched the journey from her pussy to his tongue. Her lips were cherry red and swollen from his bruising kisses.

He laved her honey from his fingers. "Delicious." Oleg licked his lips before he slid his hard fingers back inside her pussy.

Her body gripped his hand. She was desperate and nearly weeping from desire.

"Do you want to come now?"

She nodded helplessly.

"Good." He brushed a kiss over her lips. "Now bite my lip like you promised me, volchitsa. I want to feel your teeth."

Frustration and desire flared in her eyes, and Tatyana sank her blunt little teeth into Oleg's lower lip as he stroked her harder and faster, flicking her clitoris with the flat of his thumb.

He hummed in pleasure as her teeth broke his skin. He curved his fingers up and pressed harder.

Tatyana released his lip, nearly choking as her climax came in crashing waves. He felt her muscles release and contract against his hand, her thighs pressing together as her body shuddered and a hoarse cry erupted from her throat.

"Too much!" She panted and gripped his wrist. "Too much, too much."

Oleg smiled in satisfaction and eased back his strokes even as his cock raged with unsated desire.

There was nothing like watching a woman come. The only thing that could improve the experience was taking her blood at the same time. Tatyana didn't know it yet, but when she gave him her blood, the pleasure would be even more intense.

She clung to him, pressing her face to his neck and murmuring silent words against his skin.

After a few lingering aftershocks, Oleg took his fingers from between Tatyana's thighs and licked them clean. Then he pulled her skirt down and straightened her suit before he pushed the car door open and lifted her in his arms.

Tatyana tensed as soon as the cold night air hit her skin. "You didn't—"

"Not tonight, volchitsa." He kicked the door closed and strode toward the dark and empty house. "You need to rest, and I need to make some calls."

Chapter Twenty-One

Tatyana closed the door to her room in Oleg's house, set all three locks, and pressed her back to the door before she slid down to the floor, her knees giving out under the storm happening in her mind and body.

What have you done?

What have you done?

What, what, what have you done, Tatyana?

She was shaking and exhausted and wired all at the same time. Her skin felt like it might fly away from her body. The top of her head was going to float off. When she closed her eyes, she could still feel Oleg inside her, stroking her to a pleasure so extreme she couldn't wrap her brain around it.

Her body began to shake again, likely an aftershock from stress. Her anxiety spiked, and she gripped the seams of her skirt with tight hands.

"Breathe." She inhaled through her nose and let the air into her lungs in a slow and deliberate stream.

Breathe.

She opened her eyes and looked around the room.

It was a luxurious suite with a balcony that overlooked the ocean. When she'd woken that morning, the sun was shining at an angle through the wide French doors. There was a silver thermos of coffee and a tray of fruit and pastries under a sterling silver dome on the table outside.

None of it felt real. Not the luxury. Not the intrigue. And definitely not the romance.

Romance?

No, Oleg wasn't a romantic. None of what had happened in that car had been romantic. It was hunger and desire and power. He'd given Tatyana pleasure and taken none for himself, and yet somehow all of it had felt... selfish?

What was going on? She didn't understand him. The moment he'd seemed even a little bit human in the car, when she'd reached out to him—finally understanding how his feud with Zara would end—he'd taken control back and pushed her into giving him everything.

And she'd *wanted* it. She'd asked for every touch, then craved more. She felt like an animal, her body operating on sheer instinct. She could still taste his blood in her mouth.

What have you done?

Tatyana had behaved like a vampire, biting into his lip until she could feel his flesh give way and his blood entered her mouth.

Oh God.

She'd tasted vampire blood. Her heart started to race and sweat bloomed on her forehead. She put her hands to her cheeks. Did she feel different? Was she hotter than normal? Colder?

What did drinking vampire blood mean? She didn't feel any different, but she didn't know and she didn't know who to ask. Who could she ask?

She reached for her phone and scrolled though her texts.

Not Elene.

Definitely not her mother.

Her stylist's name caught her eye.

"I'm here to help, Tatyana. I hope you can trust me even though I know that everything must feel very strange right now."

Lorala would know, wouldn't she?

She tapped Lorala's number and quickly typed in a question.

> If I tasted vampire blood by accident… She racked her mind for some kind of explanation that wouldn't give her away. …if there was a fight and some flew into my mouth, what would happen? I'm not going to become a vampire now, am I? Will I be sensitive to the sun or anything?

It was a few moments before she saw Lorala typing back in her messaging app.

> Definitely not. Vampire blood will heal surface wounds or scratches. If you ingested a lot of it, it might make you throw up, but you're not going to become a vampire. You'd have to be nearly dead from blood loss and then drink a lot of vampire blood for that to happen. It's not something that happens by accident.

Tatyana let out a breath and pulled her knees up as she rested her forehead on them in relief. She let Lorala's information sink in for a few moments before she responded.

> Thank you. I didn't know what might happen, and I was going a little bit crazy.

> Are you okay?

How to answer that?

Well, Lorala, I saw the world's oldest vampire tonight, and she scared the crap out of every vampire in the tavern. Then I found out that my new boss is going to kill my old boss and that doing that will mean killing a part of himself, which made me feel sympathetic to him and hold his hand and he took that as an invitation to pull me onto his lap and give me the most unearthly powerful orgasm I've ever experienced.

She couldn't tell Lorala any of that.

> It's been a strange night, but I'll be okay. Thank you for calming my panic before I spiraled. I better get some sleep.

Let's get a drink in the daylight when you get back to Odesa.

> Yes. That sounds great.

She tossed her phone on the floor and covered her face with her hands.

Tatyana, what have you done?

After a few more self-pitying moments, Tatyana dragged herself from the floor and stood. She eased off her jacket, kicked off her shoes, and scooted her skirt to her ankles before she kicked her clothes into a heap by the closet. She stripped to her panties and grabbed her giant hooded sweatshirt, pulling it over her head as she dragged the blankets from the bed over to the window.

Making a nest for herself where the sunlight would touch her skin when the morning came, she curled into a ball and pulled a blanket over her body, hiding under the blankets while she waited for daylight.

She wanted her mother. She wanted her cat.

And she desperately wanted to *not* dream about Oleg Sokolov.

TATYANA WOKE THE NEXT MORNING WITH THE SUN SHINING ON her face. She'd kicked off her covers during the night and was bare from the waist down, wearing only her hoodie and a pair of underwear.

Glancing at the balcony, she saw that the silver coffee carafe and domed tray was back on her balcony, so either the French doors were shaded from the outside or whoever had delivered her food had gotten a show.

Tatyana couldn't bring herself to care.

Whatever servants existed in Oleg's home, they were basically invisible. She hadn't seen more than a shadow of them since she'd arrived. Food appeared like magic. Fresh towels were hung on a warming rack in the bathroom. Full size bottles of luxury-brand shampoo and conditioner were in the bathroom.

It all seemed excessive for a two-night trip, but what did she know? Oleg lived like royalty, and she had become attached to him by some twist of fate.

She rose and walked to the bathroom, taking off her hoodie and underwear to take a shower in the marble walk-in.

As she stood under the rain-like shower, she closed her eyes and tried to focus.

She had one day to herself in Sevastopol. When she arrived, Oleg told her that a driver would be available to her but she would need to be accompanied by bodyguards since Zara was still roaming around.

She thought about visiting her mother but decided against it. In the mood she was in, she'd probably try to grab her mother again and run.

Then Oleg would track her down again, drag her back, and she'd be even further behind in looking for his money.

"Work," she whispered. She could work. That's what she was going to do. She was going to get her computer, try to forget the night before, and sink into analyzing spreadsheets with money transfers from two years ago, looking for patterns.

She slapped the shower lever down and shook her head before she wrapped a towel around her hair, put on the plush bathrobe, and left the bathroom.

Good, she had a plan. She would work, find Oleg's money, and then...

No, she wasn't going to think that far ahead. She was going to focus on work.

She rubbed the excess water from her hair and combed it out before she walked to the balcony and poured some coffee to start the day. Sitting in the sunlight, she surveyed Oleg's mansion, and it was nothing less than a wonder.

Isolated on a jut of rocky beach that stretched into the Black Sea, the property was surrounded by trees and the house itself reminded her of a massive cruise ship, each story built back into the hill behind the house with balconies and staircases twisting around lush gardens and private patios.

It reminded her of houses she'd seen on the Greek islands, only instead of blue domes, the roof was baked red tile, and the whitewashed walls of the mansion were decorated by intricate mosaics that must have taken years to install.

The sound of waves and gently trickling water was everywhere, burbling from blue-tiled fountains that reflected the sky, falling from waterfalls that flowed from one story to the next, and bursting in joyful splashes from reflecting pools that lined the walkways that led down to the ocean.

She nibbled on the croissants and the fruit provided by the unseen servants, wondering if she could get more and who she could talk to about eating a real meal.

The night before, she hadn't had much of an appetite, but now she was ravenous. Pastries and fruit weren't going to cut her hunger.

Her stomach growled, and Tatyana walked back inside to dress and go in search of food.

Armed with jeans, a T-shirt, and a perfectly appropriate business-casual jacket, she left her barricaded room and walked down the staircase that led to the main living area of the house.

There were fountains in the living area too and a massive fireplace that dominated a sunken conversation pit surrounded by windows that looked out over the sea.

"Hello?" Her voice echoed on the plaster walls and tiled floor. "Is anyone awake?"

In moments, a woman appeared from a hidden hallway under the stairs.

"Miss Vorona," she said. "I am Leni, the house's day manager. May I assist you?" Her appearance and accent told Tatyana she was a Crimean native, probably a Tatar woman.

"Yes, please." She walked toward Leni. "The fruit and pastry on the balcony is delicious, but I am wondering if there is something more? Maybe some eggs or even a kasha?" Tatyana found herself missing something as simple and hearty as her grandmother's buckwheat porridge.

Leni's eyes brightened immediately. "Of course! The chef will enjoy having a human guest to cook for."

"Vampires don't eat much, do they?"

The woman smiled. "They don't need to. But our chef cooks for the staff too, and Pavel makes wonderful pancakes. Would you like blini with smoked salmon, perhaps? Or pancakes with fresh fruit? Both would be more filling than pastry."

"Blini with salmon sounds amazing." She looked around the room. "I was hoping to work today before we fly back. Is there a room with a large table where I can plug in my laptop and spread out some files?"

"Of course, Miss Vorona." Leni nodded. "Perhaps the second dining room would suit you. There is a large table, but not as large as the banquet room. I can show you to it after I tell Pavel your breakfast order."

"Perfect." She walked back to her room and grabbed her computer and files before she returned to the main room where Leni was waiting.

"This way." She led Tatyana down another beautifully decorated hallway where green-and-gold tile mosaics decorated the bottom of the walls.

"The artwork in the house is magnificent. All the fountains and the murals."

Leni looked over her shoulder and smiled. "Yes, Mr. Sokolov has taken great care in their design. He employed some workmen for the outside, but the mosaic of the sirens over the fireplace is his own work."

Tatyana nearly tripped over her feet. "He... You mean he made them? Himself?"

"Oh yes." Leni nodded. "Mr. Sokolov is a very talented artist and creates work for most of his homes."

A fuzzy memory tickled her mind.

"What do you do for fun?"

"I work on my art."

"You're an artist?"

"Mosaics. I make mosaics."

She knew that. Or she *had* known that. Oleg had told her about his art—there was a verdant forest scene in her mind—but she had forgotten.

Or he had made her forget.

They were going to have a conversation about that when he woke.

"Here you are." Leni opened a pair of double doors to reveal a gilt-edged room with oil paintings decorating the walls and an amber chandelier hanging from the ceiling. "Pavel is preparing your breakfast right now. Please make yourself comfortable and I'll serve you shortly."

SHE WAS NECK-DEEP IN CRYPTOCURRENCY TRANSACTIONS WHEN she heard his voice.

"Excellent. You're making yourself at home."

She looked up to see Oleg leaning against the double doors of the dining room, his arms crossed over his chest.

Tatyana blinked and looked out the window. "I didn't even realize the sun had gone down."

"Did you spend all day in here? Studying your numbers and accounts?" He walked toward her, and she felt it again, the magnetic force of everything he was bearing down on her. "You should have made use of the grounds. There are several pools, a grotto, and a boat available should you want to use it."

Tatyana saved her work, closed her laptop, and scooted her chair back from the table. "I had work to do."

"You can't work all the time."

She was desperate to change the subject from herself. "You're a mosaic artist. You told me that and then wiped my memory."

He stopped walking. "In my defense, you touched my hand and passed out." He looked her up and down. "I do love your reaction to my hands."

Tatyana's cheeks burned, but she ignored his provocative words and continued with the statement she had decided to make. "I don't want you to alter my memory again. I know I can't stop you. If you really want to do it, you will. But I am asking you not to, and if you have any respect or regard for me, you will not do it again."

Oleg smiled. "So businesslike, my little wolf." He walked over, bent down, and placed a chaste kiss on both her cheeks. "I regard you highly, and I will not alter your memories again unless I deem it necessary for your safety."

That was likely the only concession she was going to get out the overbearing vampire lord. "Thank you."

"You're welcome."

"I have spent all day working, but I did eat lunch out on the main balcony, and the fountains are beautiful."

Oleg pulled out a chair and sat next to her, stretching his legs out and crossing them at the ankle. The position made Tatyana very aware of just how tall he was. His physical presence dwarfed hers.

"This was the house I built for Luana." Oleg looked around. "And Zara. Water vampires prefer to live near their element. They resided here for many years after they became lovers."

She let out a slow breath. "I don't think I knew that before. So your mate and your..."

"Child." He lifted one shoulder. "The tie between Zara and me was completely independent of her relationship with Luana. We were in no way a family. Zara was Luana's lover first. My mate asked me to change her lover so Zara could remain at her side."

Wow. Just... wow.

"That is... very twisted."

"Perhaps from a human perspective, but we are not human."

"Wait. I'm confused." Tatyana remembered what Mika had told her. "Zara is your child, but you're a fire vampire who comes from an... earth vampire. Right?"

Oleg stared at her with a blank expression. "You listen well."

"But how—"

"My mate was a water vampire. It's not common, but when one exchanges blood with a vampire of another element—and Luana and I exchanged a lot of blood—then sometimes unpredictable things happen with amnis."

"So you had Luana's blood when you changed Zara." Something about that felt so wrong to Tatyana, but she didn't know why. Oleg was right—she was trying to assign human morality to creatures that were not human. "That means Luana had your blood too."

He lifted one eyebrow. "That's what a mate bond is."

She felt a twisting pain in her heart. She looked at Oleg's cool grey eyes. Calculating. Cold. Predatory. He didn't like this subject, but he was indulging her curiosity. "Did it hurt you physically when Luana died?"

There was a twitch under one eye. "It was excruciating."

Which meant that killing Zara would be just as painful to him. Maybe more.

"And Luana didn't change Zara herself because then she would be like a mother?"

He raised an eyebrow. "You've been asking questions."

"Maybe," Tatyana said. "But you were mated to Luana and—"

"If you, for example, wanted to become a vampire, I would never turn you, Tatyana Vorona." His eyes traveled down her body. "Then I would never be able to taste your lovely breasts."

Turning the conversation toward the provocative meant Oleg was finished with the subject of his dead mate and his daughter.

"Not to worry." She smiled. "I have no interest in becoming a vampire."

"Hmm." The corner of his mouth ticked up. "You would make a good one. You are practical." His eyes met hers. "And you bite."

Tatyana felt like Oleg had spread his fire over her skin. "Last night, when we—"

"Not the time to speak of such things." He kept his voice low. "Not with so many ears in this house. Many of the people here were hired by Zara."

Tatyana's entire body felt hot. "Do you think some of them still speak to her?"

"Not willingly, but she knows who they are, which means she might try to use them."

"Why didn't you fire them?"

"You would have me put a seventy-year-old gardener out of work because my daughter hired him? You are even more practical than I thought."

"No." How did he turn things around on her so quickly? "I only meant—"

"I know what you meant, and you're not wrong. But I haven't spent time in this house since Luana died. Choosing staff was not a high priority."

She looked down at her spreadsheets and her notes before she looked back at Oleg. "Do you think Zara would care that we were lovers?"

Oleg's smirk turned into a smile. "We're not lovers yet," he whispered. "That was just a little taste." He winked at her, and in the blink of an eye, he rose and was walking toward the door. "We need to return to Odesa tonight. You should get your work things together, but leave whatever personal items in your room that you would like. That suite is yours now. I'll instruct the night manager to give you a key."

Tatyana had the feeling she was teetering on a bicycle that had started rolling down a hill. "I don't need a key to your house. And I'm not leaving anything here. I already have a house in Sevastopol."

Oleg turned when he reached the door and spread his arms. "And now you have the use of a second. I've already called the pilots. Be ready to leave at nine."

Chapter Twenty-Two

While they were flying back to Odesa, Oleg read through the report Tatyana had prepared, but most of it was gibberish to him.

Planning an armed assault on a river fortress with a dozen vampires, a few human soldiers, and eliminating his enemies before dawn? That was well within his skill set.

Interpreting the intricacies of twenty-first-century banking was not.

"Mika."

"He's already in Odesa, boss."

Oleg glanced up and realized that the only people on the plane were him, Seban, and Tatyana. "Right."

Seban asked, "You need anything from the galley?"

"No." Oleg turned to Tatyana, who was sitting in the back row of seats nearest the Faraday cage. "What is a cryptocurrency?"

"Oh..." She glanced at Seban, then back to Oleg. "Um, how much do you know about blockchain?"

"Nothing."

"Then this is going to take a while to explain," she murmured.

"It's made-up money from computer programs," Seban said. "You know how countries switched from gold coins to paper money?"

"Yes. A foolish decision."

"Yeah." Seban nodded. "This is kind of like that but with computers. Numbers on a screen, boss."

Tatyana raised a hand.

Oleg frowned. "We're not in school."

"It's slightly more complex than that, but one thing blockchain has in common with precious metals is that it is not connected to an issuing bank or tracked by the government, which makes it very convenient for hiding money you've stolen."

"Hmm." Oleg nodded. That he could understand. "Electronic transfers of currency are still backed by human governments that have to account for them. So those currencies, even if they are only electronic, can be tracked."

"Exactly. And cryptocurrency is more like electronic gold that is mined—I'm not going to try to explain the blockchain—but it can be sent through exchanges that aren't backed by any government."

Oleg nodded. "I approve of this."

"Of course you do," Tatyana muttered.

"Like gold exchanges, boss." Seban flipped through a newspaper.

"Gold exchanges?" Tatyana looked between them. "Like public exchange markets?"

"The opposite of public," Oleg said. "Most immortals over a century keep their wealth in precious metals and jewels. Tangible items that don't lose value."

She nodded. "That makes sense."

"Because of that, we have gold exchanges that are exclusively for vampires. You can store gold with them or simply move it through their system."

"Oh right." Tatyana nodded. "So instead of having to show up with physical gold—"

"Oh no," Seban said. "You show up with physical gold. But instead of, say, having to move that gold on a ship across the Atlantic and risking it getting stolen or the ship sinking, you can show up at the gold exchange in Lagos with ten kilos of gold bars and they send a message to give someone at the gold exchange in New York the same amount."

Oleg added, "Minus a service fee."

"There's always a service fee," Tatyana said. "But that's interesting. From what I have found, I don't think Zara bought any gold with the money she took from you. I do think she bought something physical though."

"Which is?"

"Real estate."

Oleg nodded. "I taught her well."

"It's nearly impossible to track cryptocurrency exchanges, but most lawyers don't want to be paid in crypto. If I can find out who she was paying with traceable money, I should be able to find out who she was using to buy her property."

"Good. Then we can... persuade those lawyers to tell us where Zara spent her money." Oleg flipped the file closed and shoved the folder through the cage. "So I don't need to read any of this."

Tatyana took it. "Not if you don't want to. I'll give this to Elene when we get back."

"Excellent."

She had a good mind. An excellent mind.

Maybe his little accountant would be able to figure out how to make Zara's trap better. "You know that you are the bait Mika is dangling to lure Zara back to me, correct?"

Tatyana narrowed her eyes. "Yes."

"How would you like that trap to snap shut faster?"

"With me and Zara in it? Not appealing."

"Just Zara, little wolf." Oleg smiled. "I have other plans for you once Zara is no longer a headache."

Seban reached over and silently put on his favorite accessory: a pair of high-tech noise-canceling headphones.

Tatyana saw them. "I need to get a pair of those."

"Not when you're traveling with me." He should have put her in the cage with him. "Zara. Trap. How do we bait it better?"

Tatyana huffed out a breath. "I don't know. What do you think she wants?"

"She wants money and to make my life miserable."

"Okay..."

"Zara likely left Istanbul because she was stealing from her new lover, so she knows Laskaris won't protect her anymore, but it doesn't matter. She's already made my business less profitable through increasing the tariffs." He leaned back. "Now she needs money."

Tatyana frowned and stared at the ground near her feet. "I'm not going to bother asking why she hates you so much—parents are complicated—but the money she stole from you is hard to access. She hid it well, stashed it in property that she can't sell without coming out of hiding. So she probably needs cash."

Oleg enjoyed watching her think. Her forehead drew two little lines between her eyebrows. Her face scrunched up in concentration.

She looked older than twenty-seven, and he suspected that she'd long been the most responsible member of her family. She had gone away to university. She had also returned when it was necessary and spent all her savings and inheritance to preserve her family property.

He approved of her work ethic and values, but he also had the very strong urge to erase those lines on her forehead. He wanted to wipe away the stress he saw in her eyes.

He had the nagging urge to watch her sleep. Would she be restless and tense? Would she relax like an exhausted child?

Oleg grimaced, irritated that this human woman was occupying so much of his mind.

Once he was rid of Zara, he would install Tatyana at the house in Sevastopol. That was the ideal situation. She could be near her mother, and Oleg could visit her like he'd visit any of his human mistresses. He'd indulge in her company when it suited him and then go about his business. She would be well cared for, and he could get back to living his immortal life.

Tatyana looked up. "Does Zara have gold? Like the gold you were mentioning earlier? Something she could take to one of these exchanges?"

He nodded slowly. "Technically? Yes. She's my daughter."

"So she has something like a trust fund she can access?"

"Ah." Oleg smiled. "Not exactly. Vampire children are supposed to spend their first years with their sire. We teach them how to control their urges, how to feed without killing. How to live inconspicuously in the human world, eliminate their enemies, and develop a ruthless business sense in order to survive for centuries."

She nodded. "So a typical family environment."

He didn't try to stop his smile. "Often vampires stay with their sires for decades or even centuries before venturing out on their own. Some never leave at all."

"Let me guess," Tatyana said. "Luana didn't want to wait a decade. She wanted Zara back."

"She did. I trusted Luana to protect her, so I allowed Zara to go with Luana instead of staying with me."

"But she has a trust fund? Something from you or from Luana?"

"She has nothing from Luana. Though we were estranged, I was still Luana's mate. All her property belonged to me after her death. But when vampire offspring venture out on their own, they are given an inheritance from their sire."

"So Zara has her inheritance from you." Tatyana nodded. "And that is in gold?"

"It's in gold and quite a lot of jewels." Oleg folded his hands together. "And she can come retrieve it anytime she wants."

Realization dawned in Tatyana's eyes. "She has an inheritance, but she doesn't *have* an inheritance."

"When she defied me and went to Laskaris, I told Zara her inheritance would be waiting for her in Saint Petersburg." He smiled. "All she has to do is go there and get it."

"And I'm guessing it's in a house or a castle there?" Tatyana was staring at the ground again. "Under guard?"

"Obviously I can't leave chests of treasure sitting around without guards."

Tatyana took a deep breath and looked up. "Then that's how you sweeten the trap. Bring that treasure to Odesa and make sure she knows about it. You want to draw Zara out? Show her the gold."

Show her the gold.

It wasn't bad advice, and it would probably work. It might escalate the conflict, but it would work.

Mika was standing in the driveway of the compound in Odesa when Oleg returned. "You left the human at the hotel?"

"Yes. She needs to sleep." Oleg handed Mika the folder Tatyana had left with him. "Read this and see if you can make any sense of it. Do you know what cryptocurrency is?"

Mika shrugged. "I've read Satoshi Nakamoto's work."

"Is he a vampire?"

Mika narrowed his eyes. "Some theories say yes. Zara put most of her money in cryptocurrency?"

"I believe that's how she moved it, but Tatyana thinks it's in real estate now."

"Hmm." Mika opened the file, perusing it as they made their way into the house. "Smart."

"Zara or Tatyana?"

"Both."

As soon as they were inside, Oleg stripped off his shirt and rolled his shoulders, allowing his fire to flicker over his skin.

Mika caught his release of tension. "We should talk about the meeting with Saba. How was being in Luana's house?"

"Strange." He'd stayed in Luana and Zara's old day chambers, and the experience was haunting. He could still smell his mate, sense her amnis. It had been unsettling. "I think I'll tear up the basement and renovate so I can use the house again. Tell Elene to find a project manager for the job."

Mika leaned against the fireplace and set the folder on a nearby table. "Are you going to keep the woman there?"

"I've thought about it. It's near her mother and sitting empty at the moment."

"She can use the house, and you can fly in and visit her when it's convenient." Mika nodded. "I approve."

"I don't care." He stretched his arms over his head and reached for a box of cedar incense he kept on the mantel. Pinching the end between his fingers, he lit the stick and set it in a holder to fill the room with the comforting smell of burnt wood. "I'm going to move Zara's treasure to Odesa. Call someone in Saint Petersburg and arrange the transport. A small truck should be enough."

Mika blinked. "You want to move Zara's treasure here?"

"It will draw her out."

"It will provoke her."

Oleg picked up a tray of tesserae from a rolling cart next to the mantel project. He picked up a handful of rounded green glass and rolled it in his palm, enjoying the sensation of cool glass against callused skin. "This is taking too long."

He felt restless and irritable. Maybe he should have kept the woman with him.

No, she needed to sleep. She hadn't slept well in Sevastopol, and she needed to stay in good health if she was going to be his lover.

Mika asked, "Since when are you impatient?"

"Since when are you so cautious?"

"Always," Mika said. "You pay me to be cautious, remember?"

They had talked about logistics and business, but Oleg still hadn't told Mika what had passed between him and the ancient vampire he'd met in Sevastopol.

Oleg poured the green glass back into the tray and turned. "I told Saba that Zara was already dead."

Mika's face went blank. "You lied to her."

"We've lied to everyone."

"I didn't think you would lie to Saba." A thread of fear in Mika's voice. "If she finds out—"

"She won't find out if we take Zara quickly. Right now there are only rumors and whispers, but this needs to end."

"Take Zara? Not kill her?"

Oleg wavered. "I haven't decided yet."

He kept going back and forth. Kill Zara? Keep her captive? After his first conversation with Tatyana about it, he'd been entertaining the idea of keeping Zara captive. But then he'd told the vampire world she was dead. He didn't mind lying, but he also didn't want to anger the ancients.

Mika's face was even paler than usual. "I don't like any of this. She needs to be dead, Oleg. I'll call Roman. He'll arrange a truck to bring Zara's gold here."

"Good. And tell Roman to include Luana's jewelry too."

Mika closed his eyes and took a deep breath. "When she hears about this, I cannot predict how she will react."

"She'll lose her mind—more than she already has—and when she does that, she'll make a mistake." Oleg turned back to the mosaic and tried to calm his mind. "Make it happen, Mika."

"I can have an armored truck by tomorrow. The truck isn't a problem."

"Talk to Radu and arrange for it to go through Minsk. I don't want that gold going anywhere near Ivan and the others in Moscow." It would be just like his brothers to hijack his truck to fuck with him. Technically they were under his aegis, but they were already angry about Oleg killing Sokolov blood; he didn't want to provoke them more.

"Understood. He owes us more than one favor."

"Then once I have Zara's gold in Odesa, it stays with me," Oleg said. "Forget dangling the human in front of her—dangle the gold. We both know she wants that more."

"I suspect she wants the human *and* the gold," Mika said. "But she might be content with the gold."

A WEEK LATER, OLEG WOKE AT DUSK, LYING IN HIS DAY CHAMBER and letting his mind drift. He kept his eyes closed and saw a picture in his mind, a floating, fuzzy image of doves flying over a field of wheat, their pearl-grey wings casting shadows on the golden waves below them.

He could use polished marble for the birds' bodies, mother-of-pearl around their necks. Amber glass to create the heads of wheat so in candlelight they would appear to move, catching the light as the flames flickered.

He saw her walking through the wheat field, her golden hair the same color as the nodding heads of grain. She turned and looked at him, her blue eyes easy and her smile wide in the afternoon sun.

Do you dance, little wolf? Do you still dance in your dreams?

Oleg opened his eyes and stared at the velvet darkness that wrapped around him.

Unlike most vampires, he preferred his day chamber to be void of all light.

Vampire sleep was one of the best and worst aspects of immortal life. Other than a few outliers, his kind was struck unconscious during daylight. Whether his mind was exhausted or frenzied, when the sun rose, Oleg slept. It was one of the reasons he preferred life in the Kievan South.

For an immortal, life in the north was a journey of extremes. In the winter, icy cold chilled his fire and slowed his already slow blood but allowed for plentiful darkness. When the summer hit and temperatures warmed, his blood quickened, but waking hours contracted to an impractical three or four hours a night, so it was impossible to get any work done.

The vampires who had remained in Oleg's northern homeland were a different breed, and he'd never felt kinship with them. He preferred the milder temperatures and lower latitudes of the Black Sea and the surrounding regions.

He snapped his fingers and brought a flame to life, directing it toward the oil lamp by his bed. The soft gold glow illuminated his day chamber and animated the walls.

He hadn't finished the mosaics in this room because he didn't spend much waking time here, but he'd sketched out a river scene he remembered from his early years with his sire, when he followed Truvor's command, conquering territory up and down the vast interior river systems of Eastern Europe.

"You want to move Zara's treasure here?"

"It will draw her out."

"It will provoke her."

His daughter Zara truly had no idea how luxurious her life had been. Oleg had indulged her because Luana had loved her. He'd never subjected her to the harsh discipline his own sire had demanded of his children.

Truvor's clan was made up of the hardest and smartest warriors he could gather from the human populations he conquered during his reign. The humans who fell under his violent hand probably had no idea the barbaric Norseman was something other than human, though Truvor acted like a vengeful god.

He demanded tributes of young men and women from every city he passed, and he used those humans to hunt, feed, and train his army.

That was the crucible that had birthed Oleg, and when he had woken as a fire vampire, his sire had been more than pleased.

For a time.

A note slid under Oleg's door, and he swung his legs over the bed, letting the sheets fall away while the cool night air kissed his bare skin.

Walking over to the door, he captured the scent of Elene on the folded paper.

He opened the note and saw his CFO's neat script.

Tatyana and I had a productive week. Another ten million recovered from bank accounts with the help of her hacker friend. I think she's made some agreement to split her commission with him, but since it's her money, it's none of our business. Our own tech people have looked into this mysterious contact and can't find any trace of him.

Oleg grunted. If his technology wizards couldn't find Tatyana's friend, Zara's people were unlikely to find him either. Elene's note continued.

I gave her the night off but told her to stay near the hotel. Mika's people told me this afternoon that Zara's Albanian allies were spotted in Malinovsky, and the delivery arrived from Saint Petersburg, so it's likely Zara is somewhere close. Tatyana doesn't need to be wandering around, even with security.

Neither do you! Oleg wanted to scream at Elene, but he knew she wouldn't listen, and the moment he got high-handed, she would quit. She'd done it before when she married Dmytro, and Oleg had stubbornly survived for all of three weeks before he begged her to come back to work.

I'm headed home, and yes, Mika put extra guards around our place, so calm down. Have a good night and don't bother the girl. She needs a break from you.

. . .

Oᴌᴇɢ ᴛᴏssᴇᴅ Eʟᴇɴᴇ's ɴᴏᴛᴇ ᴛᴏ ᴛʜᴇ sɪᴅᴇ ᴀɴᴅ ᴡᴀʟᴋᴇᴅ ᴛᴏ ʜɪs closet, tossing another flame at the lamp near the door. Once he was in his closet, he picked out some casual clothing that would be appropriate for the club at the Admiral because he had no intention of taking Elene's advice. He'd already given Tatyana a week alone.

He was hungry.

Sʜᴇ ᴡᴀs ᴛᴀʟᴋɪɴɢ ᴡɪᴛʜ ᴀ ʙᴀʀᴛᴇɴᴅᴇʀ ᴡʜᴏ ᴡᴀɴᴛᴇᴅ ᴛᴏ ʜᴀᴠᴇ sᴇx with her. Of course the stupid human bartender wanted to have sex with her—half the men in the club probably wanted to have sex with his bookkeeper, but this bartender should have known better.

The human said something to her, and her response was a pure laugh. Nothing rueful or sarcastic. There was no edge to it; it was happiness and delight.

The sudden jolt of jealous anger caught Oleg by surprise. His fangs dropped, a low flame burned along the back of his hand, and a muscle in his jaw twitched.

He quickly pulled his anger back, remembering where he was.

Admiral staff was off-limits, but the man should have known better. He was flirting with Oleg's woman. Worse, she was responding to him. Encouraging him.

Tatyana's cheeks were flushed, and she appeared to be in a celebratory mood. She should be. If he'd made a cool million dollars just by tracking down somebody else's money, he'd feel celebratory too.

"Mr. Sokolov." The hostess greeted him. "Shall I prepare your usual table?"

"Thank you."

"For one?"

"Two." Tatyana would be eating with him.

Or he might be eating her, but that wouldn't be in the club.

"Very good." She hustled away to herd her staff, and Oleg approached the bar.

Tatyana sensed him before he even got close. Her shoulders froze, and the laugh that she'd been sharing with the bartender died.

The human quickly turned when he saw Oleg's frigid expression.

"You." Tatyana pouted, and he could tell from her scent that she'd taken more alcohol than usual.

Damn. She was off the menu for the night.

That didn't mean he didn't require her company. Oleg held his hand out and snapped his fingers. "Come. You'll eat dinner with me."

Her head fell back and she sighed. "Is it impossible for you to just *ask* like a normal person?"

"I'm not a normal person."

"Obviously not."

Her lips pouted adorably, and a little of Oleg's anger died away. He stepped closer and ran a finger along her shoulder, making the hairs on her neck stand at attention for him before he trailed his fingers down her back until his hand rested in the small of her back.

"Elene said you had a successful day. Let me buy you dinner as a thank-you."

"You're paying me ten percent." She looked up, her blue eyes hooded and languorous. "That's a good thank-you."

Oleg pressed a finger to her lips. "Let's not talk about money in the club, hmm?"

Her mouth formed a small O, and she nodded.

He rubbed the small of her back and nudged her off the barstool. "Come, volchitsa. Eat with me."

"Food?"

The corner of his mouth inched up. "Do you like caviar and champagne?"

"Yes." Her voice was a little loud even for the club. "That kind of dinner I can agree to."

Oleg's fire soothed for the moment, he walked Tatyana to his booth and waited for her to settle in before he slid beside her and put his arm around the back of the booth.

She looked at his arm where it rested across her shoulders. "You're hugging me."

"I'm not." He snapped at the waiter who was hovering nearby. "Do you have a preference for the champagne?"

"I don't know enough about good champagne to care," she murmured. "You're going to order something ridiculously expensive, so just order whatever you want since you were going to do that anyway."

"Good." He ordered in Georgian, which was the language of the young man who was waiting on them. "I ordered you some salmon too."

"That's nice." She took a deep breath and leaned into his side. "You smell good."

"I'm surprised you can smell my cologne. It's made for vampire sense of smell."

"Most human perfumes are probably too strong for you."

"Yes." He enjoyed her scent though. It was the one he'd brought her from Greece. "You smell delectable."

She looked up, blinking slowly. "I should have asked if you were hungry."

"Are you offering?"

Her lips flushed, and he could see she was considering it.

Oleg bent down to her ear and spoke softly. "It's normal to be curious about new things."

She pulled away and he gave her space. He could hear her heartbeat racing.

"I think I want to go back to my room," she said. "Can we eat there?"

"Are you inviting me to your room?" Oleg's cock was already hard.

Tatyana had drunk too much alcohol for Oleg to enjoy his initial plan for the night, but he wasn't ready to take his leave, especially when the bartender was still watching her and trying to pretend he wasn't.

"Uh..." She shook her head. "I don't— Yes." She whispered, "I don't want everyone looking at me while I'm eating dinner, and when I'm with you, I can feel their eyes."

His eyes turned and swept across the room, immediately noticing that most of the vampires in the room *were* watching them.

"Fine." He slipped out of the booth and held out his hand. "We'll eat in your room."

"No, but then everyone will think we're going to have sex." She glanced nervously around the club. "They're going to think that, aren't they?"

"They think that anyway."

Her cheeks were flaming red, and now Oleg wanted to get her out of the club because she smelled like an amuse-bouche to every vampire around them.

"Come." He tugged her out of the booth. "We're leaving."

"Oleg—"

"No." He pulled her close and bent down to whisper in her ear again. "You will not argue with me in public. Ever. If you know what is good for you, you will not argue with me in public." His fire was dancing right on the edge, and he could sense his amnis roused by even the suggestion of challenge from the woman. "Don't make me use amnis to silence you, because I will."

He saw her mind doing very quick calculations despite the haze of alcohol. "Okay."

"Good." He walked with her from the club, her hand grasped firmly in his. "Please deliver our meal to Miss Vorona's suite," he told the hostess.

"Of course, Mr. Sokolov. I'll take care of it."

Oleg walked down the stairs and bypassed the elevator.

"It's five floors down," Tatyana protested.

"Do you want to be stuck in an elevator for the next few hours after I've shorted out the control panel?"

She followed him into the stairwell. "Are you saying that you walk up fifteen flights of stairs every time you come up here?"

"It's not difficult, Tatyana." He was tempted to throw her over his shoulder and walk faster, but he didn't know how precarious her belly was. "How are you feeling?"

"More sober now that I'm walking down five flights." She took a deep breath. The stairwell was open at the landings, and the night air was bracing. "I'm not sure what just happened back there. Why are you angry?"

"I'm not angry." Oleg was annoyed, but like Tatyana, he wasn't sure why.

You know why.

The bartender making her laugh. Her delight with no shadows. He wanted her to laugh like that, smile like that. At him. Only at him.

"You are angry." She squinted. "I wasn't doing anything."

"I'm not angry." He turned and swept her up in his arms. "You're walking too slowly."

She was light as a feather as he carried her, and the scent of her blood and body set his fangs on edge.

"Close your eyes."

"What?"

"I'm going to walk at vampire speed."

"What does that..."

She trailed off when he started to move.

"Oh no."

She pressed her face to his shoulder as Oleg sped down the stairs. Since they were alone, he didn't have to modify his natural speed, and they were at her door around a minute later.

"We're here." He set her on her feet, and she wobbled a little bit. "Steady."

Tatyana leaned into his chest and tilted her face up to his. "That was fast."

He trailed a finger over the soft brown wing of her eyebrow. "I told you to keep your eyes shut."

"Like a high-speed train," she murmured. "I took one of those once. In Germany."

"Hmm." He held her, enjoying the wondering expression in her eyes. "Do you have your key?"

"Are you going to kiss me again?" Her eyes were on his lips. "The way you kiss... I've never been kissed like that."

"I imagine not." He leaned down and brushed his lips over her mouth. He kissed her again and again, soft, drugging kisses that ratcheted up the delicious tension zinging between them.

Her mouth was full and swollen from his teeth. He scraped his fangs along her lower lip, enjoying the hint of blood that rose just underneath her skin.

"When I bite you" —he trailed his lips to her ear and whispered— "I will give you so much pleasure that you will come just from my teeth."

She pressed her breasts against his chest and leaned into him, her eyes clouded with anticipation. "Why does that sound so good?"

"Because you've already felt my hands and you want more." He ran his thumbs along the small of her back, trailed his fingertips over the rise of her bottom. His touch was so light she shivered, and he felt her skin prickle at the sensation he aroused. "Would you like to feel my cock, little wolf? Feel how hard it is when I fuck you?" He brought her hand to the front of his trousers. "My teeth are even harder. Sharper."

Tatyana sucked in a breath and wrapped her fingers around his heavy cock.

Oleg smiled and pulled her hand away before too many ideas grew in her mind. "You've been drinking. I'm not going to touch you more than this when you've been drinking."

"But it's the same feeling as when you kiss me," she whispered. "When you touch me. It feels like... champagne bubbles along my skin. Under my skin."

Oleg's cock was not interested in nobility. She was standing in front of him, willing, wet, and ready.

"Tatyana, open your door." He wasn't going to fuck her, but he wanted to play a little longer, and he didn't want to share. "You'll be embarrassed if someone walks by."

"What do you want from me?" She looked up at him, her blue eyes drowsy and drunk. "Is this part of the plan?"

Oleg pulled away. "Plan?"

"To catch Zara?" She frowned. "To get your money. Why are you being... sweet?"

The spike of anger tore through him again, but this time what lay behind the anger wasn't jealousy.

Her suspicion *hurt*.

Damn her.

Oleg crossed his arms over his chest. "Where is your key?"

"Okay, okay." She dug into her pocket for the key and held it out to him. "You're angry again. I can't keep track of why you're angry all the time."

Oleg took her key. Then he opened her door, shoved Tatyana inside, shut it behind her, and walked away.

Chapter Twenty-Three

"Too much celebrating over the weekend?" Elene was looking at Tatyana with an amused expression. "I gave you time off so you could rest, not so you could party."

They were sitting in Elene's office, Tatyana on her laptop and Elene at her desk. There were spreadsheets, files, and printouts scattered over the coffee table, and the remnants of dinner waited on a tray near the door.

Tatyana laughed weakly. "Well, when someone buys you an entire bottle of champagne and you have no one to drink it with, it's a crime to let it go to waste."

It had been three days since Oleg had left her slightly drunk and very sexually frustrated at her hotel door, and Tatyana was still confused by what had happened.

He had been soft and sweet and gentle with her. Yes, he'd been domineering and high-handed too, but she wasn't going to pretend that his sweeping her off her feet, ordering champagne and caviar, and kissing her senseless didn't work.

It worked. It had very definitely worked.

And then in a blink he was angry and she was alone.

Again.

She was starting to think their night in the back of his car had been a fever dream.

"Men," Tatyana muttered.

Elene's eyebrows went up.

"Sorry," Tatyana said. "My mind wandered, but I'll have those files for you shortly."

They'd been working all day, but they were waiting on an email from Grimace, who thought he could crack the last of Zara's accounts that night, leaving only the paperwork of foreign attorneys to deal with, which would be Elene's forte.

Once Tatyana found the signing documents from Zara's email server, Elene would start on the process of claiming ownership of ZOL's foreign properties under the SMO umbrella.

"Ah, men." Elene smiled a little bit. "Good men are priceless. And there is nothing worse than a bad one."

Tatyana peered through her reading glasses at the older woman she was starting to idolize. Elene Beridze was the CFO of a vampire-owned multinational corporation, trusted adviser to a thousand-year-old immortal, and commanded a staff of humans and vampires who hung on every command.

In short, she was a complete badass.

Tatyana had also seen the pictures of Elene's adorable professor husband on her desk along with pictures of their two gorgeous children.

Tatyana wanted to be Elene when she grew up, and she was starting to feel like if there was anything positive to come out of this insane situation—other than gobs of money, obviously—it was meeting Elene.

"What would you classify Oleg as?" Tatyana asked her. "A good man or a bad man?"

"Neither," Elene said. "He's a vampire." Her head popped up when she saw something on her screen. "An email from Grimace." Elene waved at her. "Translate."

Tatyana opened the messaging app that she and Grimace used to communicate and clicked on the message her old friend had sent.

—pidge, your wish is my command. You owe me a date when you're back in Kyiv and the world is a happier place.

She quickly typed back. *—you get a date when you're old enough to buy me a beer.*

—low. I turned eighteen last summer.

That was news to Tatyana. She'd been teasing—she thought he was in his early twenties—but that confirmed that the best hacker she knew had started breaking into military servers when he was fourteen.

In his own way, Grimace was as terrifying as Oleg.

—you're a wunderkind, Grimace.

As she typed, a stream of user names, passwords, and authorization keys streamed across a window that popped up in the corner of her laptop. Grimace had not only found the last of Zara's accounts, he'd grabbed the passwords and set up two-step verification on all of them so that she wouldn't be able to access them anymore.

"Get ready." Tatyana opened a secure window and started typing. "Account one is in the Maldives." She let out a sharp breath. "Five hundred thousand." That was less than she expected. She typed in the next. "The next one is Swiss."

Elene walked across the office and looked over Tatyana's shoulder. "How many accounts?"

"Five total." They'd already recovered two of them, and both those accounts had held nearly ten million. "Four in Switzerland."

Which had some of the best security in the world, meaning Tatyana would never have cracked it without Grimace's help.

But agreeing to split the commission with him still meant that SMO already owed her over a million dollars.

She keyed in the authentication code for the first Swiss account and almost fell over. "Another eight million."

"The first of four?" Elene smiled. "I knew it was over thirty million."

By the time Tatyana had finished and sent statements to Elene, the total of Zara's theft, not counting the money in real estate, was 42,560,017 Swiss francs.

Over fifty million US dollars.

She was riding back to the hotel in Elene's car, still in shock.

Elene glanced over as she drove. "We owe you over five million dollars now."

There were security cars in front of them and behind them, but Elene preferred to drive her own sleek Mercedes sedan. Tatyana was riding in the passenger seat, watching the city go by and wondering how a person's life could change so much in the space of two months.

Two months. That was all the time that had passed since she'd walked boldly into SMO's offices and made a deal with a vampire.

"As soon as we submit the paperwork to transfer the money," Elene continued, "how would you like to be paid? Have you decided? Or would you prefer to let me help you open your own Swiss account now?

"Oh my God." Tatyana was breathless. Even with Grimace's cut, she had over three million dollars now. "Um... yes, a Swiss bank account might be helpful."

Elene smiled. "I have a few connections there. I could probably find a bank that would give you one or two percent interest on an amount like that. You could easily live off the interest when you go back to Sevastopol."

"Right." She felt a knot in her chest ease. It was over. It was actually over.

She could have a life again. Her mother would be protected. The farm wouldn't be in danger from the taxes ever again. She could... She could breathe. For the first time since her grandparents had passed away, Tatyana would be able to breathe.

Elene stopped at the red light behind the guard's car. "Of course, if you'd be interested in continuing employment with SMO, I *would* hire you. You're very talented, Tatyana. Very smart."

Tatyana looked at Elene's profile in the red glow from the signal light. "Do you need to ask Oleg?"

Elene scoffed. "I am in charge of the hiring for SMO. Not Oleg."

Tatyana nodded. What would it mean? She could stay in Odesa. She could... get her own apartment. She could have her own space again.

Your mother.

That was the sticking point, wasn't it? Her little bubble of hope rose, then sank. That was always the sticking point.

"I'll think about it," she told Elene. "Thank you."

"Don't thank me." The light changed, and she started into the intersection. "You'd be an asset to—"

The delivery van came out of nowhere, slamming into the black sedan in front of them and pushing it across the intersection as Elene's Mercedes slammed into the side.

Airbags exploded; there was a sickening crunch and the sound of gunfire.

Everything went black.

Chapter Twenty-Four

There was shouting outside. Mika burst through Oleg's front door, and his fangs were already bared.

Oleg set his palette to the side. "What has happened?"

"Elene." Mika choked on her name. "Elene's car. She was going home and there were rockets." He was speaking so quickly in Estonian Oleg could barely make out what the man was saying. "They rammed the front car; she collided with the truck."

Oleg's fangs fell, and he bared his teeth as the fire on his neck and arms roared to life. Somewhere in the distance an alarm rang. "What happened?"

"It was an ambush." Mika could barely get out the words. "There were a dozen at least. Human. And then four vampires."

"Where is she?" Oleg grabbed his boyar by the collar and threw him against the wall. "How could this happen? It was your job to protect her!"

"There were three cars. A fucking rocket launcher." Mika was shaking, and the water in the air drew to his skin. It looked like he was sweating, but the water vampire's amnis was roused, and the damp sea air clung to him as adrenaline rushed through his system.

"Where is she?" The flames on Oleg's body rose, and he felt his trousers char to ashen scraps.

"Stop." Mika sent a cooling mist over Oleg. "Stop and think. They can't have gotten far."

Oleg froze. "Elene's not dead?"

Mika shook his head. "There was a human guard who survived. He was burned by the rockets, but he said the Albanians took the women and shoved them into the back of a delivery truck. But they took them *alive.*"

Oleg's fire erupted again. "Them?" He bent down in Mika's face, grabbed him by the neck, and snarled. "What do you mean, them?"

"It's Tatyana." Mika managed to choke out the words. "Zara has Tatyana and Elene. She's taken them both."

Chapter Twenty-Five

Tatyana's head was aching. Her whole body was aching. Her mind was woozy as she tried to understand what had happened. One moment she and Elene were watching Oleg's guards ease into the intersection and the next...

Crash.

Grab them!

Voices coming from everywhere. An explosion and hands grabbing her from the crumpled car. Everything happened at once.

She's no one! Elene had shouted. *My secretary. Leave her alone!*

More voices in a language she didn't understand.

What was happening?

"Tatyana?"

Elene's familiar voice cut through the haze and the pain. Why did her body ache so much? Everything had gone black. Where was she?

"Tatyana." Elene's voice again. "Are you awake?"

Drip. Drip. Drip.

Something was dripping in the background, like when a pipe burst in the bathroom. She'd woken to dripping, and she would never forget that sound.

Drip. Drip.

"Tatyana." A soft hand on her face. "Try to wake up. You've been asleep for hours."

Hours? It felt more like days.

Her eyes fluttered open, and sunlight streamed through a round window. The floor around her rocked.

"Where am I?" She squeezed her eyes shut. "Bright."

"You probably have a concussion." Elene scooted over and tried to help her sit up. "I'm sure both of us do."

Tatyana tried opening her eyes again and held a hand up to the glaring light that streamed in. "Can you turn it off?"

"It's the sun." Elene laughed bitterly. "It's probably the only thing protecting us right now."

Tatyana looked down at her clothes, but nothing made sense. She was wearing what looked like the overalls her grandfather used to wear when he was working on his tractor. "Where are my clothes?"

"They took them." Elene propped her up and held Tatyana's chin in her hands. "Look at me if you can. I want to check your eyes."

Tatyana opened her eyes and looked at Elene, who had two black eyes and a bloody lip. "They beat you up?"

Elene shook her head. "That was the airbag. You look about the same, I think. We both had bloody noses. Blood all over our clothes. Cuts from the glass." She plucked at the navy-blue coveralls that sagged on her. "That's why they put us in these. I think our clothes were covered in blood. They probably don't want the vampires to lose control."

"Who is they?" She closed her eyes again. "My head hurts so much."

"I'm sure it does." Elene stroked her cheek. "I am so sorry, my dear. This is all my fault."

"What are you talking about?"

"I was so determined..." She sighed. "It didn't occur to me that she would have that many people working with her."

"Her?" Terrifying realization dawned. "Zara has us. They were speaking Albanian." She blinked. "Zara's people took us."

"I believe so." Elene glanced at the window as the ground rocked again.

"Where are we?"

Elene was staring at the round window. "On a boat, but I don't know where. I can't see any shoreline. We're probably heading south."

It wasn't a window. It was a porthole. She and Elene were sitting on a narrow bed in what looked like a small whitewashed cabin. Crew quarters maybe?

There were no sheets on the bed. No pillows or blankets or any signs of habitation. There was a small desk built into the wall with a metal toilet underneath it, but there was no chair. There was a single door with no window.

Elene was staring at the door, her face cut, her eyes bruised.

Nothing seemed right. Nothing made any sense. "Why would Zara kidnap me? I thought she'd just kill me."

She'd been half expecting it for weeks.

Sometimes on the news, you would hear about a person who committed a horrible crime, but their friends and neighbors would say: Oh, we never would have thought! He was so quiet. She was so kind!

Not Zara. The moment Oleg had confirmed to Tatyana that Zara was a vampire, all she could think was: Yes. That makes sense.

And vampires hunted people. People were their prey. Like cows. Like deer in the forest. It was the natural order of things. A pigeon was never going to survive in a hawk's world.

"Zara won't kill us," Elene said. "She wants her money. She wants her inheritance."

Tatyana let out a long breath, and that hurt. Her entire body hurt, but letting out a breath really hurt. "What inheritance?"

"Her gold." Elene shifted and winced as she did. "Her inheritance from Oleg. He moved it to Odesa last week to provoke her into action. He said it was taking too long for her to come out of hiding."

"That was..." She grimaced. "That was actually my idea. I can't believe he took my advice."

"Well, it worked." Elene looked around the small cabin. "It worked very well."

Tatyana wanted to lie down and go to sleep again, but she didn't want to die.

Which was unfortunate because she had a suspicion that she was definitely going to die. "You know, I'm really glad we took her money. At least when she kills us, I can die satisfied that she'll spend eternity being poor. I'm poor, and it's not fun."

Wait. She wasn't poor anymore.

"Your humor is grimmer than Oleg's," Elene muttered. "Maybe you two *are* a good match."

It was a strange turn of conversation. Not that it mattered, because Tatyana was going to die. "Do you think Oleg will give my commission to my mother when I'm dead? That would be fair, right?"

Elene snapped at her. "We're not going to die."

Wrong, wrong, wrong. Tatyana grew up on a farm. She knew how the natural order worked.

The hawk ate the pigeon.

The fox ate the hawk.

The human ate the chicken.

And the vampire ate the human.

Her head was starting to swim again. "I think I'm going to pass out."

"She doesn't want to kill us. Tatyana, stay awake. She won't kill us. She's going to use us as leverage to get her gold. She knows Oleg will want us back."

"You? Maybe." She wiggled her finger like a teacher chiding a student. "But I'm the bait, remember? The bait doesn't usually survive the trap. That's the whole point of being bait."

Whatever Elene said, it drifted away as Tatyana fell back into darkness.

Chapter Twenty-Six

The warehouse lay on a deserted street on the edge of the waterfront, surrounded by barbed wire and a guard shack where two guards stood holding machine guns that were typical for private security.

Oleg and Mika waited in the shadows across the street. In a few more minutes, a dozen of Oleg's druzhina would be gathered—all the ones in the immediate area—and they would take the warehouse, the humans and vampires inside, and any information they had about Oleg's missing women.

It had been three hours since Tatyana and Elene had been taken.

"Remember," Mika murmured, "we need the leaders alive."

His boyar had identified the warehouse as the temporary headquarters of a faction of the Albanian vampire mafia that Zara had hired to abduct Elene and Tatyana.

"Waiting for Karl and Oksana." Mika signed across the dark street where Ludmila was waiting in the shadows. "They're almost here."

Ludmila and Oksana were mated. The sniper would feel her mate as she approached.

Oleg was wearing a pair of black canvas pants and nothing else. His amnis was frantic and furious. He felt a muscle in his cheek twitch, and his fangs were long and aching in his mouth. He gripped the leather-wrapped handle of his favorite axe. He hadn't used it in a decade, but he kept the edge sharp, and he would feed his old friend blood that night.

He forced himself to be patient.

Zara wouldn't kill them immediately. She would want information from Tatyana. She would want to use Elene for trade because she knew the woman was valuable to Oleg.

He blanked out what they must be suffering at that very moment and hoped that wherever Zara's people had taken them, his daughter was not yet present.

She was... unpredictable.

Oleg was doing everything possible to dampen his own energy, so he couldn't reach out and sense how many immortals were in the building, but Mika's spies said that roughly a dozen vampires and twenty or so humans were hiding out, waiting for a boat back to Sarandë. They had been hired the week before, transported by Greek freighter, and were now stranded in Odesa.

They were at Oleg's mercy, but he had none.

"They're here," Mika said. "Wind first?"

"With Rudov."

One of the few blood siblings in Oleg's druzhina, his brother was a powerful and silent earth vampire with an affinity for metal.

Mika signed across the street, and four wind vampires took to the air, shooting into the darkness and alighting on the roof of the warehouse with silent feet, Rudov carried by the largest flyer.

Oleg met his brother's eyes across the darkness and nodded. "Now."

Pouring from the shadows, Oleg's people sped across the street. Two cracks rang in the darkness—probably from Ludmila—and one armed guard's head exploded. Then the next.

Rudov gripped the metal roof in his hands, and Oleg could feel his amnis flex as the vampire tore open the roof of the warehouse before he dropped inside, followed by the four wind vampires.

Shouts came from inside the warehouse just as half a dozen water vampires scrambled easily over the gate and the barbed wire. As they passed, they scraped their flesh and the scent of blood filled the air.

Oleg's people did not stop.

Mika ran forward—Oksana emerging from the shadows to join him —and in a singular movement, the two soldiers tore open the gates and tossed the twisted metal across the road.

Oleg waited for the sound of chaos to reach his waiting ears. He walked deliberately across the street, his axe lifted to his shoulder, and let his fire come alive.

He stepped over four human bodies in the yard—several of their limbs had been ripped from their bodies.

The Albanians wouldn't have crossed into his territory without tacit permission of the Greeks. Oleg had a message to send.

Double doors were open, but no light came from the shadowy death trap where the Albanian vampire mob was caught.

He brought a ball of fire to his hands, tossing flames at the trucks sitting parked in the yard. One burst into flame, and a few moments later the second caught on fire.

There were shouts and screams from inside the warehouse as Oleg crossed the threshold, the fire burning along his arms the only light other than the occasional muzzle flash and a burning trash can.

He stepped over two twitching vampire bodies with their heads detached.

A foolish human shot at Oleg from the shadows, hitting him in the shoulder, and he charged.

He moved in the blink of an eye, grabbing the human from behind a pillar with inhuman speed. The man screamed as Oleg grabbed him, pulled his head to the side, and sank his teeth into the man's neck before he twisted it, waiting for the neck to snap before he let the body drop to the ground.

Just in time for a water vampire to come at him from the shadows, pulling a cloud over Oleg's fire in an attempt to douse his flames.

But the immortal only had the damp night air to work with, and when Oleg let his flames loose, his older amnis easily overpowered the misty element of the water vampire, who abandoned elemental attack to charge Oleg with a curved, short saber aimed at his neck.

Oleg lifted his axe, relaxed his fire, and swung, rage-filled adrenaline powering his oldest weapon as it arced toward the vampire's neck.

Sword met axe, and the ancient clang of metal rang through the dark warehouse, adding to the screams and cries of the humans and vampires fighting.

Oleg stomped his foot, bent his knee, and wrenched his axe handle, pulling the curved edge of the other vampire's saber close, slicing his own arm open as he grabbed at the sword hand of the vampire he was fighting with his flaming left hand.

Oleg's fire rushed to heal the open wound on his arm as he yanked the sword away from his opponent. Then he swung his axe down, slicing off the man's leg below the knee.

The man screamed, and Oleg had every intention of taking off his head when Mika yelled, "Wait!"

He snarled at the intrusion into his bloodlust but pulled back. Instead of his neck, Oleg sliced off his right arm and let the vampire drop to the floor, crippled but alive.

Oleg turned and surveyed the wreckage his men had left. The scent of human blood was heavy in the air, and the floor was black-red with the excess of battle.

His people were flush with the blood of their enemies, and the thrilling rush of battle permeated the air.

Oleg raised his axe and held it over his head. *"Druzhina!"* he shouted with a guttural roar.

"Krov!"

"Druzhina!"

"Zapal!"

"DRUZHINA!"

Oleg's warriors answered back with a satisfied roar.

Blood and fire. His people had fought with blood, fire, and vengeance for the humans under his aegis who had been taken by these intruders.

Now to get the information they needed from those who survived.

Mika had four vampires tied up along one wall, and Oleg grabbed the one he'd maimed, gripping his hair and pulling him to the lineup.

"Dry them." Oleg pointed at the vampire who felt the oldest and the strongest. "Start with him."

Mika and Oksana put their hands on the vampire and started pulling the water from his body until the immortal began to scream in pain.

Oleg snapped his fingers and brought the fire to his hands. Then he crouched down and looked the vampire in the eye as he placed the fire on the stump of his severed leg. "They will pull the water from your body, and then my fire will crawl through your veins, eating what's left of your blood from the inside out."

The vampires on either side of the man began to whimper and shake, but the old one stayed strong.

Until Oleg forced a thread of fire into his body.

He let out a strangled scream and his face collapsed in agony, but there were no tears to shed. It wasn't possible with his body shrinking and drying before Oleg's eyes.

"Your death can be swift," Oleg said quietly. "Or it can be prolonged, but you will tell me what I need to know before you die. Where did you take the women?"

Chapter Twenty-Seven

The next time Tatyana woke, her head was clearer and someone was screaming.

She froze when she realized that she'd been moved again. She was lying on the ground, and the dripping sound was back.

The screaming was Zara.

"Give! Me!" She paused and took a breath. "My money!"

There was a heavy thud, and something large clattered to the floor.

Tatyana looked over and saw that her old boss was standing over her new boss, who was tied to a steel chair that was lying on its side.

Elene's face was battered, and blood streamed down her head and oozed from her mouth, but despite that, she was trying to calm Zara down.

"Zara, please. I want to get you your money."

"Bitch, you're the one who took it!" The irate vampire snapped at the men standing behind Elene. "Get her up."

The two men lifted Elene's chair back up, and the older woman slumped to the side. "I can't access that money right now, but I can tell you where your gold is. Do you want to know where your gold is?"

"It's in his fucking house!" Zara, who was dressed in an incongruous designer dress, bent over and shouted in Elene's face. "You think I don't know where it is?"

"Then you know he just did this to provoke you." Elene's voice was calm and reasonable despite her face looking like someone had beat it with a mallet.

Tatyana's hands were zip-tied behind her body, she couldn't move, and when she started crying, hot tears stung the cuts on her face.

She was beyond pain now, but she still tried to stop Zara from beating Elene to a pulp. "I can get the money."

"You." Zara turned to Tatyana, and for the first time, Tatyana saw her true fangs. The woman Tatyana had once thought was so beautiful and intriguing walked over, her platform heels making heavy clunks on the hollow steel floor. "Can you?" She crouched down. "Huh? Can you get me my money? Can you get my *gold*?"

"Uh…" She frowned. "I don't know about your gold, but I know the passwords."

"Of course you fucking do." Zara slapped her across the face, and Tatyana's ears rang. "You betraying cunt. You helped me set everything up and then you go to my bastard of a father and rat me out?" She slapped Tatyana again, and her lip burst open.

Tatyana tasted blood.

"You think because he's fucking you that he cares?" Zara snorted. "He fucks anything that moves. He'd have fucked me if I wasn't his blood."

"Zara," Elene called out. "Listen to me. Leave Tatyana alone. She was just trying to help her family. She doesn't know about our world."

"Bullshit." Zara stood and turned to Elene. "How do I get my money, Elene?"

"I can help you."

"No, you won't. You never ever did!"

She was a child. Tatyana watched Zara stomp around, kicking her foot and lashing out at everyone and everything around her. The realization was almost comical.

Except it was so, so horrible.

Zara was like a lethal toddler having a temper tantrum, only she wasn't just stomping her foot and screaming, she was beating Elene to death.

"I want my money!"

Slap. Punch. Zara kicked Elene's shin, and yet the woman didn't cry out. Her silence only seemed to enrage Zara more.

"God, what kind of cock does he have that you all just *worship* him, huh?" She sneered at Elene. "He used to fuck you before you got old, right?"

"All I want" —Elene spat out blood and tried to speak calmly, but her face was so swollen that her words were starting to slur— "is for Tatyana to be able to go home and for you to get your inheritance."

"Yes. It *is* my inheritance." She pointed at Elene, grabbed her chin, and yanked down, making Elene cry out in pain. "Isn't it my right? Luana wanted *me*. He couldn't stand that, could he? She didn't want him anymore. She wanted me. And she wanted me to have her jewelry and her gold and her house, didn't she? She wanted that for me."

"It's only fair," Elene said. "Luana loved you very much. I know that, Zara."

"And he took it all because he was her *mate*." Zara spat out the word and slapped Elene again. "What the fuck did he give her? Nothing but grief! Nothing but bitching at both of us for causing problems. And then..." Zara's angry rant caught in her throat. "And then..."

Elene made her voice soft. "I know. It was wrong, Zara. It was wrong and everyone knows it."

"Not Athens!" Zara screamed. "Not the self-righteous fucking *council*."

"It was wrong." Elene repeated it over and over. "It was wrong, Zara. It was so wrong."

"I know it was fucking wrong!" Her sorrow turned to madness again, and she lifted her fist to Elene and punched her across the jaw. "But you were his right hand, weren't you? You filed the paperwork to take *everything* from me. Don't think I don't recognize your signature, dearest Elene. My father's" —slap— "dearest" —punch— "bitch."

"Stop!" Tatyana was desperate. Zara was losing it, and she was losing it on Elene. "Stop—I'll get it all back for you! I promise I'll get it all back! I promise, I promise, I promise. Zara, stop!"

"Please." Elene cast her gaze toward Tatyana and shook her head slowly as her brilliant blue eyes started swelling shut. "If you kill me, Zara, you know he will hunt you to the ends of the earth. He will take your freedom, he will lock you up, and no one will stop him. If you kill *her*, it will be even worse. He will end you."

"No, he won't. I'm his own blood, so fuck you." Zara drew her hand back punched Elene again.

Tatyana heard Elene's head snap to the side, and the chair cracked as it fell on the floor.

Elene, still tied to the chair, didn't move.

"No!" Tatyana screamed.

"Dammit." Someone in the shadows shouted at Zara in a language Tatyana didn't recognize. The man sounded pissed off.

Tatyana stared at Elene's collapsed chair, willing her body to move.

Please. Please, Elene. Please.

Tatyana felt the guttural moan crawl up from her chest and out her throat.

No, no, no, no.

Zara glanced at Tatyana, then at the man shouting from the shadows.

She wiped her hand along her mouth, tasting Elene's blood as she stretched her jaw and bared her fangs. "Well, she should have been a vampire."

Tatyana's entire body hurt from sobbing. Her eyes ached. Her head ached. Her stomach ached. She tried to throw up, but nothing came out. Her throat was parched and dry as she wept over Elene's still figure in the low light of the cargo hold.

Drip. Drip. Drip.

Zara knelt down in front of Tatyana and lifted her head. "Your turn. You're going to get my money back for me, or I'm going to beat you to death like I did your friend. It will be painful, and I will take my time. So start talking."

Tatyana's eyes watered, and her mouth split again when Zara slapped her. She was lying on her side and tried to hunch over to protect her belly when Zara kicked her. She felt something tear her skin as the heavy platform heel landed.

Something broke inside her, and there was a gush of warmth in her belly.

No. This couldn't be all. This couldn't be the end of her life.

It wasn't fair.

Her vision became blotted and spotty as lights flashed in the periphery.

She didn't want to die yet.

Tatyana heard Zara muttering under her breath.

"Shit."

A sickening numbness pulled at her mind and Tatyana's eyes flickered shut.

Chapter Twenty-Eight

Oleg raced over the black waters of the sea, staring into the darkness at the silhouette of the Greek freighter in the distance. The moon shone on the water as they followed the churning wake of the freighter headed toward the Turkish Straits.

They would not reach their destination.

The water vampires of his druzhina had already reached the vessel, and he could see them climbing up and over the sides as wind vampires began to dive-bomb the freighter from above.

It was his sniper Ludmila who had found them after his wind vampires had spread out over the Romanian coast, looking for the ship the Albanians had named before Oleg killed them all.

Oleg had put a cold wall around his emotions, cutting off everything but his rage and his need for vengeance. Anything other than that was contrary to results.

He couldn't think about Tatyana. Or her mother. Or the soft scent of saffron and amber on her skin.

He definitely couldn't think about Elene, about Dmytro, or about the two babies he'd held in a church over twenty years ago and promised to protect.

Their mother had been taken by his own blood.

He'd sent no explanation when he sent a small army of men to Elene's house. Said nothing when he sent his plane for her daughter in London and sent men to her son's house in Rome. His godchildren would know that something had happened, and he'd taught them to cooperate.

Oleg cut off any softness or human emotion as he focused on the boat that cut across the ocean. His blood surged when he heard the first cry.

"The druzhina will kill every vampire on board," Mika said quietly. "The humans?"

"Find the women," Oleg said quietly. "Then make it a ghost ship."

Mika nodded. "Understood."

His boyar dove into the water, cutting through the waves faster even than the speedboat Oleg was riding.

It was fifteen minutes later when they pulled up close enough to board the ship. Oleg jumped onto the side, grabbing the rungs of a ladder and climbing easily up to the deck. He nodded at the men and women he passed, most of whom smelled of blood and gore.

It was satisfying but not what he wanted.

Blood trails led to crumpled human bodies. Not a vampire took a breath as he passed.

Oleg met Mika at the last open door and said nothing when he saw the vampire's reddened eyes.

Mika led him down to a hold that reeked of blood, and no one said a word as Oleg took in the scene.

Someone had found a sheet somewhere and covered her body, but Oleg felt the rage gather and burst out when he smelled Elene's blood.

So much blood.

Too much blood.

His fire burst out in rage and agony, and he cursed in words that no one had spoken in centuries.

Mika walked toward him, but Oleg put a hand up as flame raged around him. He smelled his own hair singing from the ferocity of the angry inferno.

His people shouted and ran from the hold as the room filled with fire.

And Mika stood in a corner, bloody tears running down his cheeks as he drew the water in the damp hold toward himself so that Oleg's flames would not burn him alive.

Oleg didn't know how long his fire raged, but he found himself kneeling beside Elene's body, lifeless but warm from his fire. The remnants of his clothes were smoking and falling into ash. His skin was burning but his element had died back.

And Elene was just as dead.

He gathered her broken body into his arms and rocked her as his rage cooled and grief wracked his soul. He wept with no shame over a woman who had been his dearest friend.

After some time, Mika walked over; Oleg could see his old friend's pain was as great as his.

"If there had been even a hint of life," Mika said, "I would have tried to turn her."

"She would have hated us."

Mika whispered, "I wouldn't have cared."

Oleg blinked back the bloody tears that dripped onto the white sheet that covered Elene. "No sign of Tatyana?"

"According to the captain, Zara took her and left about an hour ago. He didn't know where she was going. I used amnis; he was telling the truth."

"She wants her money back." And Tatyana was the one who could find it.

"It sounds like Tatyana may be injured, but she's alive. Zara said something about getting her medical attention."

So Tatyana was injured but alive. For now.

But Zara would die. She was already dead.

There was no place in the world his daughter could go that Oleg would not find her.

Chapter Twenty-Nine

Tatyana woke to fire eating through her veins. She screamed in agony, wailing in confusion and pain.

Someone threw a bucket of water on her; then a door slammed. The water crawled over her skin, spreading and soothing the angry, itching sensation that covered her.

She opened her eyes and blinked in the darkness that wasn't dark. There was a rank sweetness in the back of her throat and an aching in her jaw.

Drip. Drip. Drip.

The dripping sound came from everywhere, and Tatyana realized she was lying on a floor pooled with red-tinged water. There was a body in the corner.

Elene?

Tatyana's throat already hurt, but she burst into another wracking sob when she remembered the still form lying on the floor of the creaking freighter.

She wasn't at sea anymore. Wherever she was, she could feel the ground steady beneath her. There was a skittering, electrical shock of energy along her skin, and her mind raced, trying to classify the new sensation.

Electricity? Buzzing. Brightness. Heat. Coursing rivers of blood in her body. She could feel her blood she could feel her heart and her heart should be racing her blood should be racing and the water surrounded her like a current flowing over her skin and scattering her senses too much too much too much.

She closed her eyes and listened to the thump of her heart.

Her heart.

Thump.

Silence.

Thump.

Silence.

Too slow.

Her heart was too slow.

Her skin was cold, and the water threaded over it like raindrops crawling along her body.

The water soothed her. It loved her. The water was her only friend.

Tatyana sucked in a breath, and the scent of sweet blood threaded the air. Her mouth watered, and something sharp pierced her tongue.

The body in the corner twitched and Tatyana rolled to her heels, crouched in readiness as she watched the body in the corner with a predatory stare.

Not Elene. Elene was dead.

Her throat was burning and the strange, manic energy skittered along her skin, making her muscles twitch and her mind spin.

Take.

Need.

Take, take, take.

The pain in her jaw became agony, and she opened her mouth, bringing her fingers to touch the elongated canines that were growing between her teeth.

She was ravenous and her throat was burning and her fangs—

Her fangs.

Tatyana screamed in realization of what she was. Of what she had become.

The blinking human flesh rolled over, his drugged eyes wide and his mouth bound with a dirty rag. His eyes went even wider when he saw Tatyana, and he tried to scream. The noise pierced her eardrums, and something in her brain snapped.

Too late.

She lunged toward him and sank her teeth into his neck.

A moment later a door slammed open, someone pulled her hair, dragging her off the body of the human, and slammed her against the wall.

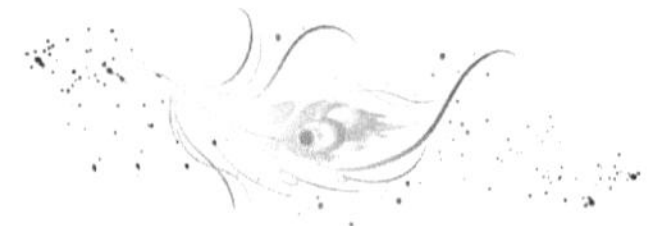

The next time Tatyana's eyes fluttered open, the incongruous image of a green mosaic fan palm filled her vision. She lay still, taking in her surroundings as her eyes slowly focused in the pearl-grey light.

It only took her a moment to remember.

Vampire.

She brought her fingers to her mouth, but though her canines were preternaturally sharp, they weren't elongated. Her throat didn't burn.

The stabbing pain was gone, but an itching sensation remained everywhere her clothes touched her body.

She lifted her head and looked down. She was dressed in another set of navy-blue overalls, but she wasn't wearing anything beneath them. She could feel the rough seams rasping against skin that felt feverish and aching.

She sat up slowly, looking around, but nothing made sense.

She was high on a hill and saw the sea in the distance, illuminated by the moon. She looked up at a sky that wasn't grey at all but swirling blue and silver, the stars nearly blinding her if she looked at them too long.

She was sitting under a massive semicircular portico in front of a house on top of the hill. There were tall columns and manicured gardens that sloped down to the rolling hills that overlooked the water.

Twisting up to the house was a serpentine drive, but there were no cars in sight. All she could see was terraced gardens filled with waving palms and citrus trees heavy with fruit. Lush green gardens rose around her, and the air was filled with the scent of earth, pine, and some heady flower she couldn't place.

She heard something moving behind her, and she sprang to her feet.

"Zara?" Had Zara turned her into a vampire? Had someone else done it?

Did it matter?

Tatyana moved like a stranger in her body.

The ground was too hard. Her footsteps too jolting. Every sense was heightened, from the bright light of the starry night to the taste of sour adrenaline that lingered at the back of her throat.

She looked around her and realized the sound she heard was the rigid frond of a large palm brushing against the house as a warm breeze swept up the hills.

The wind rolled up from the sea, laden with salt air that washed over Tatyana and soothed her anxious mind.

Water. Whatever else she was confused about, she had no doubt that her amnis came from water. She nearly wept when the humid breeze clung to her skin and soothed the burning irritation from the stiff canvas clothes.

Where was she?

The mansion at the top of the hill was old, decorated with marble columns that encircled the portico and large glass windows along the front of the house that framed the sea view. Elaborate floral murals decorated each column, each one different than the next, and those paintings crawled up to the roof of the portico, joining the vining border that surrounded the palm frond that made up the center of a massive mosaic.

As Tatyana walked, her footsteps sounded like firecrackers on the marble tile.

"Hello?"

Nothing. Her voice echoed against the tile and the marble.

She turned in circles, but there was nothing. She saw it then, the faint glow of light on the edge of the horizon.

Daylight was coming.

Thump.

Her heart gave a single thud, and she ran to the front door of the house, but when she yanked at the doors, the solid carved wood didn't budge.

Her heart beat again.

Thump.

"No." She hadn't survived all this just to burn to a crisp at her first hint of daylight. "Hello!" she yelled. "Anyone?"

Her throat was starting to burn again, and she scented something rich and sweet when the breeze turned.

Following the scent around the side of the house, Tatyana saw just how massive the edifice was, stretching two broad wings back into a dense evergreen forest filled with shadows and the flapping of birds.

As she approached, the birds fell silent.

"Hello?"

Thump thump.

The smell grew stronger and her fangs fell.

No. Oh no. "Whoever you are, please stay away."

There was a human near, and she could smell their blood, but something about it smelled... wrong. Soiled and rotten, like meat that had gone off in the heat.

Her body began to shake as she continued to walk around the mansion to the back of the left side of the house where a stone path lined with more palm trees led around carved marble steps leading to a raised terrace that spanned the back of the mansion, creating a curved crescent that embraced another lush garden.

Tatyana walked into the garden, blinking as she tried to understand the sight that met her eyes.

The body of an old man lay naked at the base of an apple tree, his blank eyes staring at the sky. His mouth was open in shock, and his body was pierced by fang marks.

Over.

And over.

And over. They were everywhere.

His man was pale, nearly blue, and his cap had fallen to the side of his head.

Tatyana felt the groan wrenching up from her belly as she realized what she was seeing. She looked at the rough work clothes she was wearing.

Smeared with the old man's blood.

"Nooo!" She screamed and fell to the ground, rocking back and forth when she realized what she'd become. And yet even over her horror and pain, she was hungry. She was so hungry her throat was burning. Even though the old man's blood was cold, she craved it.

She wept bloody tears, wiping them with the back of her hand as she stumbled to the front of the house and collapsed under the marble portico.

She wouldn't look for shelter. She *should* die. It was the only justice.

Her only release.

She didn't know what had happened with the man, but she knew in her heart he was dead because of her. She should die. She was a monster, and she'd killed an innocent old man. She was a murderer.

It would be better for her to die.

She curled into a ball as her body convulsed and she threw up the blood that curdled in her stomach. It spilled from her mouth, black and rancid to her nose.

She deserved it. She deserved to die.

"I'm so sorry," she whispered to the dead man in the garden.

Mama, I'm sorry.

Elene, I'm sorry.

She saw the sky growing lighter and felt darkness creeping over her mind. She would fall asleep. She would burn in the daylight when the sun marched across the ground.

Tatyana would die and that would be just.

She'd had enough. Enough horror. Enough blood. Enough pain.

Enough.

"Tatyana!"

The moment of her death and she heard the damn vampire's voice? Did heaven really want to torment her so much?

"Leave it and get the house open!"

Tatyana dreamed of strong arms that picked her up as if she were weightless. She was tucked against his chest, and she turned her face to his shoulder, drinking in the scent of cedar and incense that seemed to emanate from his skin.

She was dying, and this was the last vision life offered her?

"Why you?" she murmured.

"Get the doors open." His voice was just as commanding in her dreams.

Terrible. Oleg the Terrible.

"I don't care what you call me, but you're not dying just when I have you back." The sound of wood cracking and something crashed in. "I have you, Tatyana. You're safe." The brush of tender lips across her forehead. "I have you now. You're safe. I have you now."

No.

Didn't he realize?

Tatyana finally understood what was happening a moment before darkness swallowed her mind.

She would never be safe again.

Chapter Thirty

Mika stared at the sleeping newborn vampire, his eyes darting between the young woman and Oleg. "Why did Zara bring her *here*?"

Here was a country estate twenty kilometers outside Sochi, an isolated compound that overlooked the sea and backed up to one of Oleg's favorite forests. Oleg hadn't lived here in decades, but the grounds had been maintained by the old man whose body was currently being buried at the edge of the garden.

One of his oldest brothers lived in the forest behind the house and oversaw the territory for him.

Oleg had washed the crusted blood from Tatyana's body, wrapped her in silk sheets that would be the easiest on her skin, and laid her in a day chamber that only he had the key to open.

And he had no idea what was going on.

Tatyana was a vampire, and her blood smelled of Zara. Zara had sired her and then left her on Oleg's door. And he had no clue as to why.

"Why here?" Mika repeated. "If we hadn't found her—"

"I don't know."

Relieved. The moment he'd heard rumors that a ravenous newborn vampire had been dumped in front of his house in the hills outside Sochi, he had hoped that somehow his little wolf had come back to him.

It had been two weeks of searching, but Mika had come up with nothing. Oksana had come up with nothing. There were no rumors that reached Radu's ears, and Oleg's entire organization was in mourning for Elene, crippled by the loss of one of his finest people.

After killing Elene, Zara had disappeared across the sea, and Oleg had started to lose hope. His rage had torn through the streets of Odesa, crossed the sea to Sevastopol, and even brought him close to violating treaties with some of his closest allies, whom he suspected might harbor those who had taken his bookkeeper.

But according to his information wizards, none of the money had moved. Zara hadn't tried to access anything. She had no funds left after hiring the Albanians. Her resources had been drained, and she'd burned all the favors she had left. Most of the immortal world already thought she was dead.

Oleg had feared the worst. Zara had lost control and killed both of them in a rage and was hiding in the darkest pit she could find, knowing that Oleg's wrath would eventually find her.

And then.

"Leave." Oleg flicked his fingers toward the door. "Leave us."

"She's Zara's blood."

"I can smell it."

His daughter *had* lost control. That much was obvious. But why had she turned Tatyana? What did she hope to gain?

As a vampire, Tatyana's stubborn mind was now permanently resistant to Zara's amnis. She wouldn't be able to manipulate her like she would have as a human. She couldn't make Tatyana forget. She couldn't force her to give up information.

Mika huffed out a breath. "Killing Zara—"

"Has become much more complicated."

Oleg had wanted Zara's blood even if it pained him. He'd told the vampire world that Zara was already dead, and promised revenge for

Elene. But while killing his daughter might hurt Oleg, it could very well kill Tatyana. The pain would be so excruciating that a young vampire like her might not survive the loss of that bond.

"This has massive fuckup written all over it," Mika muttered.

"Know what else has massive fuckup written all over it?" Oleg snapped. "Elene's death."

Mika went silent, and a cold mask fell over his face.

Oleg glared at him. "Leave."

Mika marched out of the room without another word.

When his little wolf was awake and Oleg knew her mind was her own, he might forgive Mika. He knew Elene had resisted protection. He'd heard her stubbornness with his own ears. Mika was only partially responsible when Elene had refused to cooperate.

But ten days ago they had put Elene's body in the ground. The priests had spoken the ancient rites as her children wept. Her husband watched Oleg with a frigid glare.

Oleg had no defense; he had failed one of his dearest friends.

He would not fail Tatyana.

Oleg walked over to the bed and saw her body lax with the sleep of the newborn. He trailed a finger along her cheek, brushing a strand of her golden hair away from her eyes. Had her eyes changed? He hadn't seen them clearly before she fell into day rest. Sometimes eye color changed with immortality, but he hoped Tatyana's had remained the same glorious blue.

"You have true fangs now, volchitsa." He knelt next to her and pressed a kiss to her forehead, closing his eyes as he made a silent promise to the young woman who hadn't wanted this fate.

He would make sure she survived. He would make sure her teeth were sharp, her body prepared, and her instincts honed. He would be her master, and she might grow to hate him.

But he would make sure Tatyana survived.

Chapter Thirty-One

Tatyana woke again, but for the first time in weeks, she wasn't cold and in pain. There was no dripping sound in the background. She was warm, and the sheets around her were tucked in tightly. The fabric soothed her skin, and the warm air in the room was thick and misty with water. Someone had washed her and braided her hair in a long plait down her back.

The walls around her were a soft green color, and the floor was smooth, dark oak that settled something inside her. There were no paintings hanging, but a verdant green mosaic was inlaid along one wall, depicting a starry sky over a forest.

Oleg. Somehow she had come to be in Oleg's house. She knew it without a doubt.

There was no light save for a very low lamp in the corner with an amber bulb. It cast a gentle glow across the room and glinted against small mirrored tiles in the mosaic.

The bed she was lying on was soft, and somewhere in the distance, classical music played.

Despite the deliberately muted scene set for her, Tatyana's throat was on fire.

"Tatyana?"

She heard his voice through the door like a whisper, and her body reacted immediately. She didn't know how or why, but she felt needy and nearly desperate for him.

"Yes?" Her breasts were sensitive to the touch. She could feel her own arousal. Smell it.

What was this madness?

Had Oleg smelled every time she'd been aroused around him?

Her mind flooded with embarrassment, but part of her was only more turned on. She wanted him so badly, and she wanted him to know.

Oleg's voice was gentle and even. "I have fresh blood for you. Open the door when you're ready."

He was her monster. Her protector. And without a doubt the worst thing that had ever happened to her.

She wrapped her arms around her knees and rocked back and forth, picturing the body of the dead man in the garden. "I can't. I killed him."

"There are no humans out here. Take a deep breath. Your sense of smell is stronger than a bloodhound's now. Do you smell anyone?"

She inhaled deeply. Dust. Something green she couldn't identify. The scent of linen coming from a cabinet near the door. She could smell the sea from a distance. A hint of pine from the air outside and lemon-and-eucalyptus soap in the bathroom. There were flowers some-where close.

She breathed in Oleg's scent and wanted to wrap his body around herself like a blanket. Cedar and smoke and a hint of the incense she remembered from her childhood Sundays in church. She wanted to touch him, wanted to fuck him. She wanted to sink her teeth into his body.

This could not be happening.

Tatyana rocked back and forth, hiding her face as her fangs grew long and painful in her mouth. "I don't want this," she whispered. "I don't want any of this."

"I have donated blood," Oleg continued in the same soothing voice.

"It's fresh, but the longer you wait, the harder it will be to control yourself."

Control. Right now she would do anything that would give her back a hint of control.

Tatyana lifted her chin, set her jaw, and winced as her fangs dug into her lower lip.

She wrapped the silk sheets around her body and walked to the door. It was heavy, wooden, and bolted with old-fashioned iron locks. It took her less effort than she imagined to turn the lock, and then she cracked the door open and peered outside.

Outside the bedroom was a cozy living area with a couch and double French doors that looked out over the terrace to a garden filled with white blooms. She could smell gardenia and jasmine in the air.

Oleg was sitting on a white couch reading a book, his legs stretched out and crossed at the ankles. On the table in front of him was a large silver carafe, and Tatyana could smell the blood that it held.

Her eyes flashed toward him but settled on the blood.

"Take as much as you want." He leaned forward and set his book down before he reached for the carafe but froze when a fierce snarl erupted from Tatyana's throat.

She slapped a hand over her mouth, but Oleg raised his hands and sat back.

"Take it." He nodded at the carafe. "Drink. You'll feel more control after you've fed."

With trembling hands, she knelt in front of the coffee table and grabbed for what looked like a silver coffee carafe, twisting open the top and bringing the vessel to her lips.

She poured the blood directly in her mouth, chugging past the thickness that coated her throat as the warm blood soothed the burning pain. She could feel it dripping down either side of her mouth, but she didn't care.

It was heaven and heat and everything that she needed. It wasn't the rancid, dead blood she'd smelled the night before but fresh, warm, and soothing. She felt as if she were swallowing life itself.

Oleg silently walked to a door, opened it, and brought her another carafe before she finished the first.

"In the first month of immortal life" —he kept his voice soft and clinical— "you will need roughly the equivalent of a human body's worth of blood every night. That is not weakness or lack of discipline; that is physical necessity."

As he spoke, she continued to drink.

"Your amnis is new and developing," he continued. "Your body is burning through what is left of its human energy stores and food will no longer sustain you, though you will need to eat light meals so your stomach does not ache."

Tatyana reached for the second carafe and opened it; this time her hands didn't tremble. She was still kneeling on the floor, and Oleg walked over and grabbed a cushion from an armchair, setting it next to her.

"Relax. You'll process what you're drinking better if you relax."

Silently, she sat on the cushion, pulling the sheet around her body and crossing her legs as she started to drink the second carafe of blood. It was hotter than the first and tasted better.

"You will drink two liters of blood when you wake in the evening. You will need to pace yourself." He continued speaking as he sat back on the sofa. "Another liter halfway through the night or whenever you feel a craving again. Another two liters before you go to rest at dawn."

She took it all in, his calm recitation that almost sounded like a doctor prescribing a course of treatment.

"You should not be around humans for several months. At least. All the human staff of this house have been sent away. Only vampires I trust are on the property."

She looked at him, her eyes darting around the room, but she didn't stop drinking.

"You're at an old home of mine." Oleg answered her unspoken question. "It's some distance outside Sochi, in the middle of a forest. There are no houses around for five kilometers at least. That should be enough of a buffer to keep you contained."

Five kilometers in every direction? Not even a hound could smell blood from that distance.

Oleg leaned forward, resting his elbows on his knees. "I am assuming that this was not done as a willing choice."

She pulled the carafe from her lips and wiped her bloody mouth with the back of her hand. "Do you think I would ever want this?" Her voice was hoarse, nearly unrecognizable to her own ears.

Oleg silently handed her a linen kerchief from his pocket. "Ever? Perhaps. But not as it was done. It should never be done in anger."

"Did *you* choose to become a vampire?"

"No." Oleg shook his head. "But my sire never asked permission for such things. When I woke, I was enraged. And I was a fire vampire, so I killed a half dozen of my brothers on waking."

"Was your sire angry?" A thread of something feral and sad and angry shot through her.

"No, he didn't care about their loss. He was thrilled," Oleg said. "He'd never sired a fire vampire before. He was pleased because I was dangerous."

Was Tatyana enraged?

No. She didn't know how she felt.

"You're staring." She looked at the floor. "Do I look so different now?"

"You look the same. Your eye color didn't change."

"Should it?"

"It's not a rule. It only happens sometimes. I'm glad yours remained the same."

So did Tatyana. She didn't want a stranger's eyes looking at her from the mirror.

She wiped her mouth, did what she could to clean up the blood that had dripped down her neck and onto her breasts, but there was too much. She was going to need a shower. "I didn't want any of this, but..."

Oleg waited.

Tatyana met his steady gaze. "I didn't want to die either."

"Good." Oleg's voice was low and steady. "You're wise for your age.

I could see that the moment I met you. You're a survivor. You will survive this. And if it is up to me, you will thrive."

She took another long drink from the carafe, then rested it on the pillow she was sitting on, but she didn't let go of it.

She was confused and angry, but she could think again. Her throat wasn't on fire. "Why am I here?"

He narrowed his eyes. "I don't know. Did Zara bring you here?"

"I don't remember." She shook her head. "I was knocked out after the car crash. Then... There are chunks of time that I remember, but I don't recall anything more than flashes after Zara killed Elene." A punch of anger and sadness as tears sprang to Tatyana's eyes and her emotions swung wildly from pain to anger to longing. Her fingers gripped the carafe, and she heard glass crack as the vessel caved in. "She killed Elene in front of me."

"Give it to me." Oleg took the broken carafe from her hand and wrapped his hand around her clenched fist. "Take a deep breath and try to relax."

She whispered, "I love her so much."

"I'm sorry." Pain leached through his voice. "I loved her too, but the only thing we can do now is find—"

"Not Elene!" Tatyana started rocking again, her body shaking with an overflow of emotions like water spilling over the edge of a bowl. She felt everything and sensed everything at once.

Oleg kept his voice quiet. "Your emotions are intense right now. Your nervous system has been overloaded by your heightened senses, and your brain hasn't had the time to process—"

"I hate her!" she screamed, then slapped a hand over her mouth as a sob tore from her chest. "I hate Zara. I hate her. I want to kill her."

Oleg's voice was quiet and even. "Trust me when I say that I understand—"

"And I love her." Tatyana couldn't stop the words even though she hated them. "I *love* her so much."

Chapter Thirty-Two

"So that is why Zara brought her to you." Mika blew a stream of smoke from the thin cigar he'd lit in the library. The French doors to the back terrace were open, and the scent of oranges and lemons filled the air. "Because Tatyana will be loyal to her blood."

It was midnight and the newborn in the house was taking a bath. If Oleg knew water vampires, she could be in there for several hours.

"I always liked this house." Oleg breathed in the scent of the sea and the ripening citrus trees. "I should spend more time here. Lazlo isn't hard to be around, and he mostly wants to be left alone."

"It's not very convenient." Mika took another drag on his cigar.

He'd taken up the old habit in the weeks since they'd found Elene's body. Mika hadn't attended the funeral because he knew it would anger Dmytro and the children. He'd spent most of his nights alone or working furiously with Oksana to track down every human and vampire who'd had a part in Elene and Tatyana's abduction.

They were dead. All of them except Zara and whomever she had directly with her. Mika had personally executed them all.

Oleg had been trying to walk softly around his old friend even through his own grief after losing Elene. Because his grief was nothing to Mika's.

"It's too isolated here," Mika said. "It's not close enough to a seaport or an airport."

"It reminds me of the citadel." Oleg didn't mind the isolation. He'd been far too exposed in the past few years. His blood craved revenge, but his soul craved a decade or two away from business and politics, which wouldn't be possible anytime soon after Elene's sudden loss.

"The citadel is also too isolated," Mika muttered, "but at least there's the river."

"Luana and I had many good decades in this house. She was fond of this place." Which was probably why Oleg avoided it.

Mika set his cigar to the side and returned to the matter at hand. "What are you going to do about the newborn? She's a problem."

"She's Zara's child," Oleg said. "So she loves her sire; her feelings are completely predictable."

"But she's under your aegis, so you're bound to care for her," Mika said.

"She's not under my aegis." Oleg raised an eyebrow. "Not at the moment. Until she disavows her own sire and pledges loyalty to me, she's under Zara's."

"So you could kill her."

"Zara? I would like to, but it's complicated now."

"No, Tatyana."

Oleg wasn't prepared for the snarl that erupted from his throat, the way his fangs fell and cut his own lip, or the look of utter terror when Mika saw his reaction.

His boyar blinked. "Are you in love with—"

"Don't be ridiculous," Oleg snapped. "But that woman lost her human life because of me. Because of both of us. She didn't choose this; we *failed* her. She was a human under my protection who placed her trust in me, and I failed to protect her. Honor demands that I keep her from further harm."

"Fuck honor." Mika's voice was dead. "If anyone paid attention to honor these days, Elene would still be alive."

"I want her then." Oleg stared at Mika. "So no, I will not kill her because she's Zara's blood."

His boyar lifted a hand, opened his mouth, then shut it and slumped back in his chair. "It will be as you wish, Knyaz."

The old title mollified Oleg, and his fire calmed.

The allure that Tatyana had as a human had exponentially expanded when she became an immortal with power. Oleg had never been a man attracted to demure women. He liked power, and he liked women who knew how to use theirs. There was nothing sexier than a formidable woman, and Tatyana had the potential and the brains to be an extraordinary immortal.

But he needed to kill her sire to set her free.

And he couldn't kill her sire because it might kill her.

The thread of an idea formed in his mind, but it was a raw idea and far too personal to share with Mika.

"Tatyana loves Zara," Oleg said. "That's a completely natural response of a newborn vampire to their sire. It's born in the blood, and there is nothing we can do about it."

"But it means she's a liability." Mika leaned forward, his expression cold. "As much as I sympathize with the woman, she's a time bomb waiting to go off. Zara could have planted ideas in Tatyana's head we don't even know about."

Oleg scoffed. "Don't be ridiculous. Vampire minds are stronger than that. Hers was already resistant to manipulation when she was human. She's not Zara's puppet. It doesn't work that way."

"Fine. She's erratic. She's a newborn, and she won't be able to harm her own sire in a fight. If it came down to you or Zara, she would choose her sire no matter what she's done."

Oleg couldn't refute Mika's observations because he knew they were correct.

"She'll be completely subservient to Zara whether she likes it or not," Mika continued. "No newborn has the strength to defy their sire."

Oleg kept his eyes on the fire in the grate. "What do you suggest?"

"If you're not going to kill Tatyana—which I can accept—at least send her away. Make sure she pledges to you, then send her away. It would be a mercy."

And yet Oleg wasn't interested in mercy. He wanted Tatyana more.

Mika continued, "Send her away until we've neutralized your daughter. Either by death or captivity."

"Impossible." Oleg rose and walked to the wooden bar where he poured a goblet of blood-wine. "Zara has a sire bond with Tatyana. She will know if her child is gone. If we're going to lure her here, Tatyana should stay."

And Oleg didn't want to send her away. He had unfinished business with his little wolf, and he didn't want to let her out of his reach.

"Lure Zara here?" Mika's eyes went wide. "With what? A newborn she doesn't want to deal with? Zara had her and she got rid of her."

Which still didn't make sense. Why was Tatyana alive? Why had Zara turned her? Was it an impulse? A chaotic plan that made sense to no one but his own daughter?

Oleg slowly sipped his wine. Tatyana's turning might have been an impulse on Zara's part. She might have panicked and tried to keep alive the only link she had left to her lost fortune.

Zara might have had a searing and intense moment of pity—it wouldn't be the first time—and turned Tatyana to save her life.

Only God knew Zara's mind, and God and Oleg weren't on speaking terms.

"We don't lure Zara here with her child," Oleg said. "We move her treasure here and let Zara know about it. Whatever she's plotting, she's short on money and she won't be able to resist. She doesn't just want her gold now—she needs it."

"Fine. I'll take care of it." Mika stood. "Oksana and Ludmila are here. About half a dozen others, and I can call more of the druzhina if we need them."

"Oksana and Ludmila both?" Oleg nodded. "Good. Tatyana might prefer to have some other women around."

Mika rolled his eyes. "The house is secured. We can move the treasure on the plane since you won't need it for a while. I'm going to assume that you're staying with the woman."

"I promised to protect her." Oleg set down his glass. "Call her mother. Arrange for a video call of some kind."

"Good. That woman has been harassing my assistant anyway." Mika was already headed toward the door. "What do we tell her mother?"

Oleg shrugged. "The truth."

Chapter Thirty-Three

Tatyana sat a meter away from the video screen, staring at her mother and feeling like she was ten years old again.

"Tanya." Anna lifted her hand to the screen, touching it as her eyes went soft. "I thought they were lying to me. I thought you were dead."

"I'm a vampire," Tatyana whispered. "It would probably be better if I were dead."

"Don't say that." Anna's voice turned sharp. "Tatyana Vorona, you will banish that thought from your mind."

She closed her eyes and felt hot tears track down her cheeks.

She'd woken earlier to another raging thirst and two more silver carafes of blood. Her body was stronger than the night before, and when she turned the lock in the door, it had nearly broken off in her hand.

"Tanya?"

She opened her eyes, brushed a hand over her cold cheeks, and lifted her chin. "Yes, Mama."

"You will survive this. And you will come home."

She nodded but said nothing. She stared at her mother, seeing her in a new light.

There were silver threads at her temples now, and the lines around her eyes and mouth made her look like Tatyana's grandmother a little more every year.

Tatyana had once thought that looking at her mother and her grandmother gave her a photograph of her future selves. Middle age. Old age. She could see exactly how she would look at each stage of life.

"Look at you." Anna's mouth turned up at the corner. "You look so pale."

"Even more than before."

Her mother laughed a little bit. "Baboolya would be so happy. She'd never have to remind you to put on a hat so you don't get freckles."

Tatyana let out a hard breath. "I wish I had them. I look in the mirror and see a ghost."

"Stop." Anna waved a hand. "Just stop it. No more of this morbid talk. You could have died and you didn't. You should be grateful; it could be worse."

"Worse than being a vampire?" Listening to her mother's voice, she felt the urge to sulk like a child. "I won't be able to see you for months. Maybe longer. I don't know what's going to happen to me now. All these people are dangerous and—"

"Hush." Anna leaned closer to the screen. "You *think*, Tanya. You are a planner. You get that from your grandfather, don't you?"

Tatyana pressed her lips together and nodded.

"Good." Anna sat back. "You think. You listen and you plan. You're smarter than all of them. You know that, don't you?"

Tatyana didn't know that, but she nodded to reassure her mother.

"For now you take what is offered," Anna said. "You have people willing to help you, yes? To protect you and give you what you need?"

"Yes. My boss is here."

"Is he still your boss? From what his people told me, your contract with him was completed and you're going to be a wealthy woman."

Oh, why had they told her mother all that? Oleg's secretary probably thought she was reassuring Tatyana's mother, having no idea the number of questions it would provoke.

"Mama, I don't know when I'll be able to send you money, but—"

"I already have money in my bank account," her mother said. "More money than I know what to do with." She smirked. "I'll never have to ask Karol for money again. I could buy the whole building and kick Mrs. Lipovsky out if I wanted."

Wonderful. So Oleg had sent her mother money. Why? There was no telling. Emotional manipulation? Guilt? Maybe it was a down payment for Tatyana's work.

She rubbed a hand over her face. "I need you to tell me how much money Oleg sent you so I can pay him back."

"Good luck. He told me it was a small gift for our family's inconvenience."

Inconvenience? Was that how he thought of her?

"Just send me an email with the amount and..." Tatyana's breath caught in her chest.

Email.

Phone.

Computer.

Fuck.

"Can you email me when you're one of them now?" Anna asked.

She was completely cut off from her work. She was completely cut off from the modern world. "Oh my God."

"I can see the look on your face, and you're going to start to panic and go in circles about everything you can't control, so I'm going to—"

"I can't do anything on my own!" She stood up, shaking her arms as a current of itching electricity ran under her skin. "I can't call you without their help. I can't email you, and even if I knew where a post office was, I don't think I could get close enough to it without murdering someone and I already—"

"Tatyana Otsana Vorona!" Anna snapped at her. "Calm down."

She froze, closed her eyes, and focused on the water drops pebbling her skin. "I'm breathing."

"In."

She sucked in a breath and nodded.

"Out."

She kept her focus on her mother's voice and let out a stream of cold air from between her lips. She didn't need to breathe. She realized that when there was no pressure in her chest as she held the air in her lungs, but the human instinct to breathe hadn't stopped when her heart did.

In.

Out.

In.

Out.

When she was back in control, she nodded.

"Good girl," Anna said. "I'm going to send you some of my birds." Her mother's voice was deceptively calm. "Wouldn't you like that, Tanya? I don't think it would be good to send you Pushkin—you know how he gets around strange men—but I'm going to send you some of my lovely birds to keep you company."

Tatyana opened her eyes and stared at her mother. "What?"

"Won't that be *nice?*" Her mother's gaze was intent on the screen. "A few of my sweet birds to keep you company while you're away. A little bit of home. Don't you think that will be familiar to hear their calls at night?"

Why would her mother send her any of her precious carrier pigeons?

Oh, you idiot, Tanya. Because they were *carrier* pigeons.

Tatyana sat down again. "You know how much I love the birds, Mama."

Birds that her mother had trained over many years to fly back to her with a surety few animals possessed. Birds that could carry messages. Birds that maybe a vampire lord would not suspect.

"You'll be lonely there," Anna said, "don't you think? For a whole year I won't be able to see you. I'll send you a few sweet pets to remind you of home."

Pets, not carrier pigeons. The message was clear. The birds' skills were not to be spoken of, but if Tatyana needed to contact her mother, they would be there.

"There's a beautiful garden here," Tatyana said. "I'm sure I can build them a nice dovecote. That way they'll feel right at home."

"Good." Anna touched the screen. "Maybe they can help you think, Tanya. Help you... plan a new future, huh? You have a long time to live now." Anna's eyes narrowed a little bit. "It would be a good thing to think about what you want to do now that you have so much time."

"Yes, Mama." She swallowed the burn in her throat. "I'll remember what you said."

Chapter Thirty-Four

Oleg had cleared the covered furniture from the ballroom and taken everything to storage. Until he was ready to entertain again, this room would be used to train the newborn.

The expansive hall had marble tile floors and a large fountain set into the floor of the room with a water channel that ran out to the series of fountains in the garden outside.

Oleg was circling the fountain, and Tatyana was on the other side of the room, watching him with suspicion.

"Ideally," he said, "your sire should be teaching you all this, but that's not possible for obvious reasons. Mika is a water vampire though. When he gets back—"

"Not him."

She was wearing a pair of overly long leggings and a loose shirt with a sports bra underneath. They were the only things Oksana had that fit Tatyana. Until her clothes arrived from Odesa, it was the best they could do.

Tatyana crossed her arms under her breasts. "Are there other water vampires besides Mika who can help me? I don't trust Mika."

"That's probably smart," Oleg said. "He suggested that I kill you."

Tatyana bared her fangs, and Oleg felt his cock stiffen.

His reaction to this woman was getting out of hand. He needed to fuck her. Soon.

"It's nothing personal," Oleg continued. "He's thinking strategically, and you're a possible asset for Zara. Right now all Mika can think about is killing Zara."

"Why?"

Oleg had no qualms telling her Mika's secrets when she already knew the man wanted to kill her. "He loved Elene. For decades. If she hadn't been happy with her husband and family, he would have pursued her, but he had too much respect for her choices."

Tatyana said nothing for a long time, but she eventually moved closer to Oleg. "I'm sorry about Elene. Zara was interrogating her, and Elene was trying to calm her down."

"That never goes well," Oleg muttered.

"She lost control. I think she just... snapped. I don't think she meant to do it. Zara knocked her over and the fall—"

"Her neck was broken. She would have died instantly." Oleg closed his eyes. "At least there was that."

"Yes." Tatyana's hands curled around her belly. "I think..." She frowned. "I think I was bleeding. I think Zara was trying to ask me questions and she kicked me and I was bleeding internally, but I have no real idea how I died." She shook her head. "I don't remember much after that."

Oleg snapped his fingers and motioned to the fountain. "Come."

Tatyana curled her lip. "I don't like the snapping thing any more now than I did when I was alive."

"You're still alive, volchitsa. Your teeth are just sharper now." He snapped again, enjoying the curl of her lip. "Like I said, a water vampire should be teaching you all this, but instead, you have me."

"A fire vampire." She walked to the fountain. "Your opposite."

"Elements don't work like that." He snapped his fingers and

brought a flame to his hand. "Ideally, they work in cooperation, not in conflict."

Tatyana reached down, splashed a stream of water at Oleg's hand, and doused his flame. "Except there's that."

He smiled. "There is that." He shook off his hand and wiped the damp on his trousers, watching Tatyana's eyes follow his hand to his thigh. Then her eyes drifted to his cock, which decided to stand at attention again now that she was admiring it.

"Do you want to learn about your amnis?" he asked. "Or do you want to fuck me? I am open to either option tonight."

Her cheeks didn't blush like they used to, but he could see the mortification in her expression.

"I'm sorry," she said.

"Don't be."

Tatyana shook her head. "I can't seem to control... anything. I'm not thinking clearly and my reaction to you is just—"

"Normal." He tried to make his voice as neutral as possible, even though the part of him that wanted her was tempted to crow in victory. "We were not indifferent to each other when you were human, Tatyana. Now you are immortal. *All* your appetites are ravenous with new power." He snapped his fingers again. "For now pay attention."

"Will you stop snapping at me?" She snarled. "I hate it."

Oleg walked over to her, held his hand in front of her face, and snapped, sparking a tiny amount of static electricity that his amnis grabbed and fed until the flame was the size of Tatyana's head.

"We may not have the same element," he murmured, "but we both have amnis. You need to become aware of yours and learn how to control it."

She crossed her arms over her chest again. "I don't feel anything like that... snapping. Or sparking."

"Yes, you do."

"I don't." She was getting angry. She was a newborn—even the slightest provocation could send her into a rage.

"It's running under your skin right now." He kept his voice calm. "It connects to the water in the air, even in your own body."

He saw the water in the fountain begin to move, pulling toward Tatyana as her emotions heightened.

Oleg glanced at the water. "Do you feel it now?"

"I don't—"

"Don't say *think*," he hissed. "Don't *think* about it. Feel. Stop thinking like a human when you're a vampire."

"I don't want to be a vampire!" She threw her arm out and the water in the fountain followed her motion, leaping from the pool and dashing him across the face as his flame went out.

Oleg grinned, and he knew his fangs were out. "Good."

Tatyana looked at her hands, shaking her head. "I don't know how I did that."

"The water is drawn to you. It *wants* to obey you."

"How?"

"Feel. It." In the blink of an eye, he was in her face. The water had drenched him, and his shirt clung to his body. "You told me once that when I kissed you, it felt like champagne bubbles along your skin."

Tatyana looked up, and her fangs were already long in her mouth. "I don't remember that."

"You'd been drinking." He grabbed her chin, yanked her face up, and kissed her. Hard. "Then you insulted me and I left you alone."

She pulled her head back. "Wait, I do remember that. How did I insult you?"

"*Is this part of the plan?*"

"*Plan?*"

"*To catch Zara? To get your money. Why are you being... sweet?*"

Her suspicion had hurt his feelings, but he wasn't going to tell her that. "You called me sweet. It was insulting."

She narrowed her eyes. "Don't worry, I take it back."

"Good. Do you feel your amnis?"

She looked down at her arms. "I feel... I don't know. There's a... buzzing under my skin. It itches."

He looked at the fireplace on the far side of the room, reached his hand out, and pulled a thread of fire toward them.

"Oleg!"

"The water is right there." He lifted his hand, slowly building the flames into a ring of fire that surrounded both of them.

"What are you doing?"

"If you don't like it, put the fire out," Oleg said. "Use the water."

The flames grew and slowly sucked the air from the room. Oleg's clothes, which had been drenched a moment before, were already bone-dry. Tatyana was looking in every direction at the flames that surrounded them.

"The water is right there, Tatyana."

She was panicking. The flames were growing closer, and she jumped in the low pool of the fountain, her eyes locked on Oleg. "What are you doing?"

An alarm sounded somewhere in the distance.

"The water is right there," he repeated. "Do you feel your amnis?"

"No!"

"Yes, you do."

"Oleg!" She looked around the room cloaked in fire. "Stop! Please stop."

He resisted the urge to give her what she wanted. There would be time to indulge her desires, but now he needed to teach her how to survive.

"The water is crawling up your body, Tatyana. Look down and think."

The fountain surged as she began to panic. "I can't think when you're going to burn us alive!"

"We're not going to burn because you're going to use your amnis. Feel it underneath your skin. Pull the water like a silk sheet over your body."

"Oleg," she cried out. "Please!"

"Grab your amnis and use it!" He roared and lifted his arms, bringing the flames up as tall as the fountain, surrounding both of them in a wall of fire.

Tatyana screamed, but he felt her amnis snap into place as her instincts connected with her element, with the current that lived within her, with the water that leaped to her command.

She lifted her arms and threw her hands out, palms flat against his fire as if she were pushing it back. The water mimicked her, gushing from the base of the fountain in a singular wave that doused the ring of flames Oleg had called, chasing it away and drenching him, the ballroom, and everything around them in the process.

"You crazy bastard!" Tatyana screamed at him, charging toward him, soaked with water and crackling with amnis. "You fucking—"

Oleg caught her around the waist and stopped her mouth with a kiss that bruised his mouth with its ferocity.

She snarled low in her throat, and her fangs cut his lip as she threw her arms around his neck, nearly climbing his body with preternatural desire.

He gripped her braid in one hand and angled her mouth to meet his. Oleg lifted her, gripping her ass and bringing the heat of her pussy to rub against his hard cock; when the bare skin of her hand touched his neck, the contact sizzled and steam enveloped them both.

He pulled her hair and tugged her mouth away, growling at the snap of her teeth as she nearly caught his mouth with her fangs.

"Good." He set her down, ignoring the pain in his groin. "Now do it again."

Chapter Thirty-Five

Tatyana sat on the edge of her bed, staring at the ground and sitting in damp clothes that rasped against her skin but somehow felt soothing.

She hated this. She hated all of it.

If there was one thing she detested, it was feeling like an amateur. She worked hard to be competent. Maybe she couldn't be the prettiest or the most popular. Maybe she wasn't good at making friends or dating.

But she was a good student. When she'd been a dancer, she'd worked harder at it than anyone in her class. She took pride in knowing what to do, even when her mother fell apart.

And now she was faced with a situation she could never have been able to plan.

There was a tapping at the door, and she knew immediately it wasn't Oleg. She walked over and cracked it open, only to see Oksana standing in the sitting room.

"Oh. Hello."

The soldier was dressed much like Mika dressed most nights, in black cargo pants and a fitted shirt. She wore her hair short and cropped close on the sides with a delightfully unmanaged curly mop on top of her head that fell into her eyes, softening the severe cut of her uniform.

Tatyana asked, "Is there something—"

"I brought you this." The woman held a pile of black and white clothing. "I convinced my mate to lend you some of her clothes. Ludmila isn't usually very sharing, but you're much closer to her size than mine."

It was a small kindness, but one that Tatyana could appreciate. "Please tell her I said thank you."

"I will."

Tatyana took the clothes, but Oksana stood at her doorway with her hands in her pockets. "Was there something else?"

"If you ever want to get a drink or something," the woman said. "Just let me know. There are so many men around here, and sometimes the testosterone…" She shook her head.

"It's like it permeates the air." Tatyana clutched the clothing to her damp chest. "I'm glad I'm not imagining it."

Oksana cracked a laugh. "You're not."

Tatyana wanted to ask her more, but she already felt like she was intruding. Oksana was a serious soldier, a mated vampire, and she clearly had her life sorted out.

And Tatyana?

She was walking around in wet socks and sort of enjoying the sensation.

Oksana smiled. "You'll get it."

"Am I that transparent?"

"It's not that. We were all there once. Even him."

Tatyana did not need to ask who "him" was.

"Thank you." She lifted the clothes. "I'll try to remember that the next time he tries to burn me alive."

"He wouldn't though." Oksana narrowed her eyes. "You know that, right?"

Did she?

"I think so?"

"Oleg is..." Oksana pursed her lips. "He's complicated. But you'll figure him out. And just so you know, there's a reason that so many of us are loyal to him."

"Why is that?"

Oksana took a step back and smiled. "I think you'll have to figure that out for yourself." She headed toward the door. "Let me know if you need more clothes, but I think yours will be coming tomorrow night."

Chapter Thirty-Six

Oleg strolled along the back terrace that overlooked what Luana had once called his moon garden. The shape of the garden mimicked a crescent moon that curved out from the house, its tips leading to winding paths through the evergreen forest behind the house.

The lushness of the moon garden reflected the climate of the subtropical coast, and the plants looked more like a Mediterranean paradise than a formal European garden.

Fragrant citrus trees mingled with waving palm trees that wintered over thanks to the microclimate that survived even on top of the hill overlooking the sea.

Wrought iron arches crawled with fragrant, white-blossomed jasmine. Carefully clipped gardenias and camellias lined the pathways. All the flowers were white, heavily fragrant, and luminous under moonlight.

Now the whisper of the wind through the pine trees was joined by the cooing of six pigeons Tatyana's mother had sent her from home.

When Tatyana had told him the birds were coming, he felt an unexpected lightness in his chest. It pleased Oleg that she would keep pets in his home, and he immediately ordered supplies to build a large aviary and a dovecote at the back of the garden in a sunny spot that would be warm enough for the birds but sheltered from the wild animals that lived in the forest.

He and Mika had finished the structure in a matter of hours with the help of his brother Lazlo, just in time for the truck from Sevastopol to arrive with two heavy chests of Zara's gold, the birds from Tatyana's mother, and more homemade food than half a dozen vampires could eat in a week.

Tatyana had let the birds loose in the aviary and spent two hours sitting with them and whispering secrets as he tried not to listen in.

When she'd returned to the house before dawn, her expression seemed slightly more relaxed, and Oleg had been encouraged to see peace on her face instead of anger.

But that night as he walked through the moon garden, Oleg heard her crying.

He walked down the path, past the massive reflecting pool in the middle of the garden where a delicate fountain shot water upward in a crescent-shaped fan.

She was leaning against the trunk of the small apple tree, staring at the ground where his old gardener's body had been found on the night he came for her.

"My little wolf," he whispered. His heart ached because there was nothing that pierced the immortal soul like the sting of regret.

Oleg walked over, and just as Tatyana was turning, he bent down, picked her up in his arms, and cradled her in his lap.

"Oleg, I don't have the energy to fight with you right now."

"Stop." He pressed his lips to her temple. "No lessons tonight."

He had spent the past week teaching Tatyana the basics of using her amnis. He'd taught her to draw it over her skin like a shield. He'd watched as she learned the beginnings of control over her instincts, calling on the water with clumsy but potent power.

Every moment had been like pulling teeth.

His little bookkeeper was resistant to mental manipulation of any kind now that she had an immortal mind. She was stubborn, determined, and defiant.

And frightened.

"No lessons tonight," he repeated, pressing her head to his shoulder. "Let me be sweet with you."

She sighed and pressed her tearstained face against his shoulder. "I thought that was an insult."

"Only when I'm trying to seduce you."

"Don't try to make me laugh when I want to die."

The air caught in his lungs.

Oleg had a sudden vision of Tatyana, her skin smoking and her glorious blue eyes turning black in the sun's hateful light. The image was so repulsive that he felt fire whispering in his ear.

Lock her away.

It is for her own good.

His urge to possess her was growing stronger every night.

Oleg forced himself to breathe calmly. "Don't say things like that."

"I was walking through the garden and then all of a sudden I was here. And all I could think was: I killed an innocent man, and I don't even remember doing it. I'm a monster."

"If you'd been conscious enough to remember, you wouldn't have done it." He kissed her temple again. "It is not your fault."

"You told me that even when I'm not out of my mind with hunger, bloodlust can still overwhelm me, so how do I know—"

"Tatyana, stop." He shook her a little bit. "Even in the worst throes of bloodlust, you will still be you. I know you would never have harmed my groundskeeper if you had any kind of control over yourself."

She let out a shuddering breath but relaxed in his arms. "He's still dead."

"And I am not happy about that. But he had a long life. He was a grumpy bastard who was brilliant at pruning fruit trees and had no patience for self-pity, so stop saying you want to die. It won't bring him back to life."

She slid an arm around his waist and snuggled closer. "Don't be sweet with me."

Oleg grunted. "I will be sweet if I want to be sweet."

"You shouldn't."

He held her close and turned.

"Where are you taking me?"

"Out of the garden." He had something in mind, and if that couldn't put a smile on her face, he would have to stoop to asking Oksana for advice.

He didn't want to ask Oksana.

"I have something to show you," he said.

"I can walk."

"I know you can." He carried her toward the house. "But why walk when I am willing to carry you?"

He pushed the door open with his foot, setting Tatyana inside as he went to light the lamps that would illuminate the space properly. "Have you ever heard of the Amber Room?"

In the darkness, he heard her suck in a breath. "The room made entirely of amber panels in the Catherine Palace in Saint Petersburg?"

"I saw the original room once." He lit an oil lamp set into a niche in the wall, and gold light filled the space. "Before it was destroyed by idiotic humans."

Tatyana slowly walked to the center of the room. "I thought they reconstructed it."

"The reconstruction is not terrible, but the amber doesn't have the same quality as the original." He walked to the next lamp. They were set at even intervals around the room. "Now *this* is not a reconstruction—"

"Oleg." Her voice was breathless. "What is it?"

He lit the last lamp and turned to see her spinning in the center of the room. "This was inspired by the Amber Room, but it is my own creation."

Like the original Amber Room, the walls had been layered in gold, but instead of a pure amber overlay, Oleg had envisioned an amber glass mosaic that danced in the candlelight, a garden of mosaic flowers illuminated by flame and mirror so that every part of the room appeared lit from behind by sunlight.

"Oh my God. It's so beautiful." She wiped tears from her eyes. "Why is it so beautiful?"

"Because you see more now than you ever could as a mortal."

Oleg closed the door and latched it so they wouldn't be disturbed. Then he went to the center of the room where Tatyana was turning in place, taking in every corner of the exquisitely decorated room.

He wanted to make her smile. He wanted to make her think of anything but ending her newly immortal life.

Oleg took her hand and lifted it over her head, then spun her around. "Do you still dance?"

She looked up at him, her eyes swimming a little from the unexpected spin. "What?"

"When you were a child, you studied dance. One does not simply stop being a dancer because their mother cannot afford classes." He spun her again. "Do you still dance?"

She frowned. "No."

"Why not?"

"Because I became a bookkeeper, not a ballerina."

Oleg kept her fingers woven with his. "Take off your shoes."

"What?"

"You're wearing stockings, yes?"

"I'm wearing socks."

"Take off your shoes."

She toed them off, and Oleg kicked them to the edge of the room. "*Releve.*"

Tatyana's back stiffened, and she rose onto the ball of one foot, the other knee bent with her foot braced against her leg.

Holding her hand, Oleg pulled her arm gently away from her body and into second position. Her posture remained erect as Oleg walked her around, twirling her in the center of the glittering room like a tiny figurine in a jeweled box.

She lifted her eyes to the ceiling, watching the play of candlelight and shadow in the golden room, watching herself move in the mirrored panels that reflected the light.

She was wearing loose pants and an old T-shirt, but she was luminous. Exquisite.

"You don't stop being human when you become immortal," Oleg said. "If anything, it makes you *more* human, not less."

He didn't stop turning her, and her body, newly fortified by amnis and elemental power, didn't tire.

"Your senses are greater. Your desire is greater. Your appetite is *greater*." Oleg stopped and walked toward her, drawing her hand to his chest.

His heart wanted to thump. He could feel the cold organ warming at the feeling of her touch. *What are you doing, you sentimental fool?*

The enchanted expression on Tatyana's face made him ignore the voice in his head telling him to keep his distance.

She relaxed her feet to standing and her blue eyes were glittering. "I haven't done that in years."

"This room took me over a hundred years to make. I *couldn't* have completed it exactly to my vision if I was human."

Oleg kept his eyes on hers and saw her mouth form a small O. *Do you understand now, little wolf?*

"You didn't choose this life," he continued, "but you can make the most of it if you want. You can dance on mountaintops and pirouette on the seafloor. But you cannot do any of that if you live in regret or wish that you were dead."

He couldn't tear his eyes away from hers. Her clear blue gaze captured him, and the careful words he'd been about to say caught in his throat. A strange, creeping awareness teased the edges of his mind.

Deep behind the cage of his ribs, Oleg's heart gave a single thump. "Tatyana Vorona, I would see you dance."

She stood on her toes again, but this time she offered her mouth to him in a slow, velvet kiss that stirred his blood and drenched him in heat.

Careful.

Careful.

She was stronger now; he couldn't break her.

But can she break you?

Tatyana seduced his mouth, her lips moving with aching tenderness as she learned the curves and lines of his kiss.

She had no elemental control, so when her amnis crawled from her body and slid over his skin, Oleg hissed in pleasure, ignoring the unconscious intrusion of her energy into his.

Her amnis was as eager as her mouth.

His cock roared to life, thrilled by the naive intimacy as her power curled and melded with his own.

Tatyana had no idea how forward and how vulnerable she was being. If Oleg had his way, she would never know. He would bind her to him so thoroughly, she would never want another lover and never know what she'd offered him in innocence.

She opened herself to him, and his amnis slipped along her own, thrilling with the slow, sensual caress of power against power.

Her amnis was fresh and cool, like fog covering a banked fire. He lifted her shirt and pressed his hands to her back. "I want skin."

His fangs were down when she lifted her arms and he pulled the shirt over her head, leaving her in nothing but a thin satin slip that did nothing to hide her breasts.

Oleg picked her up and walked to the wall where candlelight illuminated the glass and the mirror mosaic, reflecting her bare skin as he drew the satin up and over her head.

She shivered in the cool night air, her nipples coming to hard little points, so he covered them with his mouth and brought the fire to his skin, heating both of them with his body.

Tatyana gasped and arched her back against the wall, pushing her breast into his mouth as he teased one with his tongue and the other with clever fingers that had spent too many months imagining this single act to rush.

"Do you like that?" He scraped his fangs along the rise of her breast. "Tell me what you like."

"I can't."

Her breath was already coming in pants, and Oleg knew she'd never felt pleasure like this because—like all her senses—this sensual storm was heightened. Her nerves were exquisitely tuned to his energy, and he was going to linger, taking full advantage of her newly primed responses.

He lifted his head and licked the top of his tongue along her collarbone. "I'm going to taste you properly now."

She tried to reach for his cock, but Oleg wasn't ready to let her out of his control.

"Not yet." He pressed her wrists to her sides. "Keep them there, or we stop."

The intimacy was so intense Oleg knew he was going to have trouble controlling his fire. His element was sparking on his skin, and she didn't have the control yet to counter him should his fire come to life.

But she would. Soon, she would.

Kneeling in front of her, he slipped his thumbs in the waistband of her leggings and pulled them down.

The scent of her arousal, potent before, enveloped him, and he growled low in his throat, lapping his tongue up the inside of her thigh as she trembled.

"Lift." He patted one leg and she raised it, allowing him to toss the leggings across the room. Oleg looked up, and Tatyana rose above him like a goddess, her gold hair falling over her shoulders and her skin lit with amber glass, mirrors, and candlelight.

She was breathtaking.

"Some night I am going to draw you like this." He trailed a single finger down the inside of her thigh as her body melted in pleasure. "You will stand just like this, and I will draw you."

"Please," she whispered. "I can't—"

"Yes, you can." He lifted her leg and put it over his shoulder, baring her sex to him, and then he didn't make her wait any longer.

Oleg feasted on her, gripping her ass and lifting the wet center of her desire into his mouth, lapping at her folds until the pointed tip of his tongue reached her clitoris and her amnis went wild.

She reached out, gripping his hair in her fists as her body exploded in pleasure. She sobbed, and he drank in the sounds of her climax, reveling in the burst of elemental energy that drew to her. The water in the room clung to her skin and spread over his, turning to steam as his body heated.

She cried out, "Enough!"

It wasn't enough, but if he kept eating her, he wouldn't stop.

Oleg pulled away from her pussy and looked up, licking his lips as he met her pleasure-flooded eyes. He tapped the inside of her thigh, just to the left of where her flesh was soft and full. "I'm going to bite you." He licked at the spot. "Just here. If you don't want me to—"

"Yes." Her lips were full and swollen with blood. Her fangs were long in her mouth.

Oleg struck without a second of hesitation, sinking his fangs into the soft flesh as the shock of her pleasure made Tatyana fall forward.

He caught her, lowering her to the ground even as he continued to drink her in.

Too much. Too much.

He felt her amnis mingle with his own.

Dangerous. Tempting. This was how blood bonds were formed.

He pierced his tongue, healing the small wounds with the blood on his tongue before he licked up her body, cleaning every drop from her thighs and her sex before he kissed her belly, her breasts, and back to her mouth.

She was drunk with pleasure as she reached for him, but he was still fully clothed.

He stood and stripped off his linen shirt and wool trousers, catching the hungry stare she sent his cock when it sprang from the confinement of his undergarments.

Oleg smiled and gripped it in his fist, shaking his head a little bit. "Ah-ah." He knelt down beside her. "You don't get your mouth on that until you can control your fangs a little better, volchitsa."

The corner of her mouth ticked up. "Fair."

She was so beautiful in that moment Oleg forgot to breathe.

Stretched across the wooden floor, lying on her side so the round curve of her bottom was mirrored back at him from a dozen angles and her breasts glowed in the gold light.

"You're beautiful."

She didn't hesitate. "So are you."

Oleg lay next to Tatyana and pulled her body over his. "The floor is cold."

"I didn't even notice," she whispered, staring at his mouth.

She was energy drunk, feeling her amnis stirring in his body as their elements mingled together. It was startling intimacy and a boundary that immortal lovers rarely crossed unless they were mated.

But Tatyana didn't know that.

He lifted her and she braced her hands on his chest, leaning forward so her breasts made his mouth water to taste her again. But his cock was screaming for relief, so he lifted her, angled her over his aching erection, and slowly invaded the waiting heat of her body.

Bliss.

Oleg closed his eyes, willing his climax to hold off until he could make her come again.

"Ride me." He gripped her hips with his hands and moved her body up and down his shaft. Once she had a steady rhythm, he kept one hand on her hip while he brought his other over to stroke the swollen bead of her clitoris with his thumb.

"Oh God." She shook her head. "I can't. Not again."

"Yes, you can." Tension was building at the base of his cock and his balls were tight and ready to come, but he held off, waiting for her to climax again.

He reached for her hand on his chest, keeping the rhythm of his thumb steady as he brought her wrist to his mouth and licked along the delicate, blue-veined skin, imagining what her fangs would feel like at his neck.

The urge to feel her teeth break his skin only ratcheted up the fire sweeping through his body. No one had bitten Oleg since Luana. Imagining Tatyana's teeth in his neck was a riotous thought.

"Oleg?" Her body began to shake, and the water in the room drew to her skin again, drenching her as it dripped on Oleg's bare body and steam rose in curling puffs where their flesh met.

The room was filled with a gold mist when Oleg slowly slid his fangs into Tatyana's wrist, lapping at her vein as her body exploded again. She convulsed in pleasure, and he let his climax rip loose.

He threw his head back and released months of pent-up energy in a surge of elemental power. The flames in the candles grew until they nearly reached the gilded ceiling, and his hips arched, driving deeper into Tatyana's body as flames burst to life over his shoulders.

Her energy rose up and matched his with unexpected control. Mist fell over them both, dousing the fire before it could burn out of control. Tatyana's climax continued to roll through her in a slow wave as she fell forward, her skin sizzling against Oleg's when she collapsed on his chest.

Oleg's mind was spinning in pleasure, release, and silent shock. His amnis twined with Tatyana's in a spiral that wrapped around them both and pulled so tight that it nearly choked him.

The fire was churning through his veins, confused and delighted by the revelation of Tatyana's amnis spinning through his system.

He felt everything. Her pleasure, her fear, her desire and the aching need for tenderness. Her energy whispered along his own, and his amnis embraced it without reservation, without doubt, and without reserve. She was in his blood, and his element didn't only accept her.

It demanded more.

"That was..." She kissed the skin on his chest, just where his heart gave a reluctant thump. "I don't have words."

Neither did he. Oleg grunted something under his breath and put his arms around the delicate woman who curled onto his chest and released a deep sigh.

The woman who might have just destroyed him.

Chapter Thirty-Seven

Tatyana woke the following night with electricity in her veins and a new resolve to make her life—whatever it was going to be—work for her. She sat up in bed, looking at her body for marks Oleg might have left, but there was nothing. No bruises, no scrapes from stubble against skin.

Her body had healed itself as she slept, and the only evidence of sex with Oleg was a new hum in her blood, as if the amnis that animated her had been fed by his own.

For a moment after their sexual storm, she had panicked, keenly aware that she'd abandoned herself to pleasure in a way she'd never done before.

She'd wanted Oleg for months. He'd teased her in the backs of cars, drugged her with gentle kisses at odds with his gruff persona. And last night, as he spun her around in the Amber Room, she'd finally been able to imagine it.

What could her life be? What could she do?

Was this what freedom felt like?

It was a heady drug combined with potent, nearly animalistic desire for the vampire who had been her captor *and* her protector.

So Tatyana had taken what she wanted. There had been no caution or calculation. No careful weighing of consequences as she'd done as a human.

No condom.

She stopped breathing for a moment.

No condom because she could not get pregnant from a vampire. Nor could she carry a baby. Ever.

There was a twisting ache in her chest when she realized that—despite her own complicated relationship with her mother—she'd wanted to have children of her own. Someday. She'd never thought about it with any seriousness. She wasn't married, and she'd never been in a long-term relationship.

Motherhood was something she'd pushed to the back of her mind, and she was a little surprised how hurt she was at the thought of losing the chance.

You could have died, and you didn't. You should be grateful.

Her mother's practical advice slapped her out of her reverie.

New life. Immortal life. The idea of family had to die if she was going to move forward.

"I could have died. I should be grateful," she whispered. Even though being grateful for her immortal life meant being grateful to the woman who nearly murdered her, she was going to try.

Zara.

A wave of irrational longing grabbed her by the throat. She closed her eyes and remembered the feel of Zara's hands braiding her hair.

"I love your hair."

They were sitting in Tatyana's bedroom, and Zara was looking over her shoulder as Tatyana worked on the books.

"Do you? I like your curls." Tatyana glanced over her shoulder and saw Zara playing with the ends of her blond hair. "I always wanted curly hair. My grandfather had curly hair, but I take after my mother and my grandmother."

"I can tell." Zara heaved a huge sigh and pulled at Tatyana's blond ponytail. "I should shave your head while you're sleeping and make myself a wig."

Tatyana laughed. "Oh, I'm sure that would look beautiful."

"Let me braid it for you." Zara scooted closer and tugged at the hairband around her ponytail. "I'm very good at braiding."

"Oh?" Tatyana felt a silly burst of pleasure.

On most nights Zara could be mercurial and demanding, but every now and then they'd share a night like this when Tatyana could imagine they were two friends. It felt like being back at university in the dormitories.

"Yes, I'm an excellent braider." Zara loosened Tatyana's ponytail and combed her fingers through her hair. "I used to braid my girlfriend's hair. She had beautiful blond hair like you." Zara's voice grew soft. "She looked a little bit like you. Maybe that's why I noticed you at the club that night."

"Your girlfriend?" Tatyana's cheeks grew warm. She had known girls in school who preferred women to men, but they weren't open about it.

"You didn't know that I prefer women?" Zara asked. "I'm not coming on to you, by the way. You're my employee, so that would be stupid."

"Right." Tatyana laughed a little bit. "Where is she? Your girlfriend. Are you still together?"

Zara's hands moved quickly through Tatyana's hair. "No, she died. She was far too young, but she died."

Tatyana's heart ached. "Zara, that's terrible. I'm so sorry."

"Thank you." Her voice was soft. "I can tell that you mean that." Zara's fingers rested briefly on Tatyana's shoulder. "I miss her every night."

"How long has it been?"

Zara let out a long breath, her fingers still moving through Tatyana's hair. "Years. But then sometimes I wake up and think she's right next to me."

"I'm so sorry. I can't imagine losing someone like that."

"You will though." Zara's voice grew clipped, and she reached for the hairband on Tatyana's desk, twisting it around whatever braid she'd created. "We all lose people. You lost your grandparents. You'll lose your mother someday. Death is inevitable."

"I suppose you're right." Tatyana could feel the turn in Zara's mood the way a flock of birds wheeled and changed direction in the sky.

She stared ahead, busying herself with the numbers on her computer. "The business is doing well. Your second quarter numbers are really impressive."

"Yes." Zara's voice was cold again. She stood and walked to the door. "I'm too busy to stay here all night talking with you. Finish the accounts and send the printouts to me. Call the regular number."

Moments later, Tatyana heard the front door of the apartment close, and everything was silent again.

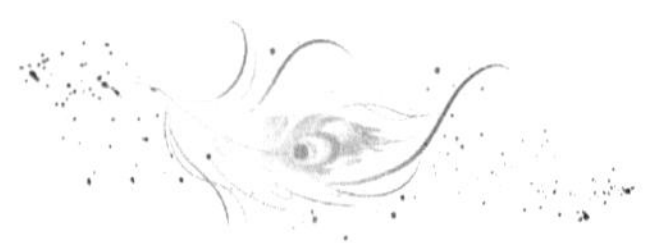

Tatyana pulled her long ponytail over her shoulder and tugged it hard. Zara was her sire, she reminded herself. Oleg said it was normal to feel this affection. It was a result of her amnis, not because she had gone insane or was suffering a mental breakdown.

There was a tapping at the door, and a woman's voice roused Tatyana from her memories.

"Tatyana?"

It was Oksana.

It was *not* Oleg, who had carried her back to her room before dawn and left her alone. She didn't know how she felt about that. Maybe she didn't feel anything.

Or maybe... a little bit of relief?

She was still processing what had happened in the Amber Room, and she wasn't sorry that he'd left her on her own. Being anywhere near Oleg was consuming in a way that still frightened her. As much as she wanted him, that desire was tempered with caution.

Her body and her amnis were reckless for Oleg, hungry for him.

Her mind?

Eh, she could wait.

"Tatyana?" Oksana's voice came again. "Are you well?"

"Yes." She stood and threw on a robe. "I'm awake."

"I have your blood. Oleg says you must drink at least a liter before you leave your quarters."

Tatyana was undoubtedly thirsty, but even in two weeks of vampire life, the burning at the back of her throat had lessened. She felt more in control. More rational.

Except for the random longing for her homicidal maniac sire, of course.

Tatyana walked to the door and opened it to see Oksana standing with a silver carafe.

"You're not snapping at my hands," the other woman said. "Progress."

Tatyana had to smile. "Thank you." Suddenly she realized something. "Oksana, you're a water vampire."

"I am." Oksana smiled. "Are you looking for a few pointers?"

"From someone who has the same element and isn't always snapping his annoying fingers at me?" Tatyana raised an eyebrow. "What do you think?"

"Finally! It's past time that you asked." She pointed to the carafe. "Drink your blood and get dressed. We can work in the ballroom."

Tatyana and Oksana worked for hours, and while the older vampire's lessons weren't as explosive as Oleg's, Tatyana's analytical mind ate them up. It helped that while no one even came close to her when she was training with Oleg, the moment she started working with Oksana, a small crowd formed along the edge of the ballroom.

Far from being intimidating, the vampires who watched them often called out encouragement or clapped when Tatyana did something correctly.

"Well done!"

"She's sharp."

"Not terrible for a newborn."

The last compliment came from a stocky man with a long beard who leaned in the doorway. He looked older than the others, and he was significantly shorter. His arms and legs looked powerful, and Tatyana didn't know how she knew, but the man wasn't a water vampire and he was far older than any other vampire in the room.

If Tatyana had to guess, she'd say he was an earth vampire, though she had no idea what instinct told her his element or his age.

"Explosions of amnis are powerful, and right now you have a lot of energy because you're young," Oksana explained, ignoring the audience around them. "Energy is good. Control is better."

"Okay." She nodded. "Control."

"You want to work toward a whisper, not a shout." Oksana stood beside Tatyana and raised her hand, putting Tatyana's right palm against her own. "Feel my amnis?"

She nodded, and her own energy immediately reached for Oksana's.

"Rude," the woman snapped.

Tatyana pulled her hand back. "Sorry."

"It's fine." Oksana grabbed her hand again. "What you did? It's like going up and hugging a stranger. Think of your amnis as an extension of your body. It's there to protect you and to feel others out. But you meet someone and you don't go up and kiss their face, do you?"

She felt a burning embarrassment. "Did I just kiss your face?"

Oksana gave her a wink. "I promise I won't tell Ludmila."

A low rumble of laughter from around the room, but once again it was congenial, not scornful.

"Don't worry," someone called. "We've all tried to kiss Oksana one time or another."

"Until she mated Ludmila, and now we're afraid of a bullet to the back of the head." More laughter from the edges of the room.

Their lesson continued, and after several hours, Tatyana was starting to droop and her throat began to burn.

Oksana tapped her chin. "Your body can't get tired anymore, but your amnis can." She nodded to the fountain. "Go sit in the fountain and recharge."

"Sit in the...?" She looked over her shoulder, then down at the sweatpants and T-shirt she was wearing. "Really?"

"If you want to get naked, no one will care and you'll recharge faster."

Tatyana glanced at the line of four men and two women standing along the wall of the ballroom. "I don't think I'm *that* comfortable with everyone yet."

Oksana laughed and clapped her on the shoulder. "At least take off your shoes. I'm going to go check on the perimeter with this gang. I'll have someone send over another liter of blood."

"Thank you." She walked over to the marble fountain in the center of the ballroom and sat on the edge, leaning down to take off her shoes before she sank her feet into the cold water.

The relief and refreshment were nearly instant.

She closed her eyes and felt her amnis react to her element like a dry plant sucking up moisture through the roots. A moment later she smelled fresh blood at the door, and her head swung toward the scent.

The stocky vampire paused, lifting one eyebrow before he spoke to her in Russian with a heavy accent. "Your senses are good for a newborn."

"Thank you?"

The older man grunted. "I'm Lazlo."

"Tatyana Vorona."

He set the silver carafe on the marble ledge where Tatyana was sitting. "I'm Oleg's brother. I live in the forest behind the house."

"Really?"

"Yes," he growled. "And I'm older than him, so if you want to complain about his manners, talk to me."

Tatyana couldn't stop her smile. The vampire was dark-haired and olive-skinned. He appeared to be in middle age, but for vampires that could mean anything. Elene had once told her the older a vampire looked, the younger they might have been when they were turned since people historically aged so much faster.

Elene didn't know how old Oleg had been in his human life, but since he appeared to be in his forties, he was probably only in his twenties or thirties when he was changed.

Tatyana held her hand out to Lazlo and snapped. "That thing he does when he wants your attention."

"The snapping?" The older vampire grimaced. "It makes me want to grab my axe."

"*Yes*. Every time."

"He's an annoying shit. But we pay attention to it because..." He shrugged. "Who knows? Because we do."

"At least I know he doesn't only do it to me." Tatyana angled herself toward Lazlo as she took the carafe of blood. She was too hungry to be polite, so she simply twisted off the top and drank straight from the pitcher.

It wasn't delicate, but she was too thirsty to care.

"You have an appetite." Lazlo grunted. "That's good. Sometimes the young ones? They are too busy mourning their old life to care for themselves. They pine and complain. It's very annoying."

"Is it common? To pine like that?"

He sat next to her, leaving his feet outside the fountain. "Not so much anymore. Now the world is more civilized. It's not typical for a vampire to be turned against their will like you were." He lifted a finger. "I'm sorry I didn't find you before you killed Gregor. Oleg says you feel guilty about that."

"Yes." She wished he hadn't brought it up, but maybe it was a good reminder. "I'm going to have to live for eternity knowing that I'm a murderer."

"I mean, eternity is optimistic." Lazlo shrugged. "Aim for twenty years of this and see how you feel then. You can always walk into the sun. Or ask someone to behead you—that's probably less painful than burning."

"Right." Tatyana felt strangely comforted by the older man's morbid ruminations. It felt more honest than people painting a rosy picture of living life in darkness. "How about you? What made you decide to live?"

"My brothers." Lazlo curled his lip. "Mostly the one you're having sex with."

"Oh God." She put the carafe to her lips again and gulped the blood, which had cooled and coagulated a little bit. "You really have to drink blood fresh, don't you?"

"It's much better when you do." His bushy mustache twitched. "Everyone knows about you and Oleg. Don't feel embarrassed about it."

"Okay." She finished the carafe of blood and wiped her mouth with the back of her hand. "Did he say something?"

"No, everyone can smell him on you."

"Right." And now she wanted to bury herself in the garden and remain there for around twenty years. "Good to know."

He pointed at the door. "Half of Mika's crew are having sex with each other. Oksana and Ludmila are the only ones mated. Most vampires view it as an amusing way to pass the time when you're bored. Don't be too human about it."

Oh right. Well, that probably shouldn't be surprising. And it left her with a fresh perspective on Oleg. "Good to know."

"My brother though?" Lazlo squinted. "He's odd."

What did that mean?

Tatyana turned toward the rough man. "You really don't need to tell me... anything. About Oleg. I know..."

Lazlo looked amused. "What do you know? Or think you know?"

Honestly, not much.

"He kept me from dying," Tatyana said softly. "I guess right now that's all I need from him."

Lazlo nodded. "He does that."

"Keeps people from dying?"

"He puts things back together," the old vampire said. "Broken things." He narrowed his eyes. "Are you broken?"

None of your business.

Tatyana forced a smile. "Isn't everyone?"

Lazlo picked up the empty carafe and stood. "Probably yes." He lifted it and gave Tatyana a small salute. "You're alive, Tatyana Vorona. You should stay that way for a while. No need to make any rash decisions."

TATYANA DIDN'T SEE OLEG THAT NIGHT, AND SHE WONDERED IF the man was avoiding her after a long night of very passionate sex or if she was putting too much importance on it and he was simply busy.

She got half an answer when she walked out of the ballroom after her last hour with Oksana and nearly ran into Mika Arakis.

"Oleg is away from the house," he said. "In case you were wondering."

"Okay." She wasn't going to tell him she had been. It was none of his business, and she didn't have the warmest regard for the Estonian vampire who hadn't kept Elene and her alive.

It seemed like Mika was having thoughts along the same lines. "For the record, I am deeply sorry that you and Elene were taken by Zara's people. I take full responsibility for that failure."

She hadn't expected *that.*

Tatyana looked over Mika's shoulder to avoid his unnerving gaze.

She couldn't forget what Oleg had told her. That Mika had loved Elene deeply for many years. "She didn't blame you if that's what you were wondering. She said it was her fault. That she didn't think Zara would have so many people working with her."

"I see."

Now they were both avoiding each other's eyes, and Tatyana was fine with that.

"Also for the record, I think Oleg should send you to the citadel for a year to let you recover and train. You have little to no survival skills for our world, and it would be best, but he is ignoring my advice."

What Mika suggested sounded a lot like being locked up. "Well... I'm working on the survival skills. Oksana has been helping me train."

Mika nodded sharply. "She is very competent. I'll get a report from her on your progress. Let me know what kind of weapons training you would prefer and I will arrange it."

"Uh..." She frowned. "Weapons?"

"You're small, so some light sword training would probably be advantageous to increase your reach. Judo would also be good. Oleg prefers an axe, but he's a barbarian."

Tatyana shook her head. "I feel completely lost in this entire exchange. Can you get me a computer or smart phone that won't blow up in my hands? That's about the only kind of weapon I have any experience using."

Mika cocked his head. "I can."

Tatyana blinked. "Seriously?"

"There are devices made for us now. They are not elegant like your human electronics, but you would be able to use them with the proper precautions."

"That's the kind of weapon I want then." She held out her hand to shake his.

Mika reluctantly reached out his hand and allowed Tatyana to pump it up and down. "I don't like shaking hands."

"Well, I don't like drinking blood." She let his hand go. "Get me a computer and a smartphone that I can use with an internet connection, and I'll forgive you for letting me die."

Mika sneered. "Fine."

"Good."

He looked at her with narrowed eyes. "I don't know what you and Oleg are, but if you act cruelly toward him, I will finish the job that Zara started."

Tatyana blinked. "You're giving me the 'if you hurt my friend, I'll kill you' speech?"

"Yes."

"You're giving that to *me?*"

Mika nodded and said nothing else.

Tatyana lifted a hand and shook her head. "Everything in my life is officially backward." She started walking back to her room. "Light is dark. Up is down. Night is day."

"Drink the rest of your blood before dawn," Mika called down the hallway.

"I was going to do that anyway," she said. "So when I do it, do not think it was because you told me to."

Chapter Thirty-Eight

Oleg returned to the house before dawn, just in time to see Lazlo slipping into the forest and a carful of human guards pull up to the house. Though it was unwise for mortals to be around Tatyana during the night, he refused to leave the house unguarded during the day.

He walked into the entryway and looked for Mika, who was waiting for him.

"Is she locked away?"

"She drank the rest of her blood and locked her door half an hour ago," he said.

"I'll give them the signal." Oleg walked back to the front door and waved at the van full of humans before he ducked back inside to avoid the swiftly lightening horizon. "I'm sorry it took so long. Did you tell Tatyana that I needed to go into town to meet with Ivan's men?"

His brothers in Moscow were growing more and more arrogant, and steps would have to be taken to clamp down on them soon.

Soon, but not that night.

"I told her you were gone. She was working with Oksana."

"Ah." Oleg nodded. "Good. That's an excellent idea."

"The others are saying that the bookkeeper catches on quickly and has good instincts."

Oleg nodded as he walked down the hallway toward his office. "Her mind is keen, and that matters more in immortality than muscles or strength."

The corridors and rooms near his day chamber were light safe with heavy metal shutters that would allow him an extra couple of hours before he needed to rest. He was old enough that dawn didn't pull him under immediately; he just needed to avoid daylight.

"I should ask her what kind of weapon training she wants," Oleg said. "She doesn't know her own strength yet."

"She said her weapons of choice are a computer and a smartphone."

The corner of his mouth turned up. "Amusing, but no."

Simply by virtue of wielding amnis, Tatyana was faster, stronger, and had better reflexes than the most athletic mortal on Earth. She would be able to lift weights that would rival an Olympian, run faster than a sprinter, and take out a human commando with very little effort, but she needed to learn how to use her new body to the greatest effect.

Her new body that he was craving again.

"Clear my schedule for tomorrow night," Oleg said.

Mika was walking behind him. "Fine. I should follow up with my informants in Moscow. What did Basil say?"

"He was blustering, as usual." Oleg threw out his hands. "Ivan is testing my patience."

"He's a problem you'll need to deal with eventually."

"After Zara," Oleg muttered. "One problem at a time."

His brother in Moscow was the head of the Sokolov crime family, and Oleg had done his best to separate himself from their activities while still keeping the worst of their instincts in check.

Oleg couldn't stop them from running drugs, smuggling weapons, or collecting protection money from human and vampire criminal rackets, but he'd cracked down on as much of the human trafficking as he could. The fact that some of it was still going on—while Ivan proclaimed innocence—was an ongoing problem.

"Things seem quiet right now," Oleg said. "Fly to Moscow and talk to people. It may be time to take Ivan out. Or make an example of him to warn the others."

Oleg had been choosy with which of his horrible brothers to keep alive. He didn't want to face a full-scale mutiny when he took out his sire, so he'd allowed Ivan and some of the others to live even though he really didn't want to.

Hundreds of years later, he wished he'd made a different choice.

"I don't want to leave here until Zara is gone," Mika said. "It doesn't seem wise."

Oleg paused at the threshold of his office door. "Do you doubt that I can deal with her?"

"I don't know how many people she has working with her now. Don't be foolish. She knows you're here. Even you could be vulnerable if she storms this house with enough cannon fodder."

He put a hand on Mika's shoulder and pulled his old friend in, kissing his cheek before he patted it and pushed him away. "I appreciate the concern, but she has no money and no more loyal soldiers. Even the Albanian mob won't work for her if she's not paying them."

"Oleg—"

"Clear my schedule for tomorrow night. Then go to Moscow. I want to know what Ivan is plotting and I need your ears."

"Fine, but I'm telling Lazlo and leaving Ludmila with you."

"Good idea." He walked into his office and shut the door behind him.

He wanted Tatyana's blood and sex, but she was sleeping, so he poured himself a few fingers of vodka and sat in a leather chair near a shuttered window that overlooked the garden.

In the distance, he could hear the pigeons cooing in their cote, and the sound made him smile. Such a little, domestic thing. Why did it give him so much pleasure?

The rotary phone on his desk clanged with a metallic ring, and

Oleg reached for the black plastic receiver. Only a few people had this number, so when he put the phone to his ear, he was expecting someone from the citadel. "I'm listening."

"Hello, Papa."

Zara's voice made him freeze.

He allowed the silence to drag across the line.

"Papa?" Zara sounded slightly nervous.

Good.

"Hello, daughter."

"Ah. You *are* there."

"You know exactly where I am."

"Hmm." She laughed a little bit at the back of her throat. "Did you like the present I left for you?"

Oleg had no way of knowing what Zara knew about his and Tatyana's relationship. "You left me a mess. The newborn killed the gardener."

"I would say sorry, but I am not."

"I liked that gardener."

"I know. It's difficult to find good employees. I appreciate that you didn't fire our chef in Sevastopol. She was the only one in her family who was worth a damn, and she had four grandchildren to feed."

"I know; that's why I kept her employed at the house." Oddly enough, Oleg sensed that Zara's concern for the chef was entirely sincere. That was his daughter. She could be surprisingly generous until she wasn't, and it was impossible to predict when her generosity would hit.

"I've been meaning to call since the unpleasantness in Odesa," Zara said. "This is really your fault, you know? You shouldn't have stolen all my money. I worked hard for you, Oleg. That money was more than fair."

He managed not to crush the phone receiver in his grip. "The unpleasantness? You mean your killing Elene?"

"*That* was an accident. She fell over and she was old, Papa."

Zara's voice was whining and childish, a tone she'd used with

Luana when she wanted something. Hearing it brought a rush of memories to his mind.

"It's not my fault that she broke her neck," Zara continued. "I was just asking her questions."

Oleg closed his eyes, picturing Elene's battered face in his mind. "It was entirely your fault, Zara."

"If you were so fond of her, you should have turned her!"

"I should have..." He let out a twisted laugh as his fangs lengthened. "Is that why you turned Tatyana?"

Zara was quiet.

Oleg snapped at her. "Speak!"

"She looks like Luana." Zara's voice was still childish. "I didn't want her to lie there and rot when she looks like Luana."

Oleg said nothing, but a sick, twisting guilt curled in his belly. Elene was dead because of him. Tatyana had lost her mortal life because decades ago he had created a monster to amuse his mentally unstable mate.

All of this was his fault, so he would have to make it right.

He swallowed the bitterness at the back of his throat. "Where are you, Zara?"

"Not close to you."

"You should come back to Sochi." He picked up a pen on his desk and dragged the tip along a piece of paper Mika had left, sketching out a sunflower in the margin of a spreadsheet. "You could spend some time with Tatyana and collect your inheritance."

Zara was silent again. "You brought my gold to Sochi?"

"Maybe I'll give Luana's jewelry to Tatyana instead of you. After all, she's your child and you abandoned her."

"You bastard!" Zara screamed. "You fucking bastard!"

Ah, there she was. The childish pouting was gone, and the sociopath was back. "The sun is rising here, Zara. You should be sleeping, so I think you are to the west, huh? Am I right? How far away? Are you hiding in Kyiv? Playing with your friends in Bucharest?"

A second later his daughter hung up the phone.

He hung up the handset, then quickly lifted it and dialed a different number, waiting for his office at the citadel to pick up.

"Listening," a voice said.

"The call that just came into the Sochi office," he said. "Trace it."

"I will make sure it is done, and I will call you at nightfall."

"Thank you." Oleg hung up the phone.

Then he stared at the sunflower he'd started only to realize the round center of the flower had morphed into a sketch of Tatyana's face.

Chapter Thirty-Nine

Tatyana woke to the scent of Oleg outside her door.

She rose, wrapped herself in a blue silk robe that had appeared in her closet the day before, and walked to the door, opening it and grabbing the silver carafe from his hand.

His eyebrow went up. "May I come in?"

"Yes." She stepped back and allowed him to enter her room, trying to ignore the burst of arousal he elicited just by existing.

"I'm not in control of that." She gulped down the blood as quickly as she could so it didn't cool. "Just so you know."

"I know. I am not a man to make assumptions." He walked to the chair in the corner of the room and sat, perusing the stack of books she'd been reading on the nightstand. "Pushkin poems and Russian fairy tales."

"You don't have many current bestsellers in the library." She finished the carafe of blood and set it to the side, relieved to feel the burn in her throat was even less than the night before. "Old stories from the nineteenth century are about as current as it gets."

Oleg smiled a little bit and picked up the stout, leather-bound collection of old fairy tales. "I need to update the library here. Which one is your favorite?"

Tatyana looked at him. Something about the stoic predator felt sad that night. If she didn't know how dangerous he was, she might even call him fragile.

I don't know what you and Oleg are, but if you act cruelly toward him, I will finish the job that Zara started.

Tatyana walked to the bed and sat on the edge. "My favorite?"

She thought about it. She'd probably read about half the stories in one form or another growing up. Her grandmother had an illustrated copy of the same book at the farm, and she'd spent many nights looking through the pictures even before she could read the stories. "I don't know. Probably 'Ivan, the Firebird, and the Wolf.'"

"Oh?" Oleg kicked his feet up on the footrest by the chair and leaned on the arm of the chair. "Why that one?"

"Because Ivan gets everything he wants in the end and lives happily ever after." She stretched her legs out. "Isn't that the best kind of story? Life is depressing enough. If I'm reading a story, I want a happy ending."

Oleg nodded. "Valid point."

"What about you? Are these your fairy tales? Or did you learn different ones when you were a child?"

"I don't remember being a child," Oleg mused. "Though I must have been once. My human memories are very faint."

"Hmm."

He picked up the book. "But these are good stories. I had a mistress in Saint Petersburg at one time who had four children, and I used to read these stories to them."

"To your mistress's children?" Tatyana tried to imagine the lethal vampire reading fairy tales to children.

"Yes. She was a widow, so the children were part of the arrangement." Oleg paged through the old book. "And I enjoyed spending time with them. The little boy—there were three girls and one boy—I think he must have suspected what I was, because he loved the vampire story in this book."

Tatyana curled her lip. "That's a horrible story."

"I know." Oleg smiled. "Children are so morbid. It's the thing I like most about them. He wanted to hear it over and over. The vampire is killed at the end of the story. I probably should have guessed he would grow up to hate me."

"Why did he hate you?"

"Because I wouldn't marry his mother." Oleg snapped the book shut. "It was better that I didn't, but of course he didn't know that. I had to leave when he was sixteen. I'd been with all of them for too long."

Tatyana nodded. "They would have noticed that you weren't growing older."

"Yes. But I provided for her until she died."

"And your mate didn't mind that you had a mistress?"

He shook his head and set the book back on the table. "Luana had her own interests by then. We had separate lives, but we were still friendly."

"What is your favorite story?" She nodded at the book. "Other than the vampire story."

"'The Giant Turnip,' of course."

Tatyana burst into laughter.

Oleg smiled too. "I can't believe you even had to ask. Get dressed. I have the night off, and there is something I wanted to show you."

"Are we having more lessons tonight?" Her shoulders slumped. "I want a break."

"No lessons." Oleg stood and walked to the edge of the bed, standing in front of her and straddling her legs as he looked down to meet her eyes. "Unless you're in the mood for some very particular lessons about how to control your fangs."

Tatyana held her breath when she saw the length of his erection behind his trousers. Her mouth watered, and she felt her body soften just at the thought of more sex with Oleg.

He's trying to distract you. And himself.

She looked up and met his eyes as she reached out with a single finger and ran it over the hard length covered in merino wool. "Do you know what I really want?"

Oleg's fangs were down when he answered her. "I might be able to guess."

She put her hands on his hips and firmly pushed him back. "A proper tour of the house. This place is as big as a palace, and I'm constantly getting lost."

Oleg's rueful chuckle reassured Tatyana that he was in a playful mood. "I see your teeth are as sharp as ever, little wolf."

"Out, you turnip." She shooed him toward the door. "Let me get dressed and I'll meet you in the hall."

OLEG HELD HER HAND AS HE LED TATYANA AROUND THE HOUSE, showing her the ground floor first, which she had almost memorized. There was the ballroom, the formal dining room, and other large meeting rooms. Wide, window-filled spaces that allowed the garden into the house, and walls decorated with art and tapestries.

"The first floor was made for private quarters." He waved a hand as they headed up from the ground floor. "The grand bedrooms, suites, and sitting rooms for the master of the house and his lady."

"But I think Oksana said that now they're mostly offices."

"Correct," Oleg said. "And some storage rooms. Sitting rooms. Private spaces, but no day chambers. Only the wind vampires like sleeping this high up."

"And everyone else sleeps in the basement?"

"Yes. I expanded it when I bought the house. It's the safest place for our kind." He pointed down a hallway and kept her hand in his as they walked. "I'll show you the main bedroom. It's quite beautiful."

She watched him as he led her around the house, acting as the tour guide for the curious newcomer. When he pushed open a large set of double doors, her eyes immediately went to the ceiling, which was decorated in the baroque style with a colorful and bright scene full of angels and cherubs.

Oleg pointed up. "See? Wind vampires were parading in front of you your entire life, and you just didn't know it."

Tatyana smiled. "You said the wind vampires like to sleep high up."

"They do. And they love a good balcony."

"You have a few wind vampires living with you, but not many."

Oleg grunted. "You're perceptive."

She didn't say anything, curious if he would explain more.

"Most wind vampires in this part of the world owe their allegiance to the Fire King." Oleg continued after a few moments of silence. "Arosh. He's an ancient vampire who lives in the Caucasus Mountains not far from here."

"And he's also a fire vampire?"

"Yes, but he is far older than me." Oleg squeezed her hand. "Let's keep walking." He led her out of the bedroom and toward another set of gilt-edged stairs. "Were I to challenge Arosh, I would likely lose, and I would not say that about many."

"But if he's a fire vampire, why do most of the wind vampires— Oh. Oh." She blinked. "Was his sire a wind vampire? So his children are wind vampires?"

"Exactly. Most of the wind vampires in this area are under his aegis."

"And you two are... enemies?"

"Not enemies. But not friends." He glanced down as they started up the stairs. "Arosh is an honorable vampire—he takes care of his people and is known for having a soft heart toward human women in particular—but he has his own moral code."

"It seems like the two of you would agree on that."

Oleg raised an eyebrow. "Perhaps. But fire vampires are not friends with other fire vampires. We provoke an automatic aggression instinctively. Arosh and I coexist and try to avoid each other. He stays on his side of the Mzymta River and I stay on mine."

Tatyana pulled up a mental map. "Wait, the Mzymta is close to here."

Oleg nodded and led her toward a third flight of stairs. "Yes. This house is my most eastern residence on the Black Sea. Obviously my territory stretches across Siberia, but..." He shuddered. "Cold."

She couldn't stop her smile. "You're a fire vampire."

"Does that mean I'm supposed to like the cold?" He walked to the right when they reached the landing and turned down a narrow hallway. "There is a room at a corner of the house that I wanted to show you."

"What's up here?" She glanced out the windows to see the forest spreading across the hills. "There are so many windows." It would be a death trap during the day.

"Yes." He reached a door and turned the knob, keeping her hand firmly in his grip. "I once thought that if I was human, I would have used this room as a studio because I imagine the morning light would be very beautiful. But since I cannot see the sun in here..."

"What did— Oh!" Tatyana stepped into the center of the room and froze, her mouth agape at the beauty surrounding her. "The sunflowers, Oleg."

He released her hand and walked around the perimeter of the room, surveying an elaborate mosaic that covered the base of the walls, growing up between east-facing windows and reaching toward the ceiling.

The mosaic was a field of sunflowers that circled the room, and while the light from the stars was a pearl grey shining through the glass, Tatyana could imagine how it would look in the morning with the light glinting off the gold and orange flower heads that grew up the walls.

"It's so beautiful." She lifted a hand to touch it, then pulled back. "I don't know if I can—"

"You can touch." Oleg ran his palm along the wall. "I completed this one fifty years or so after I bought the house. I think it turned out well."

The room appeared like a floating meadow over the treetops. It was empty save for a single wooden chair propped in the corner.

"No one uses it?"

"Not right now," he said. "Luana liked this room. She used to say that if she ever chose to die, she would come up to the room at dawn and wait for the sun."

"And burn down the entire house with everyone else sleeping?"

"Possibly." Oleg nodded. "That would be something she would do."

"Morbid."

"She would think of it as romantic." Oleg nodded at Tatyana. "She could be a bit dramatic. She was a dancer when she was human. A prima ballerina."

Interesting. Was that why Oleg was interested in her?

I used to braid my girlfriend's hair. She had beautiful blond hair like you.

Tatyana wasn't keen to let questions linger in her mind and twist her guts. Zara had mentioned Tatyana's resemblance to her girlfriend, and now Oleg told her his dead mate had been a dancer.

She walked over and looked up into his cool grey eyes. "Do I remind you of Luana? Is that why you're attracted to me?"

He smiled a little bit. "I cannot lie that I was struck by the similarities the first time I saw you, but other than your coloring, the resemblance is not actually very strong. Perhaps she came from the same place that your people did, a long time ago. You could be... cousins perhaps?"

"Does that mean you have a type?"

"My type is women." Oleg lifted his hand and pulled a strand of her gold hair through his fingers. "And perhaps I am only seeing what I want to see. I don't have photographs of Luana. Only a few sketches that I don't look at anymore."

Tatyana frowned. "Why no photographs? Can vampires not be photographed?"

"Another superstition, volchitsa. We simply don't take photographs because they are permanent evidence of our immortality."

Tatyana nodded slowly. "When you talk about her, she seems…" How did Tatyana phrase this without being offensive?

"Insane?" Oleg offered. "Mad?"

"Delicate maybe?"

Oleg smirked. "Delicate is a very kind way to describe her. Luana was very unstable, particularly toward the end of her life. I believe she was ill when her sire turned her, and that can happen sometimes. Turning a human who carries any kind of infection can sometimes produce a vampire who is not… balanced."

"I'll remember that."

Oleg leaned against the wall. "Still, she was my mate. I tried to protect her and keep her happy."

"Why?"

He frowned. "Because that was my job."

Tatyana narrowed her eyes. "You do that."

"Do what? My job?"

"You try to make people happy even when you're pretending to be a bully."

He said nothing, and his face went blank.

What had she said? She started to step away, but Oleg's hand darted out and pulled her closer, wrapping around the small of her back as he pulled her to his chest.

Her heart gave a single thunk.

When he spoke, his voice was low and soft. "You think I'm a bully?"

"No." She forced the words out. "I said you pretend to be a bully."

"You're not afraid of me."

She narrowed her eyes. "Sometimes I am, a little bit."

"I would never hurt you." He lifted his chin. "Do you believe me?"

"No."

Or yes. Maybe he *wouldn't* hurt her intentionally, but that didn't mean he couldn't hurt her.

His hand slid from the small of her back down to her bottom and cupped it, pulling her into his groin. "You think I'm lying?"

"Maybe you're telling the truth." Tatyana stared into his stormy grey eyes. "But remember Ivan and the firebird. Even when you start with the best of intentions, things will go wrong. That's the way of life."

Oleg reached down and lifted her, swiftly turning them and pressing her back against a wall of sunflowers as Tatyana wrapped her legs around his waist.

She could feel his hard erection against her eager, heated sex.

Take him. Take this.

For as long as you can.

The whisper in her mind seduced her as thoroughly as Oleg did when he took her lips with his own, teasing her mouth open to welcome his tongue and his fangs. She licked out, running her tongue along his slick fang, and felt a shudder cross his shoulders.

Her amnis slid across his, and she tasted her blood in his mouth as he pierced her tongue and sucked hard.

Oleg held her against the wall as she rode his erection between her thighs. Tatyana reached down, struggling with the loose sweatpants she was wearing and trying to figure out how to get rid of them without losing the delicious friction that was already pushing her to the edge of climax.

With a growl of frustration, Oleg put her on the ground, yanked her pants off, and then quickly lifted her again, leaving her naked at the waist.

"Unbutton my pants," he commanded as he held her against the wall.

Tatyana held her breath as she reached between them and fumbled with his trousers, eventually releasing his sizable erection. She gripped it with her hand and guided him into her body.

Oleg arched his hips and drove her into the wall, but Tatyana braced her hands on his shoulders and took the force of his thrusts as his amnis flooded her skin, heightening the arousal of them both until she felt like she might leave her body from the pleasure.

The smell of singed pine released in the air as his body heated. She drew water to her skin, grateful for the salt-laden breeze that carried the taste of the sea and the darkness.

Oleg whispered something under his breath, something in a language she couldn't understand. It was heated and fervent. The foreign words reached down into her chest, carrying an aching need that she tried to push to the back of her mind.

She didn't know the future. There was only this. Only now.

Tatyana closed her eyes and let pleasure break over her like a wave.

Chapter Forty

*S*tay with me, stay with me. Let me hold you in the darkness.

Oleg stared at the black phone sitting on his desk, trying to rid the foolish memory from his mind and grateful he'd muttered the words in a language that had been dead for centuries.

There was no need for Tatyana to know how far she had embedded herself into his mind.

He'd taken her blood twice now without giving any of his to her. It was a dangerous connection, one that tied her to him even though she didn't realize what it meant.

A third taste and she would live in his blood, perhaps for a very long time.

A third taste and he would have a blood bond to her. The beginning of a mating bond that might just keep her alive if he had to kill Zara.

A sire's bond was powerful, but so was a mating bond. With a mating bond, he could feel her pain, take some of the agony that would wrack her body if her sire was killed.

It could protect her even if it would hurt him.

The phone rang and Oleg grabbed for the receiver. "I'm listening."

"The call came from Sevastopol." The words were clipped and businesslike. "What do you want to do?"

Zara had been in Sevastopol the night before. While he and Tatyana had been touring the house and exploring each other's sexual appetites in various rooms, Zara might already be heading toward them.

"I'll take care of it." Oleg hung up the phone.

Zara was coming for her gold, of that he had no doubt. The only question was how long it would take for her to reach Sochi and who she would have with her when she arrived.

She wasn't dumb. His daughter would have a plan. She knew her strengths and her weaknesses. She had been Luana's lover, and she hadn't survived the twisted vampire courts of Istanbul and Athens because she was beautiful.

She would look for vampires who were alone or vulnerable.

She would definitely be looking for Tatyana, and she'd be able to sense her the moment she got close.

Her weakness? His daughter was severely impatient.

Oleg picked up the phone and called Mika.

"Hallo."

"I need you back here."

"Zara?"

"She was in Sevastopol last night when she called me."

"Before or after I left for Moscow?" Mika's voice dripped with irritation. "Did you know she—"

"I thought she was farther away," Oleg said. "Just get back on the plane and return to Sochi."

"It's nearly dawn."

Damn, it was. The nights were longer in Moscow this time of year, but they were still shackled to the unbending sun.

"Then have the plane ready at dusk," Oleg said. "I want you back here."

It wasn't that he was afraid of Zara, but he was afraid for Tatyana.

He had no idea how she'd react to her sire's presence, and he didn't want to take a chance.

The gold was here. Zara didn't really have any interest in Tatyana from what little he'd gathered on the phone the night before.

Perhaps he *should* load Tatyana on the plane and fly her to the citadel.

"Put a weeks-old newborn in a metal tube flying through the sky, piloted by humans," Oleg muttered. "A brilliant idea."

Tatyana would stay with him. For as long as it took to take care of Zara, Tatyana would stay with him. It was a strategic decision. Simply strategic.

Chapter Forty-One

"Sevastopol?" Tatyana felt her heart freeze. "My mother—"

"Is safe. Vera is glued to her, and I've sent guards to check on her; she'll be under surveillance until I deal with Zara." Oleg was sitting behind his desk, looking every bit like the dictator that he was. "And you will stay inside the house until I find her."

She blinked. "You're locking me inside?"

"For your own good." His tone was condescending, and it made her want to scream. "Zara doesn't have a large fighting force. She'll look to pick off isolated vampires when she attacks the house, and you're the most vulnerable right now."

"Are you sure it wouldn't be better to—" Tatyana clamped her mouth shut.

Oleg narrowed his eyes. "What were you going to say?"

"I was going to say that the gold is hers and you should just give it to her, but then I remembered what Elene's body looked like tied to that chair and I want to kill Zara again."

Oleg smirked, and it did nothing to tamp down Tatyana's fury. She just wanted to slap him when he looked like that.

"Good," he said. "I like this attitude. I told you from the beginning, I like to see your teeth."

"But I'm not staying in the house."

"I will lock you in your quarters if I have to."

"Fuck you!" Tatyana jumped to her feet and started to pace. "Is this because you don't trust me?"

He raised his eyebrows. "You said yourself that you love her."

"I don't *love* her," Tatyana snarled. "I love—" She bit her tongue to silence herself.

Oleg cocked his head, watching her with narrowed eyes, but he said nothing.

"I don't love Zara." She let out a slow breath. "And I want to call my mother. I want to talk to her. Right now."

"Ah." Oleg nodded as if he understood.

He understood nothing.

"Mika said he was getting me a phone and a computer that I could use," she said. "Where is he?"

"On his way back from Moscow right now, and I imagine he'll have your devices with him."

"Good." She crossed her arms over her chest as she paced.

Oleg was sitting calmly behind a vast dark wood desk that shone in the gold lamplight. His office was lined with bookshelves, but his desk was immaculate with a single black rotary phone on the corner and a leather portfolio to his right.

She wanted to throw the phone across the room, tear the portfolio with her teeth, and then fuck him on the top of that clean, shiny, civilized desk.

His voice was smoke and whispers. "What are you thinking of right now?"

"That I hate feeling out of control." Tatyana turned and walked out of his office before she could do or say anything she would regret. "If you lock me in my room, I will not forgive you and I will not forget."

A FEW HOURS LATER, SHE HEARD A TAP ON THE DOOR AND smelled Mika outside. She opened it, and he held out a silver carafe of blood and a large white box.

"Here and here. Oleg said you needed more blood."

She snatched the blood, grabbed the box, and slammed the door in his face.

"You're welcome," he said from behind the heavy oak. "Do you need any help setting up the computer?"

"I know more than you." She was already drinking the blood and eyeing the box with the new device.

"The phone is charged and equipped with an unlimited data plan," Mika continued. "There's no Wi-Fi in the house, but there are towers close enough that you should be able to use the phone as a hot spot if you need to get online."

"Good." She'd rooted around in the garden shed two nights before in anticipation of trying to work with electronics again. Now, as she finished gulping down the carafe of blood, she took the battered old gardening gloves made of leather from under her mattress. "Thank you."

"If you want to thank me, you'll stay in your room until I can kill Zara."

That made her stand up straight. She walked to the door and opened it. "What if *I* want to kill Zara?"

"Get in line," Mika muttered, then walked away.

She watched the dark man's retreat and decided she wasn't going to think about killing Zara just yet. Not until she put into motion the plan she'd been concocting from the moment she'd last spoken to her mother.

But first she needed access to the world.

She opened the box and saw the largest, most awkward and inelegant laptop she'd ever seen before in her life. It was glorious.

The computer was encased in a clear plastic box, and there was an additional clear bracket included in the box. When she put on the gloves and opened the laptop, she realized the clear bracket was a type of keyboard extender that rested an inch over the keyboard with striking pieces that reached down to each key. By using it, she could type on the laptop without touching the keys at all. It would not be swift or convenient, but it should work to keep her amnis away from the delicate hard drive and circuit board.

Not taking any chances, she pulled on the gloves and managed to turn on the computer. As it started, she reached for the large mobile phone in a similarly clumsy case that was in another box. On the front was the word NOCHT with a mirrored bird's head underneath it.

Attached to the phone was a stylus that made it possible to use the phone without her gloves.

Excellent.

She turned on the phone, quickly logged into the operating system with a dummy email account she used for throwaway phones, and immediately checked the software, pleased to realize that the phone already came equipped with a VPN.

It made sense that any communications company that wanted to work with vampires would have virtual private networks preinstalled, but since this operating system was a completely new animal to her, she didn't want to assume.

Within a half an hour, she had another VPN installed on the laptop, the phone tethered to the machine, and she was navigating through a rudimentary internet browser to a chat room where she suspected Grimace might be hanging out. She created a new name to use for the moment and looked for any familiar handles.

As soon as she started surfing the message boards, she felt like she could breathe again. It was the middle of the night, but that was when her people—the computer geeks of the world—came alive.

Come to think of it, they were a little bit like their own vampire druzhina. Just with code instead of blood.

It was hard to type, but Tatyana managed, and scrolling to the bottom of a board she knew Grimace liked to frequent, she dropped a line of code that she hoped would catch his attention.

Minutes later, Grimace was private messaging her.

—pidge, where are you??? wait, is this pidge?

She could sense his hesitation, and she didn't blame him for caution, so she typed a phrase that would only make sense to him.

—pushkin wants his code back.

—it is youuuuuu what the hell and where have you been? do you have my \$\$\$ or what? ru living in the maldives with all my money?

—i am not in the maldives + will have your \$\$\$ but now is not the time. need a favor and i will pay you.

—ur already making me \$\$\$ what is it?

Tatyana took a deep breath, glanced at the closed door, then back to the computer.

—if my mom needed to disappear from svstpl could you help her?

There was a slight pause, and then he typed back.

—tell me when and where.

Chapter Forty-Two

Oksana was a relentless taskmaster, but at least working in the ballroom with the water vampire worked a little bit to alleviate Tatyana's tension.

It had been four nights since Zara had called Oleg, three nights since they had sex in the sunflower room, and Tatyana was avoiding him. She wanted to feel more in control. Of her body, her mind.

Her life.

"Good." Oksana mirrored Tatyana's hand motions in the ballroom, standing on the far side of the fountain as she lifted a sheet of water from the base of the fountain. "Now hold it."

Tatyana had her hands out, and her amnis was alive. It was as if she could feel tiny tethers flowing from her fingertips to the water she held in the air. "Why?"

Oksana smiled. "I want you to feel it. Your arms won't get tired, but your amnis will. Controlling it is a combination of training and instinct. The water wants to come to you. It wants to serve you. But your amnis is new."

"Oleg told me that my strength is average for a newborn. Do you agree?"

"He's far older than me with far more experience, but yes, I'd say that is correct."

Tatyana held the sheet of water, feeling her amnis flag for a moment before she focused her attention on the energy. She'd decided that amnis was like a cat or a precocious child. The moment her attention wavered, her energy dropped. But the moment the amnis felt her attention focused back on it, it grew stronger, flowing happily between her hands and the water.

"You get strength from the water," Oksana said. "Never forget that. It's an endless well. Water is everywhere."

"Not the desert."

The other vampire smiled. "Even there, a little bit. But yes, I'm going to advise you stay away from deserts until you're older. You'll feel quite helpless there. You'd still have vampire strength, but a lot of that is augmented by your amnis."

"I almost broke off my door handle the other day."

"I'm not surprised. Fine control is going to be your biggest challenge." Oksana moved to the left. "Walk with me."

Tatyana listened to her trainer and mirrored her movements on the other side of the fountain.

"Do you knit?" Oksana asked.

"Do you need a sweater?"

"No, but it's good for control. Anything that forces you to pay attention and move deliberately. Tai chi. Knitting. Embroidery. Find exercises or hobbies that force you to pay attention to your muscles. Learn an instrument. Piano trains your mind; violin trains your amnis."

"I was never very musical," Tatyana said. "I liked dancing to music, not making it."

"Dancing is good. Instruments are better." Oksana's voice was blunt. "You have the time, and your brain is faster than when you were human. Your amnis will help you create neural connections more rapidly. You'll learn languages faster. You're a computer person, right?"

"Yes."

"You don't have the same kind of access to that life anymore, so you'll need to find something new." Oksana met Tatyana's eyes. "The good thing is? You have time. And money from what Mika said."

"There are worse ways to start over?"

Oksana smirked. "You could have been turned by a vengeful Russian aristocrat with a grudge against the communists."

Tatyana blinked. "There's a story there."

"One that needs vodka even though we can't get drunk."

"Fuck *me*," Tatyana muttered. "Not even a little bit?"

"Sadly, not even a little bit." Oksana lowered her arms. "Let the water down. Slowly."

Tatyana mirrored her movements and felt her amnis clinging to the water even as it settled back into the fountain.

"Remember," Oksana said, "if you can thread a needle with water, you can make a wave."

"A whisper, not a shout."

"Exactly," Oksana said. "You remember."

"Apparently my brain is better now." She flicked the last of the water from her hands and flexed her fingers, both tired and energized from the exercise. "Blood?"

Oksana snapped her fingers at one of Mika's men who was lounging by the ballroom door. "Pavel, get Tatyana a carafe."

"Yes, boss."

Tatyana sat on the edge of the fountain and watched the man leave. "Do you like it?"

"Like what?" Oksana walked over and sat next to her.

"Ordering men around."

The other woman barked out a laugh. "Yes. I do actually. But I like working for Oleg much better than my last boss, so even if I couldn't order people around, I'd probably be with him."

Tatyana glanced at her. "Who was your last boss?"

"Luana."

Tatyana's eyebrows went up. "Oleg's mate?"

Oksana smiled a little bit. "My sire was killed in a very stupid fight with one of the Sokholovs—that's Oleg's extended family—so I was at loose ends for a long time. No money really. No protector. I could have sworn allegiance to the Sokholovs, but I hate Ivan."

"He's Oleg's brother?"

"Older," Oksana said, "but more stupid. Conniving. He's a blunt instrument to Oleg's dagger."

"But how did you meet Luana?"

Oksana looked at Tatyana for a long moment.

"It's none of my business if you don't want to tell me," Tatyana said. "I'm being needlessly curious because all this life seems strange to me. But you can tell me to shut up."

Oksana finally smiled. "I like you, Tatyana Vorona. I appreciate that you say what you think."

"What's the point of talking if you don't say what you think?" Tatyana said. "My grandmother told me that if you don't want to share your true thoughts—or you think it wouldn't be wise—it's better to shut up rather than lie."

"She sounds like a wise woman."

"She was." Tatyana stared at the dark garden through the windows. "She's dead now. And I will not die. Not from cancer. Or a stroke."

"But you can die," Oksana said. "Never forget that. Luana thought she could never die, and look what happened to her. Killed by her own mate—not that she didn't deserve it."

Tatyana froze. "What?"

Oksana leaned to the side and looked at her with narrowed eyes. "Oleg killed Luana. It's not a secret. No one told you?"

Tatyana didn't know why the news was so shocking except...

Except.

"Did it hurt you physically when Luana died?"

"It was excruciating."

She stood, a skittering anxiety shivering over her body. "Where is Oleg right now?"

"In his office, I think." Oksana's eyebrows went up. "I'm sorry if I shocked you, but like I said, it's not a secret. It was a very public execution."

Chapter Forty-Three

Oleg stared at the black chest containing approximately ten million in gold bars.

It was always satisfying to see gold in person. He had millions in numbers on screens, but that meant very little to him. It made the humans who worked for him happy, but at the end of the day, he much preferred to see his wealth in gold.

What the chest contained was a fraction of the gold Oleg owed Zara. He'd only shipped two chests from Odesa, but this one had something much more important than gold.

This one held Luana's jewelry, and that was what Zara truly wanted.

The fine mahogany chest that lay on top of the gold bars was the real prize. The diamonds and emeralds alone were triple the value of the gold, and that wasn't counting the finished pieces of jewelry, which were impossible to value.

Oleg had spent centuries collecting wealth, and when Luana became his mate, he showered her with gifts, partly to charm his mate and partly to let the broader vampire world know the power and wealth he could bestow on those who pleased him.

To his disappointment, she rarely wore the jewelry he gave her, choosing rather to hide it away in her personal cache.

Oleg heard Tatyana's footsteps racing down the hallway and flipped the top of the chest closed. There was no need for her to see Zara's treasure until it was time.

Tatyana knocked, but she didn't wait for permission to enter.

He'd have to deal with that when she didn't appear to be so rattled. "What is it?"

She'd been working with Oksana in the ballroom, and he could see her amnis sparking. The water in the air drew to her skin, and though her face was pale, her lips were flushed. He wanted to snatch her from everyone's view and strip her naked, but she was clearly upset about something, so he sat calmly.

She couldn't seem to speak.

"Tatyana," he said calmly. "Why are you upset?"

"You killed Luana."

Oleg froze. Of all the things he'd been expecting her to say, that was not it. "I see Oksana has been chatting."

"She said it wasn't a secret."

"It's not." He saw them in his mind, the bright red tesserae adorning the walls of his day chamber in the citadel.

Sire.

Lover.

Mate.

Brothers.

Friends.

"I have killed many vampires," Oleg said quietly. "Did you think I became the immortal lord of the Kievan Rus because of diplomacy?"

"She was your mate." Tatyana started to pace. "Her blood was... it was *living* in you."

Just as your blood is living in me now. "Yes."

"You said it hurt you when she died."

Why was she so agitated? Did Tatyana think Oleg was going to kill her if he tired of her? Oleg sat back in his chair and folded his hands even though the old feelings and regrets were roaring in his mind.

"Luana had to die because she was unwell," he said. "She was erratic, dangerous, and became obsessed with taking human women off the street and feeding from them until they died, which was completely unnecessary for a vampire her age. In the week before I killed her, she had taken twenty women. *Twenty*. If I hadn't done something, the humans would have found her, and she could have exposed us."

"Yes." Tatyana nodded, but she didn't stop pacing. "I understand that."

"So why does this upset you?"

"It hurt you."

Did she care that much for him? Oleg felt a crack in his control. "Yes. It hurts when a blood bond is broken even if it is an old one."

"And it hurt Zara."

Oleg froze. Where was she going? "Yes. Zara hated me for killing Luana."

"It was wrong," Tatyana whispered, her eyebrows knitting together. "Elene told her that when Zara was beating her. She said it was wrong and everyone knew it."

"I'm sure Elene said that because—"

"She was trying to calm Zara down! Obviously."

Nothing was obvious about how this woman's mind worked. What was churning behind her blue eyes? "I do not understand why you are so agitated. Will you please—"

"It hurt Zara when Luana died because they had exchanged blood, yes?"

"No." Why was she asking about his dead mate's blood? "Luana never gave Zara her blood. They were not mated. That's why Luana remained my mate until I killed her."

Tatyana walked to the other side of his desk and stood, her amnis vibrating in the air. "But *you* did. You gave your daughter Luana's blood when you made her."

Oleg narrowed his eyes but said nothing.

"She's a water vampire, not an earth vampire," Tatyana said. "You may be her sire, but she carries a lot of Luana's blood. You said that."

She wasn't wrong. Oleg's daughter carried the last of Luana's amnis in her veins.

He shrugged. "And?"

"Zara has your blood. She has *Luana's* blood. She is a part of both of you. When the time comes to kill her, are you actually going to do it?"

Obviously not because it might kill you too. Not that Oleg was ever going to tell her that.

"Is this why you're angry?" Oleg unfolded his hands and slowly stood. "Because you think I won't have the strength to kill Zara?" The corner of his mouth turned up. "Really?"

"I *know* you have the strength," Tatyana spat out. "But do you have the will? You accuse me of loving her, but *you do too.* She's your blood, Oleg. And the last blood of your mate." Tatyana locked eyes with him. "Tell me you're going to kill her."

Oleg crossed his arms over his chest and tilted his chin up, looking down his nose at the angry woman. "I haven't decided yet."

Her eyes went wide and her mouth fell open. "You're not going to, are you?"

"I am leaning toward... no. I will keep her in the citadel. Don't you remember what you told me once? It would be crueler to her—harsher —to keep her alive for a century or two. I can confine her—"

"She needs to die!"

Something in his chest roared in defiance. *Nothing* could happen to Zara that might hurt Tatyana. It was unacceptable. He would not stand for it. His fire had tasted her amnis, and it wanted more. It was protective. Possessive.

Oleg watched Tatyana carefully. "When I knew she killed Elene and robbed you of your mortal life, I admit I wanted to kill her. But death is swift and merciful, volchitsa. Wouldn't it be better to let Zara suffer?"

"How can you be so cold?" Tatyana shook her head. "Zara has to die."

"So you'd have me give her mercy with a swift death? What lesson would that teach those who challenge me?"

"The whole world already thinks she's dead!"

"Still, it would be far better to let her scrape the walls and bloody her fists against stone while I keep her in prison for a century." Oleg shrugged. "Let her think about Elene's death and regret it. Maybe when she understands remorse, I will kill her."

"I don't want her to control me!" Tatyana pounded a fist on her chest. "Don't you see that?"

He did see it, and she wasn't wrong.

But Tatyana didn't know that Zara's death could kill her too.

"It's not your decision." Oleg walked out from behind his desk and toward the door. "You're irrational right now. You need blood. Let me get you something to—"

"I'm not being irrational! I'm being *very* rational and very clear. I want Zara dead." She ran and put a hand on his chest. "Are you going to do it?"

He covered her hand with his and held it there. "I will deal with Zara. You are her child; it's not your decision."

She curled her hand into a fist and drew back. "I cannot believe you."

"I don't know why you're shocked, Tatyana." He cocked his head. "Zara is my child, under my aegis. You're not my peer in any way."

"You want to keep a monster alive."

"And you think of only of yourself," Oleg murmured. "While I have to think..." *Of you.* "I must think of the hundreds of vampires and humans who *need* my power. And sometimes my cruelty."

She stepped back, shaking her head. "No one needs cruelty."

"You're still thinking like a human. Other vampires need to fear me if my people are going to be safe. My druzhina calls me lord because I am strong, not because I am merciful." He leaned down and murmured, "Just as you will call me lord when your sire is under my thumb."

"What?" Tatyana's head jerked back. "Call you *lord?* Is that what this is about for you?"

"Once Zara is captured, you will be alone, volchitsa. You will have no sire, no clan. You will be fair game to any vampire who wants to prey on you."

"And tell me how that is different from every other point in my life." Tatyana lifted her chin, her lip curling. "I've *always* fended for myself."

"But you don't have to anymore." Placing a hand on her cheek, he stroked his thumb over her silken skin.

Oleg leaned down and gently pressed his lips against hers. He flooded his amnis over her skin, spreading the pleasure of the kiss from his body to hers.

And he felt it. He felt the nascent bond in his blood, the pleasure in her blood answering his. He felt the aching want and the simmering passion that lived in her, the banked purity of her desire for him.

Oleg stepped closer and opened his mouth, waiting for her kiss to meet his.

After a moment of hesitation, she opened her mouth, kissing him back, lifting her hand to the nape of his neck and pushing her tongue into his mouth to stroke against his fangs.

A low growl in his throat when he tasted it. His arms slid around her waist and he drew her body to his, pressing them together so he felt her heart beat against his chest.

Her blood in his mouth, swallowed and captured in his own body. Her amnis threading with his. The bond grew and deepened, elevating her pleasure until he could feel it ringing through his own body like a plucked string.

She was his now. Her passion. Her anger. Her fear. He felt it all in his own blood.

Lifting his mouth from hers, he kept their bodies pressed together as he whispered in her ear. "Call me your lord, Tatyana Vorona. Give me your loyalty. Ask me for my protection, and you will have it. You will be my lover. No one will touch you. You will be cared for, your family will be protected, and you will want for nothing ever again."

Her hand gripped the hair at his nape. "All I have to do is call you lord and my family will be protected?"

Oleg pulled back and stared into her eyes, willing her to come to him. To surrender. He wanted it. He wanted to take care of her. He wanted to give her everything.

The realization twisted something tight in his chest.

"Call me your lord." He spoke softly. "And I swear you will never be alone again."

She would be his. Truly and only his. He would have no other, and he could be content because in this unexpected woman—his little book-keeper with her sharp teeth—were multitudes. Her mind was a collection of gleaming tessera he could spend eternity learning.

"You want me to call you my lord?" The corner of her mouth turned up. "Bend to you. *Bow* to you?"

He frowned. "Tatyana—"

"You said you like my fangs," she whispered. "Was that because you want to yank them from my mouth?"

Oleg saw the fire in her eyes, and he couldn't bring himself to hate it even as she rejected him. "So sharp, little wolf." He dropped his hand and took a step back. "Make sure you don't chew off your own leg trying to escape from someone who wants to keep you safe."

Tatyana walked out of the room, and Oleg felt every step she took as she walked away from him.

Chapter Forty-Four

Tatyana woke up in a haze of hunger and torment. Her gut was still churning from her fight with Oleg, and a tearing sensation in her chest told her she'd broken something delicate and irreplaceable.

Ask me for my protection, and you will have it. You will be my lover. No one will touch you. You will be cared for, your family will be protected, and you will want for nothing again.

The temptation to give in, to bend to him and fall into the safety of his power, had been nearly too much.

Call me your lord, and I swear you will never be alone again.

In the watery consciousness of dusk, she curled into a ball, realizing that it would be so easy, so *so* easy, to fall into his arms.

He would give her safety, but it would be false safety. His clan would be her clan. His army, her army. But it would all depend on Oleg's pleasure. The moment he became angry with her, disinterested or detached, she would be alone again, only this time it would be isolation for eternity.

She couldn't do it, not even to protect her mother.

Love shouldn't feel like a trap.

Her grandmother's words came back to her tormented mind, and Tatyana took a deep breath and felt her resolve settle.

Love should not feel like a trap. And every moment with Oleg Sokolov felt like she was walking into a trap. A beautiful, soft, pleasurable trap.

But always a trap.

A familiar scent filled the air, tugging at her attention while she mentally composed a short message to her mother. Tatyana would write it out as soon as she fed.

She already had the small cylinders the birds could carry on their legs. Her mother had secreted them into the clothes she'd packed.

Tatyana and her mother's phone were monitored because of course they were. Mika wasn't going to take chances again after Elene.

And her mother didn't know how to troll anonymous message boards under an alias like Grimace.

She would write out her message and release all the birds tonight. And then...

Voices outside her room.

She bolted up in bed when she realized what she was smelling.

Humans.

Her mouth grew bloody as her fangs grew long, cutting her lips and whetting her appetite. Human blood. Fresh blood. Warm, living, delectable blood.

Thoughts of contacting her mother flew from her mind, and she could only think about the blood outside her door.

Tatyana slid out of bed, clad in a pair of silk shorts and the camisole she wore to sleep. At the scent of humans, her instincts moved to the front of her mind. She barely comprehended how she came to the door, pressing her hands against the cold wood, reaching out her amnis at the scent of fresh prey.

Tatyana knew there were humans who patrolled the house during the day, but Oleg sent all of them away at night.

There shouldn't be any humans outside her door.

Her blood hummed at the scent and the challenge.

"...wait here?" They were speaking in Russian. "When are we supposed—"

"They'll be awake soon." The other voice sounded nervous. "Shouldn't we be trying to break down the door?"

"Is the sun down? It's early."

"This isn't Moscow, you idiot. We need to go in *now*. She might already be—"

"Shhh! Did you hear something?"

Tatyana stared at the brass knob as she unlatched the heavy bolts securing her door.

"Fuck, she's awake!"

"Don't kill her. Remember what Zara—"

"Fuck that crazy vampire." There was a crack against the door, as if a heavy weight had been smashed against it.

Tatyana crouched down and twisted the knob so that when the crash came again, the two men fell through the doorway, both tumbling over her body crouched near the threshold.

Her heart gave a fast thump, and she leaped on the first man, tearing the black mask from his head and yanking his neck to the side to sink her teeth into the soft, scented flesh of his neck.

"Dmitri!" the other man screamed.

Something burned across her shoulder, but she ignored it, drinking like a glutton at the human's neck.

A second burn, however, caught her attention, and she lifted her head from her kill, snarling at the wide-eyed man who was holding a gun on her.

A gun? Was that the burning sensation? She looked at her shoulder and saw a red trail scraping down her arm while a fire burned down her back.

She didn't wait for him to fire again. The man looked like he was moving through water as Tatyana leaped on him, batting away the irritating firearm as she tackled him to the ground and straddled his chest.

She ripped away the dark mask and didn't look at his face once she saw the racing vein at his neck.

The scent of his blood was metallic, but she didn't care. This was hot, living elixir and she was born to prey on these animals. She yanked his shoulders up as she straddled him and sank her fangs into the base of his neck.

The man screamed, and something in her chest crowed like a rooster at dawn.

Yes, this.

Yes, this death.

Yes, this terror.

The scent of his adrenaline was as fragrant as his blood.

She thrilled in his struggle as he tried to shove her off, but though he was twice her size, his efforts felt as helpless as a bird battering a window.

She was so powerful, and the intoxicating rush of it only made her drink faster.

The heated blood slid down her throat and left her amnis flush. The water in the air drew to her skin, and she could feel the silk clinging to her.

"My, my."

A familiar voice at the door sent Tatyana to her feet, spinning around in search of its source. Her heart leaped in her chest when she saw her.

Her sire's hair, a wild cacophony of dark brown curls in a halo around her head. Her voice soft and soothing like a mother comforting a child.

"Zara?"

"Look at you." The pride in Zara's voice nearly sent Tatyana to her knees. "You're even more gorgeous than I thought you'd be."

Tatyana dropped the body of the man she'd been feeding from. "You came."

She longed to run to Zara's arms. She wanted her to hold her. Please her. She wanted...

Zara held out her arms. "My daughter." Pink-red tears rose in her eyes. "I didn't know. I didn't know how I would feel, but I missed you so much."

"I missed you too!"

Tatyana ran to her, and Zara's embrace was fierce as Tatyana fell into her arms.

She sobbed, the cleansing tears wiping away her fear and uncertainty. This was her family. This was her blood. Everything else meant nothing. Her pathetic human mother? She was nothing compared to Zara. The humans she'd killed? They were only food for this living, pulsing bond.

Zara nuzzled Tatyana's temple. "I'm so glad you're safe."

"Why did you leave me?" Tatyana sobbed. "Why?"

"Shhhh." Zara pulled back and brushed Tatyana's hair away from her face. "Look at you. I don't know why I didn't think of it when you were working for me before. I was blind." She kissed Tatyana's forehead. "Forgive me, Tanya. I couldn't imagine how valuable you could be."

"What do you want?" Tatyana was desperate to make Zara happy. "What should I do?"

"You know." Zara smiled. "Of course you know. I can smell him on you." She leaned into Tatyana's neck, inhaling the scent of her skin before she drew her into a gentle embrace. "My lovely girl, you're going to help me kill Oleg."

Chapter Forty-Five

Oleg smelled them before he opened his eyes, and without a word, he rose from bed, swiftly dressed in heavy black canvas pants and nothing else. He walked barefoot to the door and searched for any scent that resembled a familiar human, but none of the men outside the door were his or Mika's.

Without waiting a second, he wrenched open the heavy walnut door, snapped his fingers, and brought the fire to his palm, throwing a swirling ball of flame into the silly, navy-clad soldiers who had gathered in his sitting room.

"What the—"

It was the only utterance that escaped them before the screaming started.

The ball of fire exploded in the center of the men, who immediately lifted their weapons and commenced firing at him even though his upper body was already engulfed in flames.

Oleg's fire wasn't hot enough to melt the bullets, but the heat warped their trajectory, sending them far over his head. Only one shot hit, glancing along his thigh, and that came from a man who had already fallen to the ground to escape the fire that filled the room.

Oleg lifted his arm and sent a wave of flames across the room, lighting up every man who wore a black fabric mask.

The scent of melting polyester brought a smile to his lips.

The bravest of them rushed him with a hunting knife, but Oleg reached out, twisting his wrist and plucking the knife from his hand.

He dropped the blade, spun the man around, and gripped him from behind, pulling the burning mask from his head and yanking it to the side before he sank his fangs into the man's neck, drinking deeply from fresh blood as the room around him burned.

When he'd had his fill, he dropped the man, picked up the hunting knife, and waded through the writhing bodies on the floor as he made his way out to the hallway where a battle had already commenced.

Where had Zara collected so many soldiers? Who had given her money?

These were questions to ask after he'd rid his house of his daughter's infestation.

He heard a bullet coming toward his head and ducked out of the way before he raced toward the gunman, tackling him from behind and twisting his neck to kill him before he stabbed the hunting knife through the human's eye.

Oleg continued down the hallway and toward the stairs, hearing commotion in the entryway along with Mika's skeleton crew.

In retrospect, they probably should have had more people stationed around the house. It looked like all the soldiers Mika had hired had been eliminated by the navy-clad mercenaries Zara brought.

Where *had* she gotten the money?

Oleg leaped from the landing to the marble-tiled entryway, walking toward Oksana, who had a human solder in one arm while she battled a wind vampire who was trying to throw her off-balance.

"The ballroom!" Oleg shouted. "Go. There's water."

"For this?" She grinned through bloody lips. "He's a lamb." She tossed the human toward Oleg and he caught the man in his arms, twisted his neck, and sent a ball of flame toward the wind vampire, who shrieked and immediately flew toward the windows, shattering the glass, which rained down on the humans and vampires battling below.

"Get to the ballroom and gather the rest of the druzhina there," Oleg snarled. "I'll take care of these ants."

"Áno, Knyaz!"

Oksana and the other two vampires who'd been holding the entryway raced toward the ballroom while Oleg brought the flames to his arms, coaxing his fire like a man teasing a woman.

Come now. You can feel it, can't you? He fed the flames his amnis and felt them curl around his body, teasing his skin and leaping toward anyone who threatened him. *I'll give you want you want, my darling.*

Bullets went wild. Humans screamed, and Oleg's fire gleefully danced through dry air of the entry hall, wrapping around humans who twisted and cried out as their bodies charred like so much meat.

The sound of weapons dropping to the marble was delightful. Oleg had never cared for guns.

"Oleg!" Mika shouted from the second floor, and Oleg looked up to see his second with a red gash across his neck. The gash was healing, but his face was grim.

Oleg lifted his chin as his fire smoldered around him. "Tatyana's room?"

"The door was broken," Mika said. "She's gone. Two men in her day chamber. Both dead. She fed from them."

Good. If she was feeding, she was alive. "And Zara?"

Mika shook his head. "She knows this house as well as I do. She could be hiding anywhere."

A low growl rumbled in his chest. The question was, was she hiding with Tatyana? And had the young vampire succumbed to her sire's influence? Did his little wolf still want her sire dead? Or was her ire now turned toward Oleg?

"Where would she go?" Mika asked. "She wants her gold."

"I moved it." Damn his sentimentality. He'd had visions of draping Tatyana in jewels and showering her with gold necklaces, diadems, and nothing else. "My office and Luana's day chamber. Let's start there."

"I'll take the office," Mika said. "The others?"

"I told them to gather in the ballroom."

Oleg ran to Luana's day chamber, and he knew before he entered that Zara was already there. He walked through the open doorway to see his daughter standing in the center of the room, staring at the empty bed where his mate had once slept.

Finally.

Seeing her was still a punch to the chest. Oleg didn't have many children, but most of them he treasured. He'd protected them and taught them. They were scattered across his territory, guarding his people and upholding his rule.

Except for Zara.

She was wearing a gold dress that looked like the traditional garb of the Athenian court, and her arms were bare. Her hair was long and loose, a coronet of golden brown curls that Luana had adored.

"Do you think she was happy here?" Zara knew Oleg was there, but she didn't take her eyes from Luana's bed.

He couldn't stop smoke from leaching through the air. The emotions she evoked were always so complicated. She could be as mad and as tender as Luana had been.

"She was happy for a time," Oleg said. "Like you."

Zara turned to him and smiled sadly. "We were never a very healthy family, were we?"

"I shouldn't have let her take you the way I did," Oleg said. "That was my mistake."

"It was what we both wanted." Zara shrugged. "But you shouldn't have interfered."

Oleg took a deep breath. "She was going insane. She had to be stopped."

Zara's expression transformed like a switch flipping on. "She was a goddess, and you are a barbarian!" She drew a curved sword from her dress, swinging it wildly at Oleg before she charged.

"Zara!" He batted her back but didn't release his fire even though the element tugged at his skin and his amnis went wild at Zara's assault. "Stop this. I don't want to kill you."

She laughed in his face and kept swinging the sword. "I know you don't. You could have killed me a hundred times and you didn't." She laughed again, the sound growing maniacal. "So what are you going to do, Papa? Keep me in your dungeon until I'm a good daughter?" Her eyes were lit with amusement. "Do you really think that's going to happen?"

"Zara, stop." He backed out of Luana's day chamber and into the hall. "What do you want?"

"Where are her jewels?" Zara screamed. "That gold and Luana's jewels are mine, and I want them."

"And what about Tatyana?" Oleg saw Zara's eye twitch. "Do you want Tatyana too?"

"Yes!" She shook her head. "No, I don't care about that bitch. She's your slut, not mine."

Oleg drew Zara toward the landing, knowing that though his druzhina might observe, none of them would harm Oleg's daughter without his permission.

"We need to talk," Oleg said. "And I would like an apology for Elene's death."

At the mention of Elene, Zara hissed. "Where is Mika? I'm surprised he hasn't tried to kill me yet."

"I have more control than you." Mika's voice came from the bottom of the stairs. He was staring at Zara with blood in his eyes and Ludmila was standing next to him with a rifle pointed at Zara's neck.

"Give me a single word," the woman said calmly. "Her spine will be severed."

Oleg lifted a hand. "Hold."

Zara danced down the stairs, staring at Mika and Ludmila with a defiant expression. "It's so hard to find good help when you're immortal."

Mika's expression didn't change. "Keep tempting me, and the respect I have for your sire might just crack."

Oleg held his arms out, backing toward the ballroom with Zara following him. "Come now, daughter. We have things to discuss."

Chapter Forty-Six

Tatyana was crouched in a corner of the ballroom, an axe from the garden clutched in her hand. Every other vampire around her—all in Oleg's druzhina—had a weapon. Swords and pikes. One man had a spiked ball on a long chain and a heavy shield. Most carried short blades the length of their forearms, and there were more than a few axes.

The intricately tiled mosaic floor was swimming in blood and gore. Tatyana stayed low so she wouldn't slip in her bare feet.

She felt naked and exposed in her damp silk camisole and shorts, but no one seemed to pay her any attention. Oksana ordered the other vampires around as they dragged the bodies of the humans and vampires out to the front terrace of the house where the sun would reach first.

The stench of coagulated blood and shit was nearly overwhelming.

She swallowed hard, trying to keep from vomiting up the blood she'd drank from the men who invaded her room.

Oksana walked over and sank down. "What do you need? Do you want a robe? A bath?"

Tatyana shook her head and stayed in a crouch, clutching her axe.

Oksana patted her shoulder. "You did well. I saw you fighting one of the humans. You have good instincts with the axe."

"I've never used a sword." But she'd used an axe plenty of times at the farm. Chopping firewood. Cutting branches off trees.

Oksana nodded at the small garden axe in her hand. "Then you may have your weapon. Oleg prefers an axe too. He and Lazlo are experts; they will teach you."

She didn't want to be taught. She didn't want this life. She didn't want to be afraid. She wanted peace and quiet and a computer. She wanted a serene farmhouse and a cozy library. She didn't want to be covered in blood and gore.

She wanted Oleg. And she wanted Zara too.

Emotions rocketed through her, her heart battling with her mind.

"Wait here." Oksana rose. "Just keep to this corner and protect yourself. It's almost over."

It's almost over.

Zara had told her the same thing before she sent her out into the garden to find the axe. The axe had been Zara's idea, but it had served Tatyana well. She'd slashed two humans and had seen their guts spill out in front of her. Then she'd taken off a vampire's head when he fell at her feet.

It had been similar to killing a chicken, but the scream had been louder and she knew she would never forget the blood.

So much blood.

"Come now, daughter. We have things to discuss." Oleg's voice echoed down the hallway, and Tatyana rose to her feet.

The fearsome fire vampire backed into the room, his army at his back while Zara swung a sword wildly.

Tatyana's breath caught at the sight of him. He was ferocity and beauty. His chest and arms glistened with a shimmering fire that clung to him like a second skin. He wore nothing but a pair of black pants that hung low on his hips, exposing musculature that looked like a classical statue she might see in a museum.

He was a god of fire and blood, and the punch of longing that struck Tatyana's chest almost brought her to her knees.

Zara's eyes scanned the room in a panic. She knew she was surrounded. There was no escape when her borrowed army lay in pieces at Oleg's feet. She was alone, outnumbered, and all she had was a sword to defend herself.

Tatyana wanted to run to her, protect her, but she was frozen in fear.

"Is this how you will kill me?" Zara sneered. "With your servants and lackeys watching?" She lifted her voice and shouted into the ballroom. "You cowards! You all bend to him and pray as if he's a god." She swung the sword at Oleg's neck. "He's a murderer, and he'll kill any of you the moment you fall down. The moment you are weak, he will leave you to die if he doesn't kill you himself."

There was a low murmur of voices around the room.

Mika strolled into the ballroom, his hands in his pockets and his eyes fixed on Zara. "Do you pretend to know your sire better than those who have fought alongside him for centuries?"

"I know him." Zara hissed. She raised the sword and pointed it at Oleg. "I *know* him."

"Leave us," Oleg murmured. "My loyal druzhina, I am proud of you this night. You have protected our territory and destroyed our enemies. Now leave me with my daughter."

There was more murmuring around the room and more than one expletive, but Oleg's people did not protest.

Oleg kept his eyes on Zara even as Oksana, Ludmila, and the rest of Mika's soldiers moved toward the doors, leaving at least a dozen bodies still on the floor.

Tatyana remained frozen in the corner. No one gestured for her to follow them. No one seemed to remember that she was there. She watched while Mika lingered in the doorway, shutting the double doors as the rest of Oleg's people left, leaving Oleg, Zara, Mika, and Tatyana in the ballroom alone.

And Mika's eyes weren't on Zara and Oleg anymore. They were fixed on Tatyana.

Oleg stretched his arms out and stared at Zara. "Get on your knees now. Beg for my forgiveness and I might grant it. I might give you your inheritance. I might allow you your freedom."

"Might." Zara still held the sword between them. "Not will. You *might.*"

"I guarantee nothing until I hear your apology," Oleg said. "You are part of the Sokolovs, Zara. You have always rejected this, but you carry *our* blood. The blood of Truvor and Ruda. The earth beneath us belongs to our clan, and we carry the weight and the duty of that. Honor that legacy, honor your clan. For once in your *life*," he spat out, "think of something other than your own pain."

This was not how Tatyana had expected this conversation to go. What should she do? She was torn between her sire and her lover. The axe was in her hand.

Zara lifted her chin. "I apologize..."

Oleg's shoulders released. "Good—"

"...for nothing," Zara whispered. "I apologize for nothing. I will hate you until the day I die. I apologize. For nothing." Her eyes drifted to Tatyana for a moment; then she charged.

Oleg's fire came to his arms.

Zara ran toward him, her blade lifted.

And Tatyana moved from her corner, racing to the center of the ballroom.

She slipped in blood, but she struggled to her feet, running toward the two vampires battling in the center of the room.

Oleg's fire rose over his shoulders, and as it reached, a wall of water came from the fountain, showering him and Zara both, devouring his flames. He looked at the floor, searching for a weapon as Zara ran toward him with her blade pointed at his neck.

"No!" Tatyana screamed. She lifted her axe and rushed toward Oleg.

Mika bared his fangs and arrowed toward Tatyana, a silver dagger raised.

Tatyana slipped again, the blow she'd aimed at her sire glancing off Zara's shoulder, missing her neck.

Zara's eyes went wide when she saw Tatyana strike out. "What?"

The blade that Mika had aimed at her glanced across her abdomen, raising a line of blood.

"Mika!" Oleg's roar was ferocious.

But Tatyana could only stare at Zara and the red gash on her shoulder that was not a killing blow.

Zara's eyes were wide. "What are you doing?"

Tatyana wanted her freedom. She wanted Zara gone. She wept bloody tears as she lifted the axe again, but before she could land a blow, the weapon was snatched from her hand and Oleg knocked Tatyana to the floor.

She looked up at him with pleading eyes.

Zara lifted her hands. "Papa, no!"

Oleg curled his lip, baring a fang at Tatyana, and then turned, lifted the axe, and swung it, slashing Zara across the neck. Her head detached from her body and flew across the room.

A scream ripped from Tatyana's throat as Zara's head thudded against a wall and her body fell to the bloody floor.

The pain seared through her veins like fire, and for a moment her heart felt as if it would burst before an icy pull swept through her body like a wave.

Tatyana screamed, curling into a ball on the blood-soaked floor as the water from the fountain rose and covered her, washing her clean even as she vomited the blood from her stomach and twisted with the pain of her sire's death.

The water washed over her again and again, like waves along the shore, cleaning the blood and the battle that clung to her skin. Moments after Zara's death, Tatyana's amnis was spent and a drugging wave of darkness pulled her under.

Chapter Forty-Seven

The pain of his child's death seared his veins, doubled by the pain he tore from Tatyana as her sire perished. Oleg felt his blood dying in Zara's body. He felt the last of Luana's amnis dying with her.

Though he remained standing, Oleg was frozen and his amnis was screaming in pain.

"Knyaz!" Mika ran to him and threw his arms around Oleg's torso. "I have you. I have you."

If Mika had not caught him, Oleg knew he would have collapsed.

Zara's blood spread across the inlaid mosaic floor, crimson over aquamarine and jade, the scarlet red feathering through the pooled water from the fountain until the flooded ballroom was awash in glistening, stinking rose.

Oleg stood with his feet planted wide, his chief boyar holding him up as the water coating his skin started to steam. His element finally woke and reacted to his pain. Tears that fell from Oleg's eyes turned to steam when they hit his cheeks.

"I have you," Mika kept repeating. "I have you."

After a few long moments, Oleg threw his arm around Mika's

shoulders. "Brother." He leaned down and kissed his boyar's temple. "My brother." He gently pushed Mika's arms away even though the pain still twisted in his veins. "Where is she?"

Oleg answered his own question when he turned around to see Tatyana—a vision in the water—passed out on the ground.

The silk she wore was stained pink from the bloody water she lay in, and her golden hair was matted with blood and gore. There was a red gash across her abdomen that the water was quickly healing.

Oleg looked at Mika with a raised brow. Despite his pain, the violence that had touched Tatyana offended him. "That was from your blade."

"I thought she was with Zara." Mika lowered his head. "I thought—"

"I know what you thought." Oleg had thought the same. For a moment he had thought the same, and he'd even wavered for a second.

Would death be so unwelcome if it came at her hand?

The thought of killing another gentle creature was exhausting.

He patted Mika's shoulder and walked to Tatyana, scooping her up even though the water tried to hold her. "Deal with the bodies," he commanded. "Our guards outside must be dead."

"There had to be fifty men with her," Mika said. "All Russian. Two vampires—one flew away before I could identify him, but the one I killed I did not recognize."

Oleg took a deep breath, his amnis slightly mollified with Tatyana in his arms. "We'll deal with who was supporting Zara after I clean her up."

"Yes, Knyaz."

Oleg paused at Zara's body, glancing at the head covered in dark curls that lay against the far wall. "Prepare her body for burial," he said quietly. "We will return her body to the earth."

Mika frowned. "She's a water vampire."

After three nights, if a vampire didn't burn, their body would return to its element. Water to water. Earth to earth.

"She is *my* daughter," Oleg said gruffly. "She is a Sokolov. We will return her body to the earth."

With Tatyana curled in his arms, Oleg strode through the bloody entry hall where his druzhina waited.

"Zara is dead," he told them. "Help Mika in the ballroom."

Carrying Tatyana to his own day chamber, he kicked open the door and shut it behind him. He'd deal with the locks before dawn. His druzhina was awake; no one would cross the threshold without his permission.

Tatyana was still limp in his arms as he walked to the lavish bathroom made of grey marble. He set her on a carved bench in the shower and considered how to remove her bloody clothes. Should he cut them off? Try to get them over her head?

He didn't want the blood and gore from the battle to stay on her skin any longer than necessary.

"Are you happy now, volchitsa?" He stood and walked to the faucet to turn on the water as he pictured Zara's head flying through the air. "Are you at peace?"

She was rootless now, an orphan in the immortal world. She had no clan, no family, and she refused to ask for his aegis.

"Yes."

He turned when he heard her speak.

She was awake, staring at him, and there were tears in her eyes. "Oleg."

"Shhh." He walked to her and knelt, brushing the bloody hair away from her face. "I did what you wanted. It will hurt for a while, but you will be free of her influence now."

"When she came to my room..." Tatyana hiccuped a little bit. "I... I *loved* her. She wanted me to kill you, and I forgot all about Elene. I forgot about the beatings and the violence. All I wanted was to please—"

"Shh." He put a finger on her lips and forced her chin up to meet his eyes. "She was your sire. Of course you wanted all that. Of course you did."

Her face crumpled in pain, and she threw her arms around Oleg's shoulders, her body shaking.

He held her tightly. "But you didn't kill me, did you?" The thought brought a sharp jolt of satisfaction. She was already attached to him. More even than she realized. "You didn't hurt me; you tried to kill her."

The strength it must have taken. Oleg hadn't even been able to *challenge* his sire for a hundred years. Tatyana had defied her blood bond with Zara in less than a month.

"You are stronger than I was, Tatyana. You are so strong."

Yes, his little wolf's resolve was a thing of beauty. When he made her fall in love with him, she would be his fiercest protector and his most trustworthy ally.

Oleg held her tightly as she wept, lifting her up and walking her over to the shower so she could wash the night of violence away.

He lifted her hair, pouring oils and soaps through it to wash the caked blood away until the strands were golden and the water ran clear.

"She was so angry," Tatyana murmured. "We looked all over the house for her gold, but she couldn't find it."

Oleg smiled a little bit. "I moved it to the Amber Room. I had this sentimental vision of you naked, wearing some of the jewelry I collected that Luana never wore."

She turned to him and slid her arms around his shoulders. "You wanted me to wear Luana's jewelry?"

"I wanted you to wear *my* jewelry," he growled. "Gold and silver I've collected for centuries. I gave it to Luana, but she..." He shrugged. "It was not to her liking. I thought you might enjoy it more."

"You would give all that to me?"

He met her blue eyes and didn't look away. "I would give you far more than you can imagine, Tatyana Vorona."

All she needed was to surrender to him.

So why did it feel like he was the one begging?

Her eyes were impossible to read. "So in this vision, I was wearing gold and jewels... and what else?"

Oleg could feel her hunger, and he couldn't hold back the smile. "Skin."

He slid slick hands down the sides of her body. The water on his shoulders began to steam with the heat of his element, and he felt his blood move. The pain of Zara's death was leaching away like water down the drain, and the satisfaction of victory was rising like his cock.

His soldiers would be fucking after their fight, working off their remaining energy in far more pleasurable ways than violence.

And he could feel Tatyana's amnis rising too.

"I won," she whispered. "She's dead."

"*We* won." He bent to Tatyana's ear and muttered, "They tried to kill you, but instead, you killed them. You are the victor, little wolf. Your fangs were stained with blood, and you are *alive*."

"I'm alive." Her hand slid to the back of his neck.

Oleg closed his eyes at the pleasure of the intimacy. He wanted to press her mouth to his neck and feel her teeth pierce his skin. "Yes, you are *alive*."

Her hand reached down and wrapped around his hard erection. "*We're* alive."

Oleg reached down and lifted Tatyana against the wall, the water from the shower hitting his shoulders and turning to steam.

With his fire neutralized by the flowing water, he let his amnis free, and the moment it touched Tatyana's skin, she gasped.

"Why do I want you so much?"

"It's a very ancient rule, my little wolf." He ran his fangs along her slick shoulder. "To the victor go the spoils."

"Yes." Her fingers threaded through the hair at his nape, and she wrapped her legs around Oleg's hips, pulling him closer. Her chin lifted and Oleg wanted to shout in pleasure at the triumph in her eyes.

He angled his hips, aligning their bodies before he slid inside, her tight heat grasping him more firmly than her hand. He seated his cock to the hilt and pressed her back against the wall, fucking her slowly as his amnis spread over her skin, licking his energy against hers so that every inch of her skin was stimulated.

"It feels…" She gasped.

"How does it feel?" His strokes were excruciatingly slow. He gripped her wrist in one hand and lifted it over her head, holding her to the wall so she could barely move.

Tatyana shook her head. "I can't… I can't—"

"Yes, you can." His left hand gripped her ass, angling her hips to his, while his other continued to hold her arm captive. She clung to his shoulders as her body erupted in pleasure.

He felt the flood of her amnis release over his body as she came, but Oleg waited until her eyes opened and locked with his. "Tatyana?"

Her lips were red and flushed with blood. "Yes."

He bent down, pressing his lips to her flushed mouth and biting, then licking away the sweet drop of blood at the corner before he drove his hips harder into her and moved his mouth to her ear.

"You are mine," he whispered. "I am patient. But you are mine. And when you are ready, you will *give* me your fangs."

With one last arch of his hips, Oleg closed his eyes and released.

Chapter Forty-Eight

Tatyana lay in a windowless room, staring at the clock on the wall.

Midnight. It had only been five hours since she'd woken to humans outside her room, been in the middle of a vampire battle, and made love to Oleg in a shower after he killed Zara in front of her.

It had felt like making love. He'd been tender and loving. He'd washed her hair and examined every scratch on her body before he lifted her, covered her with his electric energy, and slowly made love to her.

And for a moment she forgot everything but the safety she felt in his arms.

"You are mine. I am patient. But you are mine. And when you are ready, you will give me your fangs."

She closed her eyes and wiped away the tears that seeped from the corners. Oleg was power and possession. He was a lord accustomed to worship, and she could not give him her adoration without hating herself.

And if she hated herself, eventually she would hate him.

"Stay in this chamber until we repair your room."

Oleg had shown her to this small room in the basement of the house.

"We're going to search the perimeter and make sure there are no soldiers left, then check in town to see what we can find out about the men she sent. I'll leave Lazlo to guard the house, but I'll be back before dawn."

Back before dawn meant that she had six hours.

Six hours to get away. Six hours to message her mother. Six hours to find some place to hide from Oleg. Hide from the magnetic force of his presence, which would break down every boundary she'd erected and roll over Tatyana until she had no idea who she was.

She *could not* stay.

Tatyana sat up, swung her legs over the edge of the bed, and started to move.

She could drive one of the old trucks in the garage. They were manual transmission, but that was good, right? Less chance of breaking down. She'd learned to drive on a manual transmission on her grandparents' farm.

She dressed in jeans that rasped against her sensitive skin but would be sturdy if she had to walk far and a silk sweater Oleg had bought for her.

She could not think about Oleg.

Tatyana grabbed a notebook from her bag, scrawled out a message to her mother with the arrangements she'd made with Grimace two weeks before.

If her calculations were correct, at least one of the birds would reach Anna by dawn, hopefully not enough time for Oleg's people to move but enough time for her mother to escape.

Tatyana tore the paper into small pieces, rolling each one into a tiny cylinder before she got on her phone and sent a text to a number Grimace had given her.

Rex.

Grimace would understand the message. Tatyana stuffed the rest of her belongings into a duffel bag but left the computer and threw her backpack over her shoulders. She grabbed the phone because she couldn't abandon it yet. It was her only tie to information. Then she left her room.

She waited in the hallway, listening for any movement, but there was nothing. Creeping along the corridor and up the stairs, she paused again, but the house was deadly quiet.

She ran to the garden and the aviary, marveling at the beautiful cage that Oleg had built for her birds in only two nights.

Oh yes. Her lover was skilled at building beautiful cages. Tatyana looked at the mansion behind the garden and realized the massive bird-cage Oleg had built mimicked the lines of the house.

Beautiful. And no less a prison.

"Shhhh." She eased open the door of the aviary and woke the six birds nestled into their roosts. "How are you tonight, Rex Harrison?" She opened the first cylinder, latching it onto Rex's left leg as the bird woke and began to hop around, cooing happily when he knew he had a message to deliver. "I have a job for you and Brigitte, sir."

As soon as Rex Harrison woke, the other birds roused themselves, flapping around the aviary with excitement. Her mother's birds loved to fly, and that night they would be going home.

One by one, Tatyana affixed the messenger cylinders to each bird's leg, and then she lifted Rex first and walked outside, leaving the door open behind her.

She held the precious bird in her hands, whispering into his ear, "Fly quickly, Rex. Fly home."

Then she threw the messenger pigeon into the air and watched him soar.

Tatyana quickly launched the other five birds, but when she went to shut the gate, she saw Lazlo standing on the edge of the garden.

Her heart gave a fast thump, but she lifted her chin. "I'm leaving."

The old vampire lifted one eyebrow. "Are you?"

She gripped her duffel bag in her hand. "Yes."

"Hmm." There was something behind his bushy beard. Was it a smile? Maybe a hint of one. "He won't be happy."

"He has plenty of vampires around him who want nothing less than to make him happy."

"But that's not you." Lazlo narrowed his eyes. "I'm not my brother's enforcer. You want to go? Go. But be careful of your thirst. If I hear about dead humans cropping up, I will come after you."

Tatyana had thought about that. "I stopped. When I was feeding from that man earlier? I stopped."

Lazlo smirked. "The arrogance of the newborn." He shrugged. "Kill a human in my territory and I'll kill you. You want to take a chance? That's up to you." He turned and started walking into the forest.

She stared at him in a moment of panic, realizing that she'd been half hoping Lazlo would stop her. The dark road before her was unknown, and she had nothing.

She had nothing.

Or did she?

Oleg sat in the lobby of a hotel in Sochi as Mika interrogated a confused human who didn't realize that the busload of men from Moscow was not, in fact, a hunting party at all.

Moscow.

Ivan.

His fucking brother was involved in this. Somehow Ivan was

involved.

"Mr. Arakis, I am so sorry. I can give you keys to all their rooms so that you may examine them yourself if you would like."

"Thank you," Mika said. "That would be helpful."

The bus driver was long gone. The cars the men had hired had already been returned to the rental agency, the blood cleaned off.

Oleg had lost a dozen human employees that night but no vampires. The cracks within his empire were growing, and he could not ignore them anymore.

Luana's death had opened that crack. Zara's defiance had widened it. It was going to take a firm hand to shore up his sprawling empire, and he wasn't looking forward to another century of fighting.

At least he would have Tatyana to comfort him. In time, he knew she would be one of his wisest advisers. She had a keen mind and a head for business that would help his shipping company recover from Elene's loss.

"Oleg?"

He looked up to see Mika trying to grab his attention. "Hmm?"

"I'm going to stay here with Ludmila and Dalan to go through the rooms. Do you want to go back to the house with Oksana? There's not much else to do here."

"Yes." He rose. He wanted to feed on blood that wasn't tainted by adrenaline. He wanted to prepare his daughter's body to be buried. He wanted to hold Tatyana and feel something clean and whole. "See you at dawn."

Oksana drove the old Land Cruiser back up the hill to the mansion, dropping Oleg at the front of the house while she returned the old truck to the garage.

He walked through the front doors and realized immediately that she was gone.

Oleg froze.

He could feel the absence of her blood in his veins, the nascent tie he'd built with her thready but aware.

He had taken her blood again that night. Their bond had formed even though it was only on his side. He could feel her distance, and if he concentrated hard enough... a hint of fear.

Had she been taken? Who would take her? Was it Ivan?

Oleg stormed down to the basement only to see Tatyana's room empty, her backpack gone along with some of her clothing.

Her precious computer was left on the bed, but her phone was gone.

"Lazlo!" He roared his brother's name into the air as he marched upstairs and into the forest. "Lazlo!"

His brother sauntered out from between the trees as Oleg stared at the empty dovecote.

Not doves. Pigeons. *Messenger* pigeons.

If he weren't so angry, he would admire her.

"Yes, brother?" The bushy-haired barbarian looked amused, and Oleg resisted the urge to punch him.

"Where is she?"

"She took one of the trucks and left."

"You were told—"

"You told me to keep threats *out* of the house" —Lazlo lifted a finger— "not to keep pretty young vampires in."

"She's a newborn," he hissed. "What were you thinking?"

"I warned her that if she kills anyone, I'll hunt her down." Lazlo shrugged. "More than that? I am not her keeper."

"Fuck you." Oleg was seething. "She was alone?"

"She had a bit of luggage with her, but I couldn't see anyone else."

No one else meant that she had a plan. Tatyana was too cautious to take off into the night without having a plan. He marched back into the house and yelled for help. "Druzhina!"

Moments later, Oksana and another one of his men appeared in the entryway.

"Boss," Oksana said, "one of the trucks is missing."

"I know," he said. "Tatyana took it. Someone call Mika and have him track her phone. I think she still has it." The phone had not been on the bed in her room. The phone could be traced.

"She left?" Oksana's eyes went wide. "She's a newborn."

"You think I don't know that?" And she had nothing. She had money in the bank, but did she have any idea how to use gold exchanges? Did she even have any...?

Oleg blinked.

Gold.

He walked upstairs, then down the hallway where he'd once carried her when she had wanted to die.

The Amber Room.

When Oleg opened the door, the chest was still sitting there, but the lid was open and the mahogany box containing all the jewels was gone along with a row of gold bars, probably all she could carry in a duffel bag.

"Clever girl." The giant chest of gold was far too heavy to carry even for a vampire, but a box of priceless jewelry and loose stones?

Oh yes. That could get her quite far in the world if she were smart. And his little wolf was very smart.

He closed the top of the chest and looked around the room, remembering the first time he'd taken her against the wall, the taste of her blood, the gasping hitches in her breath when pleasure overtook her.

"My clever Tatyana," he muttered. "Do you really think this makes you any less mine?"

Oleg's anger cooled to resolve.

She was his. She could run, but he would find her.

He simply hoped she wouldn't leave a trail of dead humans in her wake.

Oleg shut the Amber Room and locked the door behind him, then walked downstairs to see Mika already in the foyer.

"I ran back as soon as I heard. She's on the main road heading east."

Oleg snapped at Oksana. "Start the Land Cruiser. We're going after her."

East meant Adler and the airport.

East also meant the river.

East meant... Arosh's territory.

Chapter Forty-Nine

She sat in a parking lot on the edge of the border crossing, sucking down a bottle of blood-wine and knowing that there was no way she could make it into Georgia on the main road.

She had no papers. No ID. She was terrified to leave the truck when the scent of humans was all around her. She'd raided the blood stores in the kitchen before she left Oleg's house, and she had a case of blood-wine in the old truck, but even as she drank, her throat was starting to burn.

She grabbed her phone, quickly turned it on and looked at the map, searching for a road that might lead away from civilization. The truck would drive over rough terrain. If she could find a place to cross the river, she could probably make it into Georgia and then contact Grimace.

Or maybe she would simply lose herself in the mountains for a while. She could find a cave. Hunt animals for blood. She knew animals were an option. She couldn't die from exposure unless it was the sun. If she could find a cave, she might be safe.

There were lots of caves in the mountains, right?

She just needed to get far enough away from Oleg that she could make a plan.

But right now she needed to get away from this border crossing because Oleg might have come back to the house before dawn. And if he came back before dawn? All bets were off.

She saw a road on the map that ran parallel to the river, weaving through warehouses and residential areas. She turned off her phone and decided to follow it.

It was four in the morning and she had just over two hours to find some kind of shelter before dawn. She had the case of blood-wine and a duffel bag of gold and jewels. She already knew she'd need help to sell any of the jewelry, but she could deal with that later.

Later?

She nearly laughed at her own foolishness.

This was the stupidest thing she'd ever done in her life save for the time she'd walked into a vampire's office building in Odesa, thinking she had leverage.

Why hadn't she just taken the loss? Forgotten her back wages?

She could be back in Sevastopol right now, listening to her mother complain about life, chatting with friends online whom she would never meet in person, and looking for work to supplement her mother's meager pension.

Instead, she was running from a possessive vampire lord after she stole his treasure, hoping that she'd find shelter before the sun burned her alive.

"Tatyana, you're an idiot." Okay, yes. She was an idiot. But she was her own idiot. That was something.

Right?

She maneuvered through the border town, avoiding the glances of any passing cars as she drove like she knew where she was going.

She had no idea where she was going.

A rush of panic nearly choked her.

She couldn't turn back now. Oleg was going to be furious. She'd stolen from him and taken off, risking exposure and maybe embarrassing him in front of his druzhina.

She had to keep going.

Tatyana wiped the tears from her eyes with the back of her hand and turned left, still heading north though the road twisted and turned.

She missed him already. He was like an addiction in her veins, a longing hunger she wanted to sate even more than her thirst.

She couldn't do it.

Tatyana could see the river on the other side of a barbed wire fence. It snaked across a shallow riverbed under the moonlight, a threaded channel of rocks, water, and mud.

She turned right onto a gravel road, heading into a dark stand of trees.

A pair of lights appeared behind her.

Fuck.

She pushed down on the accelerator, willing the car to go faster. If there were humans in the car, she was a danger to them, and she hadn't forgotten Lazlo's warning.

Kill a human in my territory and I'll kill you.

She knew he wasn't joking. Not even a little bit. This was still Oleg's territory, right? And Oleg's territory meant Lazlo's territory.

More than that, she didn't want to kill anyone. The soldiers breaking into her room were one thing—they'd been there to kill her—but a random police officer patrolling the border? They were just doing their job. She didn't want to be a murderer. She didn't want to be a monster.

Tatyana turned left as the road twisted, and she saw a black silhouette in the distance, a massive warehouse completely devoid of light. Beyond that, there was another gravel road and what looked like it might be a bridge.

Yes.

Somehow, on the other side of the river, there was shelter. The mountains were there. She could find isolation. She could be lost.

The lights behind her seemed to speed up.

Tatyana punched the engine, racing toward the river on the other side of the chain-link fence. She braced herself as the truck crashed through the fence, somewhat surprised by how easily the old gate fell over. She gripped the wheel as the road turned into gravel and then into mud.

She could see the river in front of her, gleaming in the moonlight. The water looked shallow, and the truck was built for off-road. It wouldn't be the first time she'd plowed her way through mud. The key was to pick up enough speed to make it across.

She floored the truck as the vehicle behind her started honking wildly.

Tatyana ignored it, and her heart raced as she crossed the first part of the river. The water splashed up around her, soaking the windows and flowing under the base of the doors.

The truck behind her kept honking. The driver was leaning on the horn, and she could see lights on the other side of the river switching on. Someone had spotted her truck.

Shit!

Whoever was following her was not afraid of attracting attention, which meant it was Oleg or it was the Russian authorities.

Damn it, damn it, damn it.

Not once did she let her foot off the accelerator. Not when the truck jostled her and she nearly hit her head on the roof. Not when it went sliding over the mud and started to fishtail.

She steered into the spin and righted the truck only to gasp when she went over a particularly large boulder in the middle of the river and something caught the axle, bringing her to a cold stop.

Tatyana grabbed for her duffel bag and backpack, forcing the door open as she stepped from the truck into knee-deep, frigid water.

"Tatyana!"

She heard Oleg shouting in the distance. She glanced over her shoulder and saw fire lighting up the far edge of the river.

"Tatyana Vorona, stop!"

She scrambled to an island in the middle of the river, a small outcropping of rock that would probably be submerged when the rainy season came, but for now it was an island in the middle of the rushing water. She slung her backpack over her shoulders, gripped the duffel bag to her chest, and turned to him.

Go back.

Walk across the water.

He'll be angry. But he'll forgive you.

The voice whispering in her mind was insidious and tempting.

Oleg was pacing on the far bank of the river, his Land Cruiser parked on the edge of the water, the front wheels barely dipping in.

"Tatyana." He walked to the edge of the river and held out his hand. "Come back. I promise I will not harm you."

The only person with him was Mika, who slowly got out of the Land Cruiser, his eyes fixed on Tatyana.

She couldn't read Mika. And she couldn't read Oleg either.

Tatyana was standing in the middle of a river, and she had no idea what to do.

"Come back now, while you can." Oleg held out his hand. "You're crossing into the Fire King's territory, volchitsa." He shook his head. "And even for you I will not start a war."

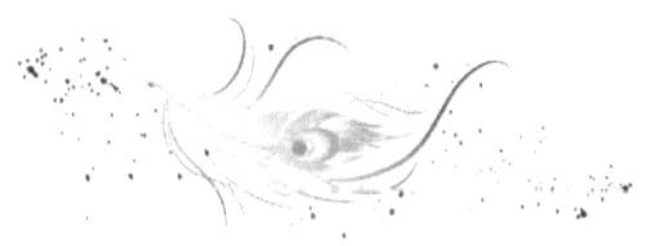

Oleg was lying. He *would* start a war for her, but it would be stupid to start one with the Fire King over something as minor as a runaway newborn vampire.

"What are you doing?" Mika was irritated. "She wants to leave and take her chances with Arosh? Fine. Leave her to him. She's caused enough trouble already."

"Shut up." Oleg glared at the truck in the distance and the thin woman clutching a backpack and a duffel bag. She was soaked to the skin, and her face was pale as the moon. "Tatyana, come back. We need to find shelter. Dawn is coming."

He already had a safe house picked out within driving distance, but there wouldn't be enough time if she kept walking.

"Tatyana!" Oleg's patience snapped. "I command you to return to me!"

She lifted her chin and turned her back to him, facing the opposite bank of the river.

"How could that not have worked?" Mika muttered.

Tatyana started trudging over the rocks, and a moment later Oleg felt it.

"Fuck."

Mika felt them too. "Oh good. Arosh's children have arrived."

Oleg watched as two wind vampires landed on either side of Tatyana.

They looked at Oleg, then at Tatyana. One had silver-grey hair and didn't speak. The other was a beautiful dark-haired woman with flowing black clothes and a sword on her back.

Tatyana took a step backward even as the silver-haired wind vampire held up his hands.

"Hold," the dark-haired woman said. "Are you in danger?"

Tatyana looked at Oleg, then back to the two vampires. She shook her head. "No. I mean... I don't know."

The silent wind vampire cocked his head and stared at Oleg.

"She is a vampire under my aegis." Oleg raised his hands. "There has been a miscommunication, and she took a wrong turn. We mean no offense to your lord. She is a newborn, and this is a misunderstanding. Tatyana, come back to this side of the river."

"If she is under your aegis," the woman said, "she is trespassing on Arosh's territory, Varangian." She drew her sword. "That would be an act of war."

"I'm not under his aegis!" Tatyana shouted, still clutching her duffel bag. "Please! I'm not. I'm..." She looked at Oleg, who held out his hand.

Come back. He pushed his longing through the thin bond he could feel tugging on her like a silken string. *Please come back.*

If she walked away from them, if she returned to him, nothing would happen.

"Tatyana, just stay calm and come back."

Oleg knew that as dangerous as Arosh's patrols were, they were not overly aggressive. He and the Fire King had lived without conflict for centuries.

"This is a misunderstanding," he repeated. "This young vampire is mine. She will walk back to me now, and when she has returned to me, I will send a token to Arosh to apologize for this tres—"

"I'm not his," Tatyana said, clutching her duffel bag to her chest, her eyes darting between the silver-haired vampire and Oleg. "My sire is dead. I have no aegis. I was turned into a vampire against my will only a few weeks ago, and I don't want to fight with anyone."

Tatyana, what are you thinking? How could she trust them? She was taking a chance. Making a gamble.

Just as she had done with him.

Tatyana took a small step toward the dark-haired woman. "I have heard that the Fire King will protect human women. I was human less than a month ago. Will he still protect me?"

"Tatyana!" Oleg's fire leaped at her words, and a burst of flames rose between them.

The dark-haired vampire kept her sword raised, but she turned it away from Tatyana and toward Oleg. "Are you telling me that you run from this vampire's wrath? That you seek protection from him?"

"I don't..." Tatyana's face was pale in the moonlight as she looked at Oleg, then back to Arosh's guard. "I just want a safe haven. Just for a little while, until I can find my place."

Your place is with me! Oleg paced, his fire growing hotter and higher. Mika was shouting at him, but he could hear nothing, see nothing, nothing but Tatyana slipping from his grasp.

"Young one," the dark-haired woman asked, "who killed your sire? Was it the fire vampire who chases you?"

Oleg bared his fangs and froze, glaring at Tatyana.

"I did it," she whispered. "I killed my sire."

The dark-haired vampire took a step back, and Oleg could see the stiff set of her shoulders. "*You* did?"

Oleg's fire died, but his rage still burned, shot through with fear for Tatyana's safety. Tatyana had no idea what she had just admitted to, and she had only her youth and obvious distress as a defense.

Mika grabbed water from the river and sent a calming mist over Oleg, enough that he could think clearly.

The two wind vampires were signing to each other in a language that Oleg didn't speak.

The dark-haired woman let out an audible sigh. "Young one, Samson, son of Arosh the Fire King, has offered you sanctuary in the Fire King's court under his personal protection." She was looking between Oleg and Tatyana as if she knew there was more to the story. "As long as you harm no one, you may claim shelter."

Tatyana's eyes turned to the silver-haired vampire. "Your name is Samson?"

The silent vampire nodded.

"And you're offering me a safe haven?" Tatyana looked back to Oleg. "What is the price?" She clutched her duffel bag to her chest.

"There is no cost," the woman said. "What you have heard is correct. The Fire King's court has long been a place of sanctuary for women in need."

Women in need. Oleg scoffed. As if he would ever hurt Tatyana.

Tatyana looked over her shoulder, then took a step toward Samson. "Really?"

"I am Daria, and I can guarantee that my brother Samson has no ulterior motive." She held out her hand. "Come. Leave this vehicle, and we will fly you to our father. Dawn is coming. We don't have much time."

"Okay." Tatyana's eyes were locked on Oleg's. "I will go with you."

"No!" Oleg shouted. "Tatyana, come back."

Tatyana walked to the edge of the water and stared at him. "I can't."

You can.

She was a mystery, and she always had been. Every time Oleg thought he understood her, she turned and slipped away from him like water running through his fingers.

Oleg took another step into the river. "You won't hide in Arosh's harem forever." The cold water cooled his rage as he kept his eyes locked on Tatyana's. "And don't forget: I am a very patient man."

Tatyana's gaze never left his, not even as the silent wind vampire wrapped his arms around her body and lifted both of them into the air. She and Oleg stared at each other until Tatyana disappeared into the darkness.

And then she was gone.

Mika tugged his arm. "Come, Knyaz. Both of us know this isn't over."

She left.

She left him.

Oleg's fangs pierced his lip, and he felt her flying away, the thread of their bond stretching into the sky and deep into the mountains.

Stretched but not broken.

She might have left him, but he would find her.

And she *would* be his.

Chapter Fifty

Tatyana flew over mountains so high that the wind cut her cheeks and her breath frosted in the air. She could see the beginning of dawn on the horizon, and she felt the pull of sleep and forced it back.

"We are not taking you to our sire's main compound," the dark one said. "There are humans there. But there is another castle high in the mountains where only immortals go. It is reserved for our sire's dearest friends, but Samson told me he would vouch for you."

Tatyana looked over her shoulder at the silent, silver-haired vampire who carried her. "Do you not speak?"

Samson shook his head, but he smiled.

"My brother does not speak with his mouth," Daria said. "But do not mistake his silence for lack of an opinion."

A few minutes later, they landed in a stone fortress high in the mountains where sharp cliffs rose around them, creating a natural courtyard where two men stood as if waiting for their arrival.

"Our sire will have felt your approach," Daria said. "Let me introduce you."

One vampire was a raven-haired man with light brown skin, a black beard, and swirling tattoos riding high on his arched cheekbones. Like Oleg, he was utterly beautiful *and* utterly terrifying. Also like Oleg, she could sense that his elemental energy was tied to fire.

Beside the dark-haired vampire stood a towering man with russet hair that flowed down his back. Tatyana looked at him instead of at the Fire King because, while this man was a giant, his blue eyes looked at her with kindness.

Tatyana, what have you done?

She could hear Oleg's voice in her mind, as if the angry fire vampire had somehow become her conscience.

She knew she was taking a chance, but the moment she'd seen the two wind vampires flying toward her, she remembered what Oleg had told her.

"Arosh is an honorable vampire—he takes care of his people and is known for having a soft heart toward human women in particular—but he has his own moral code."

She was taking a chance. It was reckless, but she'd tried being cautious in her life and what had happened? She was a vampire now. If she was ever going to survive on her own in a world of predators, she was going to have to take chances.

Daria walked across the courtyard and bowed deeply. "Father, we bring you a newborn searching for sanctuary. She was sired against her will and... she killed her sire. I do not know the circumstances, but she has no aegis. She was running from the Varangian's territory when we caught her. Samson has offered her sanctuary."

The man called the Fire King stepped forward, and if Tatyana had thought Oleg was powerful, she nearly dropped to the ground when this vampire looked at her.

He was old. So old, so commanding, and so frightening.

Tears came to her eyes, and Tatyana bowed her head.

"I am Arosh, ancient king of this territory," the immortal said. "What is your name?"

She forced the words from her mouth. "My name is Tatyana Otsana Vorona."

"I also killed my sire, Tatyana Otsana Vorona," Arosh said. "Or at least I think I did. There were burnt bones in the cave where I woke."

"She killed me." Tatyana kept her eyes on the ground. "She stole my human life, so I killed her."

"And you survived," the vampire next to Arosh said. "Unusual and rare."

Arosh chuckled a little bit. "I am no modern, tame immortal who abides by laws and customs. Your life for her life. A fair trade." He leaned forward and took a deep breath. "You carry the Varangian's scent. You were his lover."

"Yes." Tatyana looked up cautiously. "But I do not want to be his property."

Arosh's eyebrows went up. "A sentiment I can respect." He stepped back and swept his arm wide. "Very well, Tatyana Vorona. As my son has offered you sanctuary—and I trust Samson with my life—I will accept you on my mountain for now. Samson likes you, and he is my favorite child."

The taller vampire chuckled a little bit, and Tatyana felt a pull that drew her eyes up and to the right to meet the brilliant gaze of the towering vampire to Arosh's left.

"I *know* you," the giant said in a soft voice. "I saw you when you were a human."

Months ago. Tatyana blinked. "You were with Saba. In the tavern."

His brilliant blue eyes looked sad. "And you did not want this."

Tatyana felt tears come to her eyes at the power and the warmth behind the man's voice. "I don't know what I want anymore. Right now I just want to understand who I am. And I don't want to be afraid."

The giant smiled. "You are a water vampire of Ariana's line. I know your blood, child."

Tatyana had no idea who Ariana was, but she was drawn to the tall vampire. "Who are you?"

"This is Kato." Arosh grabbed Tatyana's chin and forced her eyes back to his. "Ancient king of the old sea and father of water vampires. Including you."

Including her? Did that mean she was under this Kato's aegis?

"Arosh." The giant's gentle voice was chastising. "Can't you see she's terrified?"

"She should be." Arosh released her and stepped back. "You're soft, brother."

Tatyana needed darkness and sleep. She could feel the sun rising, and she was on the top of a mountain with no shelter in sight.

"And you are too hard." Kato held out his hand to Tatyana. "I no longer have an empire to defend, nor do I want one. I enjoy teaching the young."

Tatyana didn't know what she was doing, but when she put her hand in Kato's, all her worries fell away. He was strength and power, and something in his eyes reminded her of her grandfather.

"I'm going to sleep soon," she whispered. "I won't be able to..." Her words fell away. She was spent. She had nothing. If they wanted to kill her, she was at their mercy.

"Child." Kato smiled. "Trust me."

Tatyana was in a vampire castle on a high mountain, surrounded by icy wind as the sky lightened and the sun threatened the horizon.

Everything in her life was uncertain. She still didn't know if her mother was secure. Oleg was waiting. He would be waiting for her, and she knew that one day a reckoning with him would have to come.

"Come with me." Kato took her hand and led her into the darkness of a cave cut into the mountain. "Let me show you to shelter, Tatyana Vorona. The day is coming, and you need to rest."

Moments later, Tatyana fell onto a soft bed, a door shut behind her, and darkness surrounded her like a soft and welcoming blanket.

The silence of the mountain wrapped around her mind like a

shroud, and she had the curious feeling that for the first time in months...

She was truly safe.

**Tatyana and Oleg's story will continue in CRIMSON OATH
Coming Summer 2025**

CRIMSON OATH

Coming
SUMMER 2025

About the Author

ELIZABETH HUNTER is an eleven-time *USA Today* and international best-selling author of romance, contemporary fantasy, and paranormal mystery. Based in Central California and Addis Ababa, she travels extensively to write fantasy fiction exploring world mythologies, history, and the universal bonds of love, friendship, and family. She has published over fifty works of fiction and sold over two million books worldwide. She is the author of the Elemental Mysteries series, the Irin Chronicles, and other works of fiction.

ELIZABETHHUNTER.COM

Also by Elizabeth Hunter

<u>The Firebird & the Wolf</u>

Blood Mosaic

Crimson Oath (Summer 2025)

<u>The Shadowlands</u>

First Light

The Shadow Path (April 2025)

<u>The Irin Chronicles</u>

The Scribe

The Singer

The Secret

The Staff and the Blade

The Silent

The Storm

The Seeker

<u>The Elemental Mysteries</u>

A Hidden Fire

This Same Earth

The Force of Wind

A Fall of Water

The Stars Afire

Fangs, Frost, and Folios

THE ELEMENTAL WORLD

Building From Ashes

Waterlocked

Blood and Sand

The Bronze Blade

The Scarlet Deep

A Very Proper Monster

A Stone-Kissed Sea

Valley of the Shadow

THE ELEMENTAL LEGACY

Shadows and Gold

Imitation and Alchemy

Omens and Artifacts

Midnight Labyrinth

Blood Apprentice

The Devil and the Dancer

Night's Reckoning

Dawn Caravan

The Bone Scroll

Pearl Sky

Tin God